A B.

Dreamcatcher: Secrets

To Kaye from Donna —

blessings —

KC Pearcey

KC Pearcey

To the Darling Husband
who has made the best of all my dreams come true . . .

I am going to let you in on a secret . . . no one in this book is someone you actually know.

Not your husband, your wife, your family, your friends, or your distant kinfolk.

Not even you.

If you think you resemble someone in this book,

or you think you know someone in this book,

feel free to be flattered –

but it just isn't so.

And I would know.

They all live in Balfour . . . and Balfour is only in my head . . .

Just saying . . .

Chapter 1

The First Day: Monday

Cora was standing at the double enameled sink in her grandmother's kitchen. Soft light that might have been morning came through the sheer curtains that covered the wood-framed windows and bathed and warmed her hands as she stood.

She knew at once that this was the dream, the one she dreaded. It was the first of its kind in months, and Cora was briefly afraid.

Each dream—she had lost count of how many had come to her over the last five years—had come unexpectedly, sometimes as a singular event and sometimes in a series of vignettes that, when pieced together, created a living quilt of what had seemed at first to be unrelated information. The dreams were like vintage movies, black and white and shades of gray, with sharp lines and noticeable clarity. It was as though the memory of the room itself had come to life, without color and without a sense of time and space. Without even a cobweb's connection to reality, save in the recesses of her mind.

In the beginning, the dreams were few and far between. And except for the very first dream, they were just dreams, only with predictions and promises about mundane, everyday things. Where she had misplaced something. A premonition about a new client. What Marjorie or Thomas would say about something. Nothing earth-shattering. Sometimes she would know something that would help someone find something that was lost. But in the last six months they had taken on a deeper meaning. A purpose that involved other people's lives. Mysteries of true consequence. And Charlie. The new dreams involved Charlie.

In spite of the negative feelings Cora might have had about the dream itself, the memory of the room was a precious part of her teenaged years. It was the literal place where she had once been able to find rest and peace. Where she was loved and protected. But that was a long time ago.

Now, visiting the room in the dream had taken on a different meaning. Two people, loved ones and friends she had known in life, had come to reunite with her here in this room, in the dream. Bringing cryptic messages. And now, messages from beyond.

Seeing the dead again did not bother Cora. Listening to their often cryptic and rambling communications . . . well, that was another story.

In the beginning, only one person had sought out Cora. But then one other joined, and they became interchangeable characters who traded places depending on the content of the message. The first person was her Gramma Crawford, who had died in the fire that had also consumed the kitchen where Cora in her vision now stood. The second person was her childhood pastor, James.

For a moment Cora considered trying to wake herself, but then she surrendered to the inevitable. She knew what must be done. The message was on its way.

Making coffee was the natural and expected way to begin.

The cup she found in the drainboard was the one she always used here, as was the silver spoon with the rose-patterned stem placed conveniently on the faded Formica next to the gas stove at her left. Gramma Crawford had loved roses. And coffee. She had especially loved an old four-cup drip enamel pot, chipped from years and years of wear, that required water to be boiled separately and then poured into the top section. As the fresh, cold well water came to a bubbling steam, Cora had learned to patiently drip the liquid until it soaked through the upper section and wound its way through the freshly ground beans. Her earliest memories were of the fragrant odor of coffee filling this very room. One of the first tasks Gramma Crawford had taught a ten-year-old Cora was how to measure and brew, a talent she had perfected through the brief, happy years she had spent there before her transition to adulthood.

Cora looked down at her hands and knew that recalling the details would be critical. She took a moment to study the familiar cup in her hands, looking for anything that might have changed from the last time she had had the dream.

The cup she always used was one of the ones from her

grandmother's first set of dishes, four cups and matching saucers and four dinner plates bought from the local Ben Franklin's Five and Dime. They were a wedding gift from her grandmother's sister, Lily, in 1923. Precious and cheap at the same time.

The pattern was old-fashioned and decidedly feminine. A delicate and ornate bouquet of wild flowers twisted and flowed like lace surrounding a larger faded rose in the center. A tiny border of gold leaf circled around the edge of the plates and the top rim of the cups.

Cora had an identical single cup from that original set that graced a shelf in the kitchen of her own home. The surface of the china cup in her hands was patterned with a spider's web of tiny cracks just beneath the surface of the glazing. Cora ran her finger absently over the cup she held, feeling the cracks and the familiar pattern of the scrollwork around the rim of the china. Remembering. This room and its contents were all about remembering, both the old and the new.

Without looking, Cora knew exactly where to find everything she needed, gathering the ingredients with practiced ease. The sugar bowl in the shape of a crystal pine cone. The glass bottle of raw milk in the tiny, ancient ice-box-turned-refrigerator. The coffee grounds in their tin canister, fragrant and familiar.

Focusing on her hands, she took out a worn crochet potholder to pick up the enamel pot, only to find that the coffee had already been brewed and simply awaited pouring. With reverent hands, she filled and lifted the well-worn china cup and turned to face her latest visitor.

She knew that someone would be sitting at the kitchen table. Someone was almost always sitting at the table, waiting. Waiting just for her.

Cora was not disappointed, nor was she surprised.

Brother James was wearing a dark suit, a too-starched shirt, and a tie. That much came as no surprise. The translucent mug that held his coffee was equally natural. It had been Cora's father's favorite mug and was always Brother James's choice when he visited here. He seemed at home at the handmade wooden table, sitting in the caned ladder-back chair. Nodding, he motioned for her to join him, and she responded with a smile.

"Long time," she said, crossing the worn linoleum floor and seating herself across from him at the table. "At least five months. You look well."

"You know this is a dream," Brother James said, sipping his own steaming coffee. "I made my own coffee this time. I hope you don't mind."

He watched as she looked fondly around the room.

"You do know this is a dream, don't you?" he repeated.

She glanced at the window seat. The rows of framed family pictures. The decorative plates arranged in patterns and groups on the wall. The oilcloth tablecloth slightly wrinkled from too many washings. All since disappeared. Cora felt a sadness for the house itself, as though it were a living thing.

"Yes, I know," she replied finally. She took a tentative sip from her own cup and let go of her fears. The coffee tasted hot and satisfying, exactly as she remembered. "And you are always welcome to make your own coffee here."

"That is generous of you," he countered.

Cora couldn't help but laugh. But the very act of laughing brought her back to reality. As of late, most of what happened in the dreams did not make her laugh.

"I suppose you have come with news?"

Brother James tugged gently at the collar of his shirt and settled back into the chair, which squeaked in protest. Cora took another sip of coffee. As it had been in his eighty-three years of life, nothing hurried Brother James. He tasted more of his coffee, deliberately touched the corners of his mouth with a handkerchief, and then casually rested both the hand and the initialed handkerchief on the table. Her eyes were drawn to the initials. S.A.W. Not James's initials at all.

He's up to his usual games, Cora thought. *Clues.*

Beside the cloth square was a Bible. Not Brother James's Bible. His was much larger. She knew that from listening to years of his Sunday morning sermons and watching as he hefted the tome onto the pulpit just after the offertory hymn every Sabbath. James's Bible was a country preacher's old-fashioned volume, thick with tabs and worn bulletins, scribbled notes and reminders peeking from between the tissue-like pages.

This Bible lying on the oilcloth was more modern. Slender and less used. Cora wondered if the Bible belonged to the S.A.W. of the handkerchief.

She knew it was useless to ask what was going on until the esteemed preacher decided to tell what he had come to say, so Cora decided to try a different tactic.

"How's Martha?"

Brother James sighed. "I didn't come to discuss Martha. Or myself. You know we don't talk about those things. Not here in the kitchen."

She laughed good naturedly and countered, "So I'm a mind reader now, am I?"

"What you are, dear Cora," he leaned forward, speaking softly, "is open to many interpretations. For now, you *do* know why I'm here."

"You have a message," she answered, suddenly quiet. He was right, as always. She did know why he had come. Why he had been coming off and on for the last five years.

Her mind stilled. She thought about the last two messages James had delivered and the ensuing drama of the crimes. And Charlie. *Let's hope it's a boring message*, she thought.

But she also knew Charlie. Nothing with Charlie was ever boring.

"I have a message," he patted the sacred book with the calloused tips of the fingers on his left hand, gingerly waving the handkerchief as if performing sleight of hand. "But it isn't for you."

"I hate puzzles."

"Nonsense," he chided gently. "You love puzzles."

His dark eyes laughed over his horn-rimmed glasses before he continued.

"I have a message," he repeated, more gravely and much more in his character. He paused to continue drinking his coffee.

This is taking too long, even for Brother James, she thought.

She prodded again. "From whom? The initials aren't yours."

"Such impeccable grammar. Even in your dream."

Tilting her head to one side, she studied him. This certainly seemed to be Brother James. But how to be certain? She had often wondered in her waking hours how she would be able to tell this one particular kind of dream from all her other dreams. How she would know if she were really being visited by the people who came to bring her messages in the dream. This attitude of James's right now was almost out of his character.

Cora tried to visualize their last visit together and failed.

"You aren't certain if this is really the dream," he answered her thoughts aloud. "Or only the result of some perplexing problem from yesterday, or perhaps caused by an overindulgence in Marjorie's cooking. Or maybe just some bad fried chicken."

He paused dramatically and almost laughed at himself before continuing.

"You cannot know whether this dream is going to be important. Not until later. Much later. After the events begin to happen. You know that."

"I thought that is why you came," she said, trying not to sound like a petulant, impatient child. "Aren't you going to tell me what is going to happen?"

"No, but I can tell you who it is going to happen to. Or would that be, to whom something is about to happen?"

He gave a quiet, teasing laugh. Removing his hand from the Bible cover, he revealed the initials embossed deeply into the cover in bold block letters. With a deliberate motion, he rotated the leather cover to face her. S.A.W.

So the handkerchief and the Bible do belong to the same person, she thought. *But who is S.A.W.?*

She scanned her memory for people she knew with those initials. James's voice pulled her from her frantic thoughts.

"Quips aside, I have a message for Andrew Evans."

Cora's mind came to a halt. Just a moment before, she had felt like she was onto something. Now she was confused. And obstinate.

She had understood why James came the first time, in the first dream so long ago, when she lost the baby. She had even grown accustomed to all the dreams in between. Those were disturbing and reassuring at the same time. She had come to expect them. The messages contained puzzles to solve. Problems to unravel about inconsequential things.

Then six months ago, they began to involve Charlie. First the lost girl who was kidnapped. Then the escaped prisoner a month later. Crimes like the ones they had once solved together. The messages were always vague. But the thread that connected these new dreams—that was Charlie. He had severed their marriage five years ago, but she found herself reconnected to him through the messages in her dreams.

Dreams that solved problems. Dreams that helped people who couldn't otherwise be helped.

For these new dreams, James had set one condition: Contact Charlie.

"Do you know anyone else who will believe you and do what you ask without question?" James had asked.

Now James was changing the rules. Again. This message was different. It wasn't for Charlie. That was new. And even less convenient than reaching out to her former husband.

Cora made a small sound of disgust and frowned.

"Why can't you deliver it yourself?"

He made a clucking sort of disapproving noise she knew

well. *This is definitely Brother James*, she thought.

"Now, now. Of course I'm James, silly girl," he caught her eye and winked.

"If you are going to read my mind, I don't need to talk then, do I?"

She raised her eyebrows back at him, resisting the childish urge to stick out her tongue as she had when she was seven. The dream was much too serious for that sort of levity.

"You know better than to be short-tempered," he said. His voice held a gentle reprimand.

Cora nodded her head. Experience had taught her that it was never a good idea to be in a hurry. Not in the dream. Perhaps that was the very reason that Brother James was the primary messenger. The dream had its own unique way of delivering clues, hints, and information, and she knew she must accept this process for what it was. But she was not on the whole the least bit happy about this particular situation, and she was not going to pretend that she was.

"I don't know him, James. Marjorie goes to services and sees him every Sunday, but he and I have never met," she said flatly. "Why would I even assume that he would come to speak to me?"

"Feelings, as always, are optional." Brother James reached over and tapped the edge of her cup with his index finger. "Of course, since he is a preacher, maybe his feelings are a little less optional. Maybe he would feel obligated to come to you. Drink your coffee before it gets cold."

"What if he won't listen to me?" she asked. "What if he doesn't believe that I have anything to say to him?"

He gave her a serious, studied look, then reached across the table and patted her cold hand. "Sooner or later, Cora, everyone listens to you."

She thought about that for a long moment. Brother James was certainly right about that.

"And the message?"

He hesitated with a grimace before he continued.

"Well, this is somewhat awkward."

"The message is somewhat awkward?"

"Not exactly," he said. He paused, considering his words carefully. "You see, I don't really *have* the message." He smiled at the quizzical cloud that formed on her face. "Just that there is going to *be* a message—and that only you can encourage him to do what is right when the time comes."

She leaned back in her own squeaking chair and sighed.

"So, you came to the kitchen to deliver a message you don't have, to a person I don't even know and have never met—and you don't know what is going to happen if I don't."

"Oh, on the contrary," he said, smiling enigmatically. "I know exactly what is going to happen if you *don't*."

He paused, grasping his jacket lapels and giving them a friendly tug downward, releasing the fabric with a sigh. He took another sip of coffee.

"Cora, we deal with the truth about death here."

"Yes, I know," she said. She looked at him carefully. "You know I want to help, but it was hard enough when you asked me to involve Charlie the last two times. I don't know if I'm ready to tell someone else that my dead preacher comes and gives me messages. Is all this really necessary?"

"Someone is going to die, Cora. There will be messages for Charlie, just not this one. Not yet. I cannot tell you more than that."

"That was uncharacteristically melodramatic," she said, remembering sermons she had heard Brother James preach over the decades they had known each other. Fire, brimstone, and the gospel truth, as it were. He was always sincere and open, but seldom had James delivered his sermons with manipulation and the scenery-chewing kind of theatrical flair that plagued his contemporaries.

He smiled at the bewilderment on her face.

"I rather enjoy my work, dear heart," he said gently. "Both then and now. Even the more curious aspects. You know what I mean, funerals and—"

"And visiting with me." She finished his sentence easily, absently tracing the initials on the cover of the Bible with her well-manicured index finger, as if to bring the identity of the owner out by touch.

James put down his near-empty cup and stood up, buttoning the bottom of his jacket carefully and deliberately. He gave the Bible one last friendly pat. "This time I have come to prepare you for what you need to do."

She finished the last of her coffee. She knew she had to ask.

"James, do I tell Charlie about any of this? I'm seeing him tomorrow."

"That is another matter." His smile was gentle, his tone tender. "Don't worry, dear. When the time comes, you will know exactly what you should do."

Waking was instantaneous. A sudden splash of reality, as

though she were experiencing a dive into a pool of icy water. She was completely awake and lucid, staring up at the ceiling of her bedroom. Red block numbers from the projector clock glowed cheerfully on the white surface above her. The ceiling fan hummed softly, and she focused for a moment on the broad oak blades as they turned, pushing the air downward in a cool breeze. Almost too cool for autumn.

She looked at the time—2:32 a.m. She knew that another clue. Cora also knew better than to trust her memory, regardless of what she had told James in her dream. Reaching for the lamp beside her bed, she sat up and swung her legs gingerly over the side and onto the polished hardwood floor.

The cat stirred from his sleep on the folded quilt at the end of the bed, his yellow-green eyes blinking from the sudden light of the lamp.

"Solomon," she whispered softly, picking up her journal and fumbling for her reading glasses on the bedside table. "Go back to sleep. It's not time for breakfast yet."

The snoring body beside her turned restlessly over toward the light.

"You okay?" Thomas mumbled, awake but not quite alert.

"I'm fine," she reassured him, touching his shoulder gently with her free hand. "Just a dream."

He sighed, then yawned without opening his eyes and rolled away from the light again.

"*The* dream?" he muttered, sounding a little irritated.

"Won't be a minute," Cora said. She ignored his question and his annoyance, found a pen, then turned in the journal to a clean page. "Quick notes."

"No problem," he mumbled again unconvincingly. Then, barely aware he had spoken, he returned to snoring softly. Cora smiled. The nasal music coming from her husband reassured her.

Solomon stretched his sleek, black feline form out and then curled back into a massive black ball of fur, purring.

"I'll be quick," Cora said.

Chapter 2

Thomas found her sitting at the computer in her office at seven the next morning. Her hair was tangled and twisted into a careless bun at the back of her head, and a mug of cold, vanilla-flavored coffee sat at her elbow on the table.

"Sorry about last night," she offered sincerely, still squinting at the tightly worded content on the computer screen in front of her.

"Who?"

"James," she said, typing. "Again."

Thomas's eyebrows shot up, but his voice remained level. No point in asking questions that would only add to what confusion he could see quite clearly in her face.

"Researching?"

Cora was thankful that her husband knew her so well. Four years of marriage and he knew not to ask questions for which he knew she did not have answers. Not yet, anyway.

Cora tried not to dwell on what she didn't know. There had been many questions in the past that she still couldn't answer and might never be able to. She often told herself that she knew much more than she wanted anyway. James was fond, it seemed, of oversharing.

"More coffee?"

Thomas did not wait for her answer before picking up the cup and taking it to the kitchen, a sunny country kitchen with spotless, blue-tiled countertops and a sturdy center island table. In the center of the island, Cora had already gathered a bouquet of daisies and sunflowers in a blue-spattered antique earthenware pitcher.

"The flowers are nice," he said loudly, hoping she would hear him in the office. He opened a cabinet and reached for the Mason jar of her homemade coffee mix. With practiced ease, he took the copper kettle from the stovetop and found it already cold to the touch. *She's been up too long*, he thought. He filled the kettle with fresh water, placed it on the gas burner, and twisted the knob, watching the flames lick up over the sides before he lowered the heat. For what seemed like a long time he stared out the window at the garden and tried to decide whether or not to tell her that he was concerned about the dreams. About what he knew would happen.

Especially what had happened the last two times. He saw the toll they took on her.

"Thomas."

She had left the cozy nook that served as her home office and was standing in the doorway to the kitchen. She was still wearing what Thomas called her "comfortable clothes"—long

16

baggy black pants and one of Thomas's old T-shirts. The difference in their heights was never as obvious as when she wore his clothes around the house. The shirt covered her knees quite completely. Still, Cora loved to wear his old shirts. Enveloped in Thomas's clothes, she felt safe. His scent grounded her.

He studied her face and wondered what to say. For an experienced trial lawyer, he found himself inexplicably speechless when it came to Cora's dreams. No logical questions came into his mind. At least, no questions that would make sense in any sense of the word, so he said the first thing that came into his mind.

"Toast?"

The seriousness and intensity of the question sent giggles through Cora.

"Whole wheat," she countered, trying to control herself. Failing, she moved toward him, padding on bare feet on the cool tiles.

"Of course." Thomas opened his arms and she walked into them, pressing her face against the smooth coolness of his white starched shirt and wrapping her arms under his jacket and as far as she could reach around his waist.

"I love you," she said, swallowing a sudden sob.

Thomas kissed the top of her head, his own arms holding her as tenderly as she was holding him intensely. For several moments they stood together, as they had too often before this, the streams of sunlight crisscrossing the floor and bathing them in early morning light. At last Thomas felt her relax and make a slight movement away. He opened his arms to release her, and the kettle began to whistle impatiently, as if on cue.

"I'll just make the coffee then."

He took a second cup from the cabinet and looked around for the spoon she had used, which he found washed and drying on a napkin beside the sink. With more calm than he felt, he poured out the last of her cold coffee, rinsed the two cups quickly under the running faucet, and counted out several generous spoonfuls of mix before refilling them with boiling water.

Cora moved to the other side of the kitchen and opened the breadbox. She took out two thick slices of homemade wheat bread and inserted them into the toaster with the same deliberate calm. They both knew what it meant to have the dream. Not the meaning of the dream. That varied. But the consequences of having the dream, well, those were more known. And complicated.

Thomas had finally formulated an acceptable question.

"How long?"

Cora knew what he was asking. *How long had it been since the last time?*

"Six months or so," she responded quietly. "You remember the Trumball baby? Six months ago now." Her voice grew a little stronger. "I tell myself that that worked out for the best. She was okay."

"Because of you."

"Because of the dream. Because of prayers."

Because of Charlie. The unspoken thought hung between them.

Cora reached past her husband for the steaming mug of

coffee. "You would think I would be used to this by now."

Thomas picked up his own cup with reserved frustration.

"I don't know how anyone could ever get used to this, sweetheart."

Their eyes met. His intensely green, hers slate gray. She knew this was not the time to talk about the dream. Thomas did not understand. He did not want to understand. Those conversations would come later. Most likely with Charlie, unfortunately.

"Which case today?" she asked. She turned back to the toaster and watched as it obediently completed its work. Then she opened the glass-fronted cabinet door and removed two small white salad plates. "Wilton?"

"Finalizing the divorce," he nodded tersely. "Ugly business all the way around."

"Jelly or jam?" Cora asked as she buttered the toast.

"Too messy with the new tie," he said. He gestured to her latest gift. Cora loved buying new mail-order ties as much as Thomas enjoyed wearing them. "Just whatever butter you've already slathered on, thank you."

"You are always welcome."

He pulled out a chair at the table for her and then one for himself, waiting for her to sit before he took his place opposite, so he could study her face.

"Patients today?"

"Two." Cora took a tentative bite of toast, thick with the chunkiest of homemade peach jam. "Amy at noon. I don't know if she knew about the hearing this morning before she made the appointment." Cora took a bigger bite of toast, chewed thoughtfully and swallowed. "Then someone new at four thirty."

Cora knew she would have to tell Thomas sooner or later that Charlie had called and wanted to bring a little girl who needed trauma counseling. She hadn't even talked to him. He had left a message on her answering machine with the date and time and the fact that the child was a girl. She hoped he would just come and go like the last time.

She also hoped that she wouldn't have to tell Thomas until the visit was over.

Thomas studied his wife's face, sensing her hesitation and wondering at the odd expression of reserve. Then he knew. There was only one person she would hesitate to talk about with him. Thomas's eyebrows shot even higher this time, and involuntarily he sighed.

"I didn't know Charlie was back in town."

Cora returned his look. The dream and Charlie. Thomas's worst nightmares. Charlie was his oldest friend, but his least favorite human being.

"He left a message on the machine yesterday. I left a message back. We didn't even talk. I had no way of knowing I would have the dream when I agreed to see this new patient of his, Thomas," she said firmly. "You know that, don't you?"

"I don't care if you see Charlie," he lied. "I was wondering if you really need a new client." Thomas hoped his voice was not as petulant as he felt.

"What you mean to say is, do I really need to see Charlie." Cora's mouth was amused but her eyes were not.

"Don't do that to me, Cora," Thomas said with a hint of

warning. "I am not jealous."

"I know you're not jealous." Her eyes grew darker.

"I trust you."

"I know that you trust me."

"Are you going to keep repeating what I say?"

"Probably," she said. Her voice had taken on a tone she used with angry, damaged children in her psychology practice. "At least, I will until I think you've begun to believe what you are saying."

This argument was more than four years old, and new again every time Charlie called with another of his problems. Or when Cora had the dream and Charlie just appeared.

"Why you?"

"Because Charlie says that Marjorie and I are the best."

Cora sighed and tilted her head to watch her husband down the last of his coffee and stuff the remaining corner of his toast into his mouth before standing up.

He took his cup to the sink, rinsed it carefully, and put it on the rack beside the sink to dry.

"Other people use dishwashers, you know," he said. "Should I buy you a dishwasher?"

"I'm ready to change the subject too." Cora took another bite of her toast and licked the jam from her fingers. "Will you call if Judge Candler dismisses early?"

"So I won't run into Charlie?"

She ignored the baiting. Too early in the morning for a fight.

"So you won't have cold sandwiches again for supper," she countered sweetly.

"I like cold sandwiches." He hesitated. She couldn't help

knowing when he was lying to her, so he decided to tell her a simple truth. One she could not dispute. "I love you, Cora."

"No doubt about that." She took a long swallow from her own cup and stared at the empty china without looking up. "Don't forget to ask Susan about Sunday, please."

"Sunday?"

"She'll know what I mean. I volunteered Marjorie to make cookies for the Bible study this week." Cora looked up. "You're about to find yourself in school bus traffic, Thomas."

He glanced at his watch, realizing she was right. *How does she do that?*

"I'll call before I come home."

"Yes, Thomas."

He leaned over and kissed her sticky lips.

"Peach is a good flavor for you."

Cora smoothed his closely cropped hair before he pulled reluctantly away and was gone. She listened for the front door to close. Rather, she listened for *how* the door closed. A pleasant, determined thud. Then the key in the door, securing the deadbolt. After what had happened in Baton Rouge with Charlie, Thomas didn't take chances. Cora was clever at hiding her fears, but Thomas knew that even after five years, she was still afraid sometimes. He couldn't stop the dreams from coming, but he never wanted her to feel afraid again. Not like that.

Cora yawned. *Back to computer research*, she thought, *and working on the new book.* Trauma treatments for child victims of violence. Cora hated the topic. She loved the children more. Marjorie would be coming within the hour to clean the house and to cook for the week. Cora and Thomas usually spent their weekends alone. Faithful Marjorie came in to spend the weekdays and keep Cora company, doing the cooking and cleaning so Cora could see patients and write.

Marjorie would want to talk. There was weekend news to discuss, gossip from the Sunday prayer requests, the new patient, and what might be going on with Amy.

And Marjorie would need to know about the latest dream. What little there was to tell.

Chapter 3

Susan was wearing the loudest, brightest, wildest flowered blouse that Thomas had ever seen, covered only partially by the loudest, brightest orange, yellow, and red sweater he had ever seen. For a moment, his eyes actually hurt.

"Good morning, Thomas."

Susan's pleasant Southern drawl was in sharp contrast to her almost mannish, close-cropped white hair and piercing sapphire blue eyes, lined boldly and crowned with deep purple eyeshadow. Her hot pink nails, like tiny manicured claws, tapped efficiently at the computer keyboard as she spoke.

"They were a gift from Harry."

"They?"

"The matched set, of course. Blouse and sweater set. Found them in two different clearance sections in Goudchaux's on his last business trip to Baton Rouge. Said he saw the first one the minute he walked into the door."

"I will just bet he did," Thomas said, trying not to laugh. "I don't need to know."

Susan sighed and continued to talk, her words following the rhythmic click of the keys like a country music ballad.

"Said he wanted something I could wear to work and knew I liked to cover my upper arms, so he looked for a sweater to match the shell."

"I don't need to know," Thomas repeated cheerfully.

"I think they suit me well." The clicking stopped for a moment and Susan waited.

"I don't mean to offend you, Susan. Have I complained about your clothing?"

"I'm just making Monday morning conversation."

She fingered the gaudy appliquéd flowers, outlined in metallic sequins and glass beads, then lifted a hand to fluff a tuft of her spiked hair.

"Susan," Thomas began. He studied his secretary's face for a moment and decided this was a battle he could not win. "Are the transcripts ready?"

Susan smiled and resumed her typing.

"Case file for this morning on your desk. Andy's already been by with a copy of the deposition. That lady lawyer from Atlanta sent over the preliminary divorce papers and they seemed in order."

Business finished, she resumed her Monday morning diatribe.

"Word has it that tomorrow is Judge Candler's anniversary. The Big Five-O, so I hear. Dinner reservations at Angelo's in Atlanta at six p.m. sharp, so they are staying at some hoity-toity hotel in the city tonight. There are tickets to the Fox too."

"You are a wellspring of useful information, Susan."

"You pay me well, Boss."

Thomas put his hand on the polished brass knob to his inner office door.

"Ah, Cora said something about this coming Sunday."

Susan nodded without looking up. "No problem."

"Is that an answer?"

Susan nodded again, continuing to type.

"Woman talk," she whispered confidently. "Need to know basis, Boss."

"I don't need to know?"

"You have more important things on your mind."

That much was true. Thomas went into his office, hung his jacket carefully on the back of one of the two client chairs, and took out his cell phone to text Susan's cryptic answer to Cora. He knew Cora might not answer before lunch, but Thomas liked to take care of business. This latest dream of Cora's had reminded him unpleasantly of the last dream. Cora had been able to help find a missing child, and he certainly couldn't begrudge that blessing. But Charlie was involved. He just didn't know why Charlie always had to be involved.

Life, he had been reminded, was traveling much too fast. Some days he felt as though he had finished the day before he had really begun. The little things sometimes became the big things even as he watched.

His office was meticulously arranged. Just another reason why Susan's appearance did not concern him. Susan was the best, albeit gaudiest, assistant he had ever had. Technically, she was the only assistant he had ever had. Many of his colleagues had struggled for years trying to find just the right paralegal and administrative assistant. He had been blessed with Susan his last year at Ole Miss. Ten years his senior, she had completed her paralegal training and was looking for a job with a law firm. Susan picked him. When he got a job in Atlanta, she followed. When he left the partnership in Atlanta to hang his shingle in Balfour, she followed again. Susan called herself his personal pit bull. No one else dared repeat it.

His grandfather, a lawyer whose practice in Balfour was legendary, had always said that a man's measure could be taken in the number of people who were willing to help him succeed in life. The elder's oil portrait stood guard behind Thomas's desk, and more than one observer had noticed the strong resemblance. The old man had never been stingy with his gratitude or the sizable legacy he had inherited, and neither had Thomas. Thomas had few illusions about the sources of his success.

"Court in twenty," Susan's voice drawled pleasantly over the intercom.

Thomas picked up the bulging manila folder. Divorces were the worst. He was disgusted at how relationships could deteriorate into paperwork and pure animosity.

As a surgeon puts aside the face of the patient to focus on the disease inside, Thomas opened his leather briefcase and slid the oversized folder into an otherwise empty compartment and closed the lid securely.

Scrub up, he thought to himself. *Sedate the patient. Just cut out the cancer. Minimize the bleeding. Offer hope as a painkiller.*

Healing, he knew, was beyond his abilities.

His job was simple and generally straightforward. An obligation to his client.

Thomas pushed down on the top of the briefcase, bowing his head for a moment in sincere, grateful prayer. For his work, his secretary, his life, and, most of all, for Cora.

The cell phone vibrated an interruption. A smiley face from Cora. He shook his head. He would never stop wondering how she did that.

Chapter 4

Marjorie let herself in with her key, pausing at the door to announce herself. She hung up her hand-knit white sweater, snow-white scarf, and wide-brimmed straw hat. She set her purse, enormous and heavy with the necessities of life, on the table by the door.

As usual, Solomon greeted her from the doorway to the office, his broad black tail sweeping the floor with impatient expectancy. A soft mew rumbled from his well-whiskered face.

"He's lying to you," Cora said, her voice coming out of the office. "I already fed him."

Marjorie laughed and bent to rub the furry ears as he lifted his whole body to meet her fingers, purring louder.

"But he begs so sweetly," Marjorie protested. "I have treats in my purse."

The purring increased in volume and force.

"You spoil him, Marjorie. He knows you have treats."

"I'll clean the den and the kitchen first." She paused and straightened up. "He knows that too."

Cora appeared in the doorway, smiling at the unlikely pair.

"I'm going up to shower and dress. Two appointments today."

The wrinkles on Marjorie's worn face deepened around her eyes.

"Noon with Amy, and four thirty this afternoon," Cora continued, pretending not to see the look of curiosity and concern on Marjorie's face.

"Four thirty? That is an interesting time for an appointment."

Marjorie silently searched Cora's face for a moment.

Finally, Cora shrugged in resignation.

"So, did Thomas call you and tell you to speak to me?"

"No." Marjorie folded her arms across her ample chest. "Should Thomas have called and asked me to speak to you?"

"I don't think so."

"Cora, you have that look about you. You aren't telling me something."

"Marjorie," she returned.

"Cora, what is going on?"

There was a long, rather uncomfortably familiar pause and then, with motherly intuition, Marjorie knew.

"Why in heaven's name would you talk to Charlie?" she asked bluntly. "Have you been having dreams?"

"Marjorie," Cora began, almost apologetically. "I did have a dream last night, but this is not about that. At least, I don't think it is."

Solomon's hungry stare passed between the two women and settled on Cora.

The older woman put her hands on her well-rounded hips and scowled.

"You already know what I'm going to say about this."

"I know you don't like Charlie," Cora continued. "There was a message on the answering machine about a little girl. A little girl who needs us."

Marjorie threw up her hands in disgust.

"You aren't going to listen to me, are you?"

Cora knew any attempt at conversation was futile. Marjorie was as vocally antagonistic toward Charlie as Thomas was silently brooding.

"Marjorie, I have already discussed this with Thomas. I'm going to take a shower and dress."

Cora went up the stairs to her bedroom without looking back. As long as there were dreams and damaged children, this would be a never-ending argument that no one would win.

Five minutes later, the telephone rang from Cora's office. Fortunately for the caller, Marjorie was using the vacuum cleaner rather aggressively on the den carpet while she listened to music blaring from the local country radio station.

Marjorie had no way of knowing that Charlie was only fifteen minutes away, accompanied by the child who was supposed to be Cora's four thirty appointment.

Marjorie had missed her providential opportunity to derail Charlie's return to Cora's life. Again.

Chapter 5

The divorce hearing was proceeding exactly as Thomas had predicted.

Badly. Painfully for all concerned.

Katy Wilton sat beside him, twisting a dry tissue between her nail-bitten fingers, mostly cried out. Her older sister, Amy, sat at her other side, more matronly and sober. Amy stretched a reassuring arm across the back of Katy's chair and made soothing, motherly noises.

Across the narrow aisle of the modest, turn-of-the-century courtroom sat Steve Wilton, his jaw tightly set. He stared ahead at no one in particular. His attorney, a stunning young woman in her late twenties, sat rigidly beside him. Her expression was professional, but Thomas saw the truth in her eyes.

Thomas understood her annoyance. She was a tiny, interchangeable cog in a much larger corporate legal office whose headquarters were in Atlanta. She was a long, long way from home. Steve's father, the incumbent Georgia senator, would have insisted on a senior partner and an entourage of paralegals. Since this was Wilton's only prodigal son, a lone junior partner in the prestigious firm sufficed. Steve and his father were, after all, estranged at the moment.

The mundane paperwork that was stacked and paper-clipped on the polished oak table at the elbow of the ambitious attorney represented just another rung on the ladder of her chosen occupation. She had been summoned by her superiors. She had been sent on a messy but predictable mission. She had more or less completed the job, and Thomas suspected she was ready to go back to the urban civilization she knew best.

At this particular moment, however, Amanda Grayson was as close as she thought she had ever come to walking out on a semifamous client, her reputation and job be damned.

Judge Candler sat on the bench behind the massive oak desk, as he had for the past twenty-two years. One weathered hand held the heavy wooden gavel in what might have been construed as a threatening gesture, and his piercing eyes glared from beneath bushy white eyebrows. With a baritone growl, he cleared his throat angrily for the second time in as many minutes.

"What do you mean, your client isn't ready to sign? This is a formality. I was informed that there was an agreement," the judge snapped.

The elderly bailiff made a surprised noise and jumped slightly at the judge's tone, reaching for his hearing aid and turning the volume down a notch.

The young attorney noisily shuffled her stack of papers yet again, stalling for time, and making her displeasure with her stubborn client quite clear.

"May I have a few more moments to speak to Mr. Wilton?" she asked with all the composure she could muster. She was taken aback by the judge's harshness. Her meticulously painted eyes met his with what she hoped was not only beauty but also persuasion and professional firmness.

"If it please Your Honor," she added sweetly, pouting her lips slightly.

Judge Candler slid his glasses down to the tip of his hawkish nose, stared in disbelief, and shook his head brusquely from side to side.

"My chambers," he said firmly. "Where we should have been all along."

The occupants of the room rose rapidly as he moved out, the bailiff following awkwardly in an attempt to walk and readjust his hearing aid. Katy stood slowly with a tremor, leaning heavily on her sister's arm. The elder sister gave Thomas a searching look and leaned forward.

"Not a problem for us," Thomas reassured them, almost under his breath. "Steve's lawyer had insisted that we do this in the courtroom. I don't know why. Maybe just because it was Steve. Maybe Steve insisted."

Thomas paused and stopped himself from editorializing. The quirks of life never ceased to amaze him, especially the unpredictability of attraction. Steve delaying the proceedings was just another in a line of surprises. Thomas hadn't understood how an arrogant, selfish jerk like Steve Wilton could find someone as lovely as Katy to marry him. The fact that Steve had then wanted a divorce was a mystery too.

Life, Thomas knew from his own experience, was a puzzle.

"I'll take care of everything, Katy," he said, summoning a half-smile. "Everything."

Katy nodded blankly. Her sister tightened both her lips and her protective hold on Katy's upper arm. She frowned. Thomas followed Amy's gaze and saw that her dislike was directed specifically at Steve.

Thomas looked from one sister to the other. Amy seemed indignant over Steve's contradictory behavior, and he sympathized. Dragging out the signing would put both Katy and their toddler daughter Elizabeth through the ringer. Everyone in Balfour knew that Katy would be much better off without the louse. Besides, Katy had the reputation of being extraordinarily forgiving, especially when her husband was involved.

Not your place to judge, Thomas thought as he led them out of the courtroom.

The judge's chambers were familiar, pleasant, and comfortable for Thomas. He knew the odors well. Saddle leather chairs and polished hardwoods, well-used law books and diamond-paned glass-front bookcases. Old Spice cologne and a faint musky smell of expensive Cuban cigars. For a split second, he almost felt sorry for the young female attorney. Almost. Quite clearly she did not understand her arrogant client, or the authoritative, country-proud Judge Candler. Further, judging from the absence of a ring on her left hand, she knew nothing of the complexities of marriage from a personal point of view.

Judge Candler, having hung his black robe on the worn brass hook behind the door, lowered himself gingerly into his high-backed leather chair and slapped the edge of his desk with an open palm to call the room to attention. He waited while Thomas seated Katy into the armchair nearest the massive desk and watched as Thomas and Amy took their places, left and right, slightly behind as they flanked her sides.

"You two do not sit," the judge barked to Steve and the female attorney as they entered, arguing. Steve's tone toward the woman held a low, aggressive, controlled fury.

Candler's sharp eyes and his own firm determination turned specifically on Steve.

"Hell's bells, Steve!" The older man's voice crackled with frustration. "Give Katy the baby, half the money, all the house, and move on. What is the matter with you?"

Steve glared, his expression that of a petulant child denied a second dessert. His lawyer opened her brightly glossed lips and laid a slender, well-manicured, placating hand on Steve's arm. He jerked away, attempting to speak but managing only to sputter.

The veteran judge, however, had no intention of being deterred from his own personal tirade. No one made a mockery of his courtroom.

"When you act as though you have lost your mind, son, you can expect for people to think you have gone crazy—and they will treat you accordingly." He paused for a split second, slapping the desk yet again. "Are we clear, son? You are not dealing with your daddy here."

Candler stopped and turned his attention to the now visibly shaken city attorney.

"Is all this *your* idea, Miss . . ."

"Grayson," she offered. "*Ms.* Grayson, Your Honor. I just

wanted—"

"Not interested," the judge interrupted coldly, "in either your marital status or in what you may or may not want. Did you tell Steve that he has some sort of choice about this settlement? Because he doesn't. Not as far as the state is concerned. Not as far as I am concerned."

"Your Honor—" she began again, but this time her own client interrupted her.

"I've changed my mind," Steve said flatly. "I just told you. I'm not signing any papers. I don't want a divorce."

Katy leaned away from the familiar, strident voice and reached over her shoulder, searching for her sister's hand, her face pale with shock and surprise. Amy swayed slightly, losing composure for the first time that morning, and Thomas thought for a moment that the stronger sister was about to faint.

The young attorney's face was equally ashen.

Judge Candler, a thunderous cloud gathering around his eyes, slapped the edge of the desk, this time with both palms flat, and leaned back with a long, low exhaled bark of disapproval.

Thomas could think of nothing to say, his mind racing to no particular conclusion. He had not expected this. Obviously, neither had anyone else in the room.

From the looks of Wilton's lawyer, she had no idea what to do now.

"Steve," Judge Candler said slowly, as if he might genuinely believe that Wilton had lost his mind and might be incapable of understanding. "This is not a game. You cannot just start divorce proceedings and stop them again on a whim."

The judge stopped speaking for a moment and let his words hang in the highly charged air.

"Steve, look at me, son." The judge pushed his glasses up on his nose and tapped them against his forehead. "You aren't in charge here. Do you know that? You are in no position to make demands."

"I want counseling," Steve insisted, as though he had heard nothing at all. He took two steps toward Katy, who cowered even deeper into the chair, covering her face with her hands. Thomas stepped between Steve and his intended prey, effectively blocking Wilton's view of his wife and sister-in-law.

"I want to go to counseling," Steve persisted. "With Katy. I want to go home to my daughter. I want to save my marriage."

Katy made a small, almost frightened sound and reached again for Amy's hand. Thomas folded his arms across his chest, straightened his broad shoulders, and took another step forward.

"Mr. Wilton," his attorney's feminine, pleading voice began weakly from behind her client. "We should discuss this in private. If you will only give me—"

"Shut up," he interrupted her with a callous wave of his hand. "You'll be paid."

Wilton stopped for a moment, knowing that Thomas would foil any attempt to move past him. Momentarily resigned to his fate, Wilton addressed his soon-to-be ex-wife. To anyone that did not know Steve Wilton, his tone might have been mistaken for apologetic.

"Katy, listen to me. I don't want a divorce," he said simply. "I've changed my mind. Let me come home to you and

Elizabeth."

There was only a small, strangled sob from the baffled young girl.

Wilton thumped the buttons on Thomas's starched shirt with a provocation that the attorney stiffly ignored.

"And you," he ordered pointedly. "I want to talk to your wife, Tommy. Today. Tell her that I want an appointment. Make it happen."

Stone-faced, broad-chested, and unmoving, Thomas was not to be intimidated.

"I don't presume to speak for my wife." Thomas's voice was deceptively quiet. His emerald green eyes had gone dark and deep for the second time that morning. A personal record. "I don't select Cora's clients or set her appointments. She decides for herself who she does and does not want to help."

Steve snorted and took a swaggering step backward. He was not accustomed to refusals to do his bidding. His father had seen to that for most of his life. Most men could be bought. Most women could be persuaded. The younger Wilton believed that he had both ample money and powers of persuasion.

He was formulating a scathing retort when he felt Amanda Grayson put her hand on the elbow of his Armani suit for yet another time that morning, more firmly this time.

"May I speak to you privately?" The sentence was a question, but she did not seem to be asking a question at all. "There are several avenues we might pursue."

Steve stared coldly down at her hand until she pulled it away.

Judge Candler had heard enough.

"I will give you until the end of the week. Period. Sort this out with your Atlanta lawyer here and communicate through Thomas. Only Thomas."

Judge Candler leaned forward across his desk and met Steve's eyes.

"I won't have Katy bullied by you or anyone else," he warned. "Do you hear me?"

"Judge, sir . . ." Amanda had finally found her voice, a new target for her irritation, and a growing confidence in her ability, although much too late to do her any good.

"I'm done, young woman." Candler motioned to the bailiff, who had been waiting unobtrusively by the door for further instructions. "Now, get out of my chambers."

"But, Your Honor—" Amanda began. But Steve spun on his heel and stormed to the door. She had little choice but to follow her furious client, the mildly amused bailiff bringing both the parade and the office door to a decisive close.

"Amy," Candler said easily, turning to the older of the remaining women. "A moment with your sister and Thomas, please."

Amy did not like being sent from the room, although Candler's reputation made protest both futile and foolish. She disentangled her hand and patted Katy's shoulder absently before she left, giving Thomas an accusatory stare. When the heavy oak door had thudded shut for the second time, the judge turned to Thomas.

"What in blazes is going on?"

Thomas shook his head. He turned around and faced his client, searching. "Katy?"

She looked up with wide-eyed, tear-stained bewilderment.

"Has Steve talked to you about counseling?" Thomas hated to press her, but he needed to know. "About not wanting a divorce?"

She shook her head, random strands of blond hair escaping and falling into her puffy red eyes. Pressing her fingers to her lips, she took a long, deep breath, filling her lungs with air as if for the first time in a long time. Her mouth moved for several seconds before words came out. When the words did escape, they were faint and hesitating.

"We've been staying with Amy. Elizabeth and I have been there for the last week or so." Katy sheepishly glanced at Thomas. "I know you told me I didn't have to leave the house . . . our house . . . but Amy thought . . . "

"Go on," the judge interrupted with fatherly concern. "Were you afraid of Steve?"

"Amy wouldn't tell me when he called," she said. She began to twist the tissue again. "She said he was calling all the time. I didn't want to talk to him. Amy said I didn't have to talk to him. He was acting crazy."

She paused. "He was scaring Elizabeth."

"I understand," the judge encouraged, looking at Thomas for confirmation that this was not new information. They both knew it wasn't.

"So, when was the last time you talked?"

"With Steve?" Katy dabbed at her eyes. "Maybe two weeks. It's been so fast. One minute I was married and the next . . ." Her voice trailed off.

Thomas picked up a box from the corner of the desk and handed Katy a fresh tissue, which she began to shred methodically.

"Thomas, I didn't know what to do."

"Yes, Katy, I know. You were right to call me. Amy was right."

Wilton's multiple infidelities came to his mind. That Katy had forgiven him, over and over, was a testament to her faithfulness. Faithfulness that no one in Balfour could accept or understand. Katy was always willing to take Steve back, as though she believed that her willingness to let him do whatever he wanted had insulated her from divorce. And now, after six weeks of abandonment and legal wrangling, her errant husband had suddenly reconsidered.

Maybe he realized too late what he was throwing away in Katy, Thomas thought. *Just maybe.*

"You've known Steve since you were boys, Thomas," Katy continued between soft sniffles. "You and Charlie were his best friends. Do you think he can change?"

Thomas tried not to wince at the sound of Charlie's name. This was about Katy, and that was the problem. He *did* know Steve Wilton. He knew Steve too well, and something about this just didn't seem right. Not right at all. Hadn't seemed right from the beginning. The idea of a rushed, hurry-up divorce might seem like one of Steve's ideas on the surface. Impulsive. Thoughtless. No one was surprised the elder Wilton had pulled senatorial strings to bring in a lawyer who would be efficient and effective. Even so, Steve's initial desire for divorce was an idea that Thomas had not understood. Still did not quite understand.

Katy leaving Steve made sense. Steve leaving Katy was illogical and odd, for want of a better word.

"I asked you if you thought he could change," she repeated, watching his face.

Thomas's silence was answer enough.

Katy's hands dropped on the gathering pile of tissues in her lap, and her fingers rested absently on top of the snowy white mound.

"I thought having Elizabeth would set things right. I really did."

Thomas handed her a third tissue as she began to cry again in earnest.

Judge Candler looked at Thomas.

"I don't like this," the judge said flatly. "What is Steve up to now?"

Thomas wanted to add that he had never liked Steve. Had not liked much of what Steve had ever done. He was an egotistical playboy. A shady, unethical entrepreneur who lived on his father's money and reputation. A high school star quarterback who rested on his imaginary laurels. Only a shy, pretty girl four years younger could give him what he needed— constant adoration and loyalty.

Yes, Thomas thought, *the baby should have, could have, changed everything, as many babies do. Maybe Steve discovered he was no longer the center of his lovely wife's universe. Jealousy isn't logical.*

But the thoughtful attorney said none of the things he was thinking. Speculation was fodder for gossip, not the courtroom and a speedy resolution. The judge already knew what he wanted to happen. The town of Balfour knew. Thomas looked down at the top of Katy's head and knew instinctively what his wife would say. She would not want to help Steve, but she would do what she could for Katy's sake.

"I'll call home before lunch," he offered gently. "Marjorie is with Cora today. One of them will call you to make an appointment for later this week. Do you want to talk to someone about all this, Katy?"

Katy nodded helplessly, beginning to tremble again.

"An appointment for you, and maybe Elizabeth," Thomas emphasized. "You know how Cora is with children."

Katy nodded again, this time with a smile at her daughter's name.

"Not Steve. You understand, don't you? This is not marriage counseling."

Katy did understand. No one in Balfour believed her marriage was worth saving. Except for her beloved daughter, Katy didn't believe that much in her life right now was really worth saving either. Even Steve.

Judge Candler reached for his intercom.

"Mrs. Duncan?" He paused to hear the dependable drawl of her answer. "Ask Amy to come back to my chambers, please."

"Katy," he said, turning back to the emotionally battered girl before him, his voice grandfatherly and kind.

"You just take care of little Elizabeth. Nothing else. You don't have to talk to Steve unless you *want* to talk to Steve. And if you do, Thomas should be with you."

"Yes, Judge," she whispered quietly.

There was an impatient knock. Candler nodded at Thomas, who reluctantly pulled open the heavy door. Amy swept in with an air of maternal protectiveness, like a lioness protecting her cub, and took Katy's arm. Thomas had a sudden impression that poor Katy was exchanging one tyrant for another. When the sisters had gone, the men shared a long silence before Candler finally spoke.

"Lunch? Thought I'd have the usual at Sam's. Separate booths, of course."

Thomas finally smiled.

"Sure." His word was a sigh. "See you there in thirty minutes or so. Just need to keep my promise to Katy and call Cora about that appointment first."

"I'm glad," Candler nodded. "And tell Cora that I send my love too. We miss seeing her at church, you know. I know it has been a long time, which of course I understand."

He stopped when he noted the sadness in Thomas's eyes.

"Maybe we need to plan a visit instead. Just let her know we are praying for her."

"I will," Thomas said, looking at his watch and thinking about the dream and about Charlie. And unwelcome surprises. "I will indeed."

Chapter 6

Andrew Evans's office staff was skipping lunch. Again.

The receptionist, Donna Phillips, and the church secretary, Alice Lee, had a combined sixty years of church staff service between them. Traditionally Southern in all the ways that counted, the sweet, steely pair had weathered a long succession of pastors, associate pastors, interims, and assorted ministers with grave dignity, but these last six months with Pastor Evans had put their piety to the test and had come close to being their collective last days in service at Emmanuel Baptist Church.

A stack of articles from various church committees, which all required editing, sat on Alice's usually immaculate desktop. Beside the stack was yet another neatly organized pile of youth lock-in forms, signed and dated, for sorting and filing away. Sunday's bulletin, also requiring further editing, occupied the center of the desk, recently spattered with the preacher's blood-red revisions and corrections.

Neither woman, by unspoken agreement, complained within the inner sanctum of the church offices. Both knew that resentment and discontent spread like flies on banana pudding at dinner on the ground. The same restraint could not be attributed to their long-suffering deacon husbands. As the perpetually elected church treasurer, Thad Phillips had spent the first months of the new pastor's tenure objecting strongly and often to what he saw as Pastor Evans's extravagant spending. Retiling a baptistery that was used only two or three times a year was not high on Phillips's priority list. Neither was, to his mind, funding the Tuesday Ladies Missionary Study monthly luncheons.

"Let the blue-hairs buy their own mixed green salads and cheese garlic croutons," he would complain to Donna in the afternoons when he came by to pick her up from the office. Retired from his half-century as a local banker, he and Donna lived a frugal life. Thad had retired fully vested with a modest but adequate income. They shared a single car and a quiet home and were quite well-known among their friends for also sharing a singular way of thinking.

Andrew James Lee, chairman of the deacons, knew less about the finances and a great deal more about the inner workings of the deacons and their fundamentally rocky relationship with the new pastor. The deacons had borne most of the difficulty of finding a suitable pastor for the tiny rural church, and they were now bearing the brunt of the congregational ire over their choice of Evans.

Oh, Evans had the credentials. The nominating committee had been certain of that. His first sermons were biblical and theologically sound. No question. What Andrew Lee and the other deacons were not quite able to do was to define exactly what did bother them about Andrew Evans. Too many changes too quickly made, perhaps. Too much of a city-style arrogance that just irritated the older men, who were almost as attached to their traditions as they were to their religious dogmas.

The first change to raise eyebrows was the removal of the communion table and the weekly arrangements of flowers on Sundays. Those Evans had the custodial staff, mainly one ancient handyman named Frost and his equally antique wife, Beryl, move to the vestibule and away from what many thought to be the preacher's allergy-prone nasal passages.

Next came Evans's insistence on female greeters, added to the list of males who had not generally attained the rank of deacon but who performed the duties of passing out the bulletins at the double doors on Sunday mornings and collecting the offering plates during the services. When confronted, Evans raised his own eyebrows in mildly mocking surprise and asked if his opposition thought that accepting a bulletin from a female hand rather than a male hand somehow altered the character of worship. Or maybe that the membership thought their tithes and offerings were less holy in the hands of the women of their numbers. This temporarily, although awkwardly, silenced the most audible of objections.

Then there was the argument about the music between Billy Bob and Frank.

The addition of a drum set and two acoustic guitars, followed within the week by a flute and a violin, had almost sent the choir members into apoplexy. Although in fairness those specific changes, though Pastor Evans himself had approved, had come at the request of the church choir director, Billy Bob Morris.

Brother Billy Bob had been recently radicalized by a youth group mission trip to Memphis, the Birthplace of the Blues. He seized the advantage brought on by the pastor's chaos, and in addition to his attempt to create a band had also tried to slip in an electric keyboard at one Wednesday night rehearsal. Unfortunately for Billy Bob, the organist for Sunday morning services for the last thirty-odd years had put a quick stop to that with a simple refusal to play any contraption that had to be plugged into the wall to make music. Frank was a traditionalist and a classically trained instrumentalist.

The choir members universally backed Frank, and Billy Bob was forced to return to the more conventional and time-honored methods of making music in a Baptist church. The drum set went back to the rental place in Griffith the following Tuesday. The guitars were allowed to stay, on condition of good behavior.

The office had been silent for the last hour, except for the almost imperceptible ticking of the wall clock and the occasional clicking from the keyboards of the respective computers. Both women were working together and through their lunches by common consent. Neither would have left the other to do the work that needed to be done. Though their job titles were different, their abilities to perform those jobs were equal.

When the telephone unexpectedly interrupted the determinedly plodding work, Donna lifted the receiver to her carefully salon-finished hair and answered with a sweetness that belied her present state of mind.

"Emmanuel Baptist Church, Donna Phillips speaking."

There was a long pause as she listened, but her expression did not change.

"Of course, Mrs. Evans. I think the pastor has gone to a lunch meeting." She paused. "No, I don't know with whom." She tried to keep her voice level. "I could take the message myself?" Another pause. "No? Have a blessed day. I'll connect you to the pastor's line."

To her credit, Donna did not flinch at the word "lunch," even though Alice's eyes met hers with a twinkle and the friends exchanged a conspiratorial eye-rolling before Donna hung up her receiver and went back to editing. Andrew Evans was a taskmaster. As senior pastor, he held lots of meetings, which was both expected and encouraged. Those meetings included food, of course. Most Baptists believed passionately in the power of potato salad, fried chicken, green beans, and macaroni and cheese. However, a meeting with Preacher Evans that also included food did not imply that there would be the camaraderie that most Baptists would expect from a working lunch.

Evans expected more work that eating, and that caused many to question his denominational loyalties.

Evans had made his mark on Emmanuel Baptist Church as an unwarranted innovator, thoughtless taskmaster, and socially impaired administrator.

Outsiders who were not members of the church wondered, as close-knit small-town people will, why a preacher as disliked as Evans had managed to gather the requisite number of votes to be called to the pastorate, or to keep his job after the membership came to fully understand the man they had accepted as their shepherd. The gossipers and gripers were given the same answer by almost every member, an answer which was obvious to anyone who attended the church.

As much as Pastor Evans was disliked, his wife, Virginia, was beloved. Her sturdy, country stature and pleasant spirit encouraged and uplifted everyone whose life came into contact with hers. There were no citified airs, and there was no pretense in Virginia Evans.

She wore sensible shoes, grew vegetables and flowers in a garden she tended with joy and generosity, washed and set her own naturally silver-white hair, and loved all children, although the Evanses apparently had no children of their own. There were rumors, but no woman in the church really felt she knew Virginia well enough to pry into what seemed to be a private and possibly painful subject.

Evans's tender love and affection for his wife, and hers for him, was quite honestly the reason that neither Donna nor Alice had walked out the first two weeks after their new pastor's arrival. If Virginia Evans loved this man, there must be something the rest of the world just could not see—a virtue by which he was redeemed.

In a private and rare moment on the second day of Evans's tenure, the two secretaries had quietly confessed to each other that this was indeed a remarkable marriage, and while they had never met a preacher as ornery as Andrew Evans, they had also never met a woman quite as saintly as Virginia "Ginny" Evans.

Both secretaries unabashedly envied the devotion so clearly present in Virginia's marriage to the preacher. It was what gave the two women the strength to keep working with a man they did not like. They covered for his unexplained absences. They trusted him. Which was exactly what they had to remind themselves just before the telephone call arrived in the church office several hours later.

Chapter 7

Marjorie had finished the routine Monday morning vacuuming and was about to slide supper into the oven when the doorbell rang for the first time. She carefully closed the oven door and grabbed the red plaid kitchen towel, rubbing it between her hands, and was on her way to the door when it rang for the second time.

"Coming!" she announced with her accustomed cheerfulness, beginning to hum a favorite hymn and finding herself a bit out of breath. Passing the doorway to the study on her left, she noted that it was still empty. Cora had not yet come downstairs.

From the top of the staircase to her right she could hear sounds coming from the master bedroom, classical music and the sound of water from the shower.

Good, Marjorie thought. Part of the reason Thomas paid her to come during the week was her basic bulldog skills, the ones that had served her so well in her years first as a nanny and later as a substitute teacher.

The doorbell had rung for the third insistent time when she reached the door and peered through the stained glass at the form outside. Marjorie's expression soured immediately. She knew what needed to be done.

"The appointment is for four thirty, Charlie," she snapped through the glass, her irritated breath leaving a film of condensation. "Go away until Thomas gets home."

"Tried to call," Charlie retorted calmly. "Check the answering machine, Marjorie."

"Try Ted Freud. He needs the business."

"That's Floyd, Marjorie, not Freud. Ted Floyd. He is brilliant, but he only works with adults. Stop trying to change the subject."

"Let him in, Marjorie."

The voice from the top of the stairs was firm and understanding at the same time. "You know perfectly well he isn't going to leave until we talk to him."

"I did just talk to him," Marjorie grumbled. But she unlocked the door and opened it anyway, standing just inside and hovering.

Charlie was not a tall man, nor was he particularly muscular. People who knew him only by his reputation were often surprised by his slight appearance and boyish demeanor, and that surprise pleased Charlie. He used his appearance to its best advantage for deception and deflection. If keeping people off guard were an Olympic sport, Charlie would have swept the field of gold medals.

"Tried to call to warn you," Charlie repeated, leaning nonchalantly against the doorframe. His heart was pounding in his chest, and it took all his effort to keep his voice level.

"So I heard." Cora did not make any move to come down the stairs. "What do you want, Charlie? You're hours early."

His eyes met hers and from behind him he drew a reluctant child, positioning her at his side. He looked down, and she followed his gaze to his right hand, which was being clutched by a much, much smaller hand. There, dwarfed by Charlie's masculine frame, was a tiny girl with straight, waist-length ebony hair and an almost bone-white complexion. Her almond-shaped eyes were clear and vacant of emotion, and she was wearing a cherry-red silk pajama suit with red and gold embroidered slippers.

"This is Cherry Blossom," Charlie offered with a forced smile, his eyes returning to Cora's face. He wondered if Cora and Marjorie saw what he saw. Diminutive, raven-haired, dark eyed. The little girl was a doll-like version of the woman at the top of the stairs.

Cora gave him a stern look, followed by a grunt from Marjorie.

"She told you her name is Cherry Blossom?" Cora tried not to smile.

"She won't tell me anything. She won't talk to anyone," Charlie retorted matter-of-factly. "Precisely my reason for being here. Protective services told me there was paperwork to fill out before I could come by and see you. I went by to fill out said paperwork, and the powers-that-be have changed their minds. They apparently only want paperwork from the attending psychologist. Saved me hours of drudgery, but not good news for you."

He stopped and looked down at the child. The flippancy was gone. His eyes met Cora's again, and then he looked back to the girl who was still standing like a miniature stone statue at the end of his arm.

"I told them you would help, Cora."

She tried to ignore the emotion in his voice. She knew what he wanted. He wanted to be told he was forgiven. To be told that she understood that he felt that somehow these little lost souls could replace the baby she had lost. That they had lost. Together.

Cora took a deep breath.

"Marjorie, what time is it, please?"

"Almost nine thirty, I think."

Marjorie knew what Cora was thinking. Cora needed time to prepare for the twelve o'clock appointment with Amy, who was a first time client. They both needed to get rid of Charlie quickly and quietly, and both knew that was something only Cora could do. Marjorie reached a soft, wrinkled hand toward the child.

"Would you come with me, sweetheart?"

The little girl looked up expectantly at Charlie, who nodded at her and gave her another smile. This time a real smile.

"It's okay," he said gently. "Marjorie is a nice lady. You'll be safe here."

"There are cookies in the kitchen," Marjorie offered. She took a tentative step closer. "And milk, or maybe lemonade."

"I'd like a cookie," Charlie announced, opening his fingers

and releasing the hand in his, giving the child a slight push of encouragement. "And I'll take milk with mine."

"You aren't staying," Marjorie replied almost cordially.

The child gave Charlie a hesitant look before obediently taking Marjorie's outstretched hand to follow her down the darkened hallway.

Charlie waited until they were gone before he spoke again.

"This feels familiar," he began. "You at the top of the stairs. Me in the doorway, leaving. Or was I coming in?"

"You were never coming home, Charlie. You made that clear."

"I suppose I did, didn't I?"

Charlie was glad that Cora could not read his thoughts. For all her perception, he hoped she had no clue how much her words stung. He deserved them. Every word. But he had decided long ago that if he really did love her, he would have to put his own selfishness aside. He had made the decision for both of them. She was better off without him, and safer. That was all that mattered.

There was another long pause. Like so many other moments in their past, Cora was ready for this moment to be over. For a split second she considered telling Charlie about the dream, but she remembered what James had said. The message she had was not for Charlie.

"Tell me about the little girl," she said instead. "Before you go."

Charlie sadly shook his head and lowered his voice.

"Only witness, if you could call her that, to a multiple homicide. Found alone in a house with five adults, all relatives.

Killed execution-style in Savannah about three weeks ago."

"Why wouldn't you call her a witness?"

"Seems she didn't actually *see* anything. They found her sedated and locked in an upstairs bedroom. Completely unharmed except for the meds, and they were really mild. Glass of milk by the bed. Homicide sent for protective services, and they carried her out before she woke up."

"Gangs? Drugs?"

"Just speculation at this point."

"She seems to be about four years old."

"That's what we think, but she hasn't told us. According to Lisa, there is nothing physically preventing her from speaking. Most I have gotten is that look she gave Marjorie. No physical harm or apparent injuries."

"Emotional trauma is often worse than physical," Cora said, making a disgusted face. "Has she been in protective services all this time?"

"Wheels of justice and all that." Charlie paused. "She doesn't have any other relatives."

"Are they certain?"

"Yes."

Cora sensed there was more he wasn't saying, but she knew he would tell her if he thought she needed to know.

"Is her suitcase in the car?"

Charlie nodded. "I know how you work," he said and flashed a grin. "I know you."

"Yes, Charlie." Cora was tired. "You always did know me. There was never a question about that."

If she had hit a nerve, he gave no sign.

"I'll just leave the suitcase inside the door."

He reached inside his sports jacket for an overstuffed envelope and placed it on the small mahogany table by the door.

"Paperwork's in here. You've done this before."

"Unfortunately, yes, I have." Her eyes focused on the envelope. "Are you certain there is not anything else I should know?"

"No. Just update Lisa, please. I am now officially out of the loop. This is the Savanah PD's case. Detective Mark Maclin. Truthfully, I wasn't sure why they even called me until I found out there was a child involved. They need you, Cora. They know me from other cases, and that we have history together, and they wanted me to ask. The investigation has gone cold without her. She won't talk."

"No promises, Charlie."

"You are the only one I still have any faith in, Cora," he said, not looking away. "I'll get that suitcase now."

When the door closed Cora went into the study to text Thomas, and when she came out again a few minutes later there was a tiny blue canvas suitcase just inside the door. On top of the case was a small stuffed black kitten with a large red silk bow. Solomon, with his usual cat-like curiosity, was investigating the toy interloper.

Cora double-checked that the door was securely locked and lifted the live cat gently into her arms, rubbing her chin against the soft fur of his purring neck.

Her mind raced with possibilities. She knew patience was the best plan—not just for the child, but also for Charlie and for sharing the cryptic details of her dream.

Her mind snapped back to the issue at hand. Three weeks in protective custody was a long, long time. And unlike Charlie, she had a much more realistic view of her own abilities. She knew she needed to focus.

With a deep breath, she closed her eyes and offered up a silent prayer for wisdom. After a moment Solomon struggled in her arms with a muffled yowl, and when she opened her eyes she had a sudden craving for chocolate chip cookies and milk.

Chapter 8

Lunch at Sam's was deliciously predictable. Thomas ordered the loaded potato soup in a house-made bread bowl. It came steaming and chunky, the top sprinkled with chopped green onions. If Cora had been there, she would have guilted him into a green salad too, but he preferred to save that room for Sam's famously fattening chocolate swirl cheesecake.

Judge Candler was much more gastrically responsible. His chef salad contained generous servings of homegrown vegetables, lean turkey, perfectly boiled eggs, and low-fat house special vinaigrette dressing on the side. Both men had already downed a Mason jar each of Sam's infamous honey-sweetened iced tea and were waiting for Sam herself to return to refill the glasses.

Scrupulously aware of appearances and the stipulations of law, the two men did not sit together but instead sat back-to-back in the matching booths at the back of Sam's. With the

Wilton case delayed and the expected pressure from the Senator, they could not afford rumors of conspiracy against Steve.

During trials, this was their usual lunch spot because it was public and professional. From the high-walled booths, the men had a panoramic view of the rest of the rather smallish restaurant, especially the ornately carved wooden-front double doors, inlaid with panels of thick, Tiffany-like glass that was original to the red brick building. Through the multicolored glass, diamonds and rainbows of light from the noonday sun danced across the deeply scarred hardwood floor.

Except for the customary fast food eateries that were found closer to the interstate and near the gas stations and a few chain eateries that had been voted by the town counsel to be built far away from the historic town center, there were not many choices about where to eat in Balfour.

Sam's was the only place that might be counted as a real restaurant, and certainly the only one with Southern home cooking. An overly optimistic Mexican place at the edge of the town center had lasted for almost two years before being replaced by a Chinese restaurant that lasted half as long.

Henson's Pharmacy and Soda Fountain, which occupied the opposite corner of the square, appeared to have emerged unchanged from the 1950s and offered ice cream sundaes, fountain sodas, and a variety of quick and standard sandwiches. Many tourists came through Balfour just to sit at the red vinyl-covered stools at the old-fashioned counter, watch a well-trained young man concoct cream sodas, and admire the highly polished black and white linoleum floors.

Almost everyone, tourists and locals alike, agreed that the

best vantage point in Balfour to watch the ever-changing seasons was from one of the shop windows on the square, looking out on the tree-filled park in the middle of the old town.

Sam's front window views were a frequent tourist destination, as well as her legendary food. She boasted a full hot and cold lunch menu every day, except Sundays, and a more extensive menu for dinner on most Friday and Saturday nights.

Sam, actually Samantha, had been known to randomly refuse service to anyone who used her given name. She had taken over the running of the restaurant from her grandfather, who was also called Sam.

Grandpa Sam, actually Samuel Elias Simmons, had established Simmons' Restaurant almost fifty years ago, based solely on the merits of great-grandmother Bessie's blue ribbon chicken pot pie recipe. Grandpa Sam had first leased, then purchased, the building on the downtown square across from the Balfour courthouse. The space had originally housed the first Ace Hardware store in Balfour, which had expanded and moved two blocks over from the square into newer and much larger quarters.

Simmons' Restaurant proved to be an excellent fit for the town square. It sat nestled between a quaint old bookstore cryptically named Dragons, whose sign boasted hard-to-find first editions and current popular paperbacks, and an equally unique jewelry store, Copperfield's Jewelry and Collectibles, that featured handmade gifts from local designers.

Both the bookstore and jewelry store owners were octogenarians who eyed Sam suspiciously when she took over the business, but they were soon placated when they realized she saw no need to alter the décor or the historic traditions the elders in town had come to expect from her grandfather.

In more than ten years, Sam's changes extended mainly to some healthier, more vegan options on the menu. What remained in the transformation was an interesting assortment and veritable smorgasbord of local offerings that were creative and had no discernible overall ethnicity.

Sam both managed and served, along with local teenagers looking for part-time work, but the bulk of the cooking was done by Bill. Bill was himself a confusion of character and ethnicity. His long, waist-length hair, streaked with browns and grays, was braided in one long, thick tail down his back and secured with a strip of black leather. His weathered, quite wrinkled face was of indeterminable age. On first glance, Bill might have appeared to be a Native American, but the bottle green eyes under bushy salt and pepper eyebrows were almost Asian.

Rumor had it that in her youth a rebellious Sam had met the reticent, enigmatic Bill one night in a questionable back alley in Memphis, Tennessee, and that neither of them were sober. While no one doubted that possibility, that was about as far as the rumors were allowed to go. At any rate, for the residents of Balfour, Georgia, Bill's history was as murky as Sam's was crystal clear.

Born in Balfour, Sam had led a more or less typical childhood. An only child of prominent wealthy parents, brought up in a Christian church, obedient and quiet in her teens, Samantha Sue Simmons had gone off to Memphis State. There she became simply "Sam" and traded her farm boy high school sweetheart for a fast-paced Tennessee drummer. Some say her senior year in college was responsible for nearly driving her loving parents to the gates of Woodlawn Memorial Cemetery when her father had his second heart attack in a year and her mother resorted to a diet of valium and gin fizz. Although both parents survived Sam's final unfinished year, the long-term damage was done.

No matter. Everyone in town over the age of twenty-one had heard and could recite from memory the story of how Bill, the silent stranger in a plaid flannel shirt and faded jeans, arrived at the family's front door at seven o'clock on Easter Sunday morning with a subdued, red-eyed Sam clutching his elbow.

Versions of the story vary from there, but most agree that the pair were inside Sam's childhood home—a beautiful antebellum mansion—seated side by side on the red velvet Victorian sofa in Marybeth Simmons's front parlor for several hours that morning. Everyone knew that something monumental had happened, since the Simmons, churchgoers and regular attendees at Balfour United Methodist Church, were not in their appointed pew at eleven o'clock when the services officially began. Everyone also agreed that there was some sort of religious transformation that morning behind the white columns of the family mansion.

As the housekeeper later whispered the story to her sister in Griffith, remorse, repentance, and eventual regeneration flowed from the prodigal twenty-one-year-old daughter in a way that her stunned parents accepted with tears and gratitude. The story spread over Balfour like kudzu on the banks of a swollen creek.

Sam had changed. There were collective "Hallelujahs" from

friends and family. Bill, whoever he was, had had something to do with the transformation. Maybe everything to do with the change, although Bill himself took neither the credit nor the blame for anything that happened. For the Simmons family, nothing else mattered to them except that their errant daughter was home. Nothing else for them would ever matter.

Sam returned to college the following semester in a determined attempt to finish what she had begun. Regretfully, in the next year, Marybeth and Harris Simmons died in an unavoidable automobile accident on the mountain roads of North Carolina. The townspeople consoled themselves that if theirs was not a peaceful passing, then they were surely content in the knowledge that their daughter had resumed the path to her salvation.

Bill, for his part, steadfastly refused all compensation for his services, real or imagined, including the offer of a night in one of the many rooms in the mansion, even though Sam insisted that he had no place else to go. Grandpa Sam was, however, able to persuade the apparently rootless stranger to accept an offer of work in the restaurant as a busboy and general handyman.

Within the first week, Bill's affinity for hard, honest work and his imaginative cooking skills made themselves apparent. Within two weeks, Bill had gratefully accepted a renovated room over the restaurant in exchange for a modest pay, and within the month he and Grandpa Sam became inseparable friends, working long hours in the kitchen together during the day and spending countless hours in white-washed wooden rocking chairs on the upstairs balcony overlooking the trees in the square.

Night after night they sat, playing checkers, sharing stories and secrets, and rocking in easy companionship. From time to time they also shared the guilty pleasure of a beer or two that they surreptitiously smuggled up the wrought iron exterior fire escape, but mostly they enjoyed their cold Royal Crown colas and their conversations.

No one ever knew what they talked about, or what they might have had in common. When Grandpa Sam suffered from a stroke that put him in a local nursing home and his checker-playing nights became the absentminded days of an invalid, Bill continued their tradition. At the end of every day, Bill appeared promptly at six o'clock in the doorway of the old man's room, the checkerboard and pieces under his arm and a special dessert or delicacy in a small white takeout container from the restaurant. The quiet conversations continued, sprinkled with laughter that echoed down the halls and a joy that did not escape the attention of the nursing home staff. Bill gave Grandpa Sam an easy round of checkers and hope.

When the days ended altogether, Grandpa Sam's will left his wishes clear. The house and everything he owned went to Samantha, specifically the restaurant. Oddly enough, the will further stipulated that although the restaurant itself was left to Sam, the entire upstairs second floor of the building was left to Bill.

Thomas, who had overseen the draft of the will, had been only mildly perplexed at the grandfather's request, but then decided that this sort of craziness was as much Southern as it was Simmons and accepted the situation without further question.

As for Sam, after spending two weeks of self-imposed solitude and grief in her old bedroom at the mansion, she rejoined the world of the living as a changed person once more. She abandoned what little was left of her college career in Memphis, finished a few business courses at the nearby junior college, and took over Grandpa Sam's bookkeeping from the kindly old crony of her grandpa's, who was more than happy to be shed of the burden. Eventually, with some tutoring from Bill, Sam took over the day-to-day running of the restaurant as well as waiting tables.

Rumor had it that Grandpa Sam made Bill a full partner in Simmons' Restaurant, but Thomas would not confirm anything of the sort.

No one ever saw Sam and Bill together except for their working time in the restaurant, and even then they seemed to communicate more by telepathy, gestures, and pointed facial expressions than in words or normal conversation.

They could also be seen on Sunday mornings at Balfour United Methodist Church, where they regularly attended on Sundays and for absolutely any other additional services and programs.

They arrived and departed separately and always alone.

Sam always sat on one end of the third pew, closest to the stained glass window of the Virgin and Child, where she cherished fond memories of her parents. She remembered her early years when she sat with her mother's arm against hers, sharing the hymnal as they sang in harmony together.

Bill sat on the other end of the same pew, the end nearest the center nave, in the place the elderly Sam had always occupied, dutifully rising and resuming his seat with the congregation, but politely and firmly refusing either to share a hymnal or sing a song. If the sermons or the music ever moved him, no one knew nor dared to ask.

The space between them on the pew was always empty, although neither Sam nor Bill seemed particularly lonely or even sad. Everyone thought there must be much more to the story, but like most of the secrets in Balfour, no one was brave enough to ask.

The sound of Sam tapping the edge of the table with her index finger startled Thomas, and he realized that he had been lost in thought and loaded potato soup. His bread bowl was empty. He suddenly realized that she was leaning over him to refill the Mason jar of sweet tea.

With an absentminded wave of his hand, he motioned her away.

Sam continued to stand where the booths joined and surveyed both sides, trying not to appear impatient or overly curious, a heavy, cut glass pitcher of sweet tea cradled in her hands. The expression on her sharp-featured face was one that both men knew well. Samantha Sue Simmons wanted answers.

Anticipating the onslaught, Judge Candler held up his hand almost comically to stop what both he and Thomas knew was coming.

"You know, Sam," he announced in his best booming courtroom voice, "that we absolutely cannot discuss ongoing cases."

"So you admit that it isn't settled?" Sam leaned persistently closer, her eyes narrowing. "Has Steve Wilton lost his mind?

What about Katy? Is it true she is in the family way again and Steve doesn't know? Do you think the baby is even his? What about Amy? She never approved of that marriage in the first place."

"Well, since you seem to be in a talkative mood," said Thomas, rolling his eyes dramatically and lifting his Mason jar for a refill, "I have been curious about that new recipe you have for cornbread muffins. Is it true you got that online from some Facebook site in West Texas that claims to be authentically Mexican?"

"Hush, Thomas." Sam thudded the table again, this time with the bill under her clenched fist. "Don't you make fun of me. Everyone knows the only reason people tolerate you is because of Cora."

Judge Candler chuckled and rose gingerly from the booth, sensing his opportunity for escape and slipping a twenty-dollar bill under the receipt on his table.

"No further comment from either of us, young lady," he admonished. "See you Friday, Thomas. If not, then on Sunday. Taking a few days in the city with the wife. Our fiftieth. Can you believe that?"

Thomas nodded, crammed the last bite of his crusty bread bowl into his mouth, and prepared to make his own escape from Sam's inquisition. Sam, on the other hand, neatly blocked his attempt to stand, staring blankly at the judge's back before returning determinedly to the still-seated attorney.

"Thomas," she began firmly. "I was just wondering—"

"You were wondering," he interrupted almost paternally, "what juicy tidbit you might serve as a garnish with the rib eyes on Friday night. Sorry, Sam. Try to find something growing in the garden out back."

"But, Thomas—"

He took his leather wallet from his suitcoat pocket, removed a twenty-dollar bill, and placed it under the still-empty Mason jar on his own table.

"I hear my wife calling me."

Thomas stood awkwardly despite Sam's closeness, and she stepped reluctantly back to let him exit the booth.

"Ha! You are lying, counselor!" Her voice resumed her usual teasing and good-humored tone. She knew better than to alienate one of her best customers. "You cannot hear Cora calling you. Your cell phone is always on silent."

"Some people only use their ears for listening, Sam," he countered. "I am gifted with superior listening skills that also include my intuition. You of all people should know that."

"You are just too darn cryptic, Thomas."

"I'm just a lawyer, Sam."

"That's what I just said!"

Sam playfully slapped his sleeve as he passed her. Truth be told, she found it both frustrating and reassuring to realize that some things in Balfour just never changed. Especially Thomas.

Thomas paused at the cash register to deposit a quarter on the counter and scoop two wrapped soft peppermints from the clear fishbowl that had never actually held any goldfish. Out of the corner of his eye, he could see Sam and Bill standing uncharacteristically close by the booths he and Candler had just left.

Sam, the receipts and bills crumpled in her hand, was

whispering intently to Bill, his tall form bent down and his bushy eyebrows coming together in a salt and pepper thundercloud over his equally striking eyes. Their heads were almost touching.

Thomas thought he knew exactly what they were talking about. Rather, who they were talking about.

Steve Wilton had never been a popular man in Balfour, and his latest antics were only fuel for the eventual bonfire that would surely be used to burn him in effigy, at the very least.

Now more than ever he knew that Cora needed to talk to Katy, if he could get her away from Amy and everyone else who seemed to have an opinion about what she should do about her failing marriage. The tide of public opinion was already swinging wide and high against Steve, and Katy needed to be prepared for whatever craziness Steve had in store for their immediate future. Hiding at Amy and Dan's house was not going to protect her or Elizabeth from Steve, the Senator, or the battalion of lawyers they could collectively amass.

Thomas felt no guilt about his callous disregard for Steve's sudden desire for reconciliation or for the resulting problems. Steve caused his own messes, and it was time someone stood up to him and forced him to accept the consequences.

Without a tinge of remorse, Thomas stepped out onto the recently renovated sidewalk into the crisp autumn air and headed back to his office, a brisk ten-minute walk away. He decided quite calmly that he didn't care what happened to Steve Wilton at all, as long as it didn't involve making anyone else's life, including his, more difficult.

Chapter 9

Marjorie's chocolate chip cookies were elegant and simple, childlike in both ingredients and style. First, they were huge— man-palm sized—and thick with gooey chips. Second, the consistency held up well not only to little fingers but also to the prerequisite dunking, which Marjorie herself never did except in the privacy of her own kitchen at home in her apartment at the Piney Woods.

Today she was violating her own unspoken rule and had broken off several pieces of cookie, dunking them gently into a short, heavy glass of cold milk in an attempt to lure the child into tasting a cookie of her own. Tiny head bowed, one might suppose in sleep or meditation, and hands folded obediently in her lap, the little girl sat unmoving on the high stool at the butcher block kitchen island.

Marjorie, ever cheerful, refused to push or to pretend that her feelings were hurt by the rejection. She simply paused after every futile attempt and bustled around the kitchen again, washing and drying breakfast dishes, watering the herbs growing in the many-potted window garden, taking inventory of the modest pantry, and making lists of the staples needing replacement.

She knew, as did Cora, that the last place the child was likely to feel safe or comfortable was in an office or even the warm, home-like study. Who knew how many sterile hospital rooms and impersonal offices the tiny girl had already been made to endure. There was probably a great deal of well-meaning and unintentional damage to be undone. Treatment for childhood trauma needed to be tailored to the child.

Marjorie turned from the windowsill and found that the little girl was watching her, as she had done several times already that morning. Her blank, empty eyes were locked behind a face for which Marjorie did not yet have the key.

A genuine smile lit the older woman's eyes, crinkling her entire face, as the melody of a familiar children's Bible song began in her throat and hummed softly up through her upturned lips. *Patience*, she thought. *Lots of patience. At least she isn't looking away. Or crying.*

While Marjorie was considering whether to suggest a walk in the garden, there was an odd noise in the doorway, something between a low growl and a grunt. Marjorie covered her mouth with the corner of her apron to stifle her instinctive laughter.

Solomon, in a valiant attempt to bring the stuffed kitten along with him, had secured his teeth into the red-ribboned neck in a mama cat's maternal carrying position. The synthetic black fur hung from his mouth like a misshapen goatee.

At the sound of Marjorie's poorly muffled laughter, he dropped the prize and threw himself onto the floor lengthwise in apparent exhaustion. Then, in the fluid motion of a ballet dancer, he stretched and threw out his paws to pull the kitten close again against his own furry black chest.

The girl's head turned, expressionless, as she watched to see what the cat might do next. With a yawn that gave full view to the rows of tiny, shark-like teeth and his rough pink tongue, the black cat stretched again to his full length and then curled again into a protective ball around the kitten.

The little girl slid from the stool. For a moment, Marjorie was afraid that she was going to run away. Instead, the little girl took two or three tentative steps, apparently with the intention of retrieving her property, and reached out a tiny hand toward the purring puddle of black fur.

Solomon had been chosen for a specific purpose. He was well-accustomed to the children who came in and out of his private domain. He knew what was expected of him.

Solomon was a fully domesticated Maine Coon, exceptional in size and in his unfailing tolerance and love for people—specifically small, emotionally injured people. If Solomon knew he had claws and teeth, he was completely unaware that they had any sort of ulterior purpose.

As the child watched, the tomcat released his prize, pushing the stuffed toy slightly away from him and almost within reach of the little girl's outstretched fingers. Then, with an air of innocent nonchalance, he began to groom himself, licking his paws and pulling them over the top of his head and against his ears. The result was that the damp of his rough tongue wet the long hairs of his face and created amusing spikes and clumps all over his hairy face.

Any other child would have laughed. This child merely sat down on the floor and cautiously leaned forward to pull the stuffed toy into the safety of her waiting arms. Solomon observed her just as carefully and cautiously as she watched him and then simply got up from his ministrations, ambled over to where she sat, and began bathing the stuffed kitten where it lay.

Since the girl still clutched the kitten, Solomon's persistent tongue also began to absently wash her fingers and hands as well. At first, she let out a little gasp and stiffened noticeably in fear, so Marjorie moved to lift the cat away, but then something odd and unexpected happened. Solomon began to purr. Softly at first, and then louder. The rumbling, roaring purr came from deep inside his hairy chest and rolled outward and up his throat, having a strangely calming effect upon the child. Instead of pulling away, her tiny fingers began to stroke the cat's fur. The touches were tentative at first, and then the child was opening and closing her whole hands rhythmically against Solomon's warm, vibrating ribs, until he nudged aside the stuffed kitten and climbed into the child's lap himself.

The sound of the ringing telephone interrupted the moment. The child's face, which had momentarily relaxed, tensed again. Solomon, oblivious to the interruption, continued to purr as his body stretched again and fit itself across the child's legs, spilling over on either side onto the kitchen floor, a head to one side and a swishing black tail to the other. Then he arched backward, his midsection completely covering the lower half of her body and filling all the available space.

Neither Marjorie nor the child moved. The telephone rang again, but the older woman still made no move to answer. *That's what answering machines are for*, she thought. The telephone insisted for the third time when Marjorie heard Cora quickly moving down the stairs to the office.

Marjorie was confident that Cora was not going to answer either. She would listen to the message first and then decide what to do. They both knew that anyone close to Cora had her cell phone number and would call that number instead of the home phone. This practice allowed her to avoid strangers with information she did not need and to ignore well-intentioned salesmen with information she did not want.

Cora closed the study door behind her and waited for the fifth ring, when her own friendly but impersonal greeting began to play and the machine sat ready to record the caller's message. The strident, demanding voice of Steve Wilton announced itself boldly, dictatorial and petulant, barking orders from the square black box on her desk. But Cora subconsciously refused to listen to what he was saying. She had never met Steve personally, but she felt she knew enough about him through what Thomas and Charlie had told her. She had known many men like Steve. She recognized that his wealthy, entitled mentality and arrogance came from being the spoiled only son of a powerful and successful career politician. Cora remembered Marjorie's judgmental recanting of all the details of Steve's marriage to Katy. That thought brought back memories of too many painful events in her own life. *Sweet, innocent Katy.* She remembered the morning message from Thomas. *Katy.*

Cora shook the negative thoughts from her head and

realized that she really had not been listening to the rude message at all, and that she probably needed to replay it.

Or not. Steve did not seem like a man who needed or wanted anyone's help, or who would appreciate any advice she might give him. She could not imagine that he would even consider allowing her, a total stranger, to help him. She would certainly rather not be involved. In any case, maybe the call was not even about help.

A pleasant thought occurred to her. Since she was married to Thomas, and Thomas was Katy's attorney, there was quite possibly even a conflict of interest that would prevent her from doing anything on Steve's behalf.

She decided she certainly did not have to listen to what he had to say. Not at all.

With only a mild twinge of guilt, she erased the message. Her conscience and training told her not to ignore what was potentially a cry for help. Her reason and logic refused to be bullied by a man like Steve. Before she could second guess her decision, Marjorie knocked at the office door and, without waiting for an answer, opened it and stopped thoughtfully in the doorway.

"You really need to see this." Marjorie was smiling.

Steve Wilton, Cora decided unemotionally, *will just have to call back.*

Chapter 10

Thomas spent the next three hours in a pleasant, confused fog, only half-listening through his open office door to Susan's running commentary on her plans for rearranging their newly renovated space into some sort of traditional, Southern vintage style. Thomas had learned long ago that Susan did not really expect him to listen or comment on what she called thinking out loud, so he was more than capable of working patiently on his afternoon project, a contract between a local landowner and an out-of-state timber company, while she babbled contentedly in the outer office area.

Susan's self-talk was a welcome break from his thoughts about divorces, disturbing dreams of dead people, and dislike for Charlie.

Despite his protests that whatever she did would suit him quite nicely, Susan paused every thirty minutes or so to enter his office, refill or refresh his coffee cup, and obtain his personal confirmation that there was nothing else she should be doing. Thomas secretly suspected that these breaks where actually her way of checking on his current mood and disposition, but he certainly would never say so to her.

Her present diatribe involved new flooring. According to Susan, there were five different shades and types of hardwood floors to be considered. Susan preferred the light oak, which she insisted would be more practical for cleaning, add value to the property, and brighten up the darker tones of the mahogany bookcases and heavy, overstuffed leather sofas and chairs.

Then there was the new artwork for the freshly painted mint green walls. As for those, Susan insisted that there be no family.

"Cora has been through enough," Susan said. "She doesn't need to have her privacy invaded any further by having pictures on the walls in public view."

Thomas painfully agreed. The only picture he kept of Cora was in his wallet. That was what she wanted. He half-listened as Susan continued to verbalize her thoughts.

What to put on the walls? Framed and matted diplomas, awards, degrees, and certificates, of course. There were plenty of those.

At this point, however, Susan began to argue with herself.

What about the little league baseball team that Thomas sponsored every spring? Should they hang the current picture of the team of nine- and ten-year-old players in their bright blue jerseys next to their winning record and the engraved plaque they had given the office? That would be adorable. Did adorable belong in a lawyer's office? What did Thomas think?

There were all the framed photographs taken by some of the talented locals too. Almost too many from which to choose.

Magnificent mountains, elegantly towering evergreens intermixed with hardwoods and their October burst of colorful leaves, breathtaking landscapes, rushing rivers, and cascading waterfalls. From Dawsonville to Hiawassee, Blue Ridge, and Tallulah Gorge, Balfour was situated in the center of some of the most beautiful scenery in the South. The railroad that was begun in 1876 in Gainesville and had been intended to reach Dahlonega ran out of time and money in 1878, ending in the strategically situated town of Balfour, Georgia. What should have been a prosperous stop on the railway line remained as a historic footnote where U.S. Highway 19 met State Route 60.

The town's first citizens were comprised of an assortment of railway workers, truck farmers, mountain men, and adventurous entrepreneurs who had hoped to cash in on the railway travelers. These men and their families elected to stay while the rest of the world moved on around them. Thomas's great-grandfather had been one of the entrepreneurial founders of the town, and, until Thomas's grandfather and then his father joined him in practice, the only lawyer in Balfour. Although Thomas had momentarily lapsed in his familial loyalty and sought his law degree out of state, the roots of his heritage were strong. He had eventually returned to Balfour, after a brief yearlong detour by way of a prestigious law firm in Atlanta.

Thomas's eyes had begun to glaze over just a bit when Susan changed direction and launched into a spirited description of Bogart's office in *The Maltese Falcon,* and why Thomas needed a hat just like Spade's. From there she digressed into a quagmire of choices for free-standing hat racks, before seating herself at her computer and beginning a Google search for antique wooden hall trees. Thomas considered saying that perhaps she should cut back on the reruns of her favorite classic detective shows, but he wisely thought better. He knew that was not really Susan's problem.

Susan's real problem was that she did not really know what to do with Harry, and Thomas knew this was her way of coping. Susan had been widowed with a two-year-old daughter when her husband, Ed, died suddenly of a heart attack in Baton Rouge. Susan picked herself up, moved closer home to her family in Mississippi, took classes, became a paralegal, raised her daughter with the help of close church friends, and found job security and fulfillment in her work with Thomas. For the last fifteen years or so, her life had been predictable and what some might consider boring, centered around church and her job.

Her daughter, son-in-law, and two grandchildren were living quite happily in Texas, although they visited her as often as their schedules allowed. They were always thrilled with her twice-yearly visits to San Antonio and the monthly boxes of homemade sweets she sent by FedEx.

Then Harry came into her life. Diabetic, determined, devoted, middle-aged Harry, who moved to Balfour to retire and sell real estate on the side. Susan met Harry over her prize pecan praline cookies at the Emmanuel Baptist Church singles social, and Harry had doggedly pursued her ever since. That was six months ago, and their relationship was moving slowly by most modern standards but rather quickly according to the Balfour gossips. Susan just kept baking cookies, candies, and pies that Harry shouldn't eat, trying to decide what exactly she was supposed to do with him. Harry just kept buying Susan interesting and rather impersonal presents and adjusting his insulin doses.

The stress of it all spilled over into Susan's work life, creating a kind of nervous energy in the office.

Thomas was on his third cup of strong, black coffee for the afternoon, and Susan had come to the doorway of the inner office to announce that she had finally found a ridiculously expensive solution to the problem of where to put Thomas's nonexistent hat when the telephone rang on Susan's desk.

Before she could turn and answer the phone in the outer office, the muted cell phone on Thomas's belt began to vibrate, and she paused.

Thomas answered, the color draining out of his face as he listened.

Susan spun and reluctantly left the doorway to answer the still ringing telephone on her desk. She listened solemnly for several minutes, then hung up and returned to the open doorway, her face equally drained of color.

"Steve Wilton," she whispered through dry lips, clasping her hands together at the front of her blouse. "Gunshot to the back of the head. That was Miranda Duncan at the judge's office. The judge has already left for the week, and she thought you ought to know."

"Charlie." Thomas waved the cell phone he was still gripping in his right hand. "I was one of the last people to see Steve this morning in court."

"Charlie is coming here?" she repeated mechanically. "Why is Charlie in town?"

Thomas knew Susan would not be satisfied without an

explanation.

"Charlie brought someone this morning for Cora to see. He probably stopped by the station to see Ben before he left."

Susan nodded. She knew exactly what that meant.

"So Ben is letting Charlie investigate? Burton and Dalton will be royally steamed about that."

"No doubt," Thomas agreed sagely. "They certainly threw a party when he left."

"You are going to need more coffee."

Susan turned in the doorway and looked back.

"I suppose it has to be Charlie."

Thomas gave her a wry smile.

"He's the best, Susan," he admitted.

Susan nodded.

"Then again," she offered. "So are you."

Thomas grimaced slightly, embarrassed by the compliment, and twisted his desk chair around to look out the picture window behind him facing a walled private garden. The newly planted fruit trees outside and boxwood shrubbery were fresh and dark green with the recent autumn rains. The rich, black earth packed at the bases of the roots was circled with thick, airy ferns and red- and pink-veined green caladiums. He was still staring absently at the view when Susan escorted Charlie into his office, and he did not turn around immediately.

When he did face Charlie, Thomas waited more or less patiently for the detective to have the first word. Charlie stubbornly thrust his hands into his pants pockets and looked absently around the office.

"Love what you've done with the place," he finally quipped.

Susan sighed, her voice recovering its soft, Southern charm despite her dislike for the uncomfortable situation.

"Do you still drink your coffee black, Charlie?"

"Yes, Susan. Thank you."

She went out and all but slammed the door behind her.

Charlie sat down without being asked and flipped open his notebook.

"You can say whatever you want to say in front of Susan." Thomas found himself feeling more irritable than usual. "She already took a call from Candler's office."

"Sure, Thomas," Charlie responded, pulling the cap off his ink pen with his bright white front teeth and replacing it neatly on the opposite end. "I'll tell you what I know. You tell me what you know."

Thomas replaced his cell phone at his waist.

"Of course." He picked up his now lukewarm coffee and took a swallow, grimacing. After a moment, there was a polite tap at the door, and they both stood respectfully as Susan returned with a steaming mug for Charlie and another for Thomas. Taking the cold cup from her boss's hands, she went back to the outer office, closing the door firmly behind her, but not before giving Charlie a chastising maternal glare.

There was a brief moment before both men sat down again.

"Steve was in court this morning for the divorce hearing," Thomas began. "You know about the divorce, yes? He was his usual self, only worse. Had a rookie lawyer from Atlanta with him. Graymore, I think. No, her name is Grayson. Anyway, she was having trouble controlling him."

Charlie lifted his eyebrows and opened his mouth to say

something sarcastic but stopped himself. There was no time for that right now.

"Why did Steve need controlling?"

"Well, apparently something happened over the weekend, and Steve experienced a change of heart. Wanted to call off the divorce. He started demanding and ordering everyone around. Judge Candler was pretty well furious."

Charlie, who had been writing up to this point, stopped, tapping the pen against his front teeth absently, his eyebrows elevated higher with a quizzical expression.

"I take it that you didn't see that coming?"

"Not at all," Thomas admitted. "Katy had pretty much agreed to everything he wanted—over my objections."

"Rightly so," Charlie nodded. "Go on."

"That's all, I suppose. Judge Candler hauled us back into chambers, and Steve tried to convince Katy to call everything off."

"I take it you and Candler disagreed."

Thomas picked up his coffee mug and leaned back in his chair, taking a swallow.

"Charlie, you and I have both seen Steve at his worst. This tantrum was something totally different. I mean, he was acting like Steve, but then he wasn't acting like Steve."

Charlie stuck his pen behind his ear and took a drink of his own coffee.

"I'm not sure I follow what you mean," he admitted.

"Fair enough," Thomas shrugged. "You figure this out. Before Steve would leave Candler's chambers, he insisted on counseling with Cora. Demanded that I arrange an immediate session with her."

Charlie let out a huffing sound of disbelief and muttered something low and unintelligible that sounded like a curse.

"My feelings exactly." Thomas's mouth was drawn into a hard, straight line. "Candler threw Steve and his lawyer out of chambers and gave them a week to figure everything out—without Katy."

"About what time was that?" Charlie began to take notes again.

"Maybe eleven? No. Had to be before eleven. He and Grayson were arguing all the way out the door. The judge and I talked to Katy for maybe fifteen minutes, then she left with Amy. Judge and I had lunch at Sam's around eleven or so, and I was back in the office a few minutes after noon."

Charlie's pen scratched across the notebook.

"I know you don't suspect Katy."

"Nope." Charlie did not look up from his writing. "Already have a timeline. Amy drove Katy straight from the courthouse to Elizabeth's preschool at the United Methodist Church. Some fall festival program with cute kids and carved pumpkins. Amy left her there and went to run errands. There are any number of witnesses who saw both Katy and Elizabeth at the Forrest Park playground after the program."

Thomas set his coffee cup firmly on the desktop and leaned forward.

"Charlie, what are you *really* doing here?"

The pen stopped, but the detective did not immediately look up.

"Seriously, Charlie. Has it come to this? What aren't you

telling me?"

Charlie stretched his arms over his head and leaned back into the chair, then took a long swallow of the hot coffee before speaking.

"Steve Wilton was shot at point blank range in the back of the head. In his own house. In his office. Sitting at his desk."

Thomas gave a long, low whistle of astonishment.

"So he had to know whoever killed him?"

"I'm saying that he had a pen in his hand, and he seemed to be in the process of writing or signing some sort of document or letter."

"Some sort of what? You don't know?"

"Steve's head landed on the desk. Whatever he was writing isn't quite legible at this point. Forensics is working on it, but we may need someone from Atlanta up here."

"For a little blood?"

"Apparently the bullet exited through the bulk of his brain and lodged itself into the top of the desk. Nothing is legible at this point."

Thomas swallowed another low, strangled gasp.

"So not only was he murdered, but someone walked up behind him as he was in the process of writing? There's half your mystery right there, Charlie. There can't be more than five people in the whole state of Georgia that Steve Wilton trusted . . ."

Thomas's voice drifted off and he stopped, staring at the notebook in the other man's hands.

"You've already made that list, haven't you?"

Charlie sighed, rolling the pen between his fingers. "Made

it. Checked it. Made it again."

He picked up his coffee and cradled the cup.

"Therein," the detective announced sagely. "Therein lies the rub."

"No," Thomas objected. "That still doesn't explain why you're sitting in *my* office, Charlie."

"Well, if you need more . . . Burton and Dalton have agreed to do a preliminary investigation of the scene, but they want nothing to do with questioning witnesses or finding the murderer. Ben thinks they just like their jobs and don't want to rile up the rest of the community with accusations."

Thomas frowned, picturing the two former Marines in their suits and ties, with their military haircuts and strong jawlines. He could understand why they wouldn't want to be involved in something this political. They had to live in Balfour when it was over.

He had a strong suspicion he knew what was coming next.

"I need someone I can trust, Thomas," the detective admitted bluntly. "You know as well as I do that there are plenty of people in this town who hated Steve, and plenty more who would have done anything for Katy."

"You think someone killed Steve to save Katy?"

"At this point I don't know what I think."

"But that isn't all you need, is it?" Thomas's eyes narrowed for a moment, and he snapped forward in his chair. "If this has anything to do with Cora . . ."

Charlie held up his hands in mock surrender.

"That's not fair. I have no way of knowing whether it does or it doesn't."

Thomas knew he was right, but that didn't help how he felt.

"The bottom line is that we are assuming the paper Steve was writing was a legal document of some sort, or at least a letter. If we do manage to figure out what it is, I will need a legal expert who doesn't have some personal vendetta against Steve. Someone who is above reproach."

Charlie paused, gathered his courage, then continued.

"Then, of course, no one wants to deal with the Senator."

Thomas ran his hand through his hair and leaned back. Now he had the truth.

"You haven't told him the details yet, have you? You need someone to handle Steve's father. That's why you're really here."

Charlie smiled a crooked smile.

"We're going to need more coffee."

Thomas pressed the intercom on his desk and made the polite request to Susan. They stood again, grateful for the opportunity to stretch, and then resumed their places in silence until the secretary had refilled the cups and exited again.

They took several thoughtful swallows before speaking, and this time it was Thomas's turn to begin the conversation.

"This could explode in your face, Charlie."

"That's why I'm asking for your help."

"What do you think I can do that you can't?"

"Well, in the first place, people tend to like you, Thomas. You come from the right kind of family. The Senator even likes you. He always did." Charlie cleared his throat. "Thomas, everyone knows you have . . ."

"Tact?"

Charlie laughed. "I was going to say something else, but let it pass."

He closed the notebook, neatly emptied his cup again in a long, last swallow, and stood, tucking the pen into his inside jacket pocket.

"The Senator's private plane arrives at eight or so tonight. Anson's Airstrip. I thought he'd want to see Katy and the granddaughter first, but he says he wants to go straight to the funeral home."

"No real surprises there, Charlie."

"I suppose. Katy is sedated and staying with Amy and Dan. Some aunt is coming from Jackson to babysit Elizabeth. All family. She'd be coming to see Katy anyway. The house is a crime scene for the time being."

Thomas looked at his watch and made a decision he hoped he wouldn't regret.

"I'll meet the Senator's plane tonight, but I'm not going alone."

"Absolutely not."

Thomas hesitated.

"Pick you up at six thirty? The station or Piney Woods?"

He didn't relish more time with Charlie, but it seemed the polite thing to say.

"Nope." Charlie seemed more relaxed now. "Want to take a look at the scene before we have to talk to the Senator. Giving the guys a first crack at the clues, since they were none too happy to see me."

"I can well imagine," Thomas retorted dryly. "See you at quarter til seven?"

There was a knock at the door.

"Yes, Susan," Thomas responded.

"There's a call for you," Susan announced, waiting for his invitation before she stuck just her head inside and briefly surveyed the room. "You will want to take it, I think."

Thomas nodded and reached for the receiver, pressing the blinking button on the machine. Charlie was already up and standing next to Susan, his short, boyish form at almost eye level with the statuesque older woman. He held out the heavy cup, staring her down with his characteristically crooked grin.

"Great coffee," he said, winking and brushing her fingers with a tease as he pressed the cup into her palm. "Harry is some lucky man."

"What would you know about Harry?" Susan blushed, the roots of her white hair going bright red with embarrassment.

Charlie landed a perfunctory peck on her rosy cheek.

"I'm a detective, darling," he said. "It's what I do best."

And he was gone.

Susan pressed her palm to her flaming face and gave an exasperated sigh, her resolve to dislike Charlie only slightly diminished. She, like the vast majority of people in Balfour, wanted to dislike Charlie. Believed they had every reason to dislike Charlie. And Charlie knew it. Charlie took advantage of their dislike and really did not seem to care, which only made them dislike him more.

With a shake of her head, Susan closed the inner office door to give Thomas privacy and returned to her decorating without enthusiasm.

Steve and Charlie certainly knew how to ruin a perfectly lovely day.

Chapter 11

Pastor Evans was not at all happy with his staff, although he knew perfectly well that they were both right. He was, in truth, not happy with himself either. After what he had considered an unpleasant but necessary meeting, he had gone to a late lunch with one of the more congenial deacons. He had completed his meetings for the day, and although he was more than a little perturbed about the contents of the more serious discussions, he had still made up his mind to accept things the way they were. At least, for the time being.

That is, he was satisfied until his office staff blindsided him with the news of Steve Wilton's death as he walked through the outer office doors.

Apparently the two women had already contacted Virginia, who had offered to come right over and join in the preparations for the services. Preparations which had obviously begun without his knowledge or approval.

He stewed self-righteously. *I don't want to have Steve's funeral here. The fact that the man was murdered isn't the issue. I know what kind of man Steve Wilton was. And then there is his father.*

Evans had heard plenty of stories about the Senator on the national news and from the weekly deacons' meetings. Everyone knew stories. Knew the father and son were estranged.

Stewart Wilton was too outspoken and progressive anyway. He never missed an opportunity for grandstanding. Pastor Evans saw no useful purpose for allowing the spectacle of Senator Stewart Wilton's partisan politics to invade the modest little Christian church, or unduly influence its respectable members.

Donna Phillips and Alice Lee had combined forces to show their stubborn preacher the error of his ways.

"Katy deserves better," came the first volley from Donna. "She grew up in this church. She'd still be singing in the choir and teaching second grade Sunday School if she hadn't married Steve."

"Maybe she'll come back, now that he's gone," offered Alice sweetly, relishing this opportunity to feel superior in godliness and charity, especially to the pastor.

"Katy might even persuade Amy to rejoin," she continued, pressing her blatantly evangelical point. "Who knows? They both might bring little Elizabeth back. And then maybe even Dan."

"Dan? Amy's husband?" Donna sniffed disdainfully. "Don't get your hopes up."

"Miracles do happen," Alice chastised her friend gently. "We must have faith. Stranger things have happened in

Balfour."

Donna was forced to agree.

The final blow came from his own wife, Virginia, who kept her promise to come straight to the church office from the beauty parlor when she received the call. She slipped her hand under her irritated husband's elbow, guided him firmly into his office, and closed the door before he could say anything that might further alienate his secretaries.

"Andy . . ."

"I'll do it, Ginny," he muttered. "You know I'll do it. I just don't want to do it."

"Andrew Evans," she clucked at him sweetly, patting his frowning face. "You had better adjust your attitude about this funeral, and you had better do it quickly. Let's get to the details."

She rummaged about his desk for a pen and a piece of notepaper.

"Do you know which funeral home?"

"Maybe you should ask the secretaries," he snapped, more harshly than he meant. *This isn't Ginny's fault,* he reminded himself. *Not her fault at all.*

"I'm sorry," he apologized. "They will probably take him to Parson's eventually. Donna said she hasn't heard cause of death, so his body may still be at the morgue."

"You should call Katy right away."

"Alice tried to get her, but Amy answered the cell phone and said that Katy isn't taking calls."

"Amy is protecting her sister," she observed approvingly. "I'll talk to Donna and Alice. They are quite right to begin planning, and you know it, dear. There are formalities that must be handled quickly, especially since this was all so unexpected. Flowers. Music. A bulletin or handout of some sort for the service. The church members should be notified. Pall bearers too. Perhaps some of the deacons."

"Ginny . . ."

"Andy, you love the Lord, and you love this church, I know you do. But unless you want that Senator—and I have heard several earfuls about him since we moved here—unless you want him to turn these services into a political rally, or worse yet, a platform for some public uprising over the Good Lord knows what social issue of the day, you need to concentrate on your funeral message and let your staff and your wife handle everything else. There are going to be people who want to control this for their own purposes, and no one wants that."

Virginia Evans stopped talking. For her, this tirade was completely out of character and was the longest speech she had ever made. Normally she would have allowed her husband the leisure of realizing that she was right without pushing her points or her opinion on him. Today she knew that there was no time for such luxury. The situation could quickly escalate into an ugliness that might cause a scandal in Balfour for years to come and, in the same vein, might further scar her husband's new ministry in this quiet country church.

Virginia was a crusader for what she loved, and she loved nothing more right now than Jesus, her husband, and Emmanuel Baptist Church. In that order.

She suddenly realized that she had more to say.

"I'll call Miss Toney about playing for the funeral. The organ, I think. Frank is out of town until Saturday afternoon, but she has good judgment and can be flexible. No singing, unless Katy had a hymn, and even then . . . I know you don't see the urgency or the importance of all this, Andy."

"No, I don't, darling," he looked affectionately at his wife, the lines around his eyes crinkling in a smile that did not reach his mouth. He was a little more than taken aback by her forcefulness.

"But I can quite plainly see that you are . . . concerned. And that concerns me. I'm listening to every word you say."

He cleared his throat.

"Ginny, what do you think I should do?"

"First, sit down, Andy," she guided him around the desk to his chair. Evans obediently sat down, feeling more at peace than he had in the last fifteen minutes. Virginia picked up his pen and put it in his hand, sliding one of the legal pads that he used for writing his sermons over to him. Old-fashioned, Evans found his best thoughts came to him as he wrote them out longhand, the grip of his rugged, well-worn fingers around a fine point pen as it scratched out words across the yellow paper.

"Lazarus might be good," she offered.

"Psalms, I think," he countered, not looking up. "You are my heart, Ginny."

"As you are mine, Andy." With a tender touch she smoothed the silky white hair, whose color matched her own, back from his temple. "I'll make you a cup of black tea with extra lemons and then settle outside with Donna and Alice. You won't be disturbed."

"Thank you."

She leaned down and kissed the top of his head.

"I mean it, Ginny. Thank you."

"Stuff and nonsense," she countered.

Virginia turned at the door to remind her husband that he needed to consider his words more discreetly than usual, but she thought better of her impulse.

He had already opened the well-used study Bible and had written almost a quarter of a page in his distinctive cursive weave. Virginia watched the deceptively smooth flow of his pen as it darted its way across the yellow emptiness and reminded herself that this was not the first, or the second, or even the third time that he had written a difficult and painful eulogy. Although, she mused sadly, this would be the first for someone who had been so universally disliked.

With a silent prayer for her husband's wisdom she rejoined the waiting women in the outer office, and the three of them went straight to work.

Chapter 12

Marjorie and her quiet little charge had been sharing a companionable silence for several hours when Cora decided she needed a break from writing and joined them in the sun-filled country kitchen.

Over the last three and a half years or so, since Marjorie had made her first appearance in Cora's life, there had been at least a dozen young trauma victims who had been fostered into their care. Some for a month or two before an equally suitable long-term or adoptive home could be secured, one or two for just a little longer before they were able to return to their biological parents. For the most part, both Marjorie and Cora were considered immediate emergency care. Cora was especially valuable because of her training in trauma counseling.

Marjorie had long been a volunteer mentor through FaithBridge, a Christian foster care organization that had partnered with the United Methodist Church in Balfour. When

Marjorie suggested to Cora that they could join together in taking the advanced training that would renew Marjorie's certification, Cora saw a God-given opportunity to help children in need. Marjorie, for her part, saw a God-given opportunity not only to help precious children, but to help Cora.

Virtually all of the children who had passed through Cora's home formed an almost instantaneous attachment to the grandmotherly older woman. By unspoken agreement, the first day or two was almost always spent under her watchful care as she went about her domestic bustling in the Victorian house.

Sometimes, when the weather was as cooperative as it was today, Marjorie and her companions also visited the little garden sunroom that Thomas had created for Cora just after they married. Thomas wanted her to have her own personal sanctuary where she could go to be alone. A local contractor installed French doors to one side of the bay windows in the kitchen, and these opened out into an adjacent, uniquely charming glass-walled room.

The floor was made from salvaged bricks laid in a herringbone pattern, over which Marjorie had scattered brightly colored rag rugs. In the center of the room was a white wrought iron table and four matching chairs with cushions, and against the far wall was a cozy floral chintz love seat. Glossy ceramic pots of all shapes, colors, and sizes containing houseplants in seasonal bloom were grouped against the walls and around the room.

When the addition itself was finished, Thomas had an eight-foot cedar wood privacy fence built around the entire perimeter of the pine- and hardwood-filled back yard, planted azaleas and holly bushes around the base of the trees, and resolved never to go where he was not invited.

This past spring Marjorie had suggested the addition of a raised garden, and, with Cora's enthusiastic approval, he cheerfully complied by visiting the local Ace Hardware store and having a multilevel redwood system installed and filled with potting soil and assorted vegetable plants.

Now, as the summer drifted into fall and the temperature began to drop, the last of the harvest was disappearing and all that remained were the tendinous cherry tomatoes, assorted hot peppers, and a few cucumbers, adding their bright red, yellow, and green contributions to the changing colors of the leaves.

Cora leaned against the white frame doorway and watched. Marjorie seemed happy and content, cooking and humming hymns, coping patiently with whatever happened in her life. Cora had no explanation for why or how her friend had arrived at this particular brand of therapy. Whenever Cora asked questions about Marjorie's past, they were quite skillfully deflected. Marjorie, she knew, would tell whatever secrets she carried when the time came.

At this moment, Marjorie was bustling about from one marble counter to another, stirring a pot on the stove and wiping up invisible spills, peeling Red Delicious apples into a big blue pottery bowl with her favorite tiny paring knife and sprinkling the exposed apples with quick dashes of bottled lemon juice.

With a tentative motion, she checked a container of rising bread dough as it sat near the warmth of the gas stove, peeking under a dishtowel to check the progress of her creation. Marjorie was almost always moving—working, cleaning, cooking, sewing, and finding someone to join her in whatever she was doing.

In the center of the stone floor of the kitchen she had spread a patchwork quilt where Solomon and the child sat together amid a sea of Cabbage Patch dolls, stuffed bears, and the red-ribboned kitten. From time to time Marjorie stopped to offer the little girl a piece of fruit or drink of milk, but otherwise she left them alone. The pair seemed quite content in each other's company in the warmth of the early afternoon sun, and Cora's thoughts drifted back to Marjorie.

Marjorie was ideally suited to be Cora's housekeeper and companion.

The turn-of-the-century, Victorian-style house had belonged to Charlie's grandparents, pillars in the community of Balfour who had raised Charlie when his parents were lost in a plane crash when Charlie was only ten years old. Elderly when Charlie was ten, they had also passed on quietly within hours of each other after Charlie had gone to work as a detective in New Orleans. The house was the only real home that Charlie had ever known, and all that he had to give to Cora after their divorce was final. She stubbornly refused alimony, but Charlie convinced her that the house was hers, and that he would never use it. Charlie intended Balfour to be Cora's refuge.

In the first few weeks, left alone with her grief, Cora would brood, sitting for hours in dark thought, a melancholy sadness covering her, draped over her slender form like a black cape of bone-crushing depression. Then the day came when she refused to leave the house altogether.

Charlie, in a rare moment of insight, had prepared for this contingency. In his absence from the house after his grandparents' deaths, Charlie had appointed his boyhood friend and trusted lawyer, Thomas, to supervise the estate. Charlie appealed, as only Charlie could, to his friend's sense of loyalty and duty, insisting that Thomas continue in his role as executor.

Over the course of the first month in Balfour, Cora reluctantly accepted Thomas as a vital part of her life. Thomas, for his part, fell hopelessly in love with Cora, partly because he thought she needed him, and partly because she was the kindest, most beautiful woman he had ever known.

Cora, like Charlie and Thomas, had no close family of her own. Thomas, recently wounded by the cutthroat antics of Atlanta politics and law firms, became her protector and champion. They found that they had common beliefs and hopes, so they soon came to accept that a power beyond their own had meant they should be together. That, and Charlie's well-meaning machinations.

After six months of discreet and traditional courting, they were quietly married in a civil ceremony by Judge Candler in the front room of the Victorian house with only Candler's wife and Susan as witnesses. By mutual consent, Thomas sold his own family home and moved in with Cora, the invested proceeds providing them with more than enough income for a frugal rest of their lives.

Thomas did not know what he had expected from their marriage, but after two more months had passed, he felt his own frustrating, helpless sadness as he watched his new wife continue to sink further and further away from him. Away from life.

Then one Monday morning Charlie, with all his cocky boyish charm, appeared at the door with Marjorie at his elbow.

An efficient and blessedly determined Marjorie.

"The new housekeeper," Charlie had announced to no one in particular.

That day, Cora's life changed forever.

Marjorie dismissed Charlie with a nod and an unceremonious shove out the front door, brushed past a stunned Thomas with a cool acknowledgement of his presence, and set to work to restore Cora to her joy.

Thomas tried not to resent Charlie for knowing what to do when he himself had not known. He tried not to be angry at Charlie's accusing stare, blaming him for letting things go so far before someone intervened. But Thomas loved Cora.

Cora accepted Marjorie. Marjorie did not give her a choice.

The first thing that Cora noticed about Marjorie was the humming. Marjorie was almost always humming—generally hymns, the old ones. Ones Cora remembered vaguely as the lullabies and tunes that her grandmother used to sing as she worked in the kitchen. The kitchen of Cora's dreams.

Then there was Marjorie's special coffee, really more a frothy homemade cappuccino with vanilla and a touch of cinnamon. With the coffee came the cookies of every shape and size and flavor. Soon every room in the house began to show signs of Marjorie's loving touch—a crocheted lap blanket tossed over a chair, the aroma of a fresh fruit pie, a vase of wild flowers on the kitchen island.

Soon Cora found the solitary glass room less and less inviting. The sounds of Marjorie's bustling and humming peaked her curiosity, and she abandoned her grief for the promised companionship and contentment she remembered from the days of her youth.

Standing in the doorway of the busy kitchen, Cora studied her dearest friend and treasured housekeeper and smiled, remembering thankfully.

As if she sensed Cora's thoughts, Marjorie looked up from the cooked chicken she was chopping and returned the smile. The little girl, oblivious to the watchful adults, was focused on the friendly, furry black cat. Solomon, knowing his place, was politely chasing a dangling yarn through the folds of the quilt and off onto the floor, swatting and sliding on the smooth stone tile. He rested, sprawling, his ears and whiskers twitching with feline enjoyment.

Marjorie looked at the clock on the wall.

"Weren't we expecting Amy at noon?"

Cora frowned. It was almost twenty minutes after three o'clock.

"Yes," she mused. "I suppose I lost track of time. Haven't gotten a call to cancel. Maybe she forgot. She did just call out of the blue to make the appointment on Friday. She seemed urgent, though. Almost frantic."

"Hmm." Marjorie turned around, wiped her hands with the corner of her apron, and put her hands on her hips. "Amy frantic? I cannot imagine. She always seems so reserved, so controlled."

"You know her better than I do," Cora admitted. Her self-imposed confinement to the house meant that she had learned to trust Marjorie's instincts and insights even more than her own.

"Well, you have an excellent intuition about these things,"

Marjorie offered, returning her almost full attention to the chicken. "People in Balfour have expected Amy to emotionally explode since she was seventeen. As my grandmother used to say: The tighter a person is wound up, the farther and higher they snap."

The older woman pushed up her half-glasses, away from the tip of her nose, with the back of her wrist. "Susie here agrees. Don't you, Susie?"

"Jane," the child corrected absently, stretching out next to the cat on the floor.

"That's right," Marjorie continued, returning her attention to the chicken and showing no sign of surprise. "Jane Smith."

"Jane Chen," the child corrected her again, twirling the yarn around and over the cooperative cat's ears. "I like your cat."

"His name is Solomon," Cora said politely.

The child tilted her head sideways in thought, silent again.

Cora cautiously pressed forward.

"Do you have a cat of your own, Jane?"

"No," she said, suddenly sad. "No cat."

Cora slid immediately to the floor, cross-legged and a suitably nonthreatening distance away.

"Jane," Cora repeated softly. "I like that name."

The tom blinked his green, almond-shaped eyes at Cora's voice and, sensing a familiar location in which to nap, moved toward Cora's knee. Without thinking, the little girl also moved, climbing into the empty lap, leaning back, waiting for the cat to join her. To no one's surprise, he did.

There was little if any room left in Cora's lap, but she didn't care.

Cora's arms rested calmly at her sides, and she laid her cheek hesitantly against the top of the child's dark hair. Jane's arms hugged the cat to her, and Cora felt the girl's small body begin to tremble.

"I want my mommy," she said, her lower lip beginning to quiver. "I want Mommy."

A silent tear slipped down her cheek, and then another and another, rolling in a cleansing river of pain and longing. Then the sobs began, between the sniffs and sniffles and heart-wrenching gasps for air.

Cora looked up, but Marjorie was already kneeling down next to them, pressing a handful of tissues into Jane's hands.

Cora waited until the worst of the emotional storm subsided and the child began to breathe more normally.

"You can tell me about your mommy," she offered, feeling the exhausted girl lean backward into her arms. Gently, she pressed on. "You can cry if you feel like it, and you can talk about your mommy whenever you want to talk."

Marjorie put a box of tissues on the floor beside them and stood patiently.

The child hesitated, wiping at her face with fresh tissues and rubbing her damp chin against the cat's furry head. Solomon inexplicably began to purr.

Cora waited.

"Is that man going to come back?"

The fear in Jane's voice was clear.

"No," Cora assured her. "The man is not going to come here, Jane."

"They hurt Mommy."

"I'm sorry, Jane." Tears filled the corners of Cora's eyes, and she took a tissue for herself before she continued.

"Do you remember the man in the funny blue car who brought you here? The man who gave you the black kitten?"

"Charlie," the child offered. "He kept saying his name was Charlie."

I'm sure he did, Cora thought to herself, mildly amused at memories of Charlie's clumsy attempts at conversations with children, especially the victims of crimes.

"Well, Jane," Cora began reassuringly, "Charlie catches men who hurt people, and he puts them away in jails where they cannot hurt people again."

"Charlie likes you."

Jane innocently brushed her hair out of her face.

"Everyone likes Cora," Marjorie interrupted sweetly, lifting the chunky cat deftly from the little girl's arms and placing him, with a protesting yowl, onto the cool floor.

"The two of you should go into the playroom now and maybe draw some pictures before our supper is ready," she ordered matter-of-factly. "I'll bring you something to drink and maybe a cookie."

Jane rose, her face still pale and stained with tears, while Marjorie extended her hand down to Cora's to steady the younger woman as she too stood.

"Jane, would you like to draw some pictures?" Cora asked hopefully. "I have a new box of crayons. Or colored pencils. Maybe you like pencils instead."

Jane looked from one woman to the other before she nodded almost imperceptivity, took Cora's offered hand, and followed the counselor obediently into the office playroom.

Marjorie, her job completed satisfactorily, gathered the quilt, toys, and stuffed black kitten from the floor and deposited them in a heap on the sofa in the den before she went back to chopping chicken and listening for any other surprising doorbells, telephones, and unwanted interruptions.

Solomon, with equal satisfaction, was rewarded with a small taste of chopped chicken before he took up his daily sentinel beside the French doors and began vigorously washing his snow-white whiskers.

Chapter 13

Charlie knew exactly what he needed to do. What he had done many times before this and would do many more times afterward—take a thorough look at the crime scene. He felt certain that Thomas would keep his promise to help handle the Senator. He also knew that Thomas would expect him to have done a detailed investigation of Steve's house in anticipation of the questions the Senator would surely have. In attention to details, the two men had more in common than either would have ever admitted.

Charlie did not recognize the officer on guard duty at Steve's multimillion dollar antebellum-style estate. And to Charlie's experienced eye, he also seemed to be younger than most. His uniform a bit too new and freshly pressed. His shoulders just a bit too squared. Standing at attention in the front doorframe on the veranda, he also seemed a bit bored with his job.

Bet he didn't even go inside, Charlie thought, bemused. *The chief told him to stand here, so here he stands.*

For a moment, Charlie almost envied the ignorance of the fresh recruit. He was either too uncaring or too uninformed to be properly awed by the Wilton reputation. Apparently, he had no clue of the political firestorm that was landing at Anson's Airstrip in the next three hours or so. No clue at all.

"Smith."

"Yes, sir!"

The officer snapped his head up and almost fell over his own feet. He looked quizzically at Charlie, who pointed in explanation at the name tag on the rookie's chest.

"Detective Abbott," the uniformed man acknowledged, grumbling. His thoughts went immediately to the stories he had heard from Burton and Dalton, stories that didn't paint Charlie in a good light.

Charlie's reputation as a trouble-making maverick was notorious around the Balfour PD. Burton and Dalton, who had known Charlie all his checkered life, told hair-raising stories about Charlie's past adventures and misadventures. They also applauded the calm that descended over Balfour when Charlie left for his frequent trips to New Orleans and training sessions around the country and bemoaned the chaos that ensued when he returned.

Although rookie Jim Smith had never met Charlie Abbott face-to-face until now, he knew he did not like him, if for no other reason than the effect his presence had on the Balfour Police Department.

"Sorry I startled you," Charlie returned casually, eying the expanse of yellow crime scene tape that efficiently crisscrossed the front doorway. "Anyone come by?"

Smith knew better than to evade the questions.

"Just Doc Graham and the coroner," he began. "Burton and Dalton were here too, about an hour ago, with that new girl who took the pictures."

"I don't have to tell you not to let anyone who isn't authorized inside."

But you did just tell me, Smith thought, his opinion of Charlie confirmed. *Do I look like an idiot? You must think I'm an idiot.*

Charlie realized he was being patronizing, but he didn't care. He found small talk with minions pointless, but he knew he had to establish his right to be there and to set the ground rules for the investigation. They couldn't afford to make sloppy mistakes with the Senator involved. Balfour hadn't had a major crime like this in years.

"Yep, Chief told me the rules," the rookie nodded, warming to the opportunity to talk, even to someone who was considered something of an outlaw celebrity.

"She won't last long. The new girl, I mean." His voice dropped to a conspiratorial whisper. "No stomach for the grisly."

"No one should have a stomach for cold-blooded murder, Smith," Charlie chided, unimpressed by the younger man's attempt at establishing fraternity. "Good we haven't seen much of that sort of crime in Balfour, isn't it?"

"Well, not since—" Smith saw Charlie's look and stopped mid-sentence, stuttering apologies, realizing that he was about to repeat the one story that Burton and Dalton had warned him never to retell, to the very man the story was about. Not only that, but he had come perilously close to naming Charlie's ex-wife, Cora, in the same sentence with the headlines that had followed her arrival from Baton Rouge.

"What I meant to say was—"

"Nothing," interrupted Charlie coldly. "You meant to say nothing."

Smith stumbled over himself, removing one end of the tape and dropping it carelessly before unlocking the door, anxious to avoid Charlie's piercing stare.

"So, Detective," the nervous officer continued, "how long do you think until you are going to be—"

Charlie snorted disdainfully.

"You just cannot keep that size fourteen service boot out of your mouth, can you?"

The young man fell silent, staring at the tips of his black size fourteen service shoes.

Charlie considered feeling sorry for the boy but thought better. He had to learn.

"The Senator will get here sometime tonight, but you have orders."

Charlie paused and let the words sink in before he continued.

"The Senator may try to insist upon being allowed into the crime scene. He will demand to speak to someone in authority. If he tries to cause you problems, you can tell him to call me. I will handle it. Are we clear?"

Charlie waited to make certain that Smith was paying attention.

"Burton should make absolutely certain all the pictures have been taken before he calls in the crew from Griffith for cleanup. No one from the family is allowed into the house, especially the crime scene. Everyone needs clearance from the chief. You are understanding me, right?"

Smith nodded and pressed his lips together.

Charlie paused again and felt a twinge of pity. *This kid is too green.*

"I'll remind Dalton to send someone to relieve you in a couple of hours."

"Thanks."

Charlie's hand was already on the oversized brass knob as he turned.

"One question. Did they find the gun yet?"

Smith looked puzzled.

"I don't know, sir. Dalton didn't say. Just that they had ruled out suicide."

Charlie resisted rolling his eyes. This wasn't the rookie's fault.

"That's okay. I'll read the report later."

Highly unlikely, Charlie added to himself as he allowed Smith to close the heavy oak door behind him. Reading one of Dalton's overly dramatic reports always set his teeth on edge. Sometimes he thought the older of the two former Marine detectives was just a would-be mystery writer in disguise. At least Burton stuck to the facts. His reports were concise and to the point, much like his military appearance.

The air in the high-ceilinged foyer was frigidly cold compared to the late autumn warmth outside. He could almost see the coffee-scented clouds of his breath in the thick air. He stopped a moment to look over the report in his hand, flipping past the pages of familiar forms and photographs.

Well, he thought, *despite what appears to be another flowery literary attempt, Dalton's notes seem reasonably thorough.*

There were pages of remarks and observations in Dalton's distinctively spidery and almost illegible handwriting and copious photographs too.

Maybe, Charlie thought to himself, *he has done his job after all.*

Charlie closed the folder, arrogantly resigned to trust his own instincts about what was and wasn't important. Other people's opinions and insight were of little use to Charlie. He compared it to the difference between watching television and attending a stage play. The television's cameras told him what to see. Made his decisions for him about what was important.

The stage, on the other hand, was full of choices. He could look where he pleased and see what he wanted to see without someone telling him what he should notice and what he should not. Charlie seldom agreed with anyone else about the meaning of the findings at a crime scene anyway, and most of the detectives he knew only agreed with him after he had proven himself to be right.

And Charlie was always, to his own mind, right.

Right in every sense of the meaning of the word.

The carved oak sliding doors to the left, off the main foyer, led into the study. They were a little more than half-closed, which is how, Charlie knew, they had been found. About twenty-four inches or so. Room enough for Charlie to slide between them. Burton would have marked their position, opened them, and then replaced them again for the crime scene photographs.

The opening between the doors could accommodate a small- to medium-build man and certainly most women.

At least those women, Charlie noted grimly, *on the suspect list.*

He took out his notebook and pen and began to write down his thoughts in his own cryptic shorthand.

The massive antique cherrywood desk sat in the center of the room. On the left wall there were several panels of thick, blood-red brocade drapes, hung ceiling to floor. Charlie walked over and elbowed a corner of the curtains away to reveal a thick, double-paned picture window. No way to open that.

No sign of a struggle.

That in itself did not seem quite logical. Steve liked his privacy. For all his flamboyant life style, his home had been off limits to all but a very few. He held lavish parties at private clubs and exclusive venues all over the Atlanta area, but he had never involved Katy or Elizabeth in those events. Truthfully, there were few that Katy would have wanted to attend. Charlie wondered which friends and family had even been allowed into the inner sanctum of this office, and how many there were who might be invited to approach the desk, much less Steve himself.

Charlie began to understand why Dalton and Burton had so quickly agreed to turn over the case to him.

Whoever killed Steve Wilton had gotten close to him. Too close to him.

Someone Steve trusted. And Steve Wilton was no fool.

The sweetish odor of death pervaded the lavishly decorated study. The smell, quite predictably, was strongest near the high-backed leather chair pushed slightly back from the desk. Charlie took a shallow breath and allowed his pupils to adjust to the semidarkness before he stepped forward to take in a more comprehensive view of the room and its furnishings.

Charlie's eyes were drawn to the top of the desk.

Wilton's head had fallen to rest on a blotter in the center, at least from the look of the bare rectangular outline that had obviously been removed as evidence and the frame of dried brown blood around the empty space. From what he could tell, the bullet had exited into the hardwood through the cardboard and fabric, judging by the indentation that had been left there. The bullet had been removed, he surmised, and was well on its way to forensics.

The evidence indicated to Charlie that not only had Wilton been seated at his desk, he had also been leaning his head over the desktop, doing something.

Just what the chief had said, and what he had told Thomas.

A gilt-framed picture of Katy and Elizabeth smiled eerily from the right side of the vacant space, next to a green glass and brass banker's lamp. Both were spattered with dried dots and droplets of blood. To the left of the space was a wooden pen and pencil holder, the pen missing. Charlie noted the brand—Cross—and sighed. *Even his pencils are expensive.*

The datebook calendar was opened to today's date. Those too were equally spattered with browning red stains.

Charlie used his elbow again to pull the chair back slightly, noting its original position, and peered under the desk into the darkness for a moment. He removed his flashlight from his jacket pocket and peered a second time, the beam taking a searching tour of the hand woven, Persian carpet. *No clear plastic chair protector for Steve Wilton.*

The thick pile had taken the overflow bulk of the rapidly crusting stains.

There was little doubt how Wilton had died. Or where. Charlie clicked off his flashlight. There was nothing else under the desk. Burton must have tagged and bagged the missing pen.

He carefully replaced the bulky, blood-stained chair and turned his attention to the rest of the room. Nothing seemed out of place. Glass-fronted, diamond-paned, built-in bookcases. Turn-of-the-last-century oil-painted landscapes on the walls, random themes. A three-mast nineteeth-century sailing ship. A peaceful meadow of wild flowers with a dominating oak tree. A mountain waterfall. All probably expensive, but Charlie was not a collector or connoisseur of fine art.

On an elaborately carved side table there was a square cut glass decanter, half-filled with a brownish liquid. Charlie sniffed briefly. *Bourbon. Expensive bourbon.*

He was not particularly proud that he was an expert in knowing that.

His attention drifted to the two small glasses beside the decanter, and he studied them more closely. The faint smell of strong liquor still coated the bottom.

Not bagged and tagged? Odd.

There was clearly a pinkish tint of oily lipstick just below the rim of one of the glasses. No, Burton had deliberately left him a clue, not from carelessness but from personal preservation. Charlie made another note. Burton and Dalton clearly wanted no part in finding evidence that might convict a woman in Steve's death, especially not a woman from Balfour's close-knit community.

His eyes had fully adjusted now to the depressing semidarkness, and he could clearly see that one of the multiple glass doors on the bookcase nearest the desk was slightly ajar. Charlie took a handkerchief he kept for such purposes out of his pocket and inspected the door carefully, pulling it open further to reveal the contents.

Inside he found assorted leather-bound volumes. Some of them were grouped in sets, and he supposed the majority were first editions. The musky odor of collectibles, especially the distinctive smell of the yellowed glue and vellum, hung like an invisible curtain before the rows of shelves. The image of Steve reading anything that hadn't been required reading in high school was ludicrous. The thought that another person had opened the door to the bookcase, for whatever reason, was equally puzzling and noteworthy.

Charlie studied the neatly organized and slightly dusty rows. On the second shelf at eye level, two adjoining books leaned together slightly. A third book was clearly missing from its place between them. From the others in the series, Charlie determined that the book was part of a larger set. Dark greenish leather, gold embossed spine, with maybe three other books in the group. It was too dark to read the titles.

Charlie took out his flashlight again, pushed open the door with the rim of the cylinder, and inspected the remaining set briefly. He reconsidered. Maybe the title of the book didn't matter, but Charlie made a note anyway. The missing book was small, maybe four by six or eight inches, and less than an inch thick.

Charlie began to wonder what else Burton and Dalton might have left for him to find. He quickly inspected the other bookshelves. Finding nothing else of interest, he used the handkerchief to avoid leaving his own prints and carefully replaced the glass door as he had found it.

A noise in the doorway behind him caused him to turn.

A different uniformed officer, another newcomer he didn't recognize, stood just outside the framed threshold, hands on his hips, smirking at Charlie. Obviously, Smith had been relieved from guard duty without his intervention.

"So, this is how rich people spend their time," the second officer said, a bit too cheerfully to Charlie's way of thinking. "I bet he never read half those books."

Charlie sighed to himself. *Not another one.*

"New to Balfour, aren't you, Officer?" he said, rolling his pen deftly between his fingers and feigning interest in the answer to his question.

"Jenkins," the other man responded through a highly whitened, perfect row of teeth, as if Charlie should have known him. "I'm relieving Smith."

"No, Officer Jenkins," Charlie countered quietly. "You are disturbing my crime scene investigation."

Jenkins took immediate offense, folding his muscular arms across his equally muscular chest and glowering. His uniform, like Smith's, had the crisp appearance of never having been worn.

Great. Just what the force needs. Another untrained, obnoxious jerk.

Charlie put his hands into his pants pockets and took a calming breath.

"Look, Jenkins," he began with what he hoped was his best and most congenial tone, "I am just taking a quick look around. You know us detectives, nosy lot. Burton and Dalton have been through once, but the chief asked me to look around. I was just taking notes and concentrating, that's all. While the scene is fresh. I'll be done in a few."

Jenkins narrowed his already beady eyes, unimpressed.

"Are you ordering me out?" Jenkins had clearly made up his mind to stay.

"Me?" Charlie raised an eyebrow sardonically and twisted slowly, pretending to take in the artwork on the walls with practiced nonchalance.

"I'm just the visiting detective here." His voice was casual, friendly, and drawling. "Chief doesn't let me order anybody around, except maybe the sandwich girl, Jennifer, is she still there? And Ed, you know Ed, the cleanup crew foreman from Griffith—and then, only on random Tuesdays after five."

Jenkins frowned, confused by the sudden detour from confrontation.

"They told me about you." His sour voice was accusing. "You're Charlie Abbott."

"Guilty as charged."

Charlie's hands pushed a little deeper into his pants pockets.

"Dalton knows stories about you," Jenkins went on tauntingly, "and Burton outright hates your guts. They said that you think you're smarter than the rest of us just because you write books and used to have some overblown job with the PD in New Orleans."

"Ah, well." Charlie had stopped listening and was once

again actually inspecting the crime scene. He had heard all these criticisms before and found them only mildly annoying.

His eyes stopped on the smallest of the oil paintings on the wall, a portrait of some incredibly sad woman in a black veil. Something about the way it hung on the wall didn't seem quite right. *A hidden safe, maybe.*

He felt around in his left pocket to see if he had a pair of latex gloves, and then turned back to face the increasing irritation of the much younger officer.

"Smarter?" Charlie countered absently. "Probably not smarter. I'm just methodical."

"What?"

"Methodical. Careful. Detailed. Precise. Comprehensive." He thought of Cora. Those were some of her favorite words to describe him. At the thought of Cora, he smiled enigmatically and resumed his speech with more geniality than he felt.

"Generally speaking, and I know you understand this from your extensive training, many synonymous personality traits such as these are often confused with intelligence. I do not believe myself to be any more intelligent than most law enforcement officers, and certainly less so than many others, perhaps yourself included."

"You talk too much."

Charlie nodded in agreement. "Hence the solitary investigative practices." His hands left his pockets and made a sweeping, dramatic gesture around the room. "You invited yourself in here, Officer Jenkins. Don't complain about the quality of the company."

Jenkins let out a mild oath of disgust.

"Let me know when you leave, Detective," he snapped.

Charlie waited patiently until the footsteps echoed away on the marble tiles of the foyer before he tugged the blue latex gloves from his pocket and crossed the study to peruse the oil painting.

Indeed, just what he thought. The right side of the frame was slightly further from the wall than the left. Charlie gently pulled the bottom right corner forward.

The frame swung easily and soundlessly out to reveal a small wall safe. That too did not appear to be completely closed. Slipping the tip of his latex-covered finger along the bottom edge of the gray steel, he pulled again. The small safe opened to reveal a.45 pistol nestled in a stack of typed papers and a single bulging white envelope.

Well, Charlie thought, closing his notebook and wishing he had brought more evidence bags. *Dalton and Burton really left me the jackpot here.*

Charlie knew they had never cared for him, but it was obvious that they really despised him now.

What a mess. What an incredible mess.

Chapter 14

Thomas did not quite know how to broach the subject of Charlie when he talked to Cora about Steve's death, or about his part in helping deal with the Senator.

He only knew that he needed to let her know that he was going to be late, and that it was going to be because he was spending time with her ex-husband.

Cora hated that expression, and Cora didn't hate much. She said calling Charlie an ex-husband made it sound as though he were dead or that he was some sort of X factor, unknown and unpredictable. Thomas had suggested that the description was not too far from the actual truth. Cora had not laughed.

When Thomas had tried to say first husband, Cora had objected just as strongly. That expression, she had countered, made her sound as though there had been, or would be, a long list of husbands, like the ever-changing rosters of professional sports teams or the revolving appointed chairmen on the boards of international corporations.

Thomas had found himself uncharacteristically frustrated with his wife. "So what do you want me to call him?"

"Just call him Charlie," Cora had said. "Just Charlie."

Charlie rattled Thomas in ways that only former close friends can. Charlie had been the fatherless class clown and instigator of rebellion. Thomas had been the class president, voted most likely to succeed. Together they made an unlikely pair.

Both valued truth, loyalty, and justice, and after graduation each chose his own unique path to success. They kept in sporadic touch through Charlie's grandparents and Thomas's father and grandfather. Until Cora.

Discussing Charlie with Cora was the only subject that left him irrationally speechless and at the same time with a desire to use profanity.

Not unlike our high school years, he reminded himself grimly.

As Thomas was debating with himself about whether the current conversation should take place on the telephone or in person, he found himself turning into the driveway to Cora's house. He still struggled with calling it his house, although he had stopped thinking about it as Charlie's childhood home.

The sight of the freshly painted, deep blue, two story Victorian house only partially encouraged him. The white window boxes of purple and yellow pansies smiled at him. The broad porch and the oversized oak rocking chairs with their tufted blue cushions invited him to rest with them. The worn stone walkway beckoned him inside, all the while it chided him for his insecurities and doubts. These were all evidence of Cora's touch. Cora's love for him. Her attempt to remake what had been Charlie's house into a home for them. Their house. Their home. Together.

Love for Cora usually overcame his natural dislike for Charlie's antics, as well as his regret that Charlie had lived here as a teenager. Cora had offered to sell the house, but only once. Thomas couldn't ask her to sell what had come to be her refuge from the world, so he never asked, and she never offered again. If she wanted to live in this house and was happy in this house, then he could tolerate Charlie.

Lost in thought and unintentionally staring at the house, Thomas realized that not only was he home, but the car engine was still running. The low hum of the local country music station on the radio was numbing as he dragged his mind back to the present. In a deliberate twist, he turned the key and removed it from the ignition. Senator Wilton's plane would be at the local airport in about an hour, and Thomas had no intention of being late. There were too many unexpected detours this meeting might take.

Inside, Marjorie had been watching from a side kitchen window. She had been with Cora long enough to discern the sound of Thomas's car when it pulled into the driveway, so that she knew without looking that he had arrived home. She was concerned when Thomas did not come directly inside.

Her intuition told her that somehow Charlie was involved.

When something went wrong in this house, Marjorie was usually accurate in assuming that Charlie Abbott was at the center.

Moving away from her post at the window, Marjorie took

the hot pads from the countertop and opened the oven carefully to inspect the well-browned, bubbling chicken pies. Removing them with practiced care, she placed each on the butcher block island to cool. The delicious smell hovered for a moment and then spread about the kitchen with enticing fingers.

The front door opened, and Thomas announced himself from the doorway. His voice was strained and oddly impersonal.

Marjorie's premonition grew stronger. She tried to console herself that she had done what she could.

If Charlie *was* causing trouble again, at least dinner was ready.

With a small grimace of resignation, she poured herself a cup of freshly made coffee, took a warm chocolate chip cookie from the plate, and sat down at the kitchen table to wait. And pray.

Thomas's keys dropped into the wooden bowl, and almost simultaneously she heard Cora's responding voice in the hallway. Stilted greetings. Then, intense, low conversation. Marjorie did not strain to hear the words. She did not need to know what was going on. Not just yet anyway.

Within minutes, the couple appeared in the doorway to the kitchen. Cora, her sweet smile slightly tight but still genuine. Thomas, making no pretense of being comfortable, his handsome face an odd shade of blushing, overripe peaches.

"Hello, Marjorie."

He's attempting a normal voice at least, the housekeeper thought.

"Something smells amazing. Thank you."

"If you aren't hungry now, the chicken pies will keep until you get home later."

Marjorie ignored Thomas's quizzical look and turned her gaze to Cora. "Is little Jane still sleeping?"

"She was exhausted after the drawing session. Naps are underrated."

"Jane?" Thomas turned his quizzical look to Cora.

"Four-year-old witness to her family's murder," Cora explained. She met Marjorie's encouraging eyes for support. "Charlie brought her this morning."

Thomas's arm encircled his wife's shoulders and drew her closer to him.

"Then we have both had our own stressful encounters with Charlie today." He was trying not to sound stiff and condescending. "Well, I refuse to blame him for his taste in therapists."

Cora patted the hand that rested on her elbow.

"Marjorie worked her wonders today."

"So, she's staying with us for a while? Jane?" His voice was hopeful.

His wife was always happier with a child in the house.

"Jane Chen," Cora continued. "She doesn't remember much yet or want to share, but that will come with time—and cookies."

"And prayers," Marjorie added, turning back to Thomas. "I can fix you a plate of chicken pie."

"No time." Thomas deliberately checked his watch. "Wish I could."

He spotted the plate of cookies. "Maybe just a few of those and a travel cup of coffee. Black."

Marjorie did not need explanations, moving before he had

finished asking. She bustled about to find a small paper lunch bag and the stainless steel four-cup thermos. Cora leaned closer into the half-circle of her husband's arms.

"Please be careful." She slipped her own arm around his waist, returning his hug. "The Senator can be unpredictable, and Charlie . . . Charlie is just Charlie. Trouble loves him as much as Charlie loves trouble. I just don't like the thought of you caught in the crossfire."

"Because I can't take care of myself?" he teased gently.

"Because your first impulse is to take care of other people." Her voice was soft and serious. "Your immediate thought is for someone else. Your last thought is always for yourself."

Their eyes locked in mutual understanding for a long moment before Thomas became aware of Marjorie's patient shadow, travel cup and brown paper bag of cookies in her extended hand. She stood with her head turned away, eyes politely and discreetly surveying the fading sunlight just outside the bay window.

"Thank you again, Marjorie." Thomas released his hold on Cora and gratefully took the warm thermos and generously heavy bag.

"Cora, didn't you tell me you had an appointment with Amy today? By chance, did you see her or talk to her?"

Cora shook her head.

"The housekeeper called with apologies, but that wasn't until after four. Said both Amy and Dan were out." Cora pursed her lips. "I suppose from what you just told me, they must have left Katy alone for the afternoon."

"And you disapprove, I assume?"

Cora shrugged.

"That's not really fair of me I guess," she admitted. "I don't care for Dan, or what I have heard of Dan. I'm also not sure that leaving Katy alone was a good idea under the circumstances."

Thomas frowned. "This isn't like you to be so judgmental."

She opened her lips to protest, but Thomas stooped and kissed his wife quickly and completely, preventing all speech and effectively derailing her thoughts.

Cora was blushing to the roots of her dark hair when he finally lifted his head.

"Finish my prayers for me, will you?" he said, his face also flushed as he added a second, less ardent kiss into the bangs over her forehead.

"Always," Cora promised, finding her composure and taking his hand, walking him, as she almost always did, to finish their goodbyes at the front door.

Marjorie had continued to dutifully avert her eyes, swallowing her curiosity, and turned her attention to the dishes in the sudsy sink and the herbs growing in the matching red clay pots along the windowsill. She continued humming to herself until she heard the front door close and noted the distinctive click of the deadbolt lock.

"Ready for your chicken pie supper?" she offered, noting that the late afternoon sun had brought a coolness, a darkness, to the grove of trees in the backyard. A sudden cloud of shadow had fallen across the windows.

"You didn't really have a proper lunch, you know."

"Why don't we both wait and eat with Jane?" Cora

responded from the doorway. "We should wake her soon if she doesn't wake on her own from her nap."

"Of course," Marjorie replied. She dried her hands and returned to her coffee and cookie, breaking off a piece of the soft sweet and popping it into her mouth. "Kitchen or the dining room?"

"The dining room might be nice. With my grandmother's rose chintz dishes, maybe. What do you think?"

Marjorie smiled, her mind racing with happy thoughts of children and healing.

"A tea party of sorts," she said brightly. "I'll set the table as soon as I finish my snack. Does Jane have anything special she could wear?"

"Not in the suitcase that Charlie brought." Cora paused thoughtfully. "I could check the trunk in the extra room. The donated clothes Susan and the Methodist Ladies Auxiliary brought over from the last foster children's donation drive. As I remember there were some quite beautiful hand-smocked dresses in there."

Marjorie nodded.

"Oh, Marjorie, I think we have our answer about why Amy didn't come by today."

The housekeeper raised her eyebrows questioningly.

"Steve Wilton is dead. Murdered this afternoon in his own house."

"Murdered?" The stunned housekeeper covered her mouth with the tips of her fingers in disbelief. "Oh, dear Lord! Do they know who did it?"

"Not yet."

"Oh, dear Lord," the housekeeper repeated. "And Charlie is involved, of course."

"Of course," Cora echoed. "And Charlie involved Thomas."

"Of course he did."

The Westminster clock in the den chimed six o'clock.

"Oh, my dear good Lord," Marjorie said for the third time, but this time she meant the words as a prayer.

Chapter 15

Virginia Evans applied another light coat of floral-scented hand cream to her modestly manicured fingertips and smiled at her rapidly shortening list. Almost halfway done. She felt justifiably proud of what they had all accomplished.

Donna Philips had adroitly handled planning the music and securing the musicians for the funeral on Sunday afternoon. With Frank the organist on his annual sabbatical to Charleston, she had little choice but to ask the pianist, Lavinia Toney, to play for the special services.

Miss Lavinia was unabashedly flattered by the invitation, believing her abilities to have been sorely overlooked by the minister of music's new obsession with all things Memphis. She selfishly relished an opportunity to play for what promised to be a standing-room-only congregation, without the constant criticism she received from Frank. Miss Lavinia even suggested a dear friend she knew who could provide a violin, and Donna promised to get back to her after she talked to the family.

Virginia had managed to receive assurances from the chief of police that six days would be more than sufficient to obtain a release of the body from the coroner's office, pending the results of the autopsy and under the present circumstances.

"Without any unforeseen complications," the chief had added.

They both knew what he had meant. The murder itself was one thing. The Senator was another. Senator Wilton was the biggest of the two unforeseen complications. No one had been able to predict or to control the Senator except his beloved wife, and she had died of cancer the year Steve turned five years old.

If six days did not prove to be sufficient time for preparations, Alice suggested that the whole process could quite easily become a memorial service of sorts. Not quite the same as an old-fashioned Southern Baptist funeral, but adequate to give Katy and Elizabeth some sort of closure. And perhaps even enough to satisfy the Senator's habit of publicly displaying personal issues.

Everyone well knew the Senator's bent to spectacle. He had exploited the humble roots of his small town, homespun background with the skill of a Tom Sawyer and the notorious whitewashing episode. Senator Wilton used this deceptive persona during his multiple election and subsequent reelection campaigns.

A soft Southern accent that could be turned off and on at will. A cream-colored campaign hat with the traditional patriotic red, white, and blue ribbon. Snug brocade vests beneath an ample, long- tailed coat. Patterned bow ties, never clip-on and always pure silk. The final touch: his suspenders, which always coordinated with the ties around his neck.

Yes, the Senator's appearance was a caricature of all things Southern aristocrat, yet he was indeed one of a kind, and he preferred his position of solitude at the top of the political food chain.

Father and son were in sharp contrast in more than just appearance and were seldom if ever seen together in public and less often in private. Both were greedy, self-serving men with little regard for the opinions of others, though the father had mastered the skill of concealing his disdain for the common man under the guise of public service.

Stewart Wilton's wealth and political power had given him everything he desired, save one thing—a son who could follow in his footsteps. A son who would make him proud. Failing all that, a son who could give him a grandson who could do what his father could not. Senator Wilton loved his granddaughter, but truth be told she too was a disappointment.

Steve Wilton had failed the Senator on all counts.

Now there was no son to bear the brunt of the bitterness and disappointment. The tiny town of Balfour, Georgia, prepared to face full-on what Steve had lived with all his life— the anger of a powerful, disappointed man.

Virginia Evans had suspected all this from the bits and pieces of gossip she had overheard. Donna and Alice had taken turns during the afternoon confirming her worst fears and enlightening her as to the gravity of their afternoon plans and preparations.

Virginia had spoken to the housekeeper at Amy and Dan's,

who insisted that Katy was resting under a doctor-induced sleep and could not, must not, be disturbed. The elderly housekeeper also confirmed that the blanket of flowers for the casket would come from the family, and that white roses with blue ribbons were what Katy would want. Other flowers were not necessary or expected. There were charities that Katy routinely supported, all local, including a group home for boys and girls out in the country and an organization that built housing for veterans and low-income families. The housekeeper said money should go to those people, not to flowers. The women in the office agreed that that was what Katy would want.

There had been only minimal rearranging to the regular weekly schedule for the Sunday services, just a hasty plan for an additional walk-through immediately after the regular services by the dependable Frost and Beryl along with a second cleaning lady, Sarah, and her husband, Ben, who handled the regular lawn and gardening maintenance.

The acceptability of the building's appearance, however, was a minor issue compared to the order of services for the memorial program. Services for Steve would have to be handled delicately, because they would be under a microscope not only from the local media, limited as that was, but scrutiny from the state and national media as well.

Murder was sensational. Unsolved murder with a cast of colorful Southern characters could fuel the news furnaces for weeks, if not months. Virginia knew that it would not take much of a spark to turn the whole town into a raging wildfire of innuendo and suspicion or, worse yet, a comedic three-ring circus. The funeral itself could become a crowd-gathering spectacle, with her husband walking a tightrope without a net and the entire police force playing the part of bumbling clowns while the Senator picked up a whip and a chair and took over as the self-appointed ringmaster.

Unfortunately for the Senator, he did not know Virginia Evans. She carried an unshakeable, fierce determination to protect her husband and the church she had adopted from any such shenanigans and potential grandstanding. Virginia Evans did not know this particular senator, but she was not a novice on the field of political and social combat. And she had been forearmed with enough information on Senator Stewart Wilton to put on full armor and defend whom and what she loved.

Her duty as a preacher's wife, as she saw it, was to be loyal above all reproach. She must have membership in all organizations, by proxy if necessary, and yet leadership in few, if any. Her sphere of influence must protect his back, be ever at his shoulder, and never run on ahead of him.

Virginia worked with the children in the church, with and within the various women's groups and Bible studies. She was ever careful to avoid any hint of partiality or favoritism. Her plain vanilla pound cakes, given for any and all occasions, were famous for their simplicity and taste. Virginia Evans was a woman to be counted upon. A woman of her word. A godly woman. A woman of cast iron beneath a white-haired, matronly, velvet exterior.

When Virginia Evans spoke, people in Balfour had learned to listen. The most intelligent of people moved into the line that had, on more than one occasion in the past year, formed behind her. Donna and Alice were both grateful for her quiet, efficient direction, but they dreaded that one impending telephone call yet to come.

Several times the women had paused in their work and whispered impulsive prayers for intercession, sandwiched between the incessant ringing of the office telephone. Church members with questions. The editor of the local newspaper and a reporter from the *Sentinel* in Griffith with more questions. A few curiosity seekers asking for details about Steve's death and directions to the church.

None of the three women seemed startled then when the telephone rang for the twentieth-odd time that afternoon and the dreaded call finally came just before six o'clock.

Donna, who was closest and least busy at the moment, picked up the receiver.

"Emmanuel Baptist Church, Donna speaking."

Before she could continue, both Alice and Virginia could hear the strident male voice, interrupting and shouting in vexation from the confines of the handset.

Virginia reached for the telephone, and Donna surrendered it wordlessly, mouthing profuse apologies. Virginia held the receiver at a nominal distance from her ears and listened for a moment to the tirade without trying to speak herself. She had found that the best method for dealing with people with a problem was to let them have their say-so first, however long that might take.

The most productive and disarming method was to listen. Really listen.

Virginia Evans was the best of all listeners.

Finally the voice slowed, lowered to a growl, and then finally stopped.

"Yes, Senator Wilton," she said sweetly. "This is Virginia Evans. No, we have never met. I'm Andrew Evans's wife, the pastor here at Emmanuel Baptist Church, and I have been listening to every word that you've said. You have our deepest sympathy for this devastating loss."

There was an uncomfortable pause, and the male voice noticeably disarmed. The Senator lowered his volume and responded with a voice that was barely audible now to Donna and Alice's straining ears.

"Yes, Senator Wilton," Virginia continued smoothly. "Of course, I can understand your concerns. Tentative arrangements have been made for Sunday afternoon at two o'clock."

Pause.

"Here at the church, of course. This is where Steve and Katy were married, Senator. Little Elizabeth has been in our mother's morning out program. Darling, precious child. She has Steve's eyes and Katy's smile."

Another pause. Virginia listened again without interrupting.

"I can certainly see your point, Senator," she said. Her sincerity was genuine. "Emmanuel Baptist is much more personal though, don't you think?"

When there was no answer, she continued.

"A funeral home service is," Virginia picked her words even more carefully, "well, Senator, a funeral home service is just not the same. Emmanuel does afford a bit more room too. There will be so many who will want to pay their respects to Katy, little Elizabeth, and the family."

A much shorter pause this time. The voice on the other end

of the line was imperceptible now.

"Then, of course," the preacher's wife continued sweetly, "there is our Southern tradition to consider. And Katy's wishes, as his wife."

Donna and Alice both noted that Virginia was careful not to say that people would want to pay respects to Steve or to his father. No, Katy was the person they would come to see, most of them anyway. The ones who mattered. The rest might show up to see the Senator or to be seen themselves, for what that was worth.

"Capacity?" Virginia continued, still nonplussed. "The sanctuary seats over eight hundred since we installed the balconies five years ago. Considerably larger than Glendale's or Parson's funeral homes."

Virginia listened again.

"Well, Senator, of course the service will be tastefully brief, given the emotional and unusual nature of the circumstances. The family could always plan a more elaborate memorial at a later date."

Virginia paused briefly to listen again.

"Yes, you're right, Senator. Grief is a personal emotion, and we do indeed respect that. The local police chief has assured me that there will be ample security and consideration for the family's right to privacy."

There was an almost nonexistent pause this time.

"Then we agree, Senator. All the arrangements for Sunday will be finalized according to Katy's wishes. Special arrangements have been made for you, of course, and anyone on your staff who has accompanied you."

Virginia picked up a pen and made a note.

"Your aide-de-camp, of course. And his name?" She wrote again. "Perkins? And his first name?"

Pause. Virginia's forehead wrinkled for the first time.

"Ah, just Perkins."

Donna and Alice exchanged looks and frowned. A name they did not recognize. Someone new in the Senator's never-ending entourage from Washington, D.C., no doubt. Another Yankee carpetbagger.

"Well, if you will have Perkins contact us on Friday afternoon, I will be happy to go over all the final details with him personally."

This time Virginia Evans did not wait for a pause.

"Of course, Senator. You're welcome. We'll talk to you soon."

Virginia cradled the receiver and leaned back into her chair.

"You would think you voted for him," Alice observed admiringly.

"How do you know that I didn't?" Virginia countered diplomatically, winking, then changed the subject.

"Would you darlings mind if we go over the list again in the morning?" She turned the black band of her practical Timex watch around on her wrist to see the face. "It's after six o'clock, and we all need to get home."

"I have a roast in the crockpot with new red potatoes, carrots from the garden, and pearl onions," Donna offered. "Family favorite, but there will be plenty to share."

"My husband owes me a dinner out." Alice was already putting on her lightweight pink cardigan sweater and digging through her Vera Bradley purse for her car keys.

"We have been wanting to try that Italian place over in Willow Glen," she continued. "Cheryl Davis tried it last week and said the lasagna was homemade."

"Well then." Donna stood and stretched, putting on her own bulky hand-knit sweater. "My roast certainly can't compete with homemade lasagna—and I wouldn't dare interfere with a romantic dinner in Willow Glen with *your* Andy."

Virginia tried to picture Alice's lanky husband, resplendent in his weathered denim overalls and muddy work boots, wearing his favorite faded baseball cap and seated with his well-dressed wife at a candlelit dinner in Willow Glen.

Virginia smiled to herself. Alice's Andy was nothing like her Andy.

Oh, well, she thought to herself. *To each her own.*

The two women, having gathered their belongings, stood for a moment at their respective desks and considered with pride what they had accomplished, knowing that the worst was still to come. Their admiration for Virginia Evans was more than evident in the expressions on their faces. Both were happily planning how to share this new story with the Ladies Auxiliary on Tuesday night.

Virginia had moved to Donna's desk and was absentmindedly considering the list of what was yet to be done before she could leave for the evening, and what she and Andy would have for their supper when they finally did leave.

There is only so much sadness and stress any person can bear for very long, she thought to herself. *Only so much sorrow a person can endure before the spirit has to come up for air.*

"Virginia . . ." Donna turned, hesitating. "The invitation is open to you too. Pot roast at my house."

But the preacher's wife was already focused on the computer in front of her, the format for the plan of the funeral handout bulletin for Sunday afternoon spread across the screen, and she did not hear.

Donna went on out to her impatiently waiting husband, Thad, and was almost glad her invitation had not been acknowledged. Sharing a meal with Virginia, as pleasant as that might be, would also involve feeding the preacher, and Donna really did not like the man well enough for that.

No, not nearly well enough for that.

Chapter 16

Amy loved her sister in her own way. At least, she tried. Ten years old when Katy was born, baby Katy was everything that Amy was not. A beautiful, gifted little princess who had lived a charmed and magical life, or so it seemed to the uninformed of Balfour. Gossips frequently conjectured that there must be jealousy and sibling rivalry between the older and the younger, and they were not mistaken.

As she studied her younger sister's restless, sedated form sleeping in the four-poster bed in the guest room of her home, Amy McInnis thought about just how much she had to gain, and to lose, by Steve's death.

She twisted the thick gold band around her ring finger and made the decision not to cry. There had been enough of that already.

The call had come from the police chief just as she had gone to the daycare to pick up Katy and Elizabeth. At first she thought she should take the child home first, but Katy insisted that she needed to go. Needed to see.

Amy fought the pictures in her head. The sight of the chief, the police officers, the hysterical housekeeper, the flashing red lights and the ambulance in the driveway, the rolls of yellow crime scene tape. Katy dropping to her knees, stunned and sobbing, as they rolled out the black body bag on the gurney to the ambulance. Katy clutching a baffled Elizabeth and shielding her daughter's eyes.

Amy wanted to reach out. Wanted to do something. Wanted to feel something.

But she was numb and silent.

Amy was stoic and studious, the bookworm who wore thick glasses in the first grade and who worked hard for everything she got. Amy took life very seriously.

Amy never gave anyone cause for concern. She graduated valedictorian from Balfour High School and went on full scholarship to the University of Georgia to major in business administration. The summer after her equally stellar college graduation, summa cum laude, Amy did what was expected of her and married Dan McInnis, a successful local contractor ten years her senior, and settled into a prestigious home in Balfour's exclusive, wooded countryside on a massive lot. No one ever asked Amy if she was happy. For most of her life, Amy never even asked herself.

Katy, in contrast, was a photogenic, adorable baby. The favorite. The beauty of the family. The undisputed homecoming queen. There weren't sufficient superlatives for Katy, who as a twelve-year-old flower girl innocently took center stage at her sister's wedding. Katy was born to turn heads. To be the star. To be happy.

Amy had taken second place to Katy from the beginning. Katy garnered the kind of attention that Amy unwillingly realized she wanted. But Amy tried to love her sister as though it didn't matter. And it might not have mattered, until Steve Wilton.

Steve graduated with Amy. They had dated off and on their senior year of high school, before Steve moved on to another more attractive classmate. After graduation, Steve attended a string of colleges before finally graduating from North Georgia College. He was rewarded with a hedonistic whirlwind trip through Europe, the Senator's gift to Steve for finally finishing something he had started.

When Steve finally returned to Balfour, he dabbled in selling insurance policies and brokering stocks and bonds, but Steve was neither a broker nor a salesman. His father was wealthy and busy with political life in Washington, D.C. As long as Steve didn't generate negative news, his father was willing to support him.

Steve was bored and lazy, until one day on the streets of Balfour he saw Katy.

She had been only a child when he had dated Amy in high school. This Katy was a seventeen-year-old woman. The minute he saw her, Steve wanted to marry her. Amy was outraged. She tried to insist that Katy go to college, that the ten-year difference was too great, that she knew firsthand what Steve was like. But since Amy herself had married a man considerably older than she was, her protests fell on deaf ears. Katy was innocent and flattered.

Their parents were also enamored with Steve's promises and fairytale stories and blinded to his faults and flaws. When they died in a freak automobile accident in the winter of Katy's senior year, all the barriers to Steve's plan were essentially gone. While Amy tried to pick up the jagged pieces of life after their parents' deaths, Steve moved seamlessly into the void and offered security and a life of luxury.

Steve convinced Katy that there was no real purpose in attending college. He persuaded her to stay with her sister just long enough to help settle the estate, temporarily close up her parents' house, and complete her senior year in high school. The day after graduation, Steve proudly announced their engagement, and they were married before the summer was over.

Although Amy protested loudly and persistently, the wedding was inevitable. *Finish college*, Amy had urged. *Date other people while you're young. Travel. Learn to be your own person.* Amy tried every tactic. Katy would not listen.

Practical Amy tried to talk to romantic Katy, to no avail. Katy was infatuated.

The wedding was the social event of the decade in Balfour, maybe even several decades. Emmanuel Baptist Church was Katy's only firm stand for their wedding, winning out only after a long struggle over Steve's insistence on a more cosmopolitan setting virtually anywhere else.

The pews in the church were crammed to overflowing with invited guests and publicity seekers, including a number of newsworthy, quite famous people from the Senator's

Washington inner circles. There was no dancing, but the ostentatious reception spilled out into the grounds around the church and across the street to the Methodist church. Huge, billowing white tents covered a sea of linen over rented tables surrounded by starched, canvas-covered folding chairs. The attendants wore tuxedos, and the servers glided through the crowd in elegant black dresses with tights, dainty white lace aprons, and caps. *Worthy of a movie star*, the local newspaper had reported. *A celebrity wedding.*

Amy played the dutiful matron of honor at her sister's side, standing tight-lipped in a deep purple lace dress with a huge bouquet of stark white roses in her arms. A bevy of giggling lavender bridesmaids with matching satin gloves held single white roses. But as it was at Amy's own wedding, no one noticed anyone except Katy. The rest of the world was just background fodder for the Cinderella bride.

As Amy had predicted, if only to Dan and to herself, within the first year Katy was expecting Elizabeth. Before the baby was even born, her jaded Prince Charming was seeking out greener pastures and more interesting, but always short-lived, false fairy tale romances.

Steve's boredom and lack of attention soon became the talk of Balfour, embarrassing and further humiliating the young wife. The brutal knowledge that her sister had been right came as a final crushing blow, even though Amy did not gloat.

Having no children of her own, Amy overcame her jealousy to offer her help with little Elizabeth, a tiny, doll-like copy of her beautiful mother, and the women grew closer than they had ever been.

With Amy's loving support, Katy proved unexpectedly strong.

In the face of her husband's infidelities, a wiser, only slighter older Katy immersed herself dutifully in the joys of motherhood, charity work, and the daily life of Balfour. Elizabeth became Katy's entire world. She saw no real alternative to her situation and turned a blind eye, offering what she called Christian charity to her husband's increasingly predictable and regular indiscretions.

After their third anniversary passed, Katy announced that she had been going to a counselor in Griffith and that she wished Steve would join her. For Elizabeth's sake, she was resolved not to play the part of wounded, angry wife.

When Katy's request for professional intervention was denied by her playboy husband, who voiced his intention to continue his lifestyle with or without her consent, the sympathy of all the womenfolk of Balfour descended upon them, rallying around Katy and baby Elizabeth.

Amy was pushed aside and bitter.

Steve, stunned by his wife's continued resolve and stung by his father's repeated criticisms and disappointments, moved out of the house to an apartment in Atlanta. The Senator, furious at the abrupt flurry of tabloid publicity, commanded that if his son intended to carry on in this despicable way, he should file for divorce. Steve did, and Katy accepted it as part of a greater plan.

Amy even went to see him to try to talk to him, but she regretted that decision immediately.

Watching her sister sleep, Amy despised being right almost as much as she despised Steve Wilton. She did not tell Katy that in her own heart she had once understood Steve's charm. His power over women. She remembered bitterly from her youth what it was like to want to be with him. And Amy, now wiser, despised herself for that feeling. But that was over. She knew better than most who Steve really was, and she hated him for it.

Thinking about Steve's death, she couldn't decide exactly how she felt anymore. Her mind was crowded with too many painful, private truths, and her heart pounded with contradictory feelings she was afraid to express out loud.

No one will understand, she thought, wrapping her arms around her shoulders and hugging herself sadly. *No one will understand. Not even Katy.*

But now that Steve is dead, no one ever has to know. No one at all. She regretted the thought and tried to push it away.

She should be sad, but she could not help feeling a stab of guilty relief.

The telephone was ringing somewhere downstairs. Far away.

She knew the housekeeper would answer, but Amy got up out of the rocking chair anyway. She wouldn't know what to say to Katy if she woke up. She had already said everything she wanted to say to everyone else. She needed more time to think.

Amy closed the door to Katy's room behind her and started down the broad oak staircase to the front hall of the house, her trembling, cold hand sliding along the polished railing with a light grip.

As soon as Katy had fallen asleep, Amy made a hasty call to their Aunt Charlotte in Jackson, Mississippi, to come and care for Elizabeth. Charlotte, who had vocally shared Amy's dislike and distrust of Steve, insisted on leaving for the airport within the hour. Amy gave the housekeeper instructions to purchase more of whatever two-year-old Elizabeth might need and then prepare another guest room for her aunt. She had no idea when someone would be able to get more clothes, baby food, and diapers from Katy's house. Katy had been waiting for the hearing to make decisions about what to do and where they were going to go. Then she arranged for a driver to pick up Charlotte from Hartsfield Airport just outside Atlanta.

The chief and the detectives had explained, kindly but firmly, that even though there was no evidence that Katy was involved, she would still have to face a barrage of questions. They would all be facing a barrage of questions.

Amy reached the hardwood floor at the base of the stairs and realized that her husband was watching her from just inside the front door. From fifteen feet away, Amy could see his disheveled clothing and smell the faint but pungent odor of alcohol that so often pervaded his presence these days. Placing her index finger on her lips, she motioned for him to follow her back up the staircase.

She waited until they reached the landing before she spoke.

"It's Monday, Dan." She did not try hard to keep the distaste from her voice. "Do you really want to start the week this way?"

Dan scoffed and brushed the back of his calloused hand under his bulbous nose.

"You deal with good news your way, Amy, and I'll handle it my way." His voice was thick and hoarse. His eyes, Amy noticed, a little more bloodshot than usual.

"Dan . . ."

"Amy." His voice, an octave higher than normal, mocked her pleading tone. "I had one drink. One."

She scrutinized him through narrowed blue eyes and tilted her head to one side.

"Two drinks, then," he corrected himself irritably. "Maybe more. Maybe what I mean is that I had one drink at a time." He paused. "I have a right to my vices. You certainly have yours."

The expression on his wife's face struck him like a slap. He averted his eyes, knowing he had said too much, even for him, and fell sullenly silent.

Amy stared at their bedroom door without looking at her husband.

"Go take a shower, Dan. And for heaven's sake, get some black coffee."

He rubbed his nose again and made a grunting sound.

"Ashamed of me?" His voice was slurred. "Again? How many is that so far this month? I've stopped keeping count, but I'm sure *you* know."

Amy wanted to bite her tongue and failed.

"This is not the time." Her anger boiled just under the surface. "Not the place, and you know it. Did you spend the entire day in Griffith in that bar?"

She did not give him time to answer.

"Never mind." Amy shrugged. "I don't care anymore, where or when or how much you drink. Just not today. I don't need your problems today."

Dan leaned closer to her face, a heavy hand sliding into her tangled, dark-rooted hair.

"You haven't cared about my drinking for a long time, Amy." His guttural whiskey breath was hot against her cheekbone. "And you certainly don't care about my problems. Besides, where were *you* today?"

Amy was too weary to argue, and she was certainly not going to answer questions. Not from Dan. She pushed his hand away.

"I have things to do," she tried to reason, both with him and with herself. "I need to return a call from the church. There are arrangements to be made. They need names for pallbearers, among other things."

"Pallbearers?" His laugh was ugly. "Aren't those supposed to be a man's friends? That's going to be a joke. Steve Wilton didn't have any friends."

His next laugh sounded more like a snarl.

"Don't wake up Katy." She grabbed his arm and pushed him toward their room. "Please, Dan. Take a shower and try to sober up."

The doorbell rang and echoed hollowly through the house, interrupting what might have been another protest. He gave her a dull, questioning look.

"Probably food from the women at the church," his wife explained. "It's what people do when there is a death in the family, Dan." She gave him a withering look of disgust.

"How long will *that* go on?"

She ignored his complaint. "There will be people coming to see Katy and Elizabeth. We'll be expected to have everyone over here after the services on Sunday too."

Muffled, murmuring voices drifted up from the first floor, along with the pleasant odor of fried chicken, freshly baked bread, and casseroles. Then more voices joined.

The only voice Amy recognized immediately was the housekeeper Hannah's distinctly alto tones, giving what sounded like explanations and apologies for the absence of her employers.

Amy's hand shook noticeably as she raked through her tangled hair. A shower. She needed a hot shower too. Her long fingers rested on her tense neck muscles.

Dan stared down at his wife without pity.

The doorbell rang again, adding yet more voices to the chorus below.

With an angry oath, he turned awkwardly, stumbling down the hall, slamming the door to their bedroom behind him.

Amy took a shaky breath. She considered her options, her eyes darting between her bedroom door on the left and the door down the hallway on the right, where Katy slept. Then Amy McInnis made her choice, squared her shoulders, and smoothed her hair. She walked down the staircase to face the first of the curious onlookers from town.

Chapter 17

There was a newly constructed Holiday Inn Express on the western side of Balfour, a scant quarter mile from State Highway 19. The thirty spotless rooms were an attractive, convenient stop for travelers looking for a day's quiet adventure in some quaint North Georgia town. Or at least that's what the website promised for a bargain ninety-two dollars a night. Most of the residents of Balfour did not know, nor did they care, choosing to bask in the joy of their unique historic obscurity.

Balfour's residents and their livings depended as much on a tourist's impulsive choice as it did word of mouth. The town council had spent a sizeable portion of the yearly budget for three professionally designed, well-spaced billboards, the first just out of Gainesville, north toward Dahlonega. Each touted Balfour as a historic landmark and a step back in time to the days of the Old South.

Locals and the tourists who did their homework, who

intended more than a one-night stay on the way to a more urban location, preferred the refurbished vintage rooms at the Piney Woods to the south of town. The Balfour Bed and Breakfast, recently updated, was a third and equally viable choice, depending upon personal preferences and willingness to pay for atmosphere.

Marcie Jones was the sole owner and operator of the rustic apartments known as the Piney Woods. Her identical twin sister, Darcie Jones, owned the only bed and breakfast, appropriately dubbed The Balfour Bed and Breakfast, downtown on Main Street.

The Jones sisters had endured a lifetime of teasing and undue ridicule, due almost exclusively to their quirky, rhyming names and their round, rosy dispositions. Of the Jones children, Marcie and Darcie were the oldest in the clan of eight others, all who grew up to marry, procreate, and find successful lives in Nashville, Orlando, Dallas, and Atlanta. The twins, however, remained in Balfour to care for their aging parents and take over the family business.

The Piney Woods was the first and only apartment complex in Balfour. Marcie, older by a scant six minutes, had inherited the two buildings from their parents, who had built them in 1952 after Mr. Jones returned from his Naval duty in World War II. The Joneses had operated Piney Woods successfully for the rest of their happy and productive lives.

The Balfour Bed and Breakfast, which Darcie founded, had once been the Joneses' expansive, antebellum family home in the heart of Balfour proper. Marcie and Darcie joked that they had been genetically linked from the beginning of their lives, and that they were doomed to live out their twin existence among neighbors and friends who accepted them for who they were and refrained from laughing at them. At least to their faces. Most of the time.

Marcie, a bit more optimistic than her sister, loved her work, her life, and the people of Balfour. She was considered the more adventurous sister because she was known to leave Balfour to visit the rest of the expansive Jones clan. Darcie, on the other hand, preferred to see things realistically. She avoided both automobile and air travel at all costs. In her tidy little bed and breakfast, she was content that the world should come to her doorstep and there she would cook them buttered biscuits and hot coffee.

Marcie, having spent the morning raking freshly fallen leaves and washing the linens in her occupied rooms, squinted at the clock over the front door of her office. She had stopped to enjoy her afternoon cherry cola with a twist of lime and ponder her most recent tenants. Charlie was at the top of her thoughts today.

His message to expect him on Monday had come late Sunday night. Not that it mattered to Marcie. She didn't bother his apartment when he was away.

She had no cause. He left it in a reasonably tidy state and would have soundly disapproved of her mothering. She was busy most days anyway with basic repairs and routine maintenance, and this week she had added the task of supervising the crew of rednecks who were supposed to be repaving her parking lot.

Everyone knew Charlie did what he wanted. Marcie had

known him since he came to Balfour as a troubled orphan and teenage rebel. Knew more about him than most, and she still liked him. Since he turned over his grandparents' house to Cora, Piney Woods was his permanent address and what might be called his home. Marcie was a secret keeper extraordinaire and dog sitter for his North Carolina Plott hound, Elvira, when the dog could not join him on his travels. Only Elvira was happier to have Charlie back in town than Marcie was.

Marcie looked forward to Charlie's real-life crime sagas, even if she was never able to repeat what she knew to anyone else. That is, until they came out in the next installment of one of his crime-fighting journal articles.

Today Marcie especially wanted to talk to Charlie about her newest tenant, Amanda Grayson. Up to this point, five fifteen on a late autumn afternoon, Marcie had no complaints about Amanda, although she did not like the woman on a personal level. Marcie could not put a name to her objections, but that woman was giving her unexplained cause for acid indigestion.

The buxom older woman slurped the last of her daily dose of caffeine and crushed the can before she walked outside to dispose of it, noting a new assortment of discarded beer cans in her recycling bin.

Those rednecks better not be drunk and operating heavy machinery on my property, she thought. *I will sue them till they can't afford to drink bottled water.*

In her room above, Amanda Grayson was certainly not thinking about Marcie, even though the word redneck had crossed her mind several times.

Ms. Grayson, as she insisted upon being called, was an urban professional, forced to exist for the last week in a decidedly rural environment. She was peeved.

Her appearance was out of place in Balfour. Crisp suits in shades of green, olive, and brown were tailored in a mannish way to diminish the dimensions of her obvious femininity. Peeking seductively from the buttoned coats were contradictory, low cut silk blouses that complemented her heavily shadowed hazel eyes. She wore expensive Italian shoes, the heels just high enough to suggest sophistication. Her delicate hands gestured and fluttered gracefully as she spoke, like small, white- and pink-tipped butterfly wings.

Grumbald and Lattimer, one of the oldest, most prestigious law firms in Atlanta, knew exactly who she was—and who she was not—when they brought her along as a junior partner just two years before. Her credentials were impeccable. She graduated law school at the top of her class. Her appearance was striking, and she could read situations and people with deceptively innocent ease. Amanda had proven herself to be not just a rising star, but a comet.

She had been feeling smugly satisfied with herself. Until today.

Today in court she had been ridiculously off her game with Steve Wilton. His arrogance was to be expected. His high-handed insults were to be tolerated. His sidelong suggestive glances were to be accepted with grace. But Amanda Grayson was out of what limited tolerance she might ever have had for this type of adolescent shenanigan.

She had taken the case because Grumbald and Lattimer had pressed, at the insistence of the Senator. She had taken the case because she was not given a choice. She did not know why they wanted her to handle the problem, nor did she care. She had cut her legal canines on clients like Steve, spoiled playboys with their too-maternal, domesticated wives and their mid-life crisis issues. She had spent the last three weeks preparing the paperwork and dotting perpetual i's and crossing never-ending t's until she wanted to scream into her pillow.

Amanda Grayson had spent too many overpriced hours in this backwoods excuse for a town and had looked forward to going back to Atlanta with another triumph, although minor, for the firm.

Amanda knew she had turned the television set too loud when she turned it on. Knew that the blaring soundtrack of the action movie was likely to irritate most, if not all, of the grumpy, pedestrian residents of the Piney Woods Apartments. She didn't care. She wasn't even watching the movie that screamed across the flat screen. The chase scenes and gratuitous violence simply matched her mood.

At the moment, she was throwing her fine leather Italian shoes at the black Samsonite suitcase, splayed open in the middle of the cannonball bed. Most of the shoes had missed, littering the braided carpet on the hardwood floor. She didn't care about that either. She had been in this stinking Southern backwater too long, and she was done.

Having tossed all her shoes, she turned to make a second trip to the closet for her suits and heard pounding on the door. She ignored the interruption.

Snotty little Georgia hillbillies, she thought.

Her imagination produced the image of a well-endowed

Marcie Jones, her five-foot frame squeezed into snug capri pants and a Hawaiian-flowered shirt, a mop of blue-gray curls swirling around her rosy face.

Let her knock until her chubby knuckles fall off, thought Amanda. *She can keep the deposit. She can keep this whole ridiculous hick town.*

But the voice that called out her name above the roaring engines of another movie car chase was not a woman's voice. Amanda tossed the armload of suits into the suitcase without removing the hangers and stomped to the door, peering through the requisite peephole to see a policeman's badge covering most of her field of vision.

She pulled open the door, preparing to take the offensive.

"Were you trying to knock down the door?" she snapped at the smiling, blue-jeaned man.

"Heck, no," Charlie snapped back, tucking his badge into the side of his belt. "Last door of Marcie's I knocked down cost me a week's pay—plus she made me hang it myself."

For a split second, Amanda was speechless.

"Can I help you, Officer?" she asked, pressing her foot against the edge of the doorframe and blocking his view of her room.

"You might unclench your jaw," he advised. "You're going to give yourself a migraine." Charlie leaned in to survey the room, and she took a quick step back.

From his new vantage point against the doorframe, Charlie inspected the pile of expensive shoes littering the floor. "Taking those shoes with you?"

Amanda recovering quickly, repeating herself.

"Can I *help* you, Officer?"

"Detective," he corrected. "But thank you, I could use some help." His eyes drifted over the room again.

"You're Amanda Grayson."

She couldn't tell if he was making a proclamation or asking a question.

"You represented Steve Wilton in court today."

"I did." She pushed back a bleached strand of hair that had fallen over her face. "And he fired me about fifteen minutes after we left the court this morning. So you see, Detective, Mr. Wilton and I have no legal association anymore."

"Indeed."

Charlie's eyes returned to the young lawyer's face and studied her, watching her color rise under the veneer of foundation and cream blush on her cheekbones. Charlie enjoyed the uncomfortable moment before she turned her back deliberately and walked over to pick up the shoes, tossing them carelessly onto the bed.

"Might want to put a pair or two back into the closet," he advised.

"Really?" She turned and attempted to stare him down. "Why would I do that?"

"Well," Charlie began, shifting and leaning against the other side of the open door, "we can't take your formal statement down at the station until tomorrow morning. And then, well, there are bound to be some further questions that will need to be answered before you truck off to Atlanta."

"What did you say? Questions about what?"

"Steve Wilton is dead."

The final shoe missed the bed and hit the floor with an

expensive thud.

"Dead? How?" The color drained from her face as quickly as it had come, leaving two unattractive splotches of red blush on her chiseled cheekbones.

"Murdered. Messy business too. Best as we can determine, you were one of the last people to see him alive." He paused. "Except for his housekeeper . . . and the killer, of course. That makes you a pretty important person right now."

Amanda muffled a curse and turned her head away.

Charlie shrugged. "See there, I told you not to clench your jaw. Here comes that migraine."

"Why can't I just answer your questions now?" The thick eyelashes fluttered. "I need to get back to Atlanta."

"I just bet you do." Charlie shrugged again, unmoved. "You know better than that, sweetheart. Even in Balfour, we have protocol."

"Grayson."

Charlie tilted his head questioningly.

"Call me Grayson. I'm not your sweetheart."

"Whatever." Charlie reached into his pocket and took out a piece of gum, rolling the papered stick between his fingers. "Point is that Steve's daddy is flying into our airport tonight from Washington, D.C. Since I'm pretty sure that the Senator has been paying your fees, I'm equally certain that he will be wanting a conversation with one of the last people to see his son alive."

"I see," she said coldly.

"You lawyers often do. Given time."

Charlie unwrapped the gum and popped the stick into his

163

mouth. "On my way to the airport right now."

"I suppose you expect me to ride with you."

"I suppose."

And that was the end of that.

Chapter 18

Thomas had been munching his cookies and sipping hot coffee, waiting at the local airport for almost thirty-five minutes before Charlie arrived more or less dragging Steve's pouting lawyer.

The lawyer heard Charlie's baby blue Volkswagen Beetle before he saw it coming. The car was a public embarrassment, but, like so many other parts of his life, Charlie didn't care. He had had a longer relationship with that car than with most of his so-called friends, and certainly longer than his marriage to Cora.

Charlie never said anything like that, of course. Even after all the years, giving up Cora was the one thing even Charlie couldn't joke about.

Anson Airstrip consisted of several smallish, tin roof hangers and one main concrete block building situated in a semicircle to the far side of the lonely, infrequently used runway. No one really knew why the airstrip was named Anson, since the original strip had been built in 1953 for a businessman named

Tarleton.

Edgar Tarleton had made a good living selling wrought iron fencing and decorative pieces he made himself. A bachelor, his hobby was building single engine planes from kits. When Tarleton died in the late 1980s from a heart attack, the city of Balfour discovered that, having no legal heirs, he had left both the forty acres of land and the makeshift airstrip in the center of his property to the county. His sole condition for transfer of ownership was that the airstrip and his prized Cessna, along with one or two single engine prop planes, be maintained with the endowment his estate provided.

At first there didn't seem to be much point, at least until Senator Wilton ran for office for the first time later that same decade. The Senator decided that flying in and out of Balfour was more economical and expeditious than driving down to Hartsfield-Jackson in Atlanta or trying to find a flight into Lee Gilmer over in Gainesville.

As compensation for the exclusive convenience of what amounted to his own personal airstrip, the Senator contributed a sizable sum of money every year, added to the endowment money, for the upkeep—a practice for which he was quick to expect both service and credit.

Charlie knew exactly what to expect from Anson's Airstrip, smirking with enjoyment at Amanda Grayson's horrified expression when she entered the simple, dilapidated concrete block house that served as the main building.

Thomas was standing next to a picture window, facing the makeshift runway, and drinking the last of his travel cup of Marjorie's coffee. A single dingy bathroom, labeled simply "private," was tucked into a corner beside an equally dingy and rather neglected office area—a desk covered by assorted log books and papers in front of a sadly used office chair.

Between the sparsely filled vending machines on Thomas's right was a rusting, once-white cabinet with several shelves. The laminate was littered with assorted Styrofoam cups and a canister full of granulated sugar packets and hazelnut-flavored powdered creamers. Two coffee makers squatted side by side, one with a cracked, orange-handled carafe and the other a faded black. Each etched-glass decanter was half full of a dark, pungent liquid whose consistency appeared that of used motor oil. The odor was almost as overpowering as the smell of aviation fuel in the silver tanks outside.

Frank, part-time security, and Mike, full-time janitor and general maintenance, were chatting surreptitiously in the opposite corner. They too were as dingy and worn as the rest of Anson Airstrip and had been alive almost as long, having taken their respective jobs as second incomes after retirement.

Thomas had greeted them with a wave when he came in but had left them alone to conspire and gossip while he made mental plans for the confrontation with Stewart Wilton.

Thomas had no illusions about the kind of man the Senator really was. He, like everyone else in Balfour, had watched Steve grow up in the shadow of his famous father. Thomas had met many men from similar backgrounds in his time at Ole Miss and in the year of his successful law practice in Atlanta. The idealist in Thomas always tried to see the best in people, hoped for better, but he also knew that power was a drug as real as any other kind of addiction.

Thomas was not surprised to see that Charlie had Amanda Grayson in tow. She looked smaller and more fragile than she had in the courtroom that morning, but he decided it was probably just the clothes she was wearing. Some lawyers were uncomfortable without their suits and ties. Thomas had once heard a colleague comment that he felt empowered by an expensive suit. An armor of protection against the sins of the common criminals that he defended, and an insulation from the fire of the high-powered judges before which he appeared. Amanda reminded him of that man, and he felt suddenly sorry for her insecurity and her dependency on the value of her clothes for her self-worth. The tight jeans, cotton sweater, and leather flats were probably still designer—Thomas didn't know, nor did he care—but she seemed a totally different, much younger woman without the tailored suit.

She had let down her hair from the professional bun at the base of her neck. The loose curls cascaded in a careless flow of professionally bleached blonde over her shoulders. The kind of woman who would have been attractive—and attracted—to Steve Wilton.

Thomas was neither tempted nor impressed. He knew her type from law school and from working in the Atlanta firm. Amanda Grayson was entirely too cold and calculating for his taste.

One look at the way Charlie stood next to her told Thomas that the detective shared his opinion. Amanda Grayson was accustomed to having her way, especially with men. Unfortunately, whatever spells she had attempted to cast over Steve hadn't worked. Thomas wondered where she had spent the afternoon since she stormed out of court that morning and then decided that was Charlie's business. He would leave those kinds of questions to him.

Amanda was not only pouting now, she was at the point of seething.

Charlie was satisfied that he had accomplished his goal for the afternoon. One of his prime suspects was here, and within the hour she would come face-to-face with Senator Stewart Wilton. Charlie loved fireworks, especially the human kind.

He was glad that Thomas had agreed to come. He had great faith in Thomas's abilities as a negotiator and diplomat. Almost as much faith as he had for himself as an investigator and truth-seeker.

Charlie had good sense and a natural, healthy respect for vipers. Stewart Wilton was a viper, and a dangerous one at that. He'd had all afternoon to consider his son's untimely murder. Time to allow resentment and outrage to build. Time to prepare volleys of the politician's most powerful weapon, his arsenal of words. Charlie knew those words well, and the powerful damage they could do. His intent was to provide the Senator with multiple targets for the attack.

Thomas, having known Charlie since middle school, knew too well what Charlie was thinking. Neither of them had forgotten what Steve had been and done while he was in high school. Troublemaker. Hothead. Bolstered by his father's blind defense of whatever rebellion overtook Steve at any moment. Any and all who dared to question the son were made to feel the full wrath of the powerful, vindictive father.

Thomas considered whether or not to walk out to his

Honda and put the thermos in the car when he noticed a familiar look on Charlie's face. A conversational look, like from when they were just friends and not, well, whatever they were now.

Give me a break, Charlie, he thought. *Not now.*

Charlie knew he was poking a bear with a chain saw, but he didn't care. He could admire Thomas and still want to provoke him. The plane wasn't due for fifteen minutes, and he wasn't getting anything useful from the lady lawyer.

"Have you met Jane?" He tried to keep his voice friendly and conversational.

Thomas shot the shorter man a disdainful glare, his jaw noticeably tightening.

"Shut up, Charlie."

"I was asking professionally."

Thomas snorted with disbelief. "There is nothing about you that even pretends to be professional. You're not allowed to talk about Cora."

"I was asking about Jane." Charlie's voice held its own distain. "Come on, Thomas. Give me a little credit. I have to write a report."

Thomas suspected Charlie was lying just to amuse himself, but the other man had a poker face. He could lie about almost anything, and no one would know.

I'm tired of playing games with you, Charlie, the lawyer thought. *I've had enough games for one day.*

"You can talk to Marjorie."

"You're no fun anymore, Thomas," Charlie said, taking out more gum, unwrapping the silver foil, and stuffing it back into his pocket. "I'm only trying to make conversation."

Amanda turned from her timeout corner and stared disapprovingly.

Thomas considered and nodded.

"Okay," the lawyer conceded, lowering his voice. Fighting Charlie's curiosity was futile, at best. "What do you want to know about Jane?"

"Does she seem . . . I don't know how to put this . . . *okay* to you?"

Thomas drew himself up straight and towered, glowering again.

"Now you're just being insulting. What else would she be? You left her with my wife."

"Damn Thomas, you're sensitive today." Charlie thrust his fists into his pockets and struggled with his temper, pretending he didn't understand his old friend's anger. "Jane is a key witness in another murder case. You are an experienced lawyer. I hoped you might have an impression or something. What do you want me to do?"

I want you to go away. I want you to solve your murders and write your books and get the hell out of my life, Thomas thought bitterly. *I want my wife to stop dreaming dangerous dreams. I want a normal life.*

What he said was totally different.

"All I know is what I hear. Jane is doing as well as can be expected. Cora says Marjorie has the *'eyes of love,'* whatever that means." Thomas took a deep breath. "Jane has taken to the cat."

"That cat always hated me." Charlie tossed out the observation before he could stop himself.

Don't we all, thought Thomas.

"Is that some of Marjorie's coffee?" the detective asked

pleasantly, indicating the thermos clutched in Thomas's hand.

Before Thomas could formulate a scathing reply, they heard the sound of the single engine approaching the field. Thomas knew as much about planes as he did about having his office redecorated, which was more than he cared to know about either. Glancing over at Frank and Mike, who had stopped talking and whose gazes were now fixed on the lights of the incoming Cessna as it turned, he thought about Cora. About how much he loved her.

About the day he had seen her for the first time, here at Anson Airstrip in the pouring rain. The day that Charlie brought Cora from Baton Rouge to Balfour. Away from a past filled with violence and pain. He looked over at the detective and wondered if the same memories were in Charlie's head too, and if they ever haunted him.

No, Thomas thought. He didn't want to know about planes or interior decorating, or lady lawyers. He wanted to go home to Cora.

Charlie ambled over to stand beside the doors on the runway side of the building, trying, no doubt, to distance himself from both irritated attorneys. Amanda, like a spoiled, abandoned poodle with a recent shampoo and doggie pedicure, pranced behind him, keeping close to his elbow.

Thomas reluctantly joined the pair.

"What's the plan?" Charlie asked, popping the gum against his front teeth.

"Not a clue," Thomas replied. He refused to exert himself. "You?"

Charlie chuckled and shrugged. "Your turn. I brought the

scapegoat."

Thomas caught the detective's quick-winked glance down at the female attorney.

"Careful, Charlie," he admonished. "You could get a bad bite there."

"Had my shots," the shorter man countered. "Recently too."

Obliviously gripping his arm, Amanda had understood none of the banter. She was preoccupied, staring at the rows of runway lights lying parallel in front of them and growing brighter as the darkness fell.

"You ever met Perkins?"

Thomas looked puzzled. "Who?"

"Don't know his first name," Charlie continued. "Some community organizer and public relations guru that Wilton picked up during the last campaign. Sharp, Harvard educated, Washington savvy, with a pedigree and a résumé that would make the president blush."

Thomas didn't look impressed.

"Okay, then," Charlie amended. "Maybe just the secretary of state and a freshman congressman or two." He paused. "So, you haven't heard about Perkins?"

"Have you?"

"Nope." Charlie removed yet another fresh piece of gum from his pocket, rolled the wrapper between his fingers, and added the stick to the pieces already in his mouth.

"Lost its flavor," he continued, explaining as he chewed between words.

"You need better bait for these little fishing expeditions of yours," Thomas said, sighing and rolling his eyes. "Right now you're just drowning worms."

"Look at you!" Charlie said good humoredly, pressing the gum against the bottom of his front teeth and producing an explosive pop. "All colloquial and what not."

Thomas folded his arms across his chest. Some things never change.

Frank and Mike had turned their fickle attention from the plane's landing and had been watching the exchange with muffled snickers. Not much in the way of entertainment or visitors at the Anson Airstrip, and they enjoyed what came their way, even if this scene between Charlie and Thomas was one they had witnessed repeatedly over the years. Never a clear-cut winner, but always a memorable skirmish.

Going outside with lumbering enthusiasm, they waited patiently as the plane came to a screeching stop on the tarmac.

Mike chalked the wheels while Frank waited for the cabin door to open to greet the pilot and the passengers, offering to carry the bags to the waiting car. Mike's job was to see to the refueling and make sure the pilot had coffee and conversation before he set off again. Or, barring that, if the pilot wanted to lay over for the night, Mike would see that there was an available ride to Marcie's apartments and a stopover for a late-night snack at one of the two convenience store gas stations in town. The locals were a close-knit group, and working together was important if they all wanted to stay financially afloat.

Thomas and Charlie elected to wait inside the building, neither eager to be the first to greet the Senator and the enigmatic Perkins. Charlie was considering another clever comment when Thomas turned his head at a noise and indicated the main double doors behind where they themselves had entered. Looking outside through the dusty glass of the doors, they could see the headlights of a car that had just pulled into the parking lot. A black Lincoln Town Car, gleaming from what looked like a recent car wash. Tinted windows. Sparkling hubcaps and rims. In a moment, a youthful driver in an ill-fitting suit emerged and sauntered carelessly toward the building.

"That's Bill's boy. The one who works at the service station fixing flats." Charlie popped his gum again.

Thomas shrugged.

"People have to work, Charlie. Times are hard. Not all of us are famous detectives."

Charlie popped his gum even louder, and unsympathetically shook off the young female attorney's death grip on his upper arm, taking out his pen to take notes.

Outside, the pilot emerged first from the plane, waiting at the bottom of the steps until the other passengers had deplaned. He was followed by a young man who must have been Perkins, as arrogant and sophisticated in appearance as Bill's boy was uncultured and uncouth. Then came the Senator, moving rather slowly and beginning to show the strain of his increasing age and the pressures of political wheeling and dealing.

Considering carefully what he already knew of the Senator's stormy relationship with his son, both past and present, Thomas resisted the urge to feel too much pity for the man.

Charlie, on the other hand, was thinking quite different thoughts as he watched the two politicians walk to the building, side by side in synchronized step. He thought that these two men might just have been father and son, identical except that one was obviously much older and a bit heavier and grayer than the other.

Charlie gave Thomas a sideways glance, and for a rare moment they were both thinking the same thing. Maybe the Senator had found in Perkins the son that Steve would never have been. Maybe Steve's death was conveniently coincidental to the Senator's upcoming reelection campaign. Maybe.

Stewart Wilton was a tall man, well over six feet, broad-shouldered, and muscular despite his age. He had been a legendary linebacker at UGA who had taken down his share of opponents both on and off the field. His steel gray suit was expertly tailored, and his gray hair was full and perfectly combed around his chiseled features. He carried himself like a Julius Caesar, and it was easy to imagine Perkins as a lean and hungry Cassius at his side.

Thomas took the initiative to push open the door. No sense in waiting. But Wilton brushed past him into the building, his eyes firmly set on Amanda.

"I want to talk to you," he bellowed without ceremony.

Perkins was only a step behind his boss, advancing in goose step with a leather briefcase in his left hand and extending his right to touch his employer's shoulder.

"Senator," he began. "Perhaps Ms. Grayson could join us for a debriefing in the car on the way to the house."

Wilton glared.

"I want to see my son."

"Of course," Perkins soothed. "But you also wanted to speak to Katy, express your sympathy, sir. You told me to remind you."

"Katy's staying with Amy and Dan," Charlie volunteered. "Doctor has her sedated. Aunt is in from Jackson to take care of Elizabeth."

"Then a telephone call in the morning," Perkins nodded suggestively. His hypnotic voice was as smooth as his appearance. "It's late, and the Senator has had a long day."

Abruptly, Wilton nodded in agreement with his aide-de-camp.

Charlie nodded instinctively with them.

Good grief, he thought. *We look like a dashboard convention of bobbleheads. This Perkins is smooth. Slimy smooth.*

"Tomorrow, then." Perkins turned to Frank, who was rolling in a dilapidated luggage rack groaning under several small suitcases and two hanging bags of, judging by the labels, unabashedly expensive suits.

"The Senator's car is here, I see, so if you don't mind helping the driver load the car? Frank, was it?" Perkins removed a twenty-dollar bill from his wallet and handed it to the security guard, who joined in the nodding and gingerly pocketed the bill.

Another bobblehead? Charlie thought. *Did everyone around this Perkins always find him so persuasive?*

"We're staying with the Millers," Perkins said, addressing Charlie and Thomas for the first time. "If there is any news of any sort, would you mind contacting the Senator there? We will be staying at least through the weekend, of course. Can I assume you have their number?"

Without waiting for a response, Perkins deftly slipped the hand holding the briefcase under the Senator's elbow and the other onto the small of Amanda's back. Like an authoritative father of two recalcitrant children, he guided the pair outside and deliberately loaded them into the waiting car.

Charlie waited until they were staring at the red taillights disappearing around the bend in the country road before he spoke.

"Tornado Perkins," he remarked.

"Hurricane Perkins," countered Thomas. "Comes with too much wind and an extra dose of cold water."

"I stand corrected."

Charlie turned his attention to Frank, who was wheeling the now-empty luggage rack back into the terminal building.

"Did you get the license plate?"

"Don't I always?" Frank snapped testily, stopping the cart with a jerk and pushing it absently into the corner recently vacated by Amanda Grayson. "Not my first rodeo, Charlie."

Charlie noted Frank's resemblance to a mule his grandfather had once owned but wisely refrained from telling Frank.

"Sorry, Frank," he offered lamely. "I forgot."

"Darned right you do," Frank barked cheerfully. "Georgia license tag number 214-XKZ. Morgan County. Driver is Bill's boy, making a little money on the side. God knows that boy's got the brains of a slug. The car's a special-order rental from Atlanta. Nothing that fancy around here. Leastways, not since the last time the Senator was here with some of his highfalutin friends from Washington, D.C." Frank stopped abruptly. "Sorry, guys. There I go running my mouth again. One of these days I'm going to get myself in a world of hurt with someone who don't appreciate the finer points of conversation."

"Need some help with the plane," Mike bellowed from the runway side doorway. "You going to jaw with the Bobbsey Twins all night long?"

"See what I mean?" Frank turned away from Charlie and yelled, "Don't get your suspenders in a twist, Mike. I'll be right there." He waved his twenty in the air like a Confederate flag. "Got some money for a night over in Green Creek."

Mike laughed, waving his own twenty. "Me too."

"Well," Charlie said and took out his pad and pen. "We will just leave you two to your date, then."

Frank and Mike laughed good naturedly and went outside to take care of the plane and pilot and finish locking up for the night. Charlie pulled the cap off the pen with his teeth and turned to Thomas.

"And . . ." he began, adding the newest information to that already in his notebook. He removed the gum gingerly from his mouth and fished a handful of wrappers from his pocket, taking his time to carefully cover the wad and deposit it into the trash can with a three-point flourish.

"And what, Charlie?"

"What do you think?"

"What do I think?" Thomas folded his own arms. "What do *you* think, Charlie?"

"I don't like Perkins."

"I can't name three people that you *do* like. What's your point?"

Thomas yawned. This day needed to be over. Soon. He was too tired for Charlie's mind games. He was too tired for Charlie, period.

"What do you think of Grayson?" Charlie persisted. "First impression?"

"Not your type."

"Fair enough." Charlie laughed. "Or yours either."

Thomas frowned. Charlie seemed serious, despite the laughter.

"She's out of her depth with the Senator," Thomas said, his mood sobering. "Competent lawyer, I suppose. She dresses the part. Grumbald and Lattimer wouldn't have her if she weren't good."

"You sure about that? Even with her looks and all that?"

"Grumbald must be in her eighties by now, and Lattimer can't be far behind that. They aren't senile yet, and much too professional to be taken in by polish and looks. What are you suggesting?"

"Not sure yet." Charlie had taken out the pen and pad again and began taking sporadic notes in his tiny, almost indecipherable print. "I just don't—"

"You don't like her," Thomas finished for him. "Got that."

"She wears pink lipstick. Did you notice?"

Thomas yawned, running his hand across his forehead and back through his hair.

"Are we done here, Charlie? The guys are trying to lock up. This has been a long day."

Without looking up from his notebook, Charlie made a noise of agreement.

Thomas left him there, still scribbling into the notebook, leaving Frank and Mike to chase the determined detective out and send him on his way. Thomas was more than glad to get into his Honda and pull away from the parking lot and head home to Cora.

Chapter 19

Marjorie's long-standing tradition, especially when the weather turned cooler, was warm chocolate milk before bed. Not some mix in a bag, but actual warmed milk on the stovetop, rich with thick syrup and marshmallows. She was humming softly to herself and making her nightly cup when Cora came down the stairs and into the kitchen, holding Jane's empty cup.

"Sleeping?" asked Marjorie, pouring a second generous portion of cold milk into the saucepan on the stove and turning on a burner. On the counter sat two chunky, handmade ceramic mugs, into which she had already placed a generous handful of tiny white marshmallows. "She ate a good supper."

"You're a wonderful cook," responded Cora, admiring the older woman's ease as she moved around the kitchen. Marjorie seemed at home no matter where she was, a gift that Cora often envied.

"Jane let me say prayers with her."

"That's wonderful!" Marjorie picked up a wooden spoon and stirred the milk as it began to steam. "Do you think that means someone took her to church?"

"I don't know yet."

A peaceful silence fell between them. Marjorie was adding the syrup to the simmering milk when they heard the familiar sound of the Honda on the gravel driveway, and then the grating sound of the key in the lock of the front door.

Marjorie smiled and poured the finished hot milk carefully into the mugs and placed them onto a small wooden tray with embroidered white napkins.

"Take these up for you and Thomas," she ordered kindly. "There is plenty here for a third cup. I'll check on Jane again before I go to bed."

"It's almost nine thirty, Marjorie."

"All the more reason for you to go on up to bed."

Thomas appeared in the doorway with the travel cup in his hands.

"Let's get that rinsed out." The housekeeper took the metal thermos from his hands with easy efficiency. "I was just about to rinse the spoon and the pot on the stove."

Thomas opened his mouth to thank her, but she stopped him.

"Thomas, take your lovely wife and this hot cocoa up to bed, do you hear me? I've no time for your chitchat at this hour of the night."

Obediently, Thomas took the tray from the counter and silently followed Cora up the stairs to their room. Neither was much in the mood for conversation, specifically not any conversation that involved talking about Charlie. Cora removed her chenille robe and gently pushed the sleeping Solomon aside so she could drape the robe across the foot of the bed where he routinely slept. She folded back the handmade quilted covers and slid in, waiting patiently while Thomas quickly changed into his favorite plaid pajamas.

"You look like Cary Grant," she said lovingly. "In an old movie."

"I *am* an old movie," he admitted. "At least, tonight feels like a Hitchcock."

Cora decided not to ask for an explanation.

They settled comfortably and wordlessly after that, side by side, on the antique bed that had belonged to Cora's grandparents. The sturdy cannonball was one of the few pieces of furniture that was able to be restored after the fire that destroyed the rest of the family home. Propped among the soft pillows, they sipped from the mugs, Cora leaning slightly into his shoulder. When her cup was drained, Thomas finished his own and put them side by side on the nightstand.

Sleepily, Cora nestled her head on Thomas's chest, his arm protectively encircling her shoulders.

"Jane is precious," she said, yawning. "So full of secrets."

Thomas kissed the top of her head and hugged her closer.

"Nothing you cannot handle." He took in the sweet apple fragrance of her hair.

"And Marjorie," she corrected, yawning again.

"Yes," he agreed. "You and Marjorie."

"And Jesus." Cora's voice was a whisper now as she slid lower into the pillows, stretching. "Marjorie says we should thank Jesus."

"Yes," Thomas said softly. "I always do."

And then, with a last yawn, Cora was asleep.

For a long moment Thomas waited, his own breath relaxed and content, while he said prayers of thankfulness. Then, carefully untangling his arm, he reached over to turn off the lamp on the nightstand and lay in the darkness for a long, long time before he finally fell into his own restless but dreamless slumber.

Chapter 20

The Second Day: Tuesday

Cora realized that she was standing at her grandmother's kitchen sink for a second night in a row. Out the windows she could see the towering chinaberry tree, and beyond that the wild plum and peach trees, the crabapple tree, then further, the field, plowed deep and planted with sweet corn mostly and other truck-farming vegetables.

The window was slightly open, double-hung from the top, and she could smell the freshness of newly dug earth and recent rain. The sun was going down. For a moment, Cora studied the screened opening—feeling, smelling, watching. She thought of her grandparents. Her grandfather, who had lovingly built the tiny four-room house from lumber he and his brothers had hewn themselves from the Georgia pine that grew on the acreage. Acreage that became the planting fields. The stone fireplace, stones carried from the banks of the nearby creek bed and mortared together with promises. His and his family's wedding gift to his bride. He had planned that window. He wanted to be within her sight while he was working from dawn to dusk in the fields as she worked those same hours in the kitchen, standing at the sink. This window was her place. Her favorite place.

Cora had spent many happy hours standing at that sink, her hands in soapy water, washing the well-worn country dishes or rinsing vegetables and fruits in preparation for cooking and canning. Sharing secrets, hopes, dreams, and laughter with her grandmother.

Cora looked down. The sink was filled with hot, sudsy water. To the right was the chipped spattered enamel tub of cool, clear water for rinsing the dishes, and still further right was the drainboard. As she stared at the wire form, she noticed two upside down clean cups. James's milky-white mug and hers, the flowered cup with the gold rim. She smelled the scent of coffee, freshly dripped, and then she knew she wasn't alone.

"There's a pie in the oven," the voice at the kitchen table announced cheerfully. "Wild blackberry, I think."

"My favorite."

"I know."

Cora turned to her left, toward the cast iron gas stove. The aroma of the baking crust and hot, sweet fruit drifted over her. She took the woven potholders and opened the door of the oven, gingerly removing the cookie sheet with a small aluminum tin of pie in the center. Thick syrup oozed from the fork-patterned holes pressed into the top crust.

"You're right," she said. "Smells like blackberry."

She put the sheet on the top of the stove, removed the pie

itself with the edges of the potholders, and carefully put the tin on the ceramic hot pad to cool.

"Too hot to cut yet," she said quietly.

"Then we could have a cup of coffee and talk." Brother James leaned over and pulled out the chair to his right. "You do know you're dreaming again, don't you?"

Cora solemnly filled his mug and her cup, walked over to sit down, and placed the two coffees on the oilcloth-covered table.

"You do know that I haven't done anything with the first message yet, don't you? Someone is dead, just what you said last night. Steve Wilton."

He picked up the mug and took a tentative sip.

"I know. Nothing you could have done would have changed that, Cora." He put down his mug and studied his coffee without looking at her. "No new message really. Just keeping in touch with you."

"This isn't like you to visit two times in one week, much less two nights in a row." Cora felt a strange uneasiness. "You have also never been quite this evasive."

"I don't really decide these matters, Cora," Brother James said, looking up and meeting her eyes, the rims of his own eyes curiously glistening with unshed tears. "Although if I did make these decisions, I might come more often. I rather enjoy our visits and talks, messages about other people's destinies aside."

Cora wanted to say that talking to a man who had been dead for thirty years or more tended to be disconcerting at the very least, but she didn't. This was a dream. The dream. She had had too many of these dreams to wax philosophical about them now. She believed there was a reason for everything, so there were reasons for these dreams. Some reasons she knew, some she came to know, and some she might never know.

Brother James was intensely watching her now, but she could not anticipate what he said next. The surprise was clear on her face.

"Jane reminds me of you at that age," he said and took another sip of the coffee. "Quiet, introspective. She is a beautiful child." He twitched his nose in distaste. "This needs more sugar. Real sugar. Rather strong, don't you think?"

Cora resisted the urge to point out that she hadn't made the coffee tonight.

"More sugar?" she asked. She leaned back in her chair and shook her head in disbelief. "You have never taken sugar in your coffee for as long as I can remember. Why would you begin using sugar now?"

"People change, Cora. Remember that. People change. Sometimes they have been known to change for the better." He smiled, and she noticed that his Bible was on the table to the right of his elbow, on the edge of her field of vision. He opened the well-used book and began to turn the pages, as if searching for a verse or passage of scripture as he spoke.

"Never hurts to sweeten a situation either," he continued sagely. "People are not always who we think they are."

He stopped turning pages and smiled.

"You should plan to talk to Andrew," he said. "Talk to him soon, Cora."

"It would help if I knew what I was supposed to say."

The preacher chuckled softly at that and wiped at the corners of his eyes with the back of his hand.

"Since when have you known what you were going to say before you opened your mouth?" he teased kindly. "Trust your instincts, Cora. Keep to the sweet."

She hoped he was right, but her instincts at this moment were anything but clear.

"I think the pie is ready for cutting," he suggested, tapping a heavily marked passage in Psalms before closing the Bible. "You remember David, don't you?"

David? What does King David have to do with this?

Cora obediently got up from the table.

As she picked up the wooden-handled kitchen knife, however, to plunge the tip into the center of the pie, the dream, James, and the blackberry pie were all gone. She was awake, with a sudden craving for one of her grandmother's pies.

The lighted numbers from Thomas's cosmic clock glowed mockingly from the ceiling—2:32 a.m. That number again.

Solomon protested her stirring movements with a muted yowl from the foot of the bed, and Thomas rolled sleepily toward her, his eyes barely open in the semidarkness of the room.

"Hush, cat," he snapped, grouchy and mildly irritated at the disturbance. He and Solomon had often had their differences over Solomon's right to invade the human bedroom. Right now, using Solomon as a target for his feelings seemed perfectly reasonable.

The annoyed feline responded with another noise of protest.

"I'll take him with me downstairs," she offered, scooping the protesting cat from the side of the bed as she rose. "I couldn't sleep anyway. Might as well be working on the book."

She was lying. Thomas knew it.

"I could get up with you," he offered, trying not to sound as sleepy and irritated as he felt, but she was already in her robe and at the doorway, Solomon tucked firmly under her arm as he squirmed, their silhouettes outlined in the dim hallway nightlight.

"Go on back to sleep, sweetheart," Cora whispered without waiting for another comment. She closed the bedroom door firmly, and then she was gone. Within a minute, Thomas had unwillingly fallen back into a deep, restless, and dreamless sleep.

Chapter 21

In the morning it was Marjorie who found Cora at the computer, an open Bible at her elbow, thoughtfully studying the screen. Without being asked, the housekeeper took Cora's empty cup and went into the kitchen to put on a fresh kettle of water. She knew what this second early morning meant, and she said a silent, earnest prayer for peace and quick resolution. Marjorie would never tell Cora, but these dreams disturbed her more than any of the tribulations they had weathered in the past. Maybe because they came from the past. Maybe because they meant the past wasn't really over.

A moment later Cora joined Marjorie in the kitchen, padding on small, bare feet, and sat down on a wooden stool at the butcher block island.

"Did Jane sleep?"

"Not so much as a peep from her all night long." Marjorie smothered a yawn. "I checked before I came down, and she was all curled up with that little stuffed cat. No point in waking her yet."

As if on cue, Solomon appeared in the doorway with a soft meow of greeting and complaint. Marjorie shook her head at him and wagged her finger in accusation.

"People eat first, feline," she reminded, turning to Cora. "Grits and toast?"

"Oatmeal, please," Cora stretched. "Thank you for yesterday."

"Of course." The kettle began to scream. "I hope Charlie can find whoever murdered Jane's family. Won't bring them back, but—"

"Charlie isn't really involved, you know," Cora corrected her. "He said he only got involved because of Jane." She paused and smiled at Marjorie. "I know how you feel about him. I'll go over the pictures she drew again this morning to see if there is anything else in them that someone can use, then fax them to Savannah."

"Good." It was all Marjorie would say, secretly glad that Charlie was not really involved. Maybe if he wasn't going to be the lead investigator, he wouldn't stick around.

The only contribution Charlie had made to Cora's life that Marjorie was thankful for was her work with children. When Cora first met Charlie, she worked almost exclusively with adults. Her training, combined with natural intuition, made her an excellent interrogator. Her ability to write about her experiences made her a literary celebrity. She was careful and methodical and had an engaging beauty and charm. Charlie was the opposite. He was brash and impulsive.

When Cora was first called in to consult on a case in New Orleans, Charlie resented her almost immediately. When she helped to solve the case, he was incensed. As sparks often do, they kindled a flame between the two that turned into romance, and then to an equally spontaneous marriage. Within six months, Cora found herself expecting their first child. And six months after that, Charlie found himself embroiled in the case that changed their lives.

Cora lost the baby.

After the divorce from Charlie, she had found that she really did prefer to work with the young, the innocent. Her gift was with teenagers and children. Work that was more painful in so many ways, but for Cora so much more fulfilling.

The two of them, Cora and Marjorie, had worked with several children over the past five years. All were traumatized by various adult events that had shattered the sweetness of their youth. All were brought to the door by Charlie for Cora to mend and heal so that he could bring justice into their lives as well. Cora knew the children were important to Charlie too. She knew why.

Before Marjorie came into her life, the pictures had been the best clues, and the best therapy treatment that Cora had. The pictures the children drew from the pain of their subconscious, combined sometimes with the dreams that Cora had. Both Cora and Marjorie knew that Marjorie had added a missing and valuable third ingredient of faith and hope to the recipe for recovery.

Marjorie put the oatmeal bowl in front of Cora, a graceful flower of freshly sliced Georgia peaches in the center, and tucked a spoon with a napkin into Cora's hand.

"I don't know what the dream is about yet, Marjorie. Jane or Steve or maybe something totally unrelated to either of them. I just don't know."

Marjorie came back with two empty cups and put them on the table, then sat down.

"Real coffee will be ready in a minute. While your oatmeal cools, let's pray. Only thing I know to do."

That was how Thomas found them ten minutes later when he came downstairs—quietly joined together in prayer, heads bent, whispered words and soft sniffles. The oatmeal bowl was sufficiently cooled and the coffee maker gurgled rudely while Marjorie interceded for Jane and for Katy and little Elizabeth, for wisdom and clarity, and for Charlie. Thomas found himself unexpectedly and annoyingly grateful for Charlie, although he could muster no such sympathy this morning for Solomon and his nocturnal annoyances.

Cora was the first to look up and see Thomas in the doorway.

"I'm sorry I woke you last night," she apologized, picking up the spoon and stirring her food absently. "Never happened two nights in a row before."

"For good cause, I know," he affectionately touched her tousled hair, pulled up from her neck in a careless twist and secured with a bright-colored clip. He looked at Marjorie. "Coffee made?"

The housekeeper stood immediately. Unlike Cora's special cappuccino concoction, which required mixing and hot water, Thomas preferred his morning caffeine from a traditional coffee maker and in its strongest form.

"Sit here with Cora," she insisted, indicating her empty place on the stool. "I'll pour the coffee for you."

Thomas obediently straddled the stool next to Cora and took her hand in his.

"You're hovering like a hen over a single egg in the nest," Cora sighed. "I'm fine. God knows, I'm fine."

Marjorie put Thomas's filled coffee cup in front of him and gave their joined hands a quick pat of affection.

"I will just go check on Jane."

When Marjorie was gone, Cora faced Thomas, cradling his one hand in her two.

"James again last night."

"And that is different?"

"Everything is different this time." She saw the look of surprise and concern on Thomas's face and immediately felt guilty for burdening him. "Well, maybe not everything—but so many things. I've made notes. I've gone over the details. The things he told me don't make sense. Nothing is clear. I don't know what to do."

"Cora . . ."

She squeezed his hand and let him go, reaching for her oatmeal and stirring it before taking a tentative bite. She made a face of distaste and pushed the bowl away. *Not enough sugar.*

"How was the meeting with Senator Wilton last night?"

Thomas knew that meant the subject of her dreams was closed. She would talk again when she was ready. He knew better than to persist.

"Mostly what we expected, except for his new assistant," he

paused, mockingly dramatic. "Excuse me, his aide-de-camp. A young clone named Perkins. Thought I'd put Susan doing background research on him today. There is something not quite right about that man."

Thomas had finished the last swallow of his coffee and stood when a tiny voice of greeting came from the doorway. He turned and was momentarily taken aback. Next to Marjorie, clutching the older woman's hand, was what might have been, except for the beautiful Oriental eyes, a miniature version of Cora. The child was wearing a pink flannel nightgown covered in an old-fashioned pattern of red rose buds. From beneath the edge of the bottom ruffles peeked equally tiny pink toes.

"Good morning," Thomas greeted her before quickly turning to rinse his cup in the sink, striving to control the stunned look he knew was on his face.

"Good morning," replied the child seriously, in a voice as small and delicate as her appearance.

Thomas turned to give Cora a questioning look. That the child had spoken to him at all was remarkable. Most of the young local clients that Cora treated came only during the daytime hours when he was at work, which meant he had had little if any contact with them. The children they had fostered, even those who had stayed for several months, had mostly avoided him altogether. Many hid behind Marjorie's ample skirts when he walked into the room, or peeked from behind the sunroom door during the day. Cora and Marjorie did the caregiving, and he tried as best he could to stay out of their way.

In time, Thomas had come to accept that he didn't have the ability to connect with children. He was a little taken aback by

Jane's attention.

With cautious calm, he knelt on one leg to eye level and folded his hands on his knee to balance himself.

"Jane, I'm glad to meet you." His voice was firm, gentle, direct, and kind. At least, he hoped that it was. "Marjorie and Cora and I are happy to have you here."

Jane hesitated only a split second before she nodded, the corners of her eyes beginning to tear as her thick eyelashes fluttered.

Thomas had a rash, paternal urge to take her into his arms and hug her, to somehow make the pain and the memories disappear, but he knew better. Instead he offered his right hand outstretched, palm up. Jane looked up at Marjorie and then at Cora for some sort of direction. When neither of the stunned women spoke, the little girl made her own decision. The tiny hand trembled as Jane's fingers inched their way to the center of Thomas's open palm, where they nestled for a moment before pulling away.

Close to tears himself, Thomas cleared his throat, stood awkwardly, and made a pretense of straightening his suit jacket and tie before changing the subject.

"Do you know if anyone has made contact with Katy, other than Amy and Dan?"

Cora shook her head, still awed by Jane's attitude toward Thomas and puzzled at the apparent lack of continuity in Thomas's thought process.

"Still haven't heard from Amy. We had an appointment at noon yesterday, but I think she was with Katy. Hannah canceled for her. Why do you ask?"

"Just a random thought. I was supposed to meet with Katy this week about the divorce proceeding. Now I don't know who is going to handle the estate, assuming that Steve left a will."

Cora shrugged. The idea that Steve might consider the well-being of a fellow human, even his own wife or child, seemed remarkably out of character. She paused for a moment and was ashamed of herself for thinking such harsh thoughts about a man who had just been murdered.

Then she thought about the message on the answering machine. Would it have mattered whether or not she listened to it instead of deleting it? Steve was dead.

Her mind returned to the living.

"Won't Katy and Elizabeth inherit everything?" she offered helpfully. "Who could contest?"

"I suppose you have a point," Thomas said, his eyes still watching the little girl who had retreated to stand behind Marjorie. "Still, without a will there will be copious paperwork and all sorts of assorted other practical and legal issues. The Senator supported Steve for so long. I don't know how much the two are legally tangled."

Marjorie put a hand behind her back and led Jane further into the kitchen. She steadied the stool where Thomas had been sitting as the child climbed up and seated herself beside Cora.

"Sit right there, and I'll make you some breakfast," the housekeeper said kindheartedly to Jane. Turning to Cora, she continued, "I can check in on Amy and Katy later if you like. I should be taking over a casserole or chicken pie, or maybe a cake." She paused. "I can make something for both of us."

"Thank you, Marjorie." It was Cora's turn to stand. She

wasn't much of a cook herself, at least not under circumstances when friends were expected to take provisions to the grieving. She was much better at finding something reassuring to say than at trying to figure out what comfort foods would be appropriate and appreciated by the bereaved.

"I'll walk you to the door, Thomas," she said. "Jane, I'll be right back."

Expressionless, the child folded her hands dutifully in her lap and took on a look of Buddha-like serenity. Cora hoped that the composure did not indicate a setback in the progress that had been made the day before, but she tried to be realistic. Healing takes a great deal of time and energy and patience no matter the size or depth of the wound. Jane's wounds were both deep and wide.

At the door Thomas put his reassuring arms around his wife's shoulders and drew her close, holding her to his chest as he felt her heart beat against him.

They stood for a long moment in the tender embrace until he leaned down and kissed her tenderly and thoroughly on the lips.

"Let me know about your day," he said before he was gone.

Cora clicked the deadbolt and secured the door. Feeling somewhat optimistic for the day, she walked back to the kitchen as the telephone in her office began to ring.

Chapter 22

Andrew Evans had slept fitfully. As a pastor he had been involved in many kinds of both pleasant and unpleasant conversations in his years of ministry, but he was not looking forward to having any kind of conversation with Senator Stewart Wilton. He knew, however, as the senior pastor of the church and as a practicing Christian man, that he could not escape the inevitable for long.

Husband and wife had both gotten up earlier than usual to have a special quiet time together at the breakfast table over hot tea and English muffins, a habit they had acquired for dealing with stress during their years of marriage. Then as Evans shaved and showered, Virginia had laid out his best suit—the one set aside for funerals and particularly dignified occasions—across the end of their four-poster bed, complete with matching shirt, tie, and socks. She took care of him that way, not because he was incapable of taking care of himself or because he demanded that of her, but because Evans was completely colorblind and could not be trusted to select matching clothing. Or matching anything else, for that matter.

While there were several types of colorblindness, most of which do not interfere with most normal activities, Andrew Evans had a rare form of colorblindness. His was a more serious physical flaw that he had had from birth, and which he almost never discussed with anyone, except for the police officer who administered his driver's license renewal every six years or so. Evans said it sounded like complaining to be constantly harping on what a person did not have instead of appreciating what a person did have. Over the years, and with Virginia's help, he had devised several strategies for dealing with what could have been a serious physical handicap, so much so that no one would have ever suspected that the pastor saw much of his world in shades of gray, black, and white only.

Today Virginia was feeling some of her husband's trepidation, mainly because the situation itself was one they had never faced, together or separately. Death had touched them, but murder and the sensationalism that followed was unknown territory. Virginia had chosen her husband's clothing with especial care. Blue shirt, a darker shade than the light blue he generally wore. Wrinkle-free but freshly pressed anyway. Blue striped silk tie with several shades of blue and gray, a gift from Virginia herself. Navy blue socks. Military-polished shoes, barely worn except for the occasions that demanded the expensive black tailored suit. Weddings. And funerals.

This Senator Wilton had a reputation, she knew, a well-known and discussed reputation. Andrew had his own position to maintain, and although she did not doubt her husband's ability to handle any given situation she also wanted to be certain that he could count on her to bolster his confidence in any way she could. Virginia Evans took her husband's responsibilities and his standing in the community seriously.

So it was that when Evans walked into the church office on Tuesday morning promptly at nine a.m., his staff was suitably impressed with his appearance. Virginia was at his right elbow, also dressed in her best matronly and conservative navy blue dress, her hair combed and makeup suitable for an Easter Sunday morning. As he held the door for his wife to enter the church office, they both paused just inside and stood for a moment, surveying the well-organized chaos.

Donna and Alice had both been bustling for more than thirty minutes before the couple arrived. Donna had made the morning coffee, extra strong, and sliced her famous apple cinnamon walnut bread into thick, generous portions, which had been halved and arranged neatly on her grandmother's favorite cut glass serving platter. Alice was at the computer, reading, editing, and rereading the draft of the program for the funeral service.

For the past half-hour the two women had been debating the same question over and over: whether or not a single printed sheet would do. Normally at a funeral service a traditional verse or poem was all that was needed or expected, along with the vital information about the deceased and the surviving family members. Something brief and sincere.

In most cases, the wife decided these things. But with Katy more or less isolated and sedated, the choices had fallen to Amy and the funeral home director, a humorless little man who had recently taken over the local business for a larger corporation. Neither Amy nor the interim director really wanted to assume responsibility for a decision that might irritate or offend the Senator, so both had conceded choices to the church. Choices that ultimately fell to the senior pastor, who had with equal wisdom delegated the decisions to his wife and his office staff of two.

Pastor Evans had been quick to admit that because Steve Wilton was such a prominent man in the community, and because of the sensational way in which he had died, this service would draw an extraordinary number of people into the church on Sunday afternoon. People who might hear a message of salvation and mercy that they might never hear otherwise. There was also that evangelical part of him that hoped good would come from the tragedy and that Katy and Elizabeth would return to the church. Yet another part of the preacher hoped selfishly that he would also have the opportunity to prove himself worthy of the position he had been given, and perhaps even put to rest some of the criticisms that he had endured over the six months since he had taken the pulpit.

The one painful side effect from all the publicity that surrounded Steve's death, the one that Evans dreaded and resented most, was the potential for tawdry spectacle that surrounded the ceremony. The Senator was notorious in Balfour and well beyond the borders of the county and state for confiscating any and all events to further his own political career. From baby-kissing to grand openings and natural disasters of all shapes and sizes, Senator Wilton could be counted upon to put in an appearance and posture ad nauseam for the camera or journalists or any available microphone. Evans knew the often-reelected politician and his cronies would not hesitate to use the service as a platform and stepping stone to their own ends, even if it meant hijacking the attention of a funeral service away from the Senator's own murdered son.

Feeling a bit ashamed of his judgmental thoughts, the preacher looked up to find his wife's discerning blue eyes watching him. He thought for a moment that she had been reading his mind, which she had indeed been known to do.

"Go on into your office," she said firmly. "Donna and Alice can hold down the fort out here, and you can finish your sermon for Sunday morning and the service for after."

He nodded.

"And I'll bring in your coffee," she continued. "And a nice piece of Donna's legendary apple cinnamon walnut bread." Virginia smiled at the church secretary with honest admiration. "Thank you so much, Donna."

Donna smiled in return and blushed a little at the unexpected praise.

"Anything for you, Virginia," she responded honestly. "And I'll cut a piece for you too. Alice and I are so glad for the extra hands to help at a time like this."

"Of course," the preacher's wife replied as she pushed her husband into his office and closed the door firmly. "Whatever I can do."

Chapter 23

Amanda Grayson woke on Tuesday morning with one thought in her throbbing, headache-filled mind.

She did not like Perkins. No, it was more than that. She despised Perkins and all the well-dressed, wealthy, egotistical Perkinses in the world who were just like him.

Amanda had not liked him since the day he strutted into the executive offices of Grumbald and Lattimer with Senator Wilton. She had stood at Grumbald's side and watched him get off the elevator with his arrogant, high-handed attitude in his thousand-dollar suit and shoes that were worth twice any pair of her Italian pumps. When the senior partners had called her into the conference room, she had felt like little more than a proverbial piece of meat. The most expensive cut of prime rib, no doubt, but meat none the less. Both the men had seemed much more interested in her appearance than her credentials, and that bothered her more than she wanted to admit.

Perkins had done most of the talking, and she had understood quite clearly that her job was multifaceted. Prevent any further embarrassment to the Senator's reputation. Minimize the financial damage. Settle the divorce with as little publicity as possible and move through the situation as quickly as feasible.

Her final task was to get Steve on a plane, train, or in a rented car as efficiently as possible and get him to Washington, D.C., to deposit him under the watchful eye of his father's minions there.

It seemed simple enough on the surface, and she still did not know what had gone wrong. She couldn't imagine what she had done that caused Steve to suddenly decide to return to his wife.

The conversation in the limousine the night before had been unpleasant, to say the least. Perkins had monopolized the interrogation by questioning, poking, and prodding at her in his arrogant, demanding way in a futile attempt to find answers that she did not have. At least the aide's ranting prevented the Senator from boiling over with his own blind accusations, but just like the situation in the offices of Grumbald and Lattimer, neither the Senator nor Perkins seemed moved by her arsenal of charms or her attempts at deflection. She was their verbal punching bag, and they made it clear that they believed she bore professional blame for what had happened to Steve Wilton, directly or indirectly.

After the brief but seemingly endless ride to her pseudo jail cell room at the Piney Woods apartment complex, Perkins informed her that he would be picking her up on Tuesday night to continue her conversation with the Senator. Or, more to the point, the Senator's conversation with her concerning her absolute failure to do what he had asked her to do and what repercussions she could expect for her inadequacies.

She despised both of them, and third in the line of fire was that high-handed detective who had strong-armed her into going to the airport at all. Amanda considered plotting some kind of sweet revenge on the three of them, but right now all that mattered to her was relief from a splitting headache. She had been too annoyed and angry to take the time to get ready for bed last night and had thrown herself across the quilted covers, kicked off her shoes, and slept in her clothes.

First, she thought, *I need a hot shower and a handful of Advil.*

Sooner or later she was going to need to sort through her shoes and clothes too. *This room is a total mess, thanks to that blue-jeaned jerk detective.*

Amanda considered the floor for a moment, which was littered with the contents of the suitcase and the shoes she had shoved off onto the floor when she had returned from the airport. She decided on no shower until she had sorted clothes and found something clean and decent to wear.

Southern hell, she thought sourly. She supposed the truth was that she had nothing to do today but rehang her suits and blouses and put them back into the closet, match her shoes into pairs and put them in the shoe bags, and wait. Just wait.

With several irritated kicks, she made a pathway to the small refrigerator in the kitchenette of the apartment and took out a bottle of orange juice. Returning to the bed, she picked up the remote control and turned on the television. *Maybe there is news from the outside world,* she thought bitterly. *Maybe. Surely there are other suspects. Other people for that darned detective and the Senator and his henchmen to torture.*

But Perkins must have worked his special brand of charming magic on the media, because there was only a brief opening tease about the death of Steve Wilton, son of the state Senator, on the morning newscast. The meteorologist popped up on the screen too quickly, moving to the latest storm warnings, potential hurricanes, and flash flooding around the Atlanta area.

Thank goodness for weathermen, thought Amanda as she rummaged through her cosmetic purse for a hairbrush and a tube of lipstick. *The world could be coming to an end everywhere else, but the weathermen always seemed to be calm in the midst of the storm.*

Amanda laughed softly at her own little joke. *Well,* she thought. *At least I haven't lost my sense of humor.*

At that point, she decided that the orange juice wasn't enough. She was hungry. *Quick shower and then food,* she said to herself. *That little diner in the middle of town will do. Maybe there will be news of some sort there.*

She had seen the quaint *Simmons' Restaurant* sign several times as she rode around the town square with Steve, but he discouraged her questions. Steve insisted she wouldn't like the hicks inside, which she had interpreted to mean that *Steve* didn't like the hicks inside.

She bent over and rummaged through a few pieces of clothing at the bottom of the suitcase. She settled on a thin silk sheath dress in dark purple that seemed to be decently unwrinkled and a matching angora cardigan. Quick and comfortable. She was almost to the shower when her cell phone began to ring. She ignored it.

She was fully awake now, and she was tired of being told what to do and when to do it. Whoever was on the telephone could just wait until she was ready to talk, and that was going to be later. Much later, when she was ready and not one single minute before that.

Chapter 24

Marjorie and Jane spent a pleasant morning watching the last of the slow-moving butterflies in the garden and trying to coax them to land on flowered china bowls filled with sugared water. The hot days of summer had given way to the cool mornings of autumn, and nature seemed to understand that the lives of the flowers and the insects were quickly coming to an end. Marjorie watched Jane closely in anticipation of any obvious crisis, but despite the horrors to which she had been exposed, Jane was proving to be a sturdy little soul with a gentle spirit and a kind, outgoing heart. When a tiny yellow butterfly actually landed on her trembling fingers, the child's face dissolved into a delightful puddle of joy.

Cora had spent a less joyful morning on the telephone with Child Services and the young female officer from the Savannah PD who had been assigned to follow up on Jane's case. As a psychologist, one who had had a long-term relationship with various police and legal departments and the foster care system in Atlanta, Cora's reputation and the opinions she gave carried substantial weight. While Jane's presence in her home had been initially planned as an investigation and fact-finding process, no one objected to Cora's suggestion that Jane be remanded to her and Marjorie in temporary foster care.

The rest of her conversation with the Savannah PD consisted of Cora explaining her findings with Jane. She described Jane's artwork and suggested that, given time, some other memories might surface. The strongest and almost solitary memory Jane had was of a single man, who was assumed to be part of the group that committed the murders downstairs in the house. Jane never saw any of the others. Just the one young man, a stranger with blue eyes, who had focused almost exclusively on Jane.

Jane drew his eyes over and over. He told Jane to look at him and *only* at him. To look him in the face and focus on his eyes. And drink her warm milk.

Drugged milk.

Cora noted that in Jane's pictures, the eyes were round and deep blue, not at all like Jane's eyes. Mercifully for Jane, she remembered no details about any of the events as they had taken place. Officers speculated that she had not been in the areas where the murders happened, since she was found in an upstairs bedroom with the door securely closed and locked from the outside.

The paramedics had attributed her unusually calm behavior to the sedatives. When the police responded to neighboring calls about shots fired, they found her still sleeping in her bed. After checking her vitals, an EMT carried her to the waiting ambulance, and she did not regain consciousness until much later in the children's ward at the hospital.

Whoever he was, the blue-eyed man had intended to keep her quiet, occupied, and unaware, completely isolated from the carnage.

With the lack of more concrete information, Cora promised both Child Services and the Savannah PD that she would keep in touch but that she could offer little hope of evidence from Jane. Right now, the focus needed to be on taking care of the little girl emotionally in the loss of her family, especially her mother.

After filling out the last of the forms that Charlie had brought the day before and faxing them out to all the assorted government agencies, Cora left her office with a sense of accomplishment. She followed the faint sounds of conversation and singing through the kitchen to find Marjorie and Jane.

Stopping by the kitchen island, Cora looked out into the garden and realized that for that moment, Jane seemed happy. Perhaps the better word, the more accurate word, was *content*. Marjorie looked up from her seat on the floral sofa and gave Cora a nod. Time for Cora to continue the more formal therapy she had begun yesterday.

"Lunch," Marjorie announced and came into the kitchen.

Cora continued to watch Jane, who was thoroughly enjoying her imaginary tea party in the sunroom garden against the backdrop of floor-to-ceiling windows. Solomon, with elegant grace, was lapping real milk from a saucer at Jane's feet. The stuffed black toy kitten that Charlie had brought, named simply

"Cat," had been retrieved from Solomon's favorite napping place on the den sofa and had been seated ceremonially at the child-sized table, his furry chin resting on the edge of the table and his oversized paws propped on either side of his tiny empty saucer.

Jane was carefully pouring pretend tea into the cups in turn around the table and offering very real sugar cookies to each of the toy guests, taking small bites from the treats only she could consume.

Next to a brown teddy bear in a pink vest, Marjorie had added a vintage Cabbage Patch baby doll to the circle and family of friends. Bald and dressed as a preemie baby boy, the doll was not only nameless but also in mint condition. Marjorie had rescued him from a recent garage sale over in Griffith and had added him to the small band of therapy critters who inhabited the sunroom.

Jane accepted him with unconditional affection, placing him in a seat of honor between her own chair and Cat's. The doll's chubby hands rested as if cupped around the empty china cup.

Cora smiled. She had known since she had first seen Jane at the door yesterday morning that there was something special about this child. That this was where Jane belonged, at least on a long-term foster basis. That was possible. A deep longing in Cora's heart had begun to fill with every moment she spent thinking about Jane.

Each child she had loved brought her closer and closer to the moment when she knew she would be able to commit herself to motherhood again. Something deep inside told her that Jane was somehow a part of that answer to her prayers.

Cora was only mildly surprised at how quickly the door to her heart had been inched open. She knew from painful experience how life could change in an instant. A heartbeat.

Cora also knew instinctively that if she asked, that Thomas would agree to try. She thought about the way Jane had responded to him this morning. No other child had ever done that.

The emptiness that she had felt for these years had hurt Thomas almost as deeply as it had hurt her. Had hurt Charlie.

Maybe Jane wasn't meant to stay with her forever, but maybe Jane was meant for today. And tomorrow.

No one person could ever replace another. Cora knew that. Thomas could never replace Charlie, and he hadn't attempted to. No other child could ever replace her baby. The baby Cora tried not to think about. The baby who should have been born.

The bustling stopped, and Marjorie's hand, still damp from her dishwashing, was on her arm.

"Too much thinking." Marjorie's hand gently squeezed Cora's upper arm. "Too much feeling."

Cora wiped away a stray tear that had slipped from the corner of her eye.

"How do you always know?" she whispered.

"You are beautifully transparent," Marjorie whispered back, wiping away her own stray tear with the corner of the dish towel she was holding. "Jane is a dear old soul. She needs you."

Cora nodded wordlessly.

"Yes," Marjorie continued, nodding in agreement. "Jane needs you, and you need Jane." The older woman paused and studied her friend's face. "You've already made a decision."

"I talked to Child Services, the Savannah PD, and FaithBridge this morning," Cora admitted quietly. "Just long-term fostering. But nothing absolute until I talk to Thomas."

Marjorie smiled, then frowned.

"Have you heard from Charlie?"

"I left him a message this morning." Cora's eyes were still watching the healing drama unfold in the sunroom. "Not about Jane. I left a message about the dream last night. You know Charlie." She shrugged. "He'll call when he has questions."

Marjorie nodded again and waited. She could sense there was more.

"I just don't know what to do about the dreams," Cora said finally, and a random tear slipped down her face.

Then another tear, and another.

Outside in the garden, Jane began to confide in each of her honored guests, picking up each one in turn, hugging as only a child can embrace. A sweet, pure sharing that broke the last of the dam in Cora's heart and released the flood of tears that now flowed freely from both Cora and, empathetically, from Marjorie as well.

Healing tears flowed in happiness and cleansing and joy until Cora, spent and trembling, sighed deeply and joyfully for the first time in a long, long time.

The dreams made no more sense than they had five minutes ago, but now that didn't matter to Cora. That didn't matter at all. Only Jane mattered right now.

The dreams were for Charlie, not for Cora. He would know what to do with them.

The doorbell rang. Marjorie gave Cora a quick hug and went

to answer, humming a hymn as she went.

Chapter 25

Andrew Evans had not had so much as a minute to relax, having been summoned via telephone to the police station only ten minutes or so after his difficult meeting with the Senator and his annoying aide, Perkins. Although the meeting with Wilton had taken place in the preacher's office at precisely nine a.m., Pastor Evans had felt as though he had been an interloper who had stumbled upon a burglary in his own home.

Evans's wife and the two church staff ladies, in an impressive but not surprising display of unity and Southern hospitality, had attempted to mitigate the situation with fresh coffee and homemade pastries, but the Senator and Perkins would have none of the trappings of sympathy, religious or otherwise.

"Not so much as a social crumb!" Alice Lee had sniffed when they left, insulted on behalf of Donna's legendary apple cinnamon walnut bread and the gourmet coffee they had made.

"Even a senator should have manners!"

The meeting lasted only fifteen minutes and consisted primarily of the Senator's aide demanding certain amenities and adjustments that Alice dutifully wrote down, but to which no one verbally agreed, much to the annoyance of Perkins.

The Senator stood in the far corner of the office, a towering icon staring out the window at the parking lot as if to distance himself not only from what seemed to be negotiations but from the reality of the entire situation.

He even waved away a sample copy of the proposed agenda for the service, motioning for a disgruntled Perkins to put it in his own pocket instead.

The women wondered later in collective whispers about Stewart Wilton's state of mind, and summarily excused his behavior on the grounds that he must surely be in shock over the death of his only son. Nothing else seemed to explain his deference to Perkins over the arrangements for the funeral service. Or his refusal of refreshments.

When the two men had gone, all four church members poured well-earned cups of fancy coffee and breathed collective sighs of relief. Their relief was short-lived, the telephone call from Charlie at the police station bringing on a fresh round of speculation and conjecture. Andrew refused his wife's offer to accompany him and left his untouched coffee on the corner of Donna's desk.

Twenty minutes later he was sitting across the wooden table from Charlie in what passed for the precinct interrogation room. Although the room had been freshly painted, it was little more than a glorified storage space that would have to serve until the new addition to the building was completed sometime during the next month. The former interrogation room had been turned into storage space for the building supplies, no one having anticipated anything quite so serious in Balfour as a homicide investigation.

The latex paint smell, combined with the tightly enclosed space and his general irritation with a lack of evidence and suspects, made Charlie's annoyance with the preacher all the more obvious.

So far, all the clues he had found had turned out to be totally irrelevant. He had listened to the message from Cora, and those clues seemed even more irrelevant. Sweetness, Psalms, King David, and blackberry pies.

What the pickled pigs' feet anyway?

The gun in the wall safe was Steve's own registered handgun and, according to ballistics, had not recently been fired. The envelope, thick and information-filled, was only Steve's will, dated within the year, leaving everything he owned to his beloved wife, Katy, and consequently to his daughter, Elizabeth.

The curious thing was that what was in the envelope appeared to be a copy of the same thing Steve was signing when he was shot. The papers were still too damaged to determine if they were an exact match. But why not?

Steve had apparently gone over to Griffith and used a lawyer there to help him instead of Grumbald and Lattimer, his usual attorneys of choice. He didn't ask Thomas either.

Too many lawyers in the mix, thought Charlie. *And one uncooperative preacher.*

Charlie repeated the same question he had already asked,

less politely this time.

"So, Preacher, when did you say Steve came to see you?"

There was a long pause before Evans spoke, selecting his words with apparent care.

"I never said that he came to see me."

"Isn't there some rule in the scriptures about not lying?" Charlie snapped sarcastically. "Front of the book, I think. Right up there in the top ten."

Evans sighed and rubbed his forehead. There was nothing more frustrating for him than hearing the unchurched try to school him about religion.

"There's no need for sarcasm," he said simply. "Am I under oath?"

"Do I need to put you under oath?" Charlie's cynicism increased. "I thought preachers were perpetually under oath." He pulled at the fabric on the knee of his blue-jeaned leg and sat down on the corner of the desk. "Look, I don't know what's so difficult about cooperation. I just need some information."

Evans sighed again and gave up.

"I went to see Steve Wilton," he admitted slowly. "In his office. In his house. On Monday. No one from the church knew I was there. He asked me not to tell anyone."

Charlie made a disgruntled noise and pulled out his notebook and began to write.

"Yesterday," he repeated. "The day Steve Wilton died."

"The day he died," Evans repeated. "He said he wouldn't be there, but the door would be unlocked. The housekeeper was in the kitchen, and I waited in the study for him until he got home from court. He was pretty upset."

"Yep, that's what I heard from the housekeeper when I interviewed her this morning." Charlie paused.

"So you already knew I went to see Steve?" The preacher's voice was incredulous. "Why are you asking me what you already know?"

"You don't tell me how to interrogate," Charlie said, smirking. "I don't tell you how to preach." The detective paused to let his latest quip soak in. "So, did you touch anything while you were there?"

"Did I what?"

"Touch things—books, desk, picture frames."

"I don't know. Wait. Books. I looked at his library while I was waiting in the study. I might have touched some of the books. What difference does that make?"

"Did you take one of the books?"

"Certainly not!" Evans sat upright in the chair, and his face reddened. "Are you calling me a thief?"

Charlie looked up calmly and met the preacher's angry stare.

"Tell me, why would Steve Wilton ask to see you?"

Evans hesitated for a split second, but he saw no point in stopping now. His visit had not been a secret after all.

"I don't know exactly," he admitted. "I assumed he wanted me to help him."

"Help him? How?"

"He didn't say. He asked me to be there, and then he was angry that I was there. You can ask the housekeeper."

"Already did. Steve told you to get the hell out of his life."

"You're asking me questions when you already know the answers."

Charlie tilted his head and raised his eyebrow.

"Wilton fired the housekeeper for eavesdropping at the door. She said she heard lots of shouting but not the cause of the argument."

"So you know he was alive when I left him."

Charlie slammed his notebook onto the table with an explosive, exasperated smack.

"Preacher, I want to know *why* you went to see Steve."

"I told you, I don't know."

Charlie leaned forward, inches from the preacher's face.

"Everyone has some inkling of why other people do things," he insisted firmly. "You must have some idea why you went, why he wanted to see you. Maybe your wife thought you ought to go. Maybe you thought he needed a little Jesus in his life. Maybe he had some deep dark secret confession. Give me a guess."

Evans's face blushed a darker red.

"I went because I was asked to go," he said evenly. "I am not qualified to judge another person's motives."

"And Steve didn't tell you why he asked you to come to see him?"

"I've told you all I know. No more. No less."

Charlie gave a low whistle of disbelief.

"I think there *is* more, Preacher. I think there *is* something you aren't telling me. I know there's something you're not telling me."

Evans's sigh was explosive.

"Detective, are you charging me with anything? Any kind of crime? Going to a man's house? Responding to a call for help?

Because if you aren't charging me, I have some things that I need to attend to before the funeral on Sunday."

There was no answer from Charlie, who had picked up his notebook and begun to draw curious-looking doodles down the side of a page.

Evans stood up and impatiently straightened his suit coat and tie, wiping his sweating palms against each other.

"Can I go now?"

"Sure, Preacher," Charlie clicked his pen closed and began to tap the notebook rhythmically against the table. "We can talk again. Soon, I hope."

"Of course," the preacher retorted, regaining his composure. "We can talk again when I see you in church on Sunday morning."

Charlie stopped tapping and yawned disinterestedly, shaking his head.

"Not likely, Preacher," he said with a wry grin. "Not likely at all."

Evans gave an involuntary, exasperated snort, then turned on his heel and left, pulling the door firmly shut behind him with a slam. Charlie smiled.

Finally, he thought with satisfaction, *I'm getting somewhere.*

Chapter 26

The lunch crowd at Sam's was unusually subdued. There were no loud, cheerful greetings. No teasing catcalls with the generally effervescent Sam. Considering the atmosphere, Steve Wilton's body might have been on display, seated in the first ladder-backed chair next to the chalkboard display of daily specials.

Despite the sober mood, almost all the tables were full of locals whose Tuesdays revolved around the customary business of the day. Although most of them knew Judge Candler was out of town for the week, force of habit had brought them out for their usual Tuesday lunch at Sam's.

That and the promise of catching the latest news about Steve's murder.

Judge Candler preferred Tuesday court days for county business affairs including tax issues, land and estates, and inheritance squabbles. Sometimes the Tuesday business spilled over into Wednesdays, which had always been good for Sam's business too, since people came into town and often stayed for lunch and sometimes even an early supper.

Criminal cases, speeding tickets, petty theft, other misdemeanors, and the occasional felony, along with any other assorted crimes were all reserved for Thursdays and sometimes Friday mornings. There simply weren't that many crimes that fit into those categories of lawlessness in the country town. Except for the occasional notoriety that Charlie's investigations and Cora's dreams evoked, Balfour took pride in a reputation for being a rather quiet, sleepy sort of town. Until Steve Wilton's murder.

Visitors to court and newcomers to town sometimes questioned the wisdom of waiting all week to take care of more serious issues, but Judge Candler would say, with a spark of defiance in his eyes, that he didn't like spoiling a perfectly good week with bad news. The average man's business first, he would say. A man needed to set his affairs in order at the beginning of the week and then get on with the rest of his life.

The cloud of serious crime that hung over Sam's made the whole atmosphere seem more like Thursday than Tuesday. As was her custom, Sam had reserved the back tables for Thomas and Candler. Through the gossip vine, everyone knew that the judge had taken his wife to Atlanta for their anniversary. But most who knew the judge also knew that he would be back in time for the bulk of the investigation, and Sam did not want to take any chances with the satisfaction of her most loyal and informative customers. Or with the possibility of overhearing the latest inside stories and updates.

Only a select few were ever allowed to sit at the back corner tables. With Sam's limited serving hours, there had never been much of an issue. Local folks didn't ask to sit all the way in the back, as it was too small and rather dark. Maybe even clandestine. Tourists, the few who wandered through, were persuaded that one of the four booths that lined the front windows offered a much better perspective of life in Balfour. Besides, Sam would argue persuasively, the booths overlooked the town square and faced the courthouse just beyond.

The town square was like all other Southern town squares in its uniqueness. There were several hundred-plus-year-old live oak trees for shade, a few Georgia pines that were decorated for Christmas, hardy red holly bushes with dangerously sharp leaves, a dozen wooden benches with plaques of memorials, the prerequisite colony of talkative American red squirrels and chipmunks, and a parade of entertaining, quirky pedestrian locals. A person in search of Americana could not ask for a better homegrown, hometown show.

Amanda Grayson had been induced to take a place at one of those entertaining booths and was looking out the window, hoping for a distraction and tapping her spoon impatiently against the rim of her third cup of coffee. On her way to Sam's, she had called the Senator's assistant and left a message to meet her here with the ulterior motive of speeding up her return to Atlanta. She could see no reason at all to prolong her stay, and she hoped that, despite his attitude last night, Perkins could be persuaded to agree. Especially if she could separate him from the Senator. Now he was keeping her waiting, and she was none too happy about the latest snag in her customarily well-laid plans.

She also hoped, with the Senator's influence, she could be relieved of any future contact with that cowboy detective.

Amanda had had quite enough of the long string of uncooperative men in her recent life. First Wilton. Then the hillbilly detective. Now Perkins. She touched up her lipstick carefully, thinking vaguely that she might be losing her touch.

Sam had kept a watchful eye on her most recent exotic diner, filling the cup as soon as it appeared half-empty and hovering nearby, ignoring the darkening pink stain of expensive lipstick on her good china cup. Sam would have admitted that her attention was mostly just an excuse to move closer to see a metropolitan lawyer, hoping to catch part of a cell phone conversation or form a bond of sorts that would give her a tidbit of useful information. Sam was an unabashed gossip and busybody. Well-loved, but still a gossip and busybody.

Amanda had made it clear to Sam that she was expecting someone, but as the hour wore on Sam realized that the fancy lawyer had most likely been snubbed and stood up. Sam also noticed that the woman seemed to be annoyed at the cozy intimacy of the country patrons and the position of the tables. Everyone in Balfour greeted everyone else. No one in Balfour, at least none of Sam's patrons, had issues with the bumps and jostles that came from the servers moving among and between the wooden captain's chairs. Sam had replaced all but one of the high-backed, cane-bottomed chairs with these sturdier counterparts from the recently closed fish house just out of town. Customers seemed to like the curved wood of the arms across the top. It was more comfortable for them and less maintenance for Sam. Re-caning was expensive, and wood polish was cheap. Besides, Sam thought these better matched the sturdy, high-backed parson's wooden benches and hand-hewn tables that made up the four booths at the windows and the short row of two-person tables down the walls on both sides.

As Sam approached her picky, elegant patron for the umpteenth time with the pot of freshly made coffee, she noted that Amanda had finally relaxed a bit and had leaned back into her wooden booth seat, her forearms resting on the edge of the table. The lawyer had also unbuttoned her expensive gray suit, exposing her blood-red silk blouse like a fresh gash, which clashed oddly with both the shade of her bright pink lipstick and the tint of her freshly painted nails.

"Warm up your coffee?"

Amanda's eyes snapped to attention, covering her cup with her long fingers.

"No."

Perkins was now more than an hour later than the time she had suggested, and his cell phone kept going immediately to voicemail. Amanda's limited supply of patience was all but evaporated.

"Could I bring you anything else while you wait?"

Sam hoped she sounded sympathetic and helpful. "A salad? Maybe Greek? Or Caesar?" Sam didn't wait for an answer. "Something sweet?"

Amanda took a deep breath and considered the quite likely possibility that Perkins was not coming at all. Her face flushed, wondering if this might be the Senator's doing. She hadn't been paid. She was being ignored. It felt like some sort of mental game or possibly a strategy to punish her.

"I was just leaving," she began, looking around the bench seat to gather her briefcase and purse. Sam patted the table with a soft hand and leaned over, flashing her best confidential smile.

"Listen," she began. "I am so glad to have you in here. It adds quite a bit of sophistication to the usual clientele, especially in the front window."

Amanda evaluated the other woman, trying to decide if she felt gratitude for the unexpected honesty or if her slender, ponytailed counterpart in jeans and a T-shirt was somehow making fun of her.

"I would be happy," Sam continued, sensing her opening, "to bring you a salad—on the house, of course. Good for business."

Amanda smiled in spite of herself. She was hungry. In spite of everything. That was why she had gone to all the trouble to get dressed.

"Caesar then," she said briskly. "And a glass of water, light ice, with a twist of lemon."

"Of course." Sam nodded, expertly filling the cup to just below the rim. "Be right back."

Amanda straightened herself in the seat, feeling unexpectedly gratified. *Let Perkins and Wilton play their silly games. I'm ready.*

She knew she might be stuck here in this antebellum nightmare for the next three or four days, but she was not going to hide or spend more time in that Southern prison cell of an apartment any more than she had to. Watching people pass on the sidewalk was small entertainment, but she had been noticing the plates around her. The food here smelled really good and looked more than passable. At least it wasn't all fried. She almost allowed herself to like the owner.

Yes, she thought to herself, *there's a story with that woman.* She watched as Sam gracefully maneuvered her way to the kitchen between the patrons with the rhythm of a ballroom dancer, warmly acknowledging multiple partners along the way. *Maybe even an interesting story.*

Amanda was almost as hungry for news as Sam was. Any kind of news.

Moments later, Amanda was lost in thought watching two squirrels arguing over some acorns as Sam returned with the promised salad and silverware, wrapped in yet another starched linen napkin.

"Enjoy," Sam said sweetly and disappeared across the room.

For the first time all morning, Amanda took her mind off the window and the patrons, Perkins and the Senator, Charlie, and the annoyance of her situation and picked up the heavy, silver fork.

Other people be hanged, she decided bluntly. *I'm going to take care of myself.*

She stabbed the crisp, fresh salad with relish as her mind began to formulate a new plan. A better plan for how to handle her present situation.

Chapter 27

Perkins had had his hands full with Senator Wilton. The Washington office had been calling all morning, full of questions about the reelection campaign. Wilton had appointed a new chairperson to lead his campaign, one who had been taking the plans in an interesting and rather radical new direction that both excited and disturbed the rest of the staff members, all much older and more conventional in their views of how campaigns should be run.

Perkins's job as diplomat and aide-de-camp was to maintain a delicate truce and order between the troops and their newly appointed youthful leadership. He knew that he probably should have acknowledged the request for a lunch appointment with Amanda Grayson. He knew that talking to her was necessary—maybe even moderately important—but in the business of political triage, she was a mere paper cut among multiple compound fractures.

Perkins would have to find time to put a bandage on that paper cut later. Much later. Right now, his agenda was filled with more immediate problems.

The wealthy socialite couple with whom the Senator and Perkins were staying were the Senator's old family friends, away on their semiannual retreat at their St. Simons vacation home. They had been staunch supporters and discreetly savvy political allies since the early days of his political service, in addition to being close friends and distant relatives of his deceased wife. His devotion to Steve and to remaining single after the death of Steve's mother only added to their admiration. Wilton had been a welcome house guest at all times and seasons, and now even more so when they were told about Steve's untimely murder.

Insisting that the Senator needed privacy to grieve, they had promised to return for the services on Sunday. Until then, they said the Senator should treat their small household staff, the cook and a housekeeper, as if they were his own. Both older Southern women were well-versed in the Senator's ways and wishes, having lived their entire lives in Balfour and having known him, his wife, and Steve.

The Senator's wishes were not complicated. Lots of strong coffee, never decaffeinated and always black. Since his heart attack almost six years before, he wanted nothing fried or greasy, including crispy battered chicken or truly Southern vegetables like fried okra or green tomatoes. Certainly nothing seasoned heavily with ham or pork. He was satisfied with cold cuts of turkey or chicken and lean roast beef, baked chicken, hard cheeses, leafy green salads, and fruit. Lots of fresh, local fruit.

The Senator's favorite fruit, perhaps because of availability and habit, were the Georgia peaches from which the experienced cook made her amazing pies, turnovers, and cobblers, the Senator's one fattening weakness. Perkins only barely managed to hide his distaste for the Senator's healthy lifestyle. His own tendencies leaned toward Italian pizzas and pastas served with large loaves of garlic butter, these meals interspersed with heavy doses of Mexican fiestas with seasoned beans, chips, cheese, and salsa.

Perkins was glad, however, for the space and privacy to work and that the Senator had chosen to isolate himself in the rooms upstairs and leave him principally alone for the day. The family had effectively vacated the third floor of the antebellum house, which held the guest suite, and Perkins had taken over the formal family dining room to use as a headquarters of sorts. He had spread out his paperwork on the polished table, his laptop on one side and assorted charging cables and cords zigzagging their way across the carpeted floor like cottonmouth snakes. Briefcases filled with official-looking papers and documents were spread across the other side of the table.

A separate stack, close to one end of the table nearest the window, was information concerning Steve's murder. Initial police reports. Potential press releases and statements. Notes from the meeting with the preacher who was doing the services on Sunday. Perkins had suggested sending for more staff members to handle publicity surrounding the events, as well as the Washington, D.C., bodyguard who usually accompanied them around the Capitol, but the Senator was adamant. "More people, more complications," he had argued. "More problems. More headaches in the long run."

The Senator had insisted that life did not work that way in Balfour.

Perkins had no doubt that the Senator was grieving in a deeply and highly personal way. The aide had known only superficially about Steve's relationship with his father. There were anecdotal stories told by the cronies who surrounded Wilton in Washington, who had tried to enlighten and forewarn Perkins before he had accepted this position with the Senator. Most of the accounts were secondhand narratives surrounding Steve's youth and the multiple catastrophes he had caused. Perkins had surmised that perhaps these antics and the death of Wilton's first wife so early in their marriage had contributed to the sympathetic public opinion for the Senator.

Pundits had suggested that Stewart's success in his first attempt at election to the Senate could be directly attributed to the Senator's refusal to remarry and his willingness to share with the world and the press the difficulties of struggling single fatherhood. Perkins himself had found the Senator's celibate lifestyle, coupled with his refusal to drink alcohol, noteworthy. Almost as remarkable to the aide as Wilton's steadfast devotion to his electorate and his constituency's willingness to overlook any other character flaws he might have had.

Even before Perkins had made it his business to become a member of Wilton's staff, he admired and emulated Wilton's standards. Self-control. Discipline. Order. Dedication. The man remained above provable reproach. The method was much more obvious than the motivation, and the method worked well.

Steve's reputation was the sole blemish on his father's otherwise spotless history. For the first few weeks in Wilton's employ, Perkins had watched for some sign, some logic that might explain the relationship between the father and son, but he had remained lost in speculation, until yesterday.

There was love, of course. Perkins could see that Wilton loved his son and was more or less an adoring, overly indulgent father. Despite the fact that he and Steve were almost the same age, Perkins had come to imagine the younger Wilton as a very young boy. A child who had been spoiled and damaged by the wealth of his father and the loss of his mother.

As the hours since the news of the murder passed, however, Perkins began to see that there was more to the relationship than he had initially believed. In the Senator's uncharacteristic behavior, Perkins began to see the true evidence of the father's love for his son. He was shocked and even more admiring of the man for whom he worked.

If anyone had asked him now, Perkins would have told them that Senator Wilton's feelings for his son involved hope. Blind, irrational, unreasonable hope. Hope that someday, somehow, Steve would wake up to his father's desires for his future. Perkins sensed that the Senator's hope for Steve erased and dissolved Steve's past mistakes. The Senator was looking forward to a better, happier time for the two of them together as adults and for Steve as a devoted husband and loving father.

Perkins had no such hope nor feelings of that sort for anyone. He was a pragmatist.

Maybe the old dinosaur is a human being after all, the aide thought. *Or maybe he is just getting soft in the head as well as in the heart.*

For a moment he allowed himself a tiny spark of empathy before cold reason took over.

I can like him as a man and still do what has to be done. His time has come and gone.

Perkins looked down at the words he had already written for the speech he was supposed to be writing for the Senator on Sunday at the memorial and considered saying what he now knew to be true.

Steve's death was not so much a tragedy of a physical death, although it was of course that. It was not even the end of a father's love, because with someone like the Senator that love would continue despite any circumstances.

No, Steve's death was the death of his father's hope, and that had shaken the Senator to his roots. Perkins had for the first time witnessed a tremble to the strong hand, moisture to the dry eyes, a quiver to the determined chin.

Hope was gone, at least for Senator Wilton's only son, and until the Senator was able to cope with this loss and restore the veneer of confidence under which he had hidden his true feelings and hope, he wanted the fewest possible witnesses to his pain.

Perkins deleted everything he had typed with a determined stroke and decided to begin again. He knew that the time would soon come when he would need to stab the Senator in the back, but for now he decided not to take out a knife at the son's funeral.

The housekeeper tapped tentatively at the door before she entered the dining room with a tray carrying a fresh carafe of hot coffee and a covered basket of still-warm peach turnovers.

Perkins looked at his watch, realizing with a small twinge of guilt that he should probably text some sort of excuse to

Amanda Grayson, but he straight away rejected the notion. Instead, he nodded wordlessly and gestured the elderly woman in her simple black and white uniform to one side. The housekeeper unquestioningly placed the tray on the sideboard next to a stack of delicate porcelain plates, cups, linen napkins, and shining silver dessert forks that had been left over from breakfast.

These people eat entirely too much, he thought to himself. *Why must Southern hospitality always include so much food?*

"Thank you," he said absently. "I think the Senator is upstairs showering and trying to rest. I know he will appreciate your thoughtfulness."

The older woman nodded, barely concealing her own critical opinion of the Senator's latest assistant.

Young people, she thought. *A Yankee in attitude and a Northerner by birth. All the right words and none of the feelings. No regard for traditions. No respect for the way things ought to be done. No regard at all.*

"Let me know if you need anything, sir," she said instead, but Perkins had already proven her point by going back to his typing, not noticing when she had gone.

Chapter 28

Ben Taylor had been the chief of police in Balfour for twenty-two years, and he had better sense than to interrupt Charlie when he was in one of his moods. To his credit, Ben had had no problem recognizing one of Charlie's moods from the very beginning of their long-standing relationship, which probably explained why the relationship had lasted intact for so long.

Ben had a healthy respect for Charlie's moods.

Of all the teenagers in Balfour that Ben Taylor had dealt with over the years, Charlie had been one of the most mischievous, and one of his favorites. Never truly destructive, Charlie's youthful antics had been generally clever, and most had been known to prove a point or two. The epitome of a black sheep, Charlie finished four years in forensics at North Georgia College & State University in Dahlonega and then was accepted into the Herbert T. Jenkins Police Academy in Atlanta. He graduated with high honors and numerous awards, as well as a reputation for accuracy, ego, and pigheaded stubbornness. Ben wasn't surprised at all. Charlie spend two obligatory years in Balfour in an attempt to redeem his youthful reputation before he set out for New Orleans and a successful career. And Cora.

The chief was watching the back of Charlie's head, bent into the telephone receiver on his desk and nodding as he listened. The swivel chair was moving—always a good sign—from side to side and back and forth, rocking in a kind of musical rhythm to some rock and roll tune in Charlie's active mind.

Other uniformed officers on the force and the two seasoned detectives, Burton and Dalton, kept their distance from Charlie and his desk. He liked to work alone. He liked to *be* alone. He was not reckless or careless or any sort of cowboy, in spite of the boots he often wore. He was just Charlie. His desk was well-organized and neat. He called for backup when required, and only when required. Otherwise, he kept his own hours and his own counsel, and he got results. Impressive results.

Balfour alone did not really need three detectives, but Charlie wasn't full time. He came and went as the situation warranted. He used the extra desk in the corner when he was in town, and Burton and Dalton handled the day-to-day. They were dependable detectives, often called upon to service the tri-county area. But they weren't Charlie, who was known state-wide and frequently asked to assist in solving high-profile crimes out of state in Louisiana and the Carolinas.

Ben Taylor considered Charlie the best detective he had ever met. He frequently had to say that to people who knew Charlie by reputation only. As a matter of fact, he had just gotten off the telephone with Senator Wilton's snotty assistant and had repeated his supportive views of Charlie. Several times. With emphasis.

Apparently, Senator Wilton's aide was more interested in discussing Charlie's far distant rumored adolescent past than Charlie's record as a police detective. This was common practice in a small town and with people who did not really know the individuals involved. No matter how respectable a person might become as an adult, there were always those who refused to forgive or forget the antics that same person had instigated as a child.

Charlie hung up the telephone and stood, stretching his arms over his head and twisting the kinks out of his back. After sitting for the last three hours in the chair and making telephone calls, he was pleased with himself. The investigation into the Savannah killings was almost over. At least, his part was almost over. Cora and Marjorie had been able to coax Jane to draw pictures, which Cora had faxed to the proper authorities in Savannah late this afternoon. He hoped there were clues to the murderers of her parents, uncle, and grandparents embedded in the childish crayon artwork. The number of men, maybe. The weapons used. The details that only an eyewitness would know. Details that were hopefully locked inside the mind of the timid four-year-old child.

The fact that Jane alone had been spared was also significant. That Jane could remember a solitary man with round, blue eyes was valuable information. That it seemed this man, whoever he was, had kept her from the center of the violence. That the murderers were obviously aware of her presence and yet had left her alive. All these factors helped to further pinpoint the purpose, the reasoning—if it could be called reasoning—behind the heinous crime.

These were the painful, evil, purpose-driven details, combined with the substantial evidence that had been found at the crime scene, that would allow an experienced forensics team to bring closure to the whole investigation.

But that was not Charlie's job and they had not asked for his help, particularly not with the Wilton murder on his plate. Delivering Jane to Cora's doorstep had been the most difficult part of his work, and also the most bittersweet. Jane was now in a place where she would have an opportunity to be loved and cherished and protected. A different future than what she might have had with her own family, but a future with people who would understand and heal her personal hurts. A future, he had fervently hoped from the moment he saw Jane for the first time, with Cora. He couldn't be sure. Charlie just hoped.

Charlie put on his corduroy sports jacket and tried to shake off the unwelcome feeling of self-pity that nagged at him whenever he thought of Cora.

"What's new with the Wilton investigation?" Ben tried to sound hopeful, as if he expected an answer.

Charlie stretched again, adjusting his collar and turning toward the chief's voice.

"Not much." Charlie shrugged. "Waiting for some word from the Atlanta labs about the blood and the papers they found on the desk. Setting up more interviews tomorrow, but right now we are pretty much stymied." He picked up his notepad and tucked it into his pocket with his ink pen. "No murder weapon. Still sorting through the DNA. Housekeeper was gone for the hour when the murder occurred. Narrow window of time, but I can't tell yet if that means it was premeditated or a crime of dumb opportunity."

"What about Savannah?"

Just got off the phone with the detective in charge of the case at GBI."

"Is that one closed?"

"Our part." Charlie opened the long drawer to his desk and took out his service revolver and badge.

"Back to Wilton," he said. "I'm going by to talk to Thomas before he leaves his office. See if he has any ideas. There's no shortage of people who hated Steve."

"Good idea pulling him into this." The chief eyed him curiously. Charlie thought he might be about to mention Cora, but he didn't.

"Good work, Charlie."

Charlie shrugged. He was not fond of compliments, but he knew the chief was a student of the Bear Bryant school of motivational speeches, so he humored him by listening and feigning his own appreciation.

Ben, sensing Charlie's resistance, finished up his speech. "So, keep me informed, right?"

"Sure," Charlie said with what passed for agreement. "Sure, Chief."

"Especially if you talk to the Senator," he added. "Or he talks to you."

"Sure." Charlie holstered his gun and clipped the badge to his belt. "Sure."

Outside, opening the door to his battered blue VW, Charlie

had second thoughts about going to Thomas's office. He unclipped the cell phone from his belt and saw that he had another message from Cora. He decided to listen after he talked to Thomas. He waited while the office number rang several times, and then the answering machine picked up with Susan's cheerful recorded message to call back during office hours or leave a message. Thomas had obviously gone home early. Charlie checked his watch. Hard to believe that it had been only a little more than twenty-four hours since someone had killed Steve.

He wasn't going to call Thomas at home. He didn't need any more lectures from Marjorie. She was a bulldog when she felt as though someone might upset Cora. He would listen to Cora's message in the morning and then make up his mind when to get back to her. Too late in the day to start anything new. Most of Balfour closed up when the sun went down, including Sam's. Most of the community went home to have supper with their families, sit on their front porches, and go to bed.

Charlie started the car and shifted gears. He was tired of taking the blame for involving Cora in his life. *Damned dreams. I'm not responsible for her dreams.* He shook the memories from his head. Retrospection was too dangerous.

He made a mental list of the people he had interviewed and checked off the people one at a time: the preacher, the woman lawyer, the right-hand man, the Senator, the housekeeper. Thomas didn't count, of course.

Who else was there to talk to? Katy Wilton. Although she hardly counted as a suspect. Amy and her husband were keeping close tabs on Katy, and that made talking to Steve's wife very difficult right now.

Then there were the peripheral people who weren't really suspects at all. Marcie at the Piney Woods. She might know something about that lady lawyer and her goings on.

But what would any of them really know?

The thought prickled at Charlie's mind. There were many people who despised Steve Wilton, but only so many who could get close enough to shoot him in the back of the head. Some with alibis. Some with opportunity. Some with motive.

But what motive and to what end?

Charlie shook his head again. *Sleep*, he decided. *I need sleep.*

Too many thoughts of blood-soaked ink blotters, musty libraries, missing books and guns, compassionate killers with round blue eyes, and one delicate little girl with ink-black hair were crowding around inside his head. He rolled up the window and turned on the feeble air-conditioning.

If I ever get the time, he thought, *I'll get that fixed.*

No, he corrected himself. *No, I won't.*

Charlie took his random thoughts home to his comfortable but modest apartment at the Piney Woods and put them away for the day. He had a family sized can of chicken noodle soup with saltine crackers, which he shared with his faithful plot hound, Elvira. He half-watched a couple of rerun episodes of *Matlock*, took a few careless swipes at this teeth with a toothbrush, and fell into his bed.

It was only ten p.m., but in Balfour that qualified as the middle of the night. And Charlie needed sleep.

Chapter 29

Quite wisely, knowing the judge as he did, Thomas had refrained from calling and telling him the news about Steve's death as soon as the limited facts were made public on Monday night. Judge Candler did not often get away with his wife, and when he did he made a practice of turning off his cell phone, the television, and even the car radio in order to avoid hearing any news that might disrupt their private time together.

The judge and his wife, Linda, had little enough time to themselves. They were both active not only in the community and church but were also staunch supporters of the home for boys and girls in the countryside between Balfour and the next neighboring town. They were always in the middle of something or other for someone else and seldom left Balfour, except on occasional mission trips to Mexico and hurricane-damaged regions with hastily organized groups from the Methodist church. Both had also volunteered with Habitat for Humanity last summer and worked for two weeks in South Carolina renovating a church building with a team of other like-minded adults from Balfour.

Thomas had no problem with not calling the judge until he had some actual news, although Charlie made it clear that he was not particularly optimistic that there would be actual news anytime soon. Since it had been more than twenty-four hours, Thomas concluded that waiting any longer might seem as though he were keeping secrets from the judge. He had intended to call before he left the office, but instead he insisted that Susan go home early, and he followed her almost immediately.

He decided to call Candler around seven and leave a message on his cell phone. That would give the judge an opportunity to decide for himself what to do.

Because he left early, Thomas had time to stop at the local bakery, where he bought a dozen assorted fancy cupcakes. He always bought cupcakes when Cora and Marjorie had a foster child in the house. He knew from experience that this was one thing he could easily buy without offending Marjorie's cooking expertise. Marjorie didn't make cupcakes often, if at all, and Thomas rather enjoyed picking out the various flavors, anticipating Cora's reaction as well as the children's faces when they saw the expertly decorated sweets.

The saleslady at the bakery counter encouraged him to take his time deciding on the various kinds he wanted, although she strongly suggested pink lemonade with sprinkles and a double chocolate, along with one that contained peanut butter filling.

Thomas didn't really care. He knew red velvet with cream cheese icing was Cora's favorite, and Marjorie especially liked

German chocolate. He didn't know about the little girl. Something special. She looked so much like Cora.

Thomas absently wondered if Charlie had noticed. Charlie. He tried not to think about Charlie, but Charlie was not the sort of person who was easily forgotten.

He could see Marjorie standing at the sink in the kitchen window when he pulled into the driveway. He had hoped that Cora would be on the front porch with Jane, but he also knew that it might be asking too much of Cora to expect that she would come outside. *Maybe they're in the sunroom,* he thought.

Balancing the white bakery box carefully in one hand and his briefcase in the other, he went up the steps to the front door and unlocked it, hesitating. When he opened the door, the delicious smell of Marjorie's cooking came toward him, enticing him into the kitchen. He settled the briefcase next to the staircase on the antique coat bench and carried the cupcakes like a treasure down the hallway, checking the playroom and Cora's office as he went through the house, searching for his wife. As he put the cupcake box on the countertop, he turned instinctively to the right.

In the late afternoon, light filtered through the pines and hardwoods outside. The sunroom, built specifically for this purpose, was cool and peaceful. Cora was seated on a small wooden stool next to the child's cluttered tea party table. Her lap was full of stuffed toys and dolls, balanced on her knees and propped back against her chest. Jane was bustling happily about the table, arranging and rearranging the dishes and babbling with bits and pieces of thoughts.

This was not the first time in their marriage that Thomas

had come home to find Cora in the sunroom with a child. He was certain that this would not be the last time. His lack of experience in psychology did not prevent him from seeing that this relationship was different from any of the others. Fundamentally, delightfully different, and yet the joy he saw unfolding before him also filled him with a sense of dread. He saw himself as pragmatic and practical. Marjorie sometimes called him pessimistic. Charlie had brought this child into Cora's life. Charlie usually meant trouble. Thomas couldn't bear to see Cora hurt again. Not after she had come so far from where she was when he first met her.

Cora's face was as animated as the child's, leaning in and intent on the little girl's every word. Thomas stood in silent awe for several minutes. He had never seen his wife like this.

They saw him at the same time. Two faces. Two smiles.

Instinctively he knelt, his arms opened for them, and together they moved. With a fluid motion, Thomas caught Jane up into one arm and reached out with the other to draw Cora into his side as he stood. The adults encircled the small child together.

In the adjoining kitchen, Marjorie smiled as she took the baked macaroni and cheese from the oven and replaced it with the yeast rolls. As much as she wanted to watch the scene in the sunroom, she knew she wasn't needed, so she just looked out the window to the garden and kept her thoughts to herself.

And as they often did when she thought of Cora and the changes in her life, her thoughts turned to Charlie.

Charlie is a man who wants to fix everything except himself, she thought, offering up a silent prayer of thanks for Charlie and a mental note to bake him his favorite dessert, extra chewy brownies with thick chocolate icing. She would leave them with Marcie at the Piney Woods sometime before Friday, and he wouldn't be able to refuse her gift of thanks. He had done that before. Refused a simple "thank you." That was just Charlie's way.

Poor Charlie, she thought sadly, for the first time in a long time. *Poor, poor Charlie.*

Chapter 30

The room's light was dim and sepia colored, coming from the last red-orange rays of the setting sun through the white lace curtains and the muted autumn colors of the Tiffany lamp on the night stand. The slender form in the bed turned and moaned softly.

Amy, whose feet tingled uncomfortably from sitting so long, had been waiting in the rocking chair near the window. She got up immediately and awkwardly went to her sister's side.

"Katy?" Amy's voice was low, questioning. "Katy? Are you awake?"

"Where's Elizabeth? How long have I been asleep?"

"She's with Aunt Charlotte, just down the hall in the blue room. Charlotte and Hannah gave her some supper and are going to bathe her and put her to bed soon."

Amy paused.

"Do you want them to bring her to you?"

251

Katy sat up in bed groggily and shook her head, her thick hair falling carelessly around her pale face.

"No, no," she protested. "I must look terrible. I don't want to frighten her." She rubbed her upper arm. "Did I get a shot?"

"The doctor thought you needed to sleep." Amy hesitated. "You were . . ."

"Hysterical," Katy finished, taking a deep, ragged, almost sobbing breath.

Amy thought for a moment she was going to need to call the doctor again.

"I was hysterical," Katy continued, calmer now. She looked directly into her sister's face. "Please don't apologize for doing what needed to be done."

"Katy . . ."

The younger sister held up a trembling white hand in protest.

"There isn't anything to say right now," she leaned back against the piles of white eyelet pillows, lost in the snowy mounds of fabric and lace. "Steve is dead."

A thought struck the young woman, her eyes taking on a wide, wild look as she leaned abruptly forward, clutching the sheets.

"Where is the Senator?"

Amy patted her sister's hand reassuringly and gently pushed her shoulders back into the cushions.

"I don't know, dear, and I don't really care."

Katy put a trembling hand to her temple and tilted her head questioningly.

"What do you mean? He's going to be furious."

"That's not your concern right now," Amy clucked like a mother hen, straightening the down coverlet and tucking it matter-of-factly around her sister as she spoke. "I asked Hannah to handle all the calls right now, and you know Hannah."

"Yes," Katy mused, trying to picture the Senator deadlocked in a verbal struggle with Hannah. The thought caused her thin lips to curl upward despite herself, imagining the headstrong black housekeeper, arms crossed in defiance, telling the staunch Senator exactly what he was and was not allowed to do. "Hannah takes no prisoners."

"Remember the night you went on your first date?"

"How could I forget? I was sixteen and much too naïve. Hannah met that poor boy at the door with a cast iron skillet in one hand and a rolling pin in the other. She didn't even give Daddy time to make his speech about Southern chivalry and shotgun weddings."

"I don't think that boy ever asked you out again."

"Are you kidding me? I think he left Balfour a week later and never looked back."

Amy took her sister's cold hand in her two warm hands, and for a moment they were lost together in the sweet nostalgia of memory before the younger sister pulled her hand deliberately away. She twisted her wedding rings around her finger.

"What happened to us, Amy?"

Amy looked away and stared at her reflection in the window. The sun had gone down, and the room was suddenly quite cool and dark.

"I'll have Hannah bring you something to eat, sweetheart." Amy was talking too fast, as if she didn't want to be interrupted.

With a deliberate movement she walked over and flipped on the overhead light.

"I've got some things in the closet and the dresser there from a couple of years ago when I was a smaller size. They'll be too big for you, and certainly not your style, but maybe you can manage. There are clean towels and shampoo in the bathroom."

"Amy . . ."

"Let Hannah know if you need anything else when she brings up your supper." The older sister finally took a ragged breath. "She's been very worried about you."

"That's kind of her."

"We're all worried about you, Katy."

"Are you, Amy? Dan too?" The voice was thoughtful, gentle, probing. Katy opened her thin, dry lips to say something and then thought better of it. This was not the time.

After a pause, she said simply, "Thank you for taking care of Elizabeth."

"Of course. Aunt Charlotte was delighted to come." Amy turned toward the bed and faced her fragile sister, picking at the tiny fabric-covered buttons down the front of her flowing knit dress. "There are plans to be made about the funeral."

Katy slid out of the bed and stood shakily for a moment. She was still wearing the simple cotton dress from Monday morning, creased and wrinkled from hard sleep. She splayed her hands open against the whiteness of the duvet, steadying her slim torso against the bed frame. Her bare feet were cold against the hardwood floors.

"I'm sure the Senator will have opinions about other people's plans," she said bitterly. "He has had his opinions about everything else."

When she saw the expression on Amy's face, she stopped.

"I'm sorry," she apologized stiffly. "I'm still a little disoriented from the sedative. I shouldn't take things out on you."

"You have every right to feel any way you want to feel, sweetheart." Amy felt a sudden sympathy and protective, motherly love. "Maybe after your shower, a change into clean clothes, and some supper, you'll feel like seeing Elizabeth. Reading her a book or just rocking her."

"That's a lovely idea," Katy said, studying her sister's face. "Thank you."

Uncomfortable, Amy looked away.

Somewhere below them a telephone began to ring, and then the doorbell joined. Then, the strident, authoritative tones of Hannah taking charge in the midst of the din.

Amy shook her head from side to side, amused.

"Thank the good Lord for Hannah," she said softly. "Thank God for Hannah."

Katy continued to analyze her sister's face, but she said nothing.

Thank God for you, Amy, she thought. *I should thank God for you.*

Chapter 31

The three-sided marquee of the Fox Theatre sparkled and danced in the cool Atlanta evening air. Cars jockeyed for turn lanes in the busy metropolitan traffic, vying for a parking space in the limited lot next to the theatre itself, occasionally having to pull over and dodge the screaming ambulances on their way to the Emory Midtown Hospital emergency room.

Judge John Candler looked down at the petite, well-dressed woman at his side. Her carefully bleached platinum hair was twisted into a French bun at the back of her head, held in place with a tastefully ornate rhinestone clip. Her dress was long and form-fitting, simple and elegant black. She wore a silver-gray shawl of some shiny metallic fabric that clung to her slight form.

Candler was a linebacker sort of man, well over six feet tall with broad shoulders. His own silver-white hair was cropped close to his head. In his midnight black suit, starched white shirt, and gray patterned silk tie, they made a handsome, well-matched couple. No one would have suspected their small-town roots.

As he glanced around the moving sea of theatre patrons, he was convinced that Linda Candler was the most wonderful, beautiful woman in the world.

I am the luckiest man in the world, he told himself, taking her arm with a possessive air and drawing her hand through his elbow. *I married my high school sweetheart and she has tolerated me and my small-town ways for fifty glorious, non-complaining years.*

The telephone call from Thomas relaying the facts concerning Steve's murder had reached him in the lobby of the Fox Theatre barely thirty minutes before seating for their show began. Linda had waited months to see the Broadway touring company's production of *Fiddler on the Roof.* The judge was careful not to point out the incongruity of a good Southern Methodist woman's ability to sing along with every word of the classic Jewish-themed musical. Linda did not have that sort of sense of humor. Besides, he had to admit that he became misty-eyed at the emotional "Sunrise, Sunset," although he told himself that that was just because their eldest daughter had used it in her wedding more than ten years before.

Silencing and slipping the cell phone discreetly into his inner jacket pocket, the judge decided that there was no need at all to miss the performance. Nor any need, he thought to himself, to even mention the content of the call until after the final curtain. His perceptive wife noted the shift in his demeanor, but she also knew that he would have told her if they needed to cancel their plans immediately.

So, when the lines began to move, they entered the historic theatre and allowed themselves to be seated by the flashlight-carrying attendants. Linda leaned back in her favorite balcony center seating and allowed herself to enjoy the familiar music of the overture. Her inner being was at rest, soaking in the Arabian influence of the theatre's architecture and tilting her head back to watch the programmed stars and clouds track across the artificially darkening sky. She could almost imagine curious faces in the facades of windows and doors that lined the buildings on the walls around where she sat, and they made pleasant, undemanding company.

Judge Candler could tell whenever he had done something to give his wife happiness, and that gave him a sense of pride and accomplishment.

When the final notes died away to resounding applause and the encores had eventually ceased, they waited for the crowds to thin before they walked, arm in arm, to their parked car.

"Thomas called," the judge began, calmly opening his wife's door and settling her into the passenger seat. As he had done since their days of courtship, he pulled the seat belt shoulder buckle and leaned over her, clicking it into place.

"There's something of a situation at home."

He closed the door to walk around the car to the driver's side, allowing his words to sink in. Linda took a long, deep breath. She knew from years of experience that the expression "there's a situation" was her husband's code, his advance warning that he was about to deliver very bad news. She also knew that if it had applied to their children or grandchildren, he would not have waited after the telephone call, and that no matter what the news he could not be hurried in the telling.

So she crossed her hands in her lap and waited in silence

until he had gotten into the car and secured his own seatbelt.

"We need to go back after lunch tomorrow," he began, watching her face in the reflection of the street lights for some sort of reaction. "I'm sorry, dear, but it can't be helped."

"Of course," she said. "Tell me what happened."

He told his wife as gently as he could about Steve's death, leaving out the most gruesome of details and including quickly that Steve's wife was absolutely not a suspect.

The judge took his wife's hand in his, pressing her fingers reassuringly.

"Do you want to go ahead and go back tonight?" she asked hesitantly.

"I don't know what I could do," he said. "Thomas said that Burton and Dalton are on the case and that Charlie is helping with the investigation. The Senator is arriving—or maybe he has already arrived. I was not quite clear about that part."

"Charlie?"

He heard the disapproval in her voice.

"Charlie is the best, dear."

"Oh," she scoffed, wrinkling her nose. "Charlie is the best, alright. The best at making messes for other people to clean up. The best at getting into trouble and mucking life up."

"Are you being quite fair?"

Linda patted his hand and changed the subject. "The new Baptist pastor will be doing the service, I suppose."

He gave his wife a sidelong look.

"What difference does that make?"

"I didn't think anyone likes him." She stopped and considered her words. She knew how much her husband despised hearsay and gossip.

"Well," she continued prudently. "Emmanuel is where Katy and her family have always attended. I suppose that's the only logical choice."

The judge nodded, unconvinced. How well the celebrated Senator and an unpopular Baptist preacher would get along remained to be seen. He started the car, putting his arm up over the back of the seat, and prepared to back out of the parking space.

"I see no reason why we can't spend the night at the hotel and head back later tomorrow afternoon," he said. "If there are pressing legalities, those can wait until Thursday or Friday. Settling the rest of the estate could take considerably longer, depending upon whether there is a will and how the rest of the whole situation plays out."

"Services on Sunday?"

"Thomas didn't say. That was my assumption. If everything else is in order with the investigation."

There was a pause while she waited for her husband to merge into traffic.

"John," she said, laying her left hand gently on his forearm as he drove. "John, who could have done this to Steve?"

He remembered the furious, impassioned voice of Steve Wilton, demanding that his wife return to him. Expecting that the world would bow, as it had always done, to his desires. Then the judge remembered his own exasperating desire for Steve to just grow up and get over himself. A few hours later, Steve's life was over. Forever.

Candler patted his wife's hand, then rubbed his forehead, as if to rid his mind of his recriminating thoughts. His wife's voice cut into his thoughts with another question.

"Has anyone called Cora?"

"Linda." His voice was sharp and uncharacteristically harsh. "Let's don't spoil the night by bringing up Cora."

"You like Cora," she admonished him.

"Socially, I love Cora," he retorted. "I admire and respect Thomas. I just don't know that Balfour needs all that—well, all that whatever-it-is that Cora does."

"I am only saying what people will be thinking." She remained unruffled by her husband's blustering. "Seems to me that the investigation would want to use all of the available resources, dear."

She glanced at her handsome, scowling husband out of the corner of her eye.

"And Charlie is back in town? Now isn't that a fortunate, interesting coincidence."

I don't imagine Thomas thinks so, the judge thought grimly to himself.

"If Cora has something to say about Steve Wilton's death, Linda, I trust she will go straight to the police department and not involve the rest of the community."

"Of course, dear," she soothed, patting his forearm. "Of course, dear. You would know best."

But the tone of her voice made it rather clear to John that his wife did not think in this particular instance that he knew best.

Not at all.

Chapter 32

The Third Day: Wednesday

Cora knew that she was dreaming for the third night in a row, but she also knew that this dream was substantially different from any of the others she had ever known.

First, this place was not her grandmother's kitchen. Not anyone's kitchen, for that matter. There was a dusky darkness full of shadows and tiny slivers of light coming apparently from low lamps scattered around the room, although everything was still in shades of black and white and gray.

The air was thick with musty smells, blended together with two distinct smells Cora could not quite identify. An odd, sweet odor that made her stomach turn with queasiness, and another scent of something familiar and just beyond the edges of her memory.

Her eyes adjusted to the dream darkness as they would have if this had been a waking moment in a real place, and as she waited she began to see the room itself.

Walls of books on three of the four sides. From the smell, they were old and leathered. Floor-to-ceiling, well-dusted and yet she suspected, from their near-perfect condition and order, not well-read. She turned quickly and almost stumbled over the desk, massive and solid, a polished mahogany island in the center of the equally massive room. Pushed slightly back from the desk was an oversized leather chair, empty.

Cora could sense somehow that the room was only recently vacated by its owner and that she was alone. The heightening of her senses in her dreams was not unusual. The impressions she had from this unfamiliar room were oddly calming as well as confusing.

The dreams she had always came with a specific purpose. Some message she was meant to hear, some object she was meant to see, delivered by someone familiar but deceased.

Cora never sought the dreams, and they did not frighten her. Her most recent dreams bothered her only in the sense that she knew that they meant someone living was going to die. And that Charlie would be involved.

Her job was to interpret the messages as best she could.

But this dream was different from any of her previous experiences. She tried to remember a time when she had not met someone in the dream and couldn't think of any message that came without some sort of human explanation. An empty room was odd.

Without a guide to direct her thoughts, her eyes traveled back to the walls of books and she tried to see what it was about the books that she should notice. Moving closer to the wall on her right, she walked along the bookcases, carefully surveying the rows and rows of volumes. Their arrangement seemed to form groups and patterns, sets of similar bindings and sizes, as though some interior decorator had made decisions without regard to the content of the volumes themselves.

On the third wall on the left, as Cora ran her fingers systematically along the dust-free shelves, she noticed that one book was obviously missing from its place. A smallish book, third or fourth in the set it seemed, shelved almost eye level. Cora noted the titles of the rest of the books in that group, all familiar classics, and determined to write them in her journal as soon as she awoke.

Turning back to the desk, she half-expected to wake up, finding her mission accomplished, but found herself still standing in the room.

There must be something else, she thought. Her eyes had fully adapted to the dim light, and the fourth wall of the room had become clear. There were numerous paintings on that wall, mostly oil landscapes that seemed to be expensive, although they, like the books, seemed to be more set pieces for some stage play or window dressing than understood and appreciated.

Cora perceived that the person who owned the room did not mind that she was here. That he—she assumed this was a masculine room—would have come to greet her if he had been allowed to be here. She did not know how or why she had these feelings and instincts. She simply knew.

Oddly enough, the room did not appear to have windows, although in the corners where the walls connected there were elaborate floor-to-ceiling wall hangings whose patterns resembled medieval tapestries.

Still confused about what else she was supposed to be seeing, Cora's attention moved from the walls to the center of the space and the enormous desk.

To the right side, facing the desk, was a small cabinet flanked by two cushioned chairs. On the top of the cabinet she could see a square, half-filled crystal decanter and two thick, heavy-bottomed glasses filled to about an inch with a clear, amber liquid.

Cora picked up the glasses one a time and looked at them, searching for clues. The liquid inside was clearly alcohol. She inspected the rims for lipstick stains, but there were none, which was disappointing. Nothing interesting to add to her notes. But then she realized that neither glass appeared to have been drunk at all. Curious.

Why would someone pour a drink they did not intend to have, much less two drinks?

She walked over to the desk and sat down in the leather chair so she could see the entire room, and then she smelled the odor again. Almost sickly sweet. Not perfume exactly. Then she realized from her days investigating with Charlie that it was the smell of blood. Too much blood.

Suddenly horrified, Cora covered her mouth with her shaking hand and a small wave of nausea threatened to rise in her throat. She was sitting in Steve Wilton's study, at the desk where he had been murdered. She supposed she should have known from the beginning of the dream, although she had no real reason to know where she was. She had never been in Steve's study.

There was no sign of the killing itself, no sticky liquid that might have been blood on the chair, the carpet, or on her hands. No evidence of the brutal execution except for the compelling stench of death mixed with the odor of classic, leather-bound books, priceless oil paintings, Kentucky bourbon, and costly antiques.

She swallowed the feeling of revulsion and tried to clear her mind, trying to understand what she was supposed to see. Surely Charlie had seen everything she was seeing. Knew everything that she knew. Or felt as though she knew.

Fighting an instinctive desire to escape the chair, she leaned back in an attempt to see the room from Steve's perspective. Her eyes returned to the cabinet, and then the small oriental rug between the two side chairs. The rug was slightly crooked, as if someone had gotten up too quickly from one of the chairs and had pushed it accidentally awry.

More curious than revolted, she got up and went to the rug, kneeling down to adjust the edges. Once it was straightened, she wondered why it had been moved in the first place. Impulsively, she dropped to her knees and ran her hand across the inner edge of the rug and then further in, under the liquor cabinet table that stood between the chairs. Her fingers unexpectedly came upon an object, which she pulled out gingerly and studied for a moment.

A cell phone. Simple. Inexpensive. Small and hidden. *But not deliberately*, she thought. Somewhere that it did not belong. Perhaps it had fallen and dropped, then had been kicked so that it slid underneath the cabinet. Perhaps it was not there at all and just a figurative clue that she was meant to see. Something she was supposed to tell Charlie.

Cora picked up the cell phone and stood. As she did, the device began to quiver in her hand, without sound. Lifting the phone to her ear, she heard the line go dead, and smelled that scent again. The second one.

Cologne, she thought to herself. *No, aftershave. A man's aftershave. But whose?*

Cora was awake and staring at her ceiling.

It was 2:32 in the morning.

Chapter 33

Marjorie got up around six almost every morning. Whether it was habit or choice was open to conjecture. Marjorie insisted that the morning was the best part of the day. The earlier the better, she would say, before some foolish human got his hands on the beauty of what God had made and mucked it up.

Cora did not usually get up until seven or even eight. That is, unless something was wrong. Generally speaking, Cora could sleep unless she was having dreams. When Cora was having the dreams, sleeping at all was a luxury.

When Marjorie found Cora typing on the computer in her office at 5:45 a.m. for the third morning in a row, she knew that she needed to take some sort of action. Since Cora began having the dreams, she had shared the details of them with only three people: Thomas, once they were married; then Marjorie, over the past few years; and, most recently, Charlie. Charlie understood that the information Cora gave him solved impossible mysteries and brought criminals to justice. Thomas did not understand much of anything about the dreams but wanted to be included in Cora's life and to comfort her when they came.

Only Marjorie saw both the true value and the damage that the dreams caused to Cora's mind and soul as they dragged her into dark places she would not have chosen to go. When the worst times had come, Cora had found a faithful friend and devoted confidante in Marjorie, who had taught her to accept and to use what she saw.

Marjorie encouraged her not to be afraid of the gift. To love herself.

Although most of Balfour and the surrounding area had heard rumors and gossip that Cora had what they called "visions" from time to time and that she sometimes knew things that she simply could not have known, no one ever brought up the sensitive subject of her special abilities. Most locals chose simply to ignore the reclusive young woman who was known all over the state by reputation only.

Cora woke Charlie with a phone call in the early hours of Wednesday morning and gave him the details of the dream almost as soon as she had come downstairs, not because she wanted to talk to Charlie, but because she fervently hoped that what she saw, or thought she saw, would bring a quick end to his investigation.

Charlie dutifully took notes, adding them to the increasingly cryptic list, but unfortunately seemed almost as puzzled as she had been.

Some items he had in his notes already, the missing book

and the two glasses of hard liquor, although Cora's glass was minus the pink lipstick stain. The presence of a cell phone intrigued him, as well as the scent of man's aftershave, both of which he attributed to Steve. But, as Cora pointed out, who would Steve call on a cheap cell phone?

She also mentioned the recurring time, 2:32 a.m. Charlie confirmed it was almost certainly the time of death, although in the afternoon, according to the coroner.

The call was businesslike and brief, but talking about what she had seen to someone who might be able to solve the case, even Charlie, lifted a burden from her slender shoulders.

Thomas seldom asked for details about the dreams. Cora was willing to share because he was her husband and he was always supportive and kind, albeit bewildered. But Cora did not like to talk about what she saw to people who did not really understand, and Thomas did not really understand.

She especially disliked the notoriety, skepticism, and undue attention that came from the crimes that came with the dreams. She did not like the nosy reporters, the quackish pseudo psychologists, or the religious critics who had their pet theories to try to explain why the dreams came and what they meant.

The simple fact was that Cora did not know why she had visions, nor could she control them in any way. She had no theories, even of her own. The dreams simply were.

She simply was.

Marjorie refused to entertain random theories about what she called "Cora's special gift," or to talk to any of the curiosity seekers about the time she spent with Cora in her housekeeping work. Had Marjorie been a bit more religiously fanatic, she might have termed the process the gift of prophecy, but she never used that word.

Prophets, to Marjorie's mind, were never wrong. Sometimes what they saw took generations to come true. So it followed that no one could know for certain that a person was really a prophet until long after that person was gone on to Jesus.

Marjorie was much too practical to try to solve conundrums.

Of one thing Marjorie was certain this bright Wednesday morning: Cora had told her on Monday morning that there was a message in a dream for Andrew Evans. As far as Marjorie knew, no one had told him.

If these dreams were to come to an end, someone needed to get the preacher to come to talk to Cora. Today.

Marjorie was not a person who procrastinated what needed to be done, no matter how unpleasant the outcome might be, and to Marjorie's mind, the idea of meeting with Preacher Andrew Evans was most unpleasant.

Nevertheless, she was determined. She made a breakfast of buttermilk biscuits and crispy pork sausage, offered Solomon his customary treat, and cleaned up the kitchen. While Cora sent Thomas off to work, she helped Jane prepare for the day in another of the donated dresses from the Methodist Ladies Society, a lovely pink smocked cotton with matching leggings, and brushed back the shining black hair into a ponytail with a matching striped ribbon.

When she felt her morning duties were satisfactorily completed and Jane was fed and delivered to the playroom, Marjorie went upstairs to the guest bathroom that adjoined her weekday bedroom, showered, and dressed in her best pair of olive green slacks and a mosaic-patterned Sunday blouse with a lightweight beige cardigan. Wouldn't do to look like a domestic this morning. She inspected herself in the mirror. Preacher Evans might get the idea that Cora couldn't take care of herself if she wanted to, and the last thing Marjorie wanted for Cora was anyone's pity.

Especially pity from Andrew Evans.

When she returned to the door of the playroom, Jane was happily drawing more pictures. Cora's eyes met her friend's, and she tilted her head quizzically.

"Going somewhere this morning? Do we need groceries?"

Marjorie smiled grimly.

"You told me on Monday that Pastor James brought you a message."

Cora made a distinctly unfeminine growling sound.

"Marjorie, do you really think you're going to persuade a man like Andrew Evans to set foot in this house?"

The determined domestic hitched her heavy, shoulder-strap khaki canvas messenger bag over her right shoulder, which seemed to Cora almost like the action of a soldier slinging his knapsack onto his back before marching into battle.

Well, thought Cora as she noted the hard set of Marjorie's jaw, *judging by his reputation in Balfour, going to see this particular Baptist preacher would be much like going off to the Crusades.*

"I won't go if you don't want me to go," Marjorie offered insincerely.

"Oh, no. By all means." Cora reached out and smoothed Jane's already smooth dark hair and pulled the bow a little tighter. "You look as though you've already prepared the articles of war and planned your strategy."

Cora lifted her hand with a flourish and gave a mock salute.

"I wish you Godspeed, General."

It was Marjorie's turn to snort.

Chapter 34

Amy wanted nothing more than to help Katy, but she wasn't sure what practical things she could, or should, do. All the things that they did together—cooking and shopping, having their hair and nails done, visiting friends—these all seemed trivial and inappropriate at a time like this. Katy wasn't a little girl anymore.

Katy's attitude was reserved. Distant. Even sitting with little Elizabeth. Amy wondered if Katy was in shock, or if she could be experiencing side effects from the sedatives. Everything had become so complicated.

While Amy congratulated herself at first for sending for their Aunt Charlotte, she soon realized that she had seriously underestimated their aunt's extreme dislike for Steve, as well as her vocal hatred for the Senator. A dislike Dan shared. One tirade followed another. And another. Amy was sick of hearing about Steve Wilton and his numerous flaws, and tired of keeping Katy and Elizabeth in their self-imposed isolation away from the chaos.

Food from the neighbors and church family had been pouring into the downstairs kitchen, and Hannah had asked her sister from Griffith to come down and help her. The bulk of the food had been frozen, especially the cakes, pies, and casseroles. But between answering the condolence messages and media-seeking telephone calls, keeping the house well kept, and supervising the turning away of visitors and the curious at the door, both women were kept bustling from room to room.

Amy had made it clear that her only priority right now was her sister's well-being, and no one faulted her for that. Even, quite grudgingly, Dan.

Dan, when he wasn't sharing views with Aunt Charlotte, finally retreated to his office at work where he hoped to escape Amy's nagging about his attitude and his drinking habits. Even there his coworkers fell into two categories: those who could not stop talking about Steve, and so could not get any work done; and those who refused to talk about Steve, and by complaining about the people who were talking about Steve, still could not get any work done.

So Dan sent everyone who wasn't in the middle of a job at a worksite home until Thursday morning, took his telephone off the hook, turned off his cell phone, and locked himself in his office with a bottle of Jack Daniels. He had no intention of going home, at least until he was summoned.

Amy knew when she married Dan that he was a drinker. Sometimes more. Sometimes less. But Dan drank. He was, in his own right, an important and successful man. His construction business, initially inherited from his father and before that his grandfather, had become his own. He worked hard, as they had done. His drinking habits, unfortunately, were also part of the family inheritance. Or so Dan said.

The McInnises were Irishmen. They were builders. They were men of the earth. They were drinkers. They were quiet, simple, generally thoughtful drinkers. For the most part, their tempers were kept well in check when they were sober, and only occasionally evident when they weren't.

The original McInnis brothers, two of them, arrived from Ireland to help build the railroad that was supposed to run from Gainesville to Dahlonega in 1876. When the line stopped at the Chattahoochee River in 1878, the elder brother went West to seek his fortune in California, while Dan's great-grandfather met a local girl and settled down to construction of a different kind with North Georgia yellow pine.

In the early years of their marriage, Amy accepted the alcohol as a matter of course, a part of normal life and family gatherings. There was always beer. At company parties, especially the ones with all the holiday trimmings, there was hard liquor. With family spaghetti dinners, there was always wine.

She told herself that it was just an Irish stereotype. That once they had children, things would be different. But the years went by and there were no children and things were never different, although Amy refused to give up hope.

Dan pointed out bluntly that even her own strictly Baptist parents had always kept a medicinal fifth of whiskey containing a peppermint stick under the master bathroom sink, for emergency hot toddies to treat flu and pneumonia—an old Southern remedy. Her parents, when they were alive, had even served sparkling wine to the in-laws at Christmas dinners.

Amy tried to understand, but she really didn't.

Amy didn't like alcohol in any of its forms. She especially didn't like the change it had made in Dan over the years, into someone who was always moody and brooding. Isolating himself when they had problems instead of talking them out. Dan chose liquor. Amy chose total abstinence. Under any circumstances. So much so that many people suspected her behavior signaled a pregnancy. False alarms through the years and repeated painful denials had led to a simple acceptance that Amy did not drink, which seemed to drive Dan even further away.

The abstinence was a constant recrimination for his failure. For a time, Dan also resented Katy, who had never been a drinker either.

As Amy stood at the top of the stairs and thought about Katy, a light-headed feeling came over her for the third time that morning. She knew that she needed to tell Katy her news, but this wasn't the right time. She knew that she should tell Dan, but she didn't know quite how. After all these years, everything was about to change. She knew she should be glad, but it was so hard to be anything but somber in the midst of Katy's pain and confusion. She felt selfish that somehow she might overshadow Katy's time of grieving over Steve's death with what was now, for her at least, happy news.

Besides, there were other things to consider. Complicated things. Amy kept telling herself that they didn't have to be complicated. Not now. The problems that had been weighing on her heart had been lifted.

With increased resolution, Amy kept quiet and made her plans. There would be time for talking again. For happiness again. For Katy. For them all. Soon enough.

Chapter 35

Susan had temporarily abandoned her high hopes for redecorating the office. Life in Balfour had become both unpredictable and chaotic, and that did not suit her at all. Susan had left the stress of a high-powered Atlanta law firm for the peace and quiet of Balfour, and she enjoyed being a creature of country schedules and habits.

And time with Harry. Susan enjoyed time with Harry. Boring Harry.

When she unlocked the office door at eight thirty a.m. and arrived at work, the answering machine was blinking red and beeping obnoxiously, as if to contribute its voice to her growing irritation with the current state of her universe.

Her grandfather had always said that nothing good happens after midnight. Susan believed there were no good telephone messages before nine in the morning.

With pen and stenographer's book in hand, she listened as

the Senator's aide announced in a strident voice that he had
called on behalf of the Senator, insisting that Senator Stewart
Wilton wanted notarized copies of all the papers that had been
filed on behalf of his son Steve's estate concerning the derailed
divorce proceedings. He ended the message with some legal
mumbo jumbo about rights and properties and a flood of words
that Susan did not recognize but that sounded like political
doublespeak and a mild threat.

She wrote down nothing.

Susan turned off the answering machine with a little more
force than was absolutely necessary and proceeded to file her
nails for the next fifteen minutes.

When Thomas called to say he was running late, she told
him about the message. But the lawyer said that he needed to go
by the cleaners and run a few errands before he came to work,
and that under the circumstances, she was to be as helpful as she
could if Perkins or the Senator arrived before he did.

She might have been helpful too, if Perkins had not stormed
into the office at 8:58 a.m. making demands and attempting to
rummage on his own through the papers on her desk. Susan was
not feeling even a spoonful of Southern hospitality. She did not
like people who made demands. As a matter of fact, she was
feeling downright uncooperative. She also did not mind who
knew how she felt, including her boss.

Susan was mightily put out.

Perkins, for his part, was not accustomed to a subordinate
who did not rush to accommodate herself to the Senator's plans
and was especially peeved by Susan's effective stonewalling
procedures and insincere apologies. After twenty minutes of

listening to excuses about sluggish computers and jammed copy machines, he left empty-handed and muttering vile comments under his breath about backwoods Southern towns and barefoot, ignorant women. His expensive red rental car peeled out past Thomas's Honda, and they barely missed each other in the parking lot.

"Susan," Thomas began patiently, "what just happened?"

"Don't know. Don't care." Her fingers moved deftly over the keyboard without looking up. "He's an arrogant son of a sea serpent, and I don't have to give him papers that he is not supposed to have."

"Such language." Thomas was smiling. "What did he do?"

"Oh, more what he *didn't* do." Susan continued typing, as if the tip of each finger were driving tiny tacks into the keyboard. "He did not act like a decent human being. I am nobody's lackey around here, and I will not be treated like one."

"No, you are quite right."

Thomas put a plain white confectioners' box on the desk to her left.

Susan stopped typing.

"Is that a Bavarian cream donut from the new bakery?"

"Two."

Susan smiled.

"Well, okay then," she said. "I'm feeling better now."

"Excellent." Thomas poured himself a cup of freshly brewed coffee and headed into his office, hoping the bakery would know that he was not going to make a habit of buying fresh confections every day.

"Do you think I could have those papers the Senator

wanted before noon?"

Susan indelicately wiped away the creamy yellow donut filling from the corner of her mouth with the back of her hand.

"Of course, Boss," she mumbled, gratified. "No problem."

Chapter 36

Alice was a little surprised to see Marjorie waiting in the church parking lot when she got to Emmanuel Baptist at ten o'clock. Having worked late for the past two days, Virginia had graciously suggested that they come in an hour later today, and neither Alice nor Donna had protested. Both women were a bit fatigued with dealing with people in general, but Alice thought there was something pleasant about Marjorie. Although she attended regular services, she was not a frequent visitor to the church offices, and certainly not to this preacher.

Alice knew from previous experience that when Marjorie came bearing a problem in one hand, she generally had the solution in the other. As soon as the women recognized each other, and Marjorie saw that Alice was carrying several Tupperware containers, she got out of her own car to help carry the packages inside the church office.

Within minutes Donna arrived, and the three of them set

about to begin the morning rituals of coffee-making, housekeeping, and telephone message answering. Marjorie, in her own quiet manner, managed to be helpful and stay out of everyone's way at the same time.

Alice first adjusted the thermostat, then booted up the computer to check emails before going into the back room of the office to turn on the copier, an ancient but dependable model that required warming up before it would cooperate.

The blinds were opened and the plants watered, proper greetings and salutations given, and then the day began in earnest.

The principal debate in the office yesterday had been whether or not to print the program for the funeral on Sunday in-house or to send it to the off-site printer's office in Griffith, a more cosmopolitan company that offered professional services.

Emmanuel Baptist had never had an exceptionally large or sophisticated congregation, despite the size of the building and its recent renovations. The printing press they had had for the past thirty years and its faithful octogenarian operator had done quite nicely for Sunday bulletins, even with their frequent inserts proclaiming church socials, Vacation Bible Schools, women's studies, and mission trips and the like. No one complained about the quality of the printing. Well, not much.

The question was, exactly how different was the funeral on Sunday going to be from the normal services and announcements? Alice had insisted that the funeral home, which recommended the company in Griffith, knew the best place to print the order of services, but Donna disagreed. She argued that the church would have no control over the content or the final finished copy that way. Both women were eager to hear Marjorie's opinion, especially since the preacher's wife had steadfastly refused to take sides. No one, including the preacher, was going to ask the Senator the question, nor did they have any intention of bothering Katy with details.

Marjorie, sensing that her opinion was only a pawn to be used in a friendly game of one-upmanship, wisely refused to be drawn into the discussion and feigned deafness while she pretended to inspect the ancient silk fichus tree in the corner for dust.

Evans arrived promptly at ten thirty a.m. Because of evening services and choir practice, Wednesdays were his long days at the church. He and Virginia generally had a leisurely breakfast together, and he always arrived at the church office an hour or so later than his usual time.

From the moment he stepped in the door, it was obvious to both Alice and Donna that he was unhappy to see Marjorie. He didn't personally know much about the housekeeper, only what he had inadvertently gathered from the assorted congregational conversations he often overheard and tried not to acknowledge.

He had seen her sitting in the same pew every Sunday morning, generally by herself on the back-left side of the sanctuary. She took some sort of notes during the sermon, because she was almost always writing. She seldom picked up a hymnal to sing, but she seemed to know all the words by heart. She was never in the greeting line at the front of the church after the services, and he had made no effort to press himself upon her either.

What he did know about her for certain was that she was the live-in housekeeper for a different, perpetually absent church member—a child psychologist who had been described to him as "that mysterious local psychic woman." Virginia scolded him more than once for being so judgmental about two women that he had never met nor talked to in person, but he had little faith in the practice of psychology and even less in the so-called psychic abilities of the young woman, who apparently had something of a cult following in the town of Balfour.

Nevertheless, Andrew Evans paused in the doorway to his office and made a failed attempt to be pleasant.

"Good morning," he said through his teeth, in what looked more a snarl than a smile. "Did you want to see me this morning?"

Marjorie stood and adjusted the strap of her purse, smoothing her blouse down over her slacks with businesslike efficiency.

"Good morning, Preacher," she replied coolly. "Won't take but a few moments of your time, if you might spare them."

"Of course." He waited for Marjorie to pass him and then stepped inside, faced with a second unpleasantness. Whether or not he closed the door completely depended on several well-established rules of Southern Baptist etiquette, none of which he could remember at the moment. As the choices for what to do were running through his befuddled mind, Marjorie decided for him.

"No need to sit down or close the door," she said briskly. "I've come to give you a piece of advice."

He turned his full attention to her sharply. His astonishment was clear.

"Yes," she continued. "I know that we've never had so much as a simple conversation before, and I shouldn't expect you to take advice from a total stranger, but both Donna and Alice will be glad to tell you that you should."

Andrew sighed. He realized that he had been sighing a great deal lately.

"As my wise grandmother pointed out on more than one occasion," he began in his best preacher's intonation. "Listening to opposing views can be valuable. We seldom if ever learn anything new from our supporters."

"Oh, I don't know, Preacher." Marjorie gave him a genuine smile that said she too had a wise grandmother. "I would consider myself one of your supporters."

His eyebrows shot up. "Indeed?"

"Indeed. In the biblical sense, of course," she continued with undue seriousness. "You know, *he who is not against me is for me*. It's in Zedekiah somewhere."

Evans started to protest that she had misquoted the scriptures when he caught a flicker of teasing in her eyes and realized that she was bantering with him. Or maybe baiting him. He couldn't tell.

"All right, Miss . . ."

"Marjorie O'Quinn," she corrected, tugging her hefty purse further up on her broad shoulder. "But you can just call me Marjorie. You need to visit Cora. Soon."

Evans stiffened, adjusting his glasses up on the bridge of his nose.

"She can always come to church," he said, a little more

brusquely than he intended.

"Can she really?" Marjorie's voice was firm and mildly accusing. "You know her so well, do you?"

"I—"

"Pastor," she continued, interrupting him as if he had not spoken. "Nothing is ever clear through the fog of distance. Bet your grandmother used to say something like that too."

He knew she had a point, and that did not please him.

"What do you really want from me, Marjorie?"

"This afternoon. Two o'clock."

He thought for a moment and nodded his head slowly. He started to say he would check with his secretary, but that would be lying. Donna and Alice had made it clear yesterday that there was nothing on his calendar until after Sunday. The schedule been cleared because of the preparations for Steve's services, and even if there were any conflicts, he really couldn't refuse to go see someone who had asked for a pastoral visit in the middle of the week.

He also couldn't claim he didn't know where Cora lived. Everyone knew where Cora lived. Everyone.

Marjorie turned to go, but his questioning voice stopped her.

"I thought you came to give me a piece of advice," he said.

"Oh, that *was* my advice," she said, beginning to hum an old familiar hymn and readjusting her purse strap without turning. "This afternoon. Two o'clock. We'll see you then."

The preacher closed his office door behind her, but not before he thought he heard the faint sound of muffled laughter coming from his office staff.

Chapter 37

Cora was not looking forward to the preacher's visit. She wasn't at all sure what message she was supposed to give him from her dream and Brother James. In fact, she wasn't sure she knew what to say to him at all, about anything. Cora was fairly certain that there was no information she could give to Andrew Evans and that he wouldn't in any way be a receptive listener.

She had months ago formed an opinion of him based on the DVDs of the Sunday sermons that Marjorie brought home every Wednesday night from the midweek services. Seemed a bit odd to her that he would want DVDs made of the services every Sunday morning, as it had seemed odd to the board of deacons when Evans had first proposed the idea. The idea had struck everyone, including Marjorie and Cora, as some sort of ego on the part of their new leader.

But the rest of the preacher's behavior, however odd, didn't seem to validate the idea of self-important promotion. So when the preacher found a local college student majoring in communications who was willing to sit in the balcony and film every week for free, the congregation was willing to give the idea a try. While the process of videotaping distracted the choir for several weeks, they finally grew bored and stopped staring at the camera and went back to reading the words to the songs on the back projection screen.

Alice's husband, Andy—the chairman of the deacons who had also served on the Balfour Police Force at one time—had put it all into perspective when he said that at least the video records would keep the preacher on his toes.

"Anything the pastor says," Andy had announced to the deacons, "will be recorded as evidence against him if we ever decide that he needs to move on to another church."

Andy had said it with a smile and a country drawl, but the preacher was not at all sure that it was a joke.

For the most part, Cora was not impressed with Evans's presentation skills, although she could find no fault in his theology or his biblical knowledge. He made excellent points. His organization was easy to follow but too dry for her taste. His sense of humor, she often noted to Marjorie, was nowhere evident. Cora and Marjorie were equally suspicious of any man who did not know how to laugh, especially one who did not know how to laugh at himself.

The doorbell rang promptly at 1:45 p.m.

Early, thought Cora. *How interesting.*

Marjorie bustled to the front door, waving Cora affectionately back into the den, and reached the door with her customary musical greeting.

Evans, taken slightly aback by the sound of a single enthusiastic contralto rendering the chorus of "When the Roll is Called Up Yonder," took two quick steps back and almost fell over his own two feet.

Marjorie stifled a laugh. It seemed they were picking up right where they had left off this morning.

"Pastor," she began, "do come in. Cora is in the den. Right this way."

Evans followed the housekeeper down the wide hall, noting that the house seemed unusually cool and somewhat dark, blinds and curtains drawn, the light coming from low table lamps rather than ceiling fixtures. Built in a modern version of the traditional antebellum style, the hall was a breezeway of sorts that bisected the house into two distinct halves, a staircase leading up to a small balcony in the center and slightly to his left as he entered. Under the staircase was a door to the downstairs bathroom.

The room further to the left of the stairs appeared to be a music room with a small Baldwin console piano on the far wall, flanked by an elegant Victorian love seat on one side and two velvet-covered chairs on the other. On his right was what he supposed to be an old-fashioned sitting room with several small antique chairs and another loveseat, the walls tastefully decorated with floral wallpaper that, from its appearance, seemed to be original to the house.

That must be the waiting room for her patients, he thought.

As he walked, he also noted the polished hardwood floors with Persian carpets in vibrant colors. A few framed needlepoint pieces and simple watercolors of flowers decorated the walls, but there were no mirrors or family pictures.

The next room on the right was her office. The door was open when he passed, and he saw that the wall behind the desk was covered with an intricate, king-sized, pinwheel-patterned quilt in shades of blue, green, purple, and deep golden yellow. On the walls on either side of the quilt were floor-to-ceiling bookcases holding a library-sized quantity of books and file boxes. In the center of the room were several modern, comfortable-looking chairs along with an oversized leather sofa against the left wall.

The next door was also open when he passed. It was obviously a playroom. Evans knew Cora's patients were primarily children, so he assumed it was for their therapy playtimes. Those walls were lined with low shelves holding a pleasant but not overwhelming variety of containers with toys and books and art supplies. In the center was a children's wooden table and four small, brightly painted chairs.

When the hallway finally opened out into the large country kitchen at the back of the house, Evans could see that there was a fireplace and a small sunken den to his left, and off to his right was a sunroom with more child-sized garden furniture.

He felt growing respect for the woman he was about to meet for the first time. He believed that a house is often a true reflection of the character of its owner-inhabitant, and if Cora's house described her, the words were ones of Southern dignity, warmth, compassion, and beauty.

Cora was not what the preacher had expected. Not at all.

She stood when he came into the den. He could see that she was petite, almost childlike herself in size. Her long dark hair was pulled back into a ponytail at the back of her neck, and she was wearing an oversized man's shirt and flowing, soft slacks that almost covered her bare feet. She appeared to be wearing little or no makeup.

"Hello, Pastor Evans." She put out a small hand to shake his and confidently looked into his face. "Do you prefer to be called Pastor, Preacher, or Brother?"

"Or Andrew is fine," he said. "Whatever is comfortable for you."

She gave his hand a firm shake and waved him to the overstuffed chair beside hers.

"Then let's say Brother Evans." She smiled. "Sounds a bit more Baptist. Please sit down."

"And what should I call you?" he asked as he sat, noting that this room, like the others, resembled its owner. Warm. Colorful. Friendly. Honest.

"Cora," she said. "Everyone just calls me Cora."

For a moment there was an awkward pause, and the preacher realized to his embarrassment that he was staring at his hostess. He was surprised at himself. He had not anticipated this response. She seemed so normal. For another long moment, Cora returned his stare, and then she laughed. Her laugh was one of genuine acceptance and gentle humor.

"You aren't what I expected either, Brother Evans," she said, leaning back into her chair and pulling her feet underneath her.

"No?"

"No," she said, settling deeper into the cushioned chair. "You are much taller in person than you look on the sermon tapes."

Evans found himself laughing, a strangled sort of sound that unwillingly came from his throat and was suspended for only a moment before it escaped his mouth.

Cora's eyes sparkled with mischief.

"Everyone's uncomfortable the first time they meet me, Brother Evans," she reassured him mildly. "You'll get used to me if we become friends."

"I'm not quite sure," he managed through his embarrassment.

"That we will become friends?" she asked good naturedly.

"That I am going to get used to you," he countered.

Cora laughed, genuinely amused.

"Let me tell you why Marjorie believed that I needed to see you," she offered more quietly. "And then you can decide for yourself how we might proceed."

A moment later, Marjorie tiptoed in to deposit a plate of chocolate chip cookies, still warm, and a carafe of fresh coffee with two cups on the low wooden table between them, hoping not to disturb the conversation. As she had predicted to herself, within minutes the preacher and Cora were deep in sociable but serious talk, so she went back to her kitchen duties. All was going as she had expected.

Cora could charm the venom from a cottonmouth as easily as she could read the secrets of a broken child's heart. Only once had Marjorie known of anyone with secrets so deep and awful that even Cora could not discover them, and that was not a child. That was the one person of whom no one spoke, and the reason for the dreams that had so often revealed to Cora other people's secrets. The reason why Marjorie had come to this house in the beginning of their relationship.

Marjorie shook the negative thoughts from her head and decided it was time to check on Jane, who was found sleeping soundly with Solomon across the foot of her bed and Cat tucked securely in her arms. *Maybe this Sunday or the next Jane can attend services on Sunday with me. That would be good*, she thought. Satisfied, Marjorie came back down the stairs humming to herself a soothing "Jesus Loves the Little Children" and went back into the kitchen, casting a discreet eye at the den and the now rather congenial pair. They were still deep in conversation.

After several more minutes, Marjorie ventured into the den and retrieved the plate that had held the cookies. From the absence of crumbs on the plate, she surmised that the preacher had really liked the chocolate chip cookies. Not only that, but conversation with Cora as well.

With a satisfied shake of her head, Marjorie made a mental note to bake the preacher some of his very own cookies for the next church social.

Her list of baking gifts was growing, and nothing pleased Marjorie quite as much as that.

Chapter 38

Charlie had spent the better part of the morning catching up with Marcie in her quiet, homey kitchen at the Piney Woods. She had a few interesting and witty observations about Amanda Grayson, but nothing that he didn't already know. Still, time with Marcie was always well spent.

Besides, he owed her for taking care of Elvira, and she always fed the detective an outstanding breakfast of homemade Belgian waffles with apple cider syrup and thick slices of crispy Applewood bacon.

He went straight from Marcie's to the station, where he spent several hours at his desk doing paperwork and reviewing the evidence from the crime scene. Unlike many of the other police officers and detectives he knew, Charlie did not mind paperwork. The process helped him to think and organize his thoughts. The books he wrote were that way too. Organized. Methodical. Full of details and specifics.

When he stopped to consider whether he was hungry enough for lunch, he was surprised to find a third message from Cora on his cell phone. Apparently Marjorie was organizing a meeting with the preacher, and Cora thought he ought to know that she was not intentionally interfering with the investigation into Steve's death.

Charlie was not in a position to pass judgment. If Cora could talk the preacher into cooperating with the investigation, then that was good for everyone.

He called back and left a message that he would come by around four in the afternoon to see how the meeting went, and he hoped that was okay.

After that was settled, he wrote down the combined cryptic clues Cora had given him and compared them to the actual findings from Steve's study, looking for similarities and differences.

The afternoon was spent meticulously reorganizing his notes for the murder investigation so far, making speculations and doodling diagrams, and revisiting the notes that Cora had sent. The process gave him an appetite, and Charlie rose from his chair every hour or so to refill his coffee cup and select another pastry from the box that the dispatch lady so generously brought in every Wednesday.

Wednesday, which Charlie had always reserved for paperwork and pastries, was one of Charlie's favorite days of the week. In Balfour. In New Orleans. Wherever.

Dalton and Burton had been called out on an armed robbery down in Forsyth County, so the station was unusually quiet. The chief had his own share of paperwork and saw no reason to poke a stick at Charlie, especially since he appeared to be working so productively.

Perkins had called the front desk around noon, asking for Charlie and wanting a progress report on the investigation. Ben wisely intercepted, and Charlie didn't know about the call.

"I'm the chief, and I'm in charge," he had said to Perkins. "Everything that is possible is being done, period."

But Perkins had more questions. And then more questions.

Ben went back over his responses in his mind, growing more and more annoyed at having to answer to anyone's assistant.

"No, the case isn't going cold. . . . No, we don't need any outside help. . . . No, we haven't found a murder weapon. . . . No, we have no viable suspects yet."

When it became clear that Perkins was just getting started, the chief had resorted to a more straightforward dismissal of the aggressive aide.

"I have nothing else to say on the subject. Please feel free to call back later. Much later. Make that much, much later."

At three thirty, when Charlie began clearing his desk and was putting on his sports jacket, Ben cautiously ventured out into the bullpen.

"On your way home, Charlie?"

Charlie threw his foam coffee cup into the trash. Ben smiled at the familiar sight. Charlie did not have the patience for washing china cups and mugs the way other people did. Not when disposable made his life easier.

"Going to see Cora," he said briskly.

"Got it." Ben nodded. "Keep me up-to-date."

"Will do." Charlie gave a crisp mock salute.

He was gone before Ben could think of anything else to say.

Marjorie was waiting at the door when Charlie arrived promptly at four o'clock. She knew he would be much more businesslike than when he had brought Jane and that he wouldn't waste time. Cora didn't see him in person unless it was an absolute necessity, so Marjorie ushered the detective into Cora's office immediately.

Cora was sitting on her side of the desk, her original notes in her journal in front of her. She sat with hands folded and her elbows tucked comfortably at her side. She always typed her journal notes because Charlie sometimes asked for a hard copy to take with him so he could look over them later, and these were neatly printed and placed in a manila envelope on her right.

Charlie sat in a chair directly opposite Cora. His pocket notebook sat open on the desk, and, as usual, it was full of questions. Charlie wrote one question per page, leaving room on the sheet for any answers Cora could supply. Sometimes there were several answers. Sometimes there were none at all—just bits and pieces of information that he added on additional pages of his notebook until everything fell together.

They began. The sight of them always reminded Marjorie of two intense competitors hunched over a single jigsaw puzzle with thousands of pieces and no picture to guide them.

As usual, Cora spoke first.

"The third dream wasn't in the kitchen. I was in Steve's office."

Her voice was calm and dispassionate. Charlie's eyebrows rose as he began to write.

"That's new."

"The small book is important," she said, ignoring his concern. "A missing book that belongs to a set."

"I noticed a missing book from a set. Green. With gold on the spine."

"I can't see the colors," she reminded him. "The other books in the set are classics. *Jane Eyre. Ethan Frome. The Scarlet Letter.*"

He looked up from his notes. Those were the titles he had written down himself.

"The common theme is adultery," she said bluntly.

"Well, Steve was never a faithful husband, Cora."

Cora closed her eyes for a moment to concentrate and then looked at her notes.

"There were two glasses on a table with a decanter."

"Yes. Steve may have poured drinks for someone he was expecting on Monday. A woman who could have killed him." Charlie flipped through his own notes, warming to his theory. "Maybe they were having an affair."

"Why would you think there was a woman?"

"Because of the lipstick."

"No." Cora frowned, shaking her head. "I didn't see any lipstick. Just two glasses that didn't appear to have been touched."

"There were two glasses, but I saw lipstick, Cora."

"I don't think you are looking for a woman," she said flatly. "I think there is a woman in the story, and she might have the answers you want. But whoever she is, she didn't kill Steve. You need to talk to the preacher."

Charlie paused and looked at her.

"I already talked to Andrew Evans, Cora. He says he doesn't know anything. I know he's hiding something, but there's no evidence he murdered Steve in cold blood."

"He didn't," Cora said confidently. "But you should talk to him again anyway. I think he's protecting someone."

Charlie made a notation.

"No clue who that person is?"

She shook her head.

"There was a cell phone call in the dream," she said. "Do you have a way of checking on that?"

"Not really," he admitted. "Not without an actual cell phone."

"Maybe you should look again."

He nodded. No reason not to follow every clue since there were so few.

"Okay, so what else have I missed? Men's aftershave?"

"I know that I've smelled the scent somewhere, Charlie."

He put down the pen.

"Well, that limits our suspects, doesn't it? When you don't leave the house, how would you have recognized a man's aftershave unless he came here?"

"I don't know." She was beginning to look frustrated. "You need to talk to Andrew Evans again. Soon." She paused and leaned back from the desk. "You might even catch him before he goes home for the day."

"You're awfully insistent. What do you know that I don't know?"

"Not so much."

"Cora—"

"I understand the rules," she said, putting up a hand to stop him from continuing. "I didn't discuss the case with him. I just invited him over for coffee and cookies and we just talked. That's all."

"I know what happens when people 'just talk' to you, Cora. It isn't always pretty."

She didn't react. He didn't really expect a reaction, so he returned his attention to his notebook.

"Okay, tell me about the cell phone then."

"Under the table with the drinking glasses and the square decanter."

Charlie made another note, then flipped the notebook shut and tucked the pen away in his jacket pocket.

"I'll go look for the cell phone myself," he said. "Right after I talk to the preacher and before I go home for the night."

That finished their business, but Charlie made no effort to stand. He wanted to keep talking. He wanted to say that he knew that this was difficult for her, that he knew she was drained and sad. Personal things. Things he had no right to say anymore.

From the corner of his eye he could see that Thomas was home and standing more or less patiently in the open doorway to the office, a worried frown on his face. In one arm he was carrying Jane, who had one tiny arm of her own around his neck and the other clutching the stuffed cat that Charlie had given her only three days ago.

Three days. Seems like weeks, he thought.

Charlie saw that Thomas had a cup of coffee in his free hand, which he held out to Cora.

Charlie knew that he needed to go. Marjorie was waiting by the front door, and neither of them spoke when he turned a moment to look back at what appeared to be a happy family of three in the hallway.

Cora smiled up at Thomas with a look Charlie recognized, one she might have had for him had circumstances been different. His thoughts drifted back to the first time he saw her, and for a moment he was caught in a web of memories.

No, he stopped himself firmly. *No. That was a different time, and we were different people. I will not regret letting her go. I am a better man for loving her, and she has a better life now. If she can handle these damned dreams and work with me, the least I can do is keep up my end of the bargain.*

Charlie watched, satisfied with his decision, as the trio turned and went into the kitchen. He ran a hand through his hair and turned to Marjorie, who was still standing patiently at the front door.

Cora had given him the clues, and it was his job to do the legwork. That was as it should be.

As he went down the front steps, he could hear the housekeeper close and lock the door securely behind him. Then he got into his car and called Emmanuel Baptist Church to tell the preacher to meet him at the police station. Again.

Chapter 39

The preacher had not been enthusiastic about Charlie's call, although he couldn't say that he had not expected to be summoned again after his conversation with Cora. Charlie met him at the front desk, in an attempt to minimize any discussion with the officer on desk duty about why the minister was there for a return engagement, and escorted the pastor straight to a holding room farther down toward the end of the hallway and not yet affected by the paint fumes and construction.

Almost as soon as the door closed behind them, the preacher went on the offensive.

"I've told you everything I know about Steve Wilton's death," he said firmly.

"Perhaps you have." Charlie motioned the other man toward a chair and took out his notebook. "But right now, I'm more interested in his life. The last six weeks of his life, specifically."

Evans looked away, studying the blank wall of the room with what he hoped would appear to be indifference.

"What made you think that Steve would listen to anything you had to say to him?"

"He called me," Evans began. "We've been over this before."

"Right." Charlie sat on the corner of the table, placed strategically in the center of the room and flanked by two gray metal office chairs. "But maybe you didn't go there to talk. Maybe you went there for something else."

The color rose in Evans's neck, racing upward to his temples, and he continued to stare at the wall without speaking.

"You went on behalf of a woman. A young woman," Charlie said easily, looking down at his notes and deciding to risk a guess. "A woman with whom Steve had been having an affair."

Evans's face was flushed almost crimson red.

"What did Cora tell you?"

"Nothing, Preacher. She told me nothing I didn't already know."

The preacher looked sheepishly at the table. He hadn't told Cora about a young woman. How did this detective know?

"The woman couldn't go to see Steve," Charlie continued his speculation. "She couldn't go because no one else knew about the affair. Because she's a local and the news of the affair would ruin them both."

Charlie watched the reaction on Evans's face, much like a carnivore would study a small, trapped animal of prey before the kill. Another idea came to him.

"No," Charlie corrected himself. "Steve Wilton never cared about anyone's reputation before now, not even his own. This woman had to be someone special. Someone who was still important to him."

Evans looked around slowly, as though searching for a way of escape that was not there.

"Are you going to tell me who she is, or do we keep waltzing?" Charlie knew he was close to the answer he wanted, but he also knew not to push too hard. "I thought Baptists weren't much for dancing."

Evans squirmed in the chair and put his head into his hands, leaning heavily forward onto the table.

"I cannot say anything," he said brokenly, pulling a handkerchief from his pocket and mopping his face. "I just cannot tell you anything."

"Okay," Charlie rubbed his chin. "Let me help. Steve decided to call off his divorce, and he called to see you. He asked for counseling from Cora, so it wasn't counsel he needed from you. He wanted something besides a sympathetic ear. He wanted you to do something for him."

Charlie stopped for a moment to see what effect his words were having.

"Katy had put up with a lot," Charlie continued. "Most of the people in Balfour think she put up with too much. Did you think she put up with too much, Preacher?"

"I would rather be the confessor than the judge," he said sadly. "But if you're asking me how I felt about Steve Wilton, the truth is that I didn't like him."

"Is that the whole truth?"

"No," Evans admitted. "The whole truth is that he wanted me to act as an intermediary. I told him that I wouldn't."

"How does that make you feel, now that he's dead?"

Evans turned his face away.

"I feel guilty," he said flatly.

"Then help me find out who killed him." Charlie leaned in, his voice low. "Confession is good for the soul, or so I've been told."

Evans continued to stare without speaking.

"No one in here, Preacher," he said. "No one at all. Just you and me and Jesus."

Evans shook his head. "Are you going to arrest me?"

Charlie sat up straight and shrugged.

"Not sure I can," he admitted. "You didn't kill Steve."

"So I can go?"

Charlie sighed and shrugged his shoulders. He was close.

"Don't know what to do with you, Preacher. Yet."

Evans walked to the door and had put his hand on the knob to open it when he slowly turned and looked Charlie in the face for the first time.

"She didn't kill Steve," he said bluntly. "I know she didn't."

"No such thing as a sure thing, Preacher," Charlie said, putting away his notebook and standing up to follow him out. "We can talk again tomorrow."

Chapter 40

The Senator was not pleased with Amanda Grayson or with his aide-de-camp. He was also not pleased that there was no decent place in Balfour to eat after four o'clock on a weekday. Sam's was open for early breakfast and lunch six days a week, but only for dinner on Friday and Saturday nights, and then only until nine o'clock. Sam did not pretend to be what she was not, and she refused to overextend herself or Bill, the cook, just because other eateries could not compete either with her food or her service.

As a result, the Senator and his two reluctant dinner guests had to be driven about thirty-five miles away to Griffith, the next town up and north into the mountains along Highway 52, to have an evening meal and resume their discussion from the airport.

After some heated conversation between the poor local driver and the Senator about the various choices for eating establishments, the driver pulled into the newly paved parking lot of a quiet, clean-looking Italian restaurant.

Amanda's eyes brightened at the wine list the waiter offered but dimmed quickly when the Senator waved the page away, reached for the dinner menu instead, and ordered unsweetened iced tea with lemons for everyone at the table.

Perkins shook his head. *She should do better research on her clients,* he thought critically. *Everyone knows the Senator doesn't drink. Does she think her appearance makes up for a lack of research?*

She excused herself quickly to go to the ladies' room, and Perkins caught a whiff of her perfume as she brushed past him.

Enough is enough, he said to himself. *She knows just how to get under a man's skin.*

He stabbed at the lemon wedge with his fork and fished it out of his glass, dropping it onto the tablecloth with some annoyance. The Senator had placed himself strategically between them at the table, leaving the aide and the lawyer, when she returned, with nowhere to look except at him or at each other.

At this moment, neither choice was palatable to Perkins. He chose instead to clank his long-handled teaspoon against the sides of the glass, swirling the ice cubes until they sloshed over the side and the Senator gave him a stern look.

I wish the food would get here, he thought. *I don't know what game she's playing, but I have a distinct feeling that I am going to lose no matter what I do.*

After the veto of alcohol, everyone followed the Senator's rather forceful lead and ordered the house special, chicken parmesan with garlic toast. When a fresh Italian salad garnished with local produce had been delivered promptly to the table, the Senator picked up a fork and attacked the lettuce and the female lawyer simultaneously.

"So, Miss Grayson," he began between mouthfuls of crunchy chewing. "What exactly happened with my son?"

"I don't know," she began, looking down at her own salad and deciding she was not particularly hungry. Her mind drifted to the delicious salad she had eaten at lunch, and from there her anger flared toward the Senator's assistant sitting across from her.

"Wrong answer." Wilton took another mouthful and continued to talk as he chewed. "Was he or was he not going through with the divorce?"

"I don't think he was."

"Why?"

The question was pointed. Explosive.

"That's what I don't know," she admitted. Then, a bit sarcastically, she added, "I'm not a marriage counselor or a mind reader."

"Don't be sharp with me, young woman."

The Senator's fork clinked loudly against the plate as he continued to stab his lettuce and chase the grape tomatoes and cucumbers to skewer them.

"I'm telling you what happened," she countered coolly. "The papers were in order when I left him at his office on Friday. He was ready to sign and move on. Something must have happened over the weekend."

"That much is obvious," Perkins interjected, fixing his eyes on hers for a moment and then looking away. "Did you see him over the weekend?"

Amanda looked at him to see if he too was being sarcastic, then continued with a more subdued attitude, finally taking up her fork and balancing it between her fingers. She ignored Perkins's insinuation that her relationship with Steve Wilton was less than professional.

"Steve seemed calm at first, when we first arrived at the courthouse," she continued, randomly picking at her salad as she spoke. "Then he became more agitated when his wife and her sister came in with their lawyer."

"Do you think he had been drinking?" the Senator asked, his voice more sad than disgusted at the thought.

"No, he was completely sober. He just seemed . . ."

She struggled for a moment with the right words.

"He seemed determined. Determined and a little angry, but the anger didn't seem to be directed at a person."

"What does *that* mean?" Perkins interrupted again.

"That he just seemed angry with himself." Amanda shrugged.

"That doesn't make any sense," Perkins admonished her. He began picking randomly at his own salad.

The Senator laid down his fork and studied the lawyer's face, searching for answers. "What else did he say?"

"He asked that other lawyer . . ."

"Thomas," the Senator supplied impatiently. "I know Thomas."

"Steve asked Thomas to make an appointment for him. Something about his wife."

"Do you mean that Steve wanted to talk to Thomas's wife?

Cora? About what?"

Amanda was losing her patience, but she kept her voice low. She hated being grilled like a suspect.

"How should I know? I didn't know your son, and I know even less about these small town country bumpkins and their personal problems."

She stopped and looked at the Senator's face, momentarily regretting her lack of restraint and poor judgment. He had just lost his only son. He looked elderly and worn. Tired and old and grieving. His shoulders slumped. His eyes red and bloodshot behind his glasses. She leaned forward with what she hoped looked like empathy.

"Senator," she began with a much softer tone. "Your son said he wanted his wife and daughter back. He must have had a change of heart. He said that he wanted counseling. He seemed pretty insistent that the only person he wanted to talk to was this lawyer's wife."

"Did Thomas—did Thomas agree to call Cora?"

"He seemed angry. He said that Steve would have to make his own call."

She paused and took a sip of the tea and made a face. "That's when the judge told him to go home for a week and think about it."

"That's Candler, all right. Not the first time he has had to deal with Steve and his shenanigans." The Senator put down his fork, his voice drifting off into silence and deep thoughts. Perkins and the lawyer exchanged uncomfortable, uneasy glances as they poked absently at their food and waited for him to speak again.

"So that is really all you know?" he said finally.

Amanda met the Senator's eyes.

"Yes," she said, hoping she sounded honest. "That is all I know."

The waitress brought out the main course and placed the steaming platters on the table. The Senator picked up his fork again.

"Then finish your salad, young woman," he said, making it clear that the interrogation was over for the time being and there was to be no more conversation. "I don't have any more questions. We'll have our dinner in peace and then Perkins can see to it that you get back to your hotel room for the night."

Chapter 41

Charlie wasn't surprised that the yellow-orange crime scene tape had been doubled when it was replaced, crisscrossing the front door, nor was he surprised to find that one of the uniformed patrol officers was standing guard duty by the main entrance to Steve Wilton's house. The Senator had made it plain that if the county didn't want to pay for someone to be there from the department, he would pay for an off-duty officer himself to make certain the scene was not disturbed, at least for the rest of the week. Longer, if necessary, to preserve the crime scene until they could find his son's killer.

Something about the way he said it made Charlie think that no one would ever live in the house again. Neither Katy nor Elizabeth certainly, and the Senator had long since taken up more or less permanent residence in Washington, D.C. There was no one else in the family to take it over.

Charlie let his thoughts rest on the possibility of this

beautiful home never being lived in again. In a small town like Balfour, gossip travels at light speed, and not even a newcomer would want to live in a house with the jaded history of this one. *It's a little sad*, he thought. *This really is a magnificent mansion.*

Charlie recognized the same young police officer from Monday, when he had come to the house before. Charlie suspected that the man was working as an off-duty guard to make a little extra money, since police pay wasn't exceptionally good. The young man was leaning informally against the outside front doorframe looking tired, a glazed look in his eyes.

"Smith, wasn't it?" Charlie announced cheerfully, watching as the man jumped slightly and rubbed his eyes, snapping to attention.

"Yes, sir," he stammered. "I'm awake."

"Of course you are." Charlie patted him on the shoulder fraternally. "You didn't go for your gun. Wide awake, if you ask me."

"Detective?"

"Never mind. Just taking another quick look around." Charlie folded his arms across his chest. "If you could just let me in, I won't be a minute."

"Yes, sir," Smith managed through a stifled yawn, digging in his pockets for the elusive keys. "Right away, sir."

"Thanks." Charlie patted the young man's shoulder again. Poor kid. Charlie remembered these first years and the drudge work all too well himself.

When Smith finally produced the keys, Charlie stepped back to allow the other man to open the door, and then he went inside.

The cool air and sweet, noxious smell rushed out of the foyer as he entered. Deciding against using his trusty handkerchief, he took a moment instead to pull on a pair of blue neoprene gloves as the door closed quickly behind him. He did not really know how much searching he was going to have to do for this alleged cell phone.

There was only dim sunlight from the ornate glass panel in the door, making a sharp, diamond-shaped pattern of multiple colors on the marble floor. The house seemed dark even though it was only a little after seven o'clock and the sun would not set until around eight thirty. Charlie pulled out his small LED flashlight and clicked it on.

Hopefully this won't take long, he thought. Cora was either correct and the cell phone was a literal clue that he would find right where she said it would be, or she was correct and the cell phone was symbolic and not a literal clue.

Either way, Cora had been proven right in too many instances not to check out anything she thought was significant.

Charlie avoided the massive desk, walked straight to the short, chunky table with the glasses and decanter, and dropped to his knees, waving the beam of the flashlight in short, efficient semicircles across the floor against the expensive carpet.

At first there was nothing. But Charlie persisted, more slowly now, and then he put the flashlight down and slipped his gloved hand under the table, pressing his fingers into the legs where the wood formed hidden corners. There at the front leg of the table, tucked against the left side, he felt it. A smallish rectangle of black. What Cora had seen in her dream.

A cell phone.

Charlie cautiously pulled the prize out with one hand, flicked open an evidence bag with the other, and dropped the cell phone inside. From the looks of the phone, it was a cheap throwaway, certainly not one of those fancy new smartphones that Steve would own.

Furthermore, since they had found Steve's cell phone in his pocket, whose phone could this be? Did that person know it was missing? How did it get here?

Charlie looked at his watch. Seven thirty. That hadn't taken long. He could think best at the station, without distractions. Besides, he wanted the case dusted for prints as soon as possible, and he would have to drop that off at the station.

He also supposed, with a tinge of regret, that Elvira would just have to wait a little longer for her supper tonight. Unless, of course, he could persuade Marcie to take the hound a snack until he was able to get home.

Charlie dismissed the idea of bothering Marcie. She would have more questions that he was in the mood to answer. He was feeling a little more than satisfied with the progress the investigation was making.

Charlie clicked off the flashlight and tucked the evidence bag into his inside jacket pocket. He would just run by the station first and talk to the night officer and dispatch. And wait to check to see if the prints on the cell phone matched anyone in the database.

He could be back at the apartment before eleven, with any luck. Plenty of time then to open a can of chili to share and make it worth Elvira's while to have waited for him. Maybe even give her a can of her own, heated up in the microwave and perhaps topped with a little extra shredded sharp cheddar.

Charlie was feeling especially generous.

Chapter 42

The Fourth Day: Thursday

Cora's first feeling was the cold. Icy. The air almost crackling with static electricity. The smell was familiar, but no words came to her mind to describe how she felt. There was no doubt that she was in her grandmother's kitchen again, but this was different in a way that both dismayed and depressed her.

She was facing the sink, staring at the narrow wooden shelves just to the left of the window. Outside the window was dark, a deep winter kind of darkness. Cora's attention was drawn to the shelves. There was something odd about one shelf in particular, so she forced herself to concentrate on the objects on the center shelf. There was a thimble she recognized as her great-grandmother's on the far left. Then, in the center, were the three tiny dollhouse-sized pitchers that had been there since Cora was a young girl.

One of the miniature pitchers was more a jug that had been carved from some sort of shell, maybe walnut or pecan, and a little chunky. The second tiny pitcher was made of delicate, lightly tinted glass and only about two thumbnails tall. The last and largest, reaching almost an inch and a half high, was an elegant copy of a fluted Victorian vase with a curved handle, the body of the tiny object decorated with a bouquet of flowers. Beside the trio on the right, Cora saw a ring, lying as though someone had been doing the dishes and had taken it off for safekeeping on the shelf.

She was certain she had never seen that ring in the dream before and knew without a doubt that it had never before been on the shelf over the sink. The platinum band was small, inlaid with tiny stones that sparkled on the rough wooden surface of the shelf as though the gems were winking their eyes at her.

Cora picked it up and slipped it onto her own left ring finger. *Size five or so*, she guessed. The band fit her ring finger almost perfectly.

As she looked at her hand, she knew that she had seen the ring before somewhere else. In the real world. She closed her eyes, trying to remember. Trying to picture where she had seen it, an image came to her. A woman's slender hand with modest, well-manicured fingers and a baby's hand nestled inside the palm of the first. The baby's fingers pressed against the ring, which was lying in the palm of the woman's hand.

Then Cora, shocked, realized that she was seeing the stones of the ring in color. Sapphires. Emeralds. Rubies. Cora opened her eyes and focused quickly on the room. No. Everything else was still black and white and shades of gray. The only objects with color were the stones in the ring.

So, this is the dream and yet not the dream, she thought.

Another night of firsts.

Cora shivered as much from the cold as from the apprehension, afraid to turn and yet afraid not to turn and look at the rest of the room. She took off the ring and placed it carefully back on the shelf, then turned her head slightly to the left.

There was a cup she did not recognize, although it was set in the usual warming place in the center of the gas stove, between the burners. The copper kettle was already heated on the front left burner, waiting for someone to pour the steaming water into the drip coffee maker. A small wicker basket of tea bags sat on the counter to the right.

Tea? Cora questioned.

The sweet smell of herbal apples and cinnamon rose from the basket. The cup was cold to the touch, not warm like it should have been from being on the stovetop. She turned the cup over in her hands but did not recognize it at all. It was more a mug than a cup. Heavy, handmade pottery. Cora realized instinctively that she should begin with that mug. She dropped two of the tea bags into the bottom and added the gurgling, rapidly boiling water within an inch of the lip of the mug. Picking up a spoon, she turned to face the table and almost dropped the mug on the linoleum floor.

There—seated at the table in a dark, tailored Italian suit, a collarless silk shirt, and a thick gold chain around his neck—was Steve Wilton. He appeared to have been watching her with a sense of curiosity, as if he too had been taken aback by his presence in her dream.

Opening his mouth to speak, he paused, following her

hands with his eyes as she placed the mug before him with trembling fingers. She held out the spoon, but he looked instead at his own hands. He seemed bewildered, as if he had forgotten how to use them.

"Honey for your tea?" she managed in a soft, strangled voice.

"Cora?" he responded slowly. "Where am I?"

She pulled out the chair next to him and sat down, shivering in the bitter cold air.

"Don't you know?"

He inspected the suit he was wearing. He felt the lapel, his fingers drifting down one side and then the other across his chest, lingering on the gold serpentine chain for a moment, before lifting his hand to his right temple.

"I wanted to talk to you," he said slowly. "I needed to talk to you."

"You told Thomas," she encouraged him.

"I tried to call." He seemed puzzled at his own words. "There was no answer."

Overwhelming guilt surged from the pit of her stomach and rose in Cora's throat. She urged the steaming cup toward him.

"Have some tea, Steve. It's cold in here."

He frowned at the mug.

"I don't drink tea, Cora." His eyes searched her face. "I have never drunk tea." He pushed the mug back gracelessly toward her. "Did you find the ring?"

Cora did not know what to say. The dream was becoming more and more knotted as it progressed. Questions pushed and shoved against each other for first place in her mind as she desperately tried to understand what she was supposed to ask Steve. She knew from her experience that this time in the dream—her time to discover the clues—was evaporating as rapidly as the steam still rising from the mug.

"Steve, do you remember what you wanted to tell me?"

"Tell you?" Wilton was still looking at the cup of tea with increasing interest.

"You called me. Do you remember why you called me?"

He frowned. "Didn't I leave a message?"

Cora leaned back against the security of the wooden chair. *How can I know something that even Steve seems not to know?* She wrapped her stiff, cold fingers around the rejected mug for a moment, taking in the warmth. Then, involuntarily, her hand reached out to his with sudden regret and remorse. Her eyes filled with as yet unshed tears.

"Steve," she whispered. "I'm sorry I didn't listen to the message. I deleted it."

A single tear escaped and cascaded down her cheek, followed by another. Gripping his one hand in her two, she pressed forward.

"Please try to tell me what I need to know."

His face was still almost blank, but his eyes were focused on the mug of apple cinnamon tea. Peaceful now, and without pain or feeling. His lips tried to move, but there was no sound. He looked down at her hands gripping his and a tremulous smile curled at the corners of his handsome mouth.

"Thank you," Steve mouthed silently. The tiny smile from his lips ran up his serene, chiseled face to the corners of his eyes. "You can tell them that I'm sorry. Both of them. Just that I am sorry."

"Steve? Tell who? Katy and Elizabeth?"

He didn't seem to hear her.

"Thank you for the tea too," he added.

And in a flash of brilliant, multi-colored lights, Cora knew both who wore the multi-colored platinum ring and who always drank apple cinnamon tea.

It was 2:32 in the morning, and Cora was awake. She knew she needed to call Charlie, and once more she didn't think she could wait until the sunrise.

Chapter 43

Perkins could hear the shallow breathing somewhere in the center of his chest and feel the weight of a tousled head and the softness of a slender hand on his skin. The smell of musky perfume, dark and heavy, was on the pillow they shared and on the sheets tangled around and under them.

Perkins did not even have the excuse of alcohol to justify his present problematic circumstances, and he cursed himself under his breath for this unforeseen weakness.

Amanda Grayson had not charmed him with flattery. He was too savvy for those tactics. She had not used feminine wiles and deception. His own tricks of manipulation and clever lies, he had presumed, had hardened him to any lure that might cause him to compromise his position with the Senator.

Perkins had succumbed to the most basic instinct of any man—the desire to be the hero. The need to be the Prince Charming to a damsel in distress.

Amanda, the ambitious, power-hungry, professional lawyer, had ended the evening broken, cowering in the corner of the rented limousine while the Senator had looked coldly out the window. His silence was a mocking reprimand of her performance, and his indifference had stripped away the veneer of her limited successes in the courtroom. Senator Stewart Wilton was going to destroy her life. Publicly. He had said as much himself.

She had been reduced to what she really was, an innocent in wolves' clothing. Perkins had expected nothing less than a full-fledged inquisition by the Senator, whose ruthlessness was legendary. He had also expected a much different response from this latest verbal victim. She seemed so cold.

Perkins's sympathy was not immediate. In the initial stages of the conversation over the first course of salad, he almost enjoyed watching the cat and mouse chase.

Amanda Grayson shouldn't play with the big boys if she can't handle the consequences of her failures and shortcomings, he thought. *She deserves to be chastised and castigated to the full extent of the Senator's justifiable wrath.*

Then, reluctantly, he began to admire her stoic attitude, her silent, slightly deferential smile as Wilton continued his attack. A wounded lioness defending herself against a pack of vengeful hyenas.

Well, Perkins admitted grimly to himself, *only one vengeful hyena and one forced observer.* Perkins tried to tell himself that the Senator had been provoked by the circumstances of his son's death. That he had felt betrayed by incompetence.

Moment after moment of frigid silence seemed to push the

young lawyer farther and farther back into the corner of the expensive leather seat. He watched as her face moved from defiance to brittle confidence to her own frosty silence.

From that silence, Perkins could only imagine what she must be thinking and feeling. What he himself would fear in a similar situation. Fear for the loss of reputation, for the futility of future plans. His stomach began to churn as he considered that with one slip, he might find himself in her shoes.

The Senator had ended the night with a promise that echoed in her ears as she got out of the car—that she would never practice law again in Georgia.

The driver had put Perkins out at his own much smaller, though still ostentatious, red rental car, parked in the lower driveway of the home where he and the Senator were staying. The Senator barked a terse command for his aide to make certain that the young woman was securely in her apartment before he left her, and the Senator growled yet another order at the hapless limousine driver and then stormed into the house.

No one could accuse the Senator of lacking in Southern chivalry. Perkins was aware, however, that the Senator's primary motive for having his aide-de-camp take the lawyer home was to avoid being the last person to be seen with his son's incompetent lawyer should further questions arise.

It was a question of reputation to protect. The Senator's, of course.

Perkins initially felt no chivalry whatsoever. His duty was clearly to the Senator, and he accepted his responsibility with a relatively emotionless attitude.

The ride to the Piney Woods was also taken in frozen

silence.

When they arrived, Perkins, who always took his instructions literally, turned off the ignition completely and walked around to open her car door. Gripping her elbow with practicality and firm guidance, he virtually pulled her from the car and refused to let go until she had led him up the outer staircase to her second floor apartment.

Upon reaching her door, Amanda opened her purse to remove her key and began to fumble awkwardly with the lock. Perkins impatiently took the key from her shaky hand and easily slipped the key firmly in the deadbolt, listening for the click.

So close to the security and privacy of her room, Amanda's self-control was gone. She slumped wordlessly against the door and began to sob. Soul-wrenching sobs of despair and surrender.

What happened next surprised Perkins. Amanda moved into his arms and lifted her face to his, her tears salty against his mouth. His mind was drowning, and he knew that he was about to do something against all logic and rational thought.

That was the last logical or rational thought he had until Thursday morning when he woke up in Amanda's temporary Piney Woods apartment. At this moment, all he seemed to have were the rational thoughts he should have had the night before. His impulse for flight overcame his revulsion for his behavior and what might have been an urge to wake her and say something.

Perkins knew that there was nothing to say that would not include his own recrimination.

He looked at his watch. A little after four thirty in the morning.

Pragmatically he knew that he must deal with his mistake. On a deeper level, he knew that he should prepare to deal with the potential problems this single indiscretion might cause to his reputation, not to mention his job. The Senator would probably dismiss him on the spot, and that would prevent him from making new connections and transitioning to what he hoped would be his new position with another administration.

Amanda stirred and, as if she could sense his disgust, rolled away from him, gripping the edge of the sheet closer as she turned, tucking it under her chin.

Perkins rose and dressed efficiently, folding his silk tie carefully and placing it into his jacket pocket. He checked the pockets of his pants for his wallet and the small set of keys he carried and then swung the jacket over his shoulder before picking up his shoes, moving deliberately to the door.

He opened the outer door and closed it softly behind him. For a moment he considered stopping to put on his shoes, but Perkins was in a hurry to get back through the pre-dawn darkness to the emotional safety of his room. *Where you should have been all night long*, he rebuked himself sharply.

Twenty-five minutes later he arrived at the side kitchen door of the secluded antebellum home where he and the Senator were staying. Mercifully for Perkins's peace of mind, the house showed no signs of life. The housekeeper and the cook were both still sleeping soundly in their respective rooms at the opposite end of the house. He used his guest key to open the door and, still carrying his shoes, he tiptoed up to his bedroom.

The Senator had spent a sleepless night sitting in an armchair by the bedroom window of his guest suite overlooking the moonlit front circular driveway. He saw the headlights of the red rental car and heard his aide-de-camp's stealthy steps as he returned to the guest room across the upstairs hallway.

He did not bother to confront his aide or even to wonder too deeply where his employee had been until after five o'clock in the morning. He didn't want the burden of knowing for certain. Not until sunrise, at least. Maybe not even then.

A midnight call had confirmed what he suspected.

Right now, Stewart Wilton was in abundant supply of people he couldn't trust, and he had added his aide-de-camp to that ever-increasing list.

The only question on his mind was who else was going to be added to that inventory of individuals by the time he had discovered the name of the person who had killed his son.

Chapter 44

Thomas put the refilled kettle back on the burner and turned up the flame again. Outside there was still darkness, the darkest of the early morning after the moon set and just before the dawn, and the house was chilled with the briskness of the impending autumn air.

Cora sat at the kitchen table, wrapped in the warmth of her deep blue chenille robe and matching fuzzy socks. Thomas thought she looked like a sleepy child, cradling her cup of coffee like a favorite stuffed animal. Her eyes, however, were not those of a child. They were tearful and full of hurt he could not reach or understand.

Thomas had gotten up about an hour after Cora, concerned and guilty for sleeping when she could not. He had never seen his wife quite so concerned about the dreams. At least, not since they first began. He had a momentary desire to call Charlie himself, but thought better of his impulse. *Some ideas*, he admonished himself, *are best considered in the full light of day.*

Thomas did not know that Cora had already called Charlie, rousing him from an uneasy slumber just after three o'clock. She was, she told him when she woke him, absolutely certain about the owner of the ring. She also knew without a doubt that the same woman who wore the ring also drank apple cinnamon tea. But what *that* meant, she could not say.

She left out the part about feeling sorry for Steve. She didn't know how she felt about that, and it certainly did not seem like a clue that should concern Charlie.

Before her on the tiled tabletop lay the dream journal that Cora kept in her nightstand drawer. She was holding the pen between her fingers, twirling it and rereading all the minutiae she had managed to remember when she woke. More than two and a half pages of random, scribbled notes that now needed to be typed into some legible form.

"You should go back to bed, Thomas," she admonished her husband softly. "You have to go to work tomorrow."

Thomas turned from his coffee-making to sit on the stool beside her, taking the pen from her hands and then taking both her small hands in his.

"Not tonight," he said gently. "Tonight, we are a team. Let me be a little selfish."

Cora leaned over and affectionately rubbed her soft face against the rough stubble of his unshaven chin.

"There is still no reason for you to be up too."

"I know," he said.

Behind them there was the sound of padding feet down the hallway. In a moment, Marjorie appeared, followed closely by a tiny Jane in sleepy tow.

"Good morning," Thomas said, managing a cheerfulness he did not feel and releasing Cora's hands. He indicated the presence of the little girl with a quizzical expression.

"Not just yet it isn't a good morning," countered Marjorie, lifting the child to the stool on the other side of Cora's and smoothing back the child's silky, dark hair. "Is the water still hot?"

Thomas nodded.

Marjorie moved to the cabinets and took down two cups, an oversized flowered one and a much smaller child-size blue cup, decorated with a hand-painted basket of fluffy kittens.

Cora studied Jane's face with both maternal and professional concern, but Marjorie seemed nonplussed, and the little girl did not seem to have been crying, so she put away her questions for later in the day. No point in suffocating Jane with unfounded fears and projecting her own uneasiness and worries on anyone else.

In a moment, a hymn-humming Marjorie returned to the island counter, placing the child's cup before the little girl.

"Sip slowly," she cautioned. "Don't begin until the marshmallow melts."

Jane nodded, her eyes squinting slightly as they adjusted to the bright kitchen lights. She reached out cautiously to lay claim to her cup of hot chocolate and inch it toward her. When she had staked out her territory, she put her pajama-covered elbows on the tabletop and propped her chin on her hands, staring down at the steaming chocolate to wait for the bobbing white lump to dissolve. Her dark, almond-shaped eyes inspected the kittens on the side of the cup with innocent wonder.

"Trouble sleeping?" Cora's question was directed at Marjorie rather than the girl. Marjorie nodded her head suggestively toward Jane, collecting her own cup of chamomile tea and joining the group seated around the island.

"Cat is missing," the housekeeper offered, taking her seat next to Jane. "Perhaps a certain other feline may have taken him on a little midnight expedition."

"Ah," Cora said sagely. "So much like Solomon. Looking for a friend, I suppose."

Jane seemed to be completely oblivious to the conversation, much more concerned with her beverage than her missing feline.

"Now?" she asked, rubbing the tips of her fingers over the felines as if she were petting them. "May I drink now?"

Marjorie touched the side of the cup to check the temperature and studied the dissolving cloudy puddle of white.

"Just go slowly," she agreed, watching carefully as Jane lifted the cup and took a tentative sip, white marshmallow film coating her upper lip.

Thomas smiled at the three of them together, glad he had chosen to get up. A yawn overwhelmed his face, stretching out his chin and jaw, and he made a long, low noise of exhaustion. Jane jumped slightly, momentarily startled by the sound, and then quickly covered her mouth.

He turned to her and made a silly face, sticking out his tongue slightly and rolling his eyes. A slow smile began in her eyes and stopped just short of the pink corners of her lips.

"Well then." He stood, satisfied with himself. "I suppose I

should shower and shave to begin the day. Good morning or no good morning, there is work to do."

Cora reached out for him as he passed behind her and pressed his hand in hers.

"You're a good man, Thomas."

"And you are my heart, Cora."

There was a low, interjecting yowl at the doorway. Solomon stood in the opening, his green-yellow eyes blinking in the bright artificial light of the kitchen, the red-ribboned neck of Cat held firmly between his teeth as he pulled the black, furry, bedraggled body across the floor toward the food dish.

Chapter 45

Marcie Jones distrusted the lawyer from Atlanta. Not that she had been a really difficult tenant, certainly not like some in recent memory. Marcie was certain that the uppity woman would never walk off with the Wal-Mart linens or the Fred's Bargain Store dishes in the kitchenette, but all the same, there was something about that woman that bothered her. Marcie Jones just did not have a high estimation of Amanda Grayson as a human being.

Her sister Darcie had said that the whole situation was Marcie's fault. That there were logical discrepancies to be expected between the sorts of people who chose to stay in the two totally different types of establishments that the sisters owned.

Darcie insisted that the more refined traveler preferred a bed and breakfast in the center of a historic town over rustic apartments rented by the week or month on the outskirts of civilization between the railroad tracks and a state highway.

While neither sister had updated her property to include a swimming pool, mainly due to the overwhelming cost of various legal liabilities, Darcie had splurged last year and had the local plumber install a six-man hot tub on the reinforced back deck of her converted antebellum mansion.

Marcie insisted that it was an anachronism to attach a modern convenience to what amounted to a historic restoration, to which Darcie responded that her sister did not know the meaning of the word "anachronism." Since neither sister owned a dictionary, at that point they both agreed to disagree and dropped the subject.

Marcie's distrustful nature, coupled with her chronic insomnia and penchant for early rising, was exactly how she was able to catch a glimpse of a well-dressed man leaving Amanda's apartment just before dawn that morning.

Oh, he thinks he's a clever one, Marcie thought to herself, peeking through her bedroom drapes. She had chosen her own apartment years ago because of its strategic, panoramic view of both staircases leading down from the upper apartments.

Marcie knew what went on at the Piney Woods. She considered it her business, her God-given duty, to know. She even wrote things down and kept a notebook of comings and goings, her own included. She had learned that from Charlie. Pay attention. Take notes.

Charlie's tutorage is about to pay dividends, Marcie thought, paying careful attention to the surreptitious stranger exiting Amanda's apartment.

Carrying his shoes too, silly man! Marcie almost laughed out loud. The new construction on the set of apartments behind hers, the ones whose staircases were visible from her back bedroom window, had left both of the parking lots littered with pieces of debris and demolition. Nails and screws, lots of them. Broken pieces of glass from the old windows. Splinters too.

He'll have a nail or something equally nasty in his foot in no time, she decided quite unsympathetically. *He'll learn for himself. Sneaking around in the dark is never a good idea.*

The thought of people sneaking around in the dark and up to no good conjured more thoughts of Charlie. Marcie yawned and tightened the sash on her yellow terrycloth bathrobe.

Best tenant she had ever had, Charlie was, and the only one her sister had ever envied. She had seen Charlie spending time and talking to that lawyer lady too, but his apartment was on the bedroom window side and Charlie was always obvious about his conversations and companionship and such. She might be a tempting one, but Charlie would never have indiscretions at the Piney Woods.

Not Charlie. Not ever.

Besides, Marcie knew quite well for an absolute fact that the only female company Charlie ever entertained in his apartment was his dog, Elvira. Detective Charlie Abbott might indeed have his infamous escapades at all hours of the day and night, but when he was in Balfour, he came home at night to Elvira.

It wasn't as though Charlie didn't have his own special way with women either. Marcie, along with most of the other women Charlie knew in Balfour, liked to tease him about dating and such. He had been known to fancy about town with many a pretty woman on his arm. Visiting beauties and models who seemed much more interested in Charlie than Charlie was in them.

But anyone who knew anything in Balfour knew that Charlie had been married to Cora, and that now the only thing Charlie was married to was his work. And Elvira.

Most times now when he was out of town, Marcie offered to dog-sit Elvira. Marcie, who insisted she did not even like dogs, had almost immediately fallen in puppy love with the friendly, oversized plot hound.

"Elvira is a guard dog," she would say to anyone who questioned her policy that did not allow animals in the Piney Woods Apartments. "Elvira is a service animal and an asset to the complex."

In Marcie's opinion, Elvira was better behaved than the vast majority of her tenants, both regular and occasional.

Elvira was the reason why Marcie Jones was not the only person who knew that Perkins had spent the night with Amanda Grayson in her apartment. She was also not the only person who took notes on his departure.

In another apartment across the way from Marcie's window, Elvira's large, damp nose had awakened Charlie, nuzzling insistently under his chin until the man opened one eye to stare into the pleading, brown dog eyes.

He had already been awakened once by Cora's three o'clock call, and now he considered sleepily that he might have made an error in judgment by sharing the last of his chili supper with a dog who suffered from questionable digestion.

Charlie struggled out of bed to give Elvira a moment of outside time. When she stopped in the open doorway and showed no interest in leaving the apartment, Charlie was understandably puzzled.

At least, he was puzzled until he heard the sound of a car's engine on the other side of the complex. Elvira backed inside obediently as Charlie closed the door and went over to his front window overlooking the parking lot. Marcie had insisted that the Balfour City Council pay for installing multiple halogen security lights in that same parking lot. The bargain had been a battle, but like most, Marcie had won.

One or two residents had complained about the brightness, but Marcie ignored them, saying that she expected gratitude not griping because she was looking out for their safety.

Those lights, coupled with the slow, calculated speed of his departure, made Perkins's face clearly visible from Charlie's front window. Elvira's ears twitched at her master's long, low whistle of surprise.

"Fancy that," Charlie said aloud, reaching down to scratch behind the dog's droopy ears in apology. "Going to put you on the payroll, Elvira. You've earned a paycheck today."

Elvira yawned and propped herself against his leg.

"You're right about that too." Charlie returned the yawn and scratched his own shaggy head. "Too early to be up yet. Not much we can do until morning."

Elvira understood exactly what he meant and did not hesitate.

Within minutes, both man and beast were once more stretched out on Charlie's king-size mattress, although which one was snoring more deeply was difficult to tell.

Chapter 46

Andrew Evans had begun to have some speculations of his own about who murdered Steve, thanks to his conversation with Cora, and less thankfully, his interrogations with Charlie. Talking to Cora had given him a perspective he had not anticipated. He had found her to be intelligent, engaging, warm, and honest, which was exactly what he told his wife over their customary breakfast of multigrain toast and poached eggs around seven thirty that morning.

"Ginny," he said, watching her face carefully for some affirmation. "She seems like such a normal person. What have you heard about Cora Stone?"

His wife smiled.

"Just what you've told me." She got up from the table to pour her husband another cup of coffee, but he politely waved her away. "The women at the church think she is wonderful. The work she does. The way she has handled her life. They would never say so out loud, you know. Cora does stir up the controversy."

He tilted his head skeptically. "She doesn't leave her house, you know."

Virginia shrugged. "And I have heard people say, Donna in particular, that Cora does more good from her own home than most people do from their offices and traveling about in the world. Donna says if Baptists did that sort of thing, then Cora would be first in the line for sainthood."

"Ginny . . ."

"Andy, you know better than to ask me if you don't want an honest answer."

Andrew gave his wife one of his signature sighs that said that he was finished with the subject at hand and ready to move on. She changed the subject for him.

"Have you finished the notes for the service on Sunday?"

The preacher drained the last swallow from his coffee cup and got up to take it to the sink, along with his half-empty plate. She followed him and stood beside him, looking out the kitchen window for a moment at the early morning sunlight coming through the pine trees outside.

"I don't honestly know if I'm finished with the sermon or not," he said quietly. "I thought I knew what I wanted to say, but every time I read what I have written, I want to change it."

"That's not like you."

He nodded slowly, taking his wife lightly by the shoulders and turning her toward him. For a long moment he looked down at her sweet, familiar face. He kissed her on the forehead.

"I love you very much," he said simply. "I'm so thankful for you."

She blushed slightly and pressed her face against the starched white front of his shirt, studying the pattern of his tie. His overt affection was surprising.

"I love you too, Andy," she whispered in return.

He hugged her closer to him and rested his chin on the top of her head.

"Everyone else loves you too, you know," his voice was slightly teasing. "You do know you're the only reason that they put up with me—because they all love you."

She patted his chest chidingly.

"Now, Andrew Evans. Stop that."

"You're not the only one who hears what people say." He gave her another hug and let her go. Then he had a sudden thought.

"Ginny, do the women in my office have any thoughts about who might have murdered Steve Wilton?"

She looked puzzled for a moment, then frowned.

"I don't think so. They are just certain that it cannot be Katy. If there is a second saint in Balfour, then it's Katy Wilton. But then, from what I hear, no one in that family has had an easy time of it."

"What do you mean?"

"Katy and Amy's parents died when they were teenagers, I think. Amy married Dan when she graduated from college. People say he was a logical choice, but that Amy really didn't have other options. Donna says that Dan drinks. A lot. Years later, Katy married Steve against everyone's better judgment."

She stopped talking and went back to washing the dishes.

"Go on," he prodded.

"Are you asking me to gossip? Haven't you heard enough?"

"Not yet," he said simply.

"Well, all right, then," Virginia said, a bit flustered. Her husband was full of surprises this morning. "When Elizabeth was born, they say things were better for a little while for Katy, and everyone thought that Steve might just settle down, but then he went back to his wandering ways. Alice says the Senator told Steve that he couldn't go on acting irresponsibly and he needed to start living like a married man. So about six weeks ago, Steve announced that he wanted a divorce."

"Not Katy?"

Virginia smiled. "She's a saint, remember? Long-suffering and patient."

She paused to rinse the cup in her hand and dry it carefully with a hand towel.

"Anyway," Virginia continued, "rumor has it that things were going badly at that same time for Amy. Word was that she wanted to adopt a baby, but that Dan wouldn't hear it. Said he would have his own or none at all."

"But the sisters get along well with each other?"

"I suppose they do," Virginia said, almost without thinking. "Though I think there is something like a ten-year difference in their ages, and Alice says that Amy has always been jealous of Katy."

She closed her lips firmly, putting her hands on her hips.

"Andrew Evans!" Her tone was like a school teacher scolding an unruly second grade classroom. "I cannot tell you how uncomfortable I am standing here in our kitchen reciting gossip to you as though I have any idea whether or not I'm telling you the truth."

"Thank you, Ginny," he said, laughing softly and giving his wife a quick peck on each one of her blushing cheeks in turn.

"Whatever for?"

Andrew laughed again.

"For being yourself," he said. "I'll call you from the church later. Can we have lunch, maybe?"

"I could bring something by your office around noon," she offered, still mildly concerned with his behavior. "We have leftovers from last night."

"Leftovers would be great," he said sincerely. "I would like that very much."

Chapter 47

Charlie had been sitting at his desk at the station for almost an hour pondering the three o'clock call from Cora and the unexplained and rather interesting relationship between Perkins and the lawyer lady. Those pieces of information, combined with the resulting prints on the cellphone, had not really made the situation much clearer than it had been on Wednesday. Maybe less clear.

He had stopped by Sam's for an early bird bacon biscuit to go, and she had refused his money and insisted that he take a carryout cup of coffee too. A large one.

Unfortunately for Sam, her ploy didn't work, and he refused to let slip any insider information about the investigation, despite her delicious attempt at bribery.

Charlie's mind was racing with all sorts of theories. Cora had given him a woman's name. Perkins the aide was making time with Grayson the lady lawyer. The preacher had a secret about a woman that he could not share. Steve had asked to see both Cora and the preacher.

Charlie brushed the crumbs of his breakfast from his open notepad and began to write, focusing on his previous notes and flipping between pages, lost in his racing thoughts.

Because of his concentration, it took Charlie several minutes to realize that the rookie Smith had come into the main office area and was standing politely in front of the detective's desk, waiting patiently to be acknowledged.

Charlie, perturbed at being disturbed, ignored him for several moments until he realized that Smith was holding the evidence bag containing the cell phone from Wilton's study.

"Yes?"

Smith stood his ground despite the growled greeting.

"Did you want this in the evidence room, or did you need to see it again?"

"Fingerprints are Steve Wilton's," Charlie said. "No one else's. That's not news anymore."

Charlie continued to doodle without looking up.

"Did you want something else, Smith?"

"Tech was able to get something off the phone," Smith continued hopefully. "You asked them to check on that, and they did. There was one number."

He had Charlie's attention now.

"And? Spit it out, Smith."

Smith held out the bag, and Charlie could see that it also contained a torn yellow strip of paper from a legal pad with a series of ten numbers. The detective leaned forward, his body taunt with anticipation and optimism.

"I told them down in forensics not to bother with checking," Smith offered helpfully. "I told them that you would want to do that yourself, sir."

"Sir?" The detective mock exploded, enjoying himself too much at the rookie's expense. There was no better feeling than making real progress in a case. "Sir? Do I look like your *father,* Smith?"

Charlie eagerly snatched the bag from the young man's clammy hands as the rookie stumbled back for a moment before regaining his composure.

"No," Smith said, stuttering. "No, sir—no, Detective."

"That's right," Charlie snapped cheerfully. He was beginning to like Smith. He had some backbone, and initiative too. Charlie looked more closely at the telephone number through the thick bag, holding it gingerly in one hand while he quickly flipped through his notebook. Between the scribblings, he found what he was looking for and smiled.

Cora was right. Again. The theory was taking shape.

Now he had telephone calls to make, questions to ask, and legwork to do.

Charlie stuffed his notebook into his pocket as he shoved back his chair and stood, startling Smith, who was frozen in place several feet away.

"Smith," he barked as he removed his badge and service revolver from his desk, throwing his jacket over his shoulder as he headed for the door. "Good work. Thanks."

Charlie had announced his approval loudly enough to turn heads at the other desks and cause the chief to come to the door of his office and look out.

In the moment before Smith found his voice, his mind did a dozen double takes.

"You're welcome," he finally managed to say at the detective's rapidly departing back. "Anytime I can help!" he added.

Charlie, however, had bounded down the concrete steps into the parking lot, his cell phone pressed against his ear, listening intently to the ringing on the other end of the line.

For the first time in his brief career with the Balfour Police Department, Jim Smith understood why everyone had warned him about Charlie. Charlie didn't seem to care about anything but the case. Jim had never been so talked down to, so bossed around, so snapped at in his entire life. His high school football coaches had never spoken to him the way Charlie Abbott ordered him around. Even they managed a grudging compliment when he flattened the opposing quarterback. But not Charlie.

I just gave him a key piece of evidence, and what happens? More yelling, he thought. *Or is that his way of bantering?*

The rookie shook his head. *Nevermind. I'm hooked.*

He didn't fully understand what had just happened, but he knew one thing. That was the most invigorating thing that had happened to him in his whole life. Jim Smith wanted more.

Chapter 48

Amanda Grayson woke up embarrassed and ashamed, feeling foolish and furious with herself for her stupidity. Mercifully, in the morning light, there was no sign of the Senator's diabolical aide-de-camp. His stealthy retreat told Amanda what she needed to know—that Perkins had planned the entire episode last night, and that there was some wicked agenda that would surely culminate in the termination of her employment with Grumbald and Lattimer.

The Senator would deny her fees for services. Her expense reports would be refused. She would be blackballed and shunned.

Her chances for promotion. Her opportunities for advancement. All gone with one brief indiscretion.

How dare they? she thought, swinging her shapely legs over the side of the bed, her anger and indignation building. *Who do they think they are?*

With the energy that comes from an artesian spring of fury, she pulled on a pair of yoga pants and a T-shirt before dragging her half-filled suitcase from the bedroom closet and tossing it onto the chaotic bed.

She paused, slightly out of breath, and stomped to the refrigerator for an orange juice, which she downed quickly before returning to the work that she had begun just three days ago.

Cowboy detective, she thought. *I could have been out of this twilight zone if it hadn't been for his meddling.*

And he's not the only man, the rant continued in her head. *It's all of them. I don't care what they say anymore, I'm on my way back to Atlanta. I am an intelligent woman. I can get to Grumbald before the Senator even knows I've left town. She'll understand. She clawed her way up the good old boy network in the '70s. I can make her understand what happened. She'll be on my side. I know she will.*

With every suit she threw into the designer suitcase, with every Italian shoe she tossed, every carelessly crumpled silk blouse, her conviction of her own mistreatment at the hands of others grew.

She was on her way to the bathroom to retrieve her expansive collection of salon-quality hair and beauty products when there was a knock at the door. A hasty glance at the medicine cabinet mirror confirmed her worst fears—she looked horrible.

I look positively ghastly, she thought. *I look like a failed Halloween makeover.*

She surveyed the damage. Her thick, midnight black mascara had smeared diagonally down the sides of her cheeks into the hairline just above her ears like a dried river of coal soot. Her smoky eye shadow and matching eyeliner were smudged around her eyes like some demented, rabid raccoon. The twenty-four-hour lipstick had reached the end of its life span and had faded to the sick orange shade of rotting fruit.

There were no words at all to describe the hideous bird's nest that her hair had become. Disgusted with the sight of her own face, she held up the only obvious undamaged part of what had once been her fashionable appearance, her well-manicured hands, and waved them in mock surrender as she went to open the door.

Whatever, she thought to herself. *Things can't get any worse.*

Accustomed as she was to seeing tenants who were not at their best, Marcie Jones was still unable to prevent the tiny, high-pitched scream that escaped her lips at the sight of a disheveled Amanda Grayson. Covering her mouth quickly in an attempt to stifle her astonishment, Marcie's blue-gray curls began to bob up and down as she tried to find a respectful, dignified voice and self-control over her urge to cackle.

Amanda put her hands firmly on her slender hips and thrust out her elbows at her side defiantly.

"Did you want something?" she challenged, tossing her head. "I was packing."

Marcie held out the freshly printed invoice in her free left hand, swallowing hard to prevent the sounds of hysteria fighting to escape her mouth through the fingers of her other hand.

"I assume this is my bill?" Amanda continued haughtily, pretending to ignore the obnoxious noises coming from the shorter, portly, plain-country woman. "Should I also assume you are amused by my appearance?"

Marcie shook her head violently sideways, afraid to move her right hand.

"Well, that is just rich!" Amanda's anger overflowed, her eyes raking Marcie like a laser beam. "Rich, do you hear? And I suppose you don't ever look in a mirror, do you? Do you?"

Marcie continued to hold out the invoice, the trembling in her left hand infecting her arm and then the rest of her body as she began to vibrate visibly all over from the strain of contained laughter.

For a moment they stood there in the doorway, facing off, until, much to Marcie's relief, Amanda's cell phone began to ring demandingly from her purse on the sofa. The incensed lawyer coldly ripped the paper from the older woman's hand and slammed the door.

Finally, Marcie was able to remove her right hand and release a string of hysterical giggles.

"Do I look in a mirror?" the landlady questioned herself as her ample form, quivering in laughter, descended the staircase, her tennis-shoed feet paying particular attention to the bits and pieces of construction debris scattered across the concrete.

"Of course I look in a mirror," she answered herself between chuckles. "The difference is"—she continued the conversation as she reached the first floor—"I know what to expect when I look there."

Her response to her own cleverness sent Marcie into another fit of giggling.

In the distance she could hear the sounds of the heavy

machinery rolling up the road to begin their early morning work on the building and parking lot repairs.

Time to get back to work, she thought, deciding to call the construction company and insist that this unnecessary building mess be cleaned up immediately, if not sooner.

But maybe, she mused, *I will put on a little lip gloss first.*

Chapter 49

Susan answered the early morning call from Charlie just as she stepped out of her shower to dress for work, curious that he had not waited until the law office opened and had instead called her at home. She made careful but curious notes for Thomas, including Charlie's strident instruction that Thomas should call the judge as soon as he reached the office.

Susan stifled her curiosity and told herself she was better off not knowing what Charlie was up to, even if the plan involved her boss.

Charlie, for his part, had created a checklist and was satisfied that the pieces were already in motion. He knew he had to finish what he needed to do in the next two hours. He had already made what he considered the first two most difficult of his calls and was feeling rather satisfied with his progress so far. Two to go now.

Thomas didn't ask unnecessary questions when he arrived

at eight thirty and saw the look on Susan's face. Susan handed him the cryptic message from Charlie, and he headed directly into his office and dialed Judge Candler, asking politely if they could meet for breakfast at Sam's within the hour. When he returned Charlie's call, he got a busy signal.

Candler, never one to miss the opportunity for one of Bill's famous homemade buttermilk biscuits or the chance to hear Charlie expound on his conclusion to a mystery, agreed without discussion and set about to dress. Linda sensed an upward change in her husband's somber mood, but she did not ask questions, deciding instead to offer to lay out a starched white shirt, tailored suit, and one of his more conservative ties while he showered and shaved in order to cut his preparation time.

Thomas paused for only a moment after the busy signal from Charlie to call Cora. She too did not bother with unnecessary questions and agreed to call Katy immediately after she asked Marjorie to make her own designated call.

Across town, Evans had been at the church for well over an hour when Donna came to his office door and said that he was wanted on the telephone.

"Hello," he said, picking up his desk phone. "This is Andrew Evans."

Donna did not hide her curiosity about the unidentified caller, motioning instead for a reluctant Alice to join her in the doorway.

For a long minute the two women watched as the preacher listened without responding to the oddly familiar female voice at the other end of the line, his expression never changing.

He nodded briskly. "Of course," he agreed. "I'll be there

within the hour."

He stood and hung up the phone.

"I'll be back before lunch," he said, ignoring the women's blatant interest in what he considered his personal business and picking up his leather-bound Bible.

"What should I tell your wife?" Donna ventured hopefully.

"That I will be back before lunch," he repeated matter-of-factly, securing the Bible under his arm. "Ginny is bringing meatloaf and mashed potatoes with fresh green beans."

And without so much as a backward glance he was gone, which effectively forestalled any more questions from his inquisitive office staff.

At the Police Department, Chief Ben Taylor was not at all surprised when his desk telephone rang. Charlie gave him a quick overview of what was going on, what needed to be done, and when. Charlie specified that Burton and Dalton should casually arrive at Sam's around nine fifteen a.m.

"Not a minute before, please," Charlie instructed.

What did give Charlie's superior a surprise of sorts was that Charlie asked that the rookie Smith be included in the invitation, remaining in his uniform in a squad car just outside the building and around the corner behind the courthouse, out of sight. Ben folded his arms and leaned back into his oversized office chair, considering.

What in the world is going on with Charlie? he thought. Normally Charlie avoided any sort of situation that included less-experienced officers, especially a rookie. Even including Burton and Dalton in the situation, when no love had ever been lost between them and Charlie, was puzzling.

Almost immediately, the chief's curious mind wandered to much happier possibilities. With Smith going along, he decided, he could put in a personal request of his own.

As he called for the detectives and Smith to come into his office, he wondered how many of Bill's buttermilk biscuits it would take to feed every officer in the precinct, and whether there were enough funds in petty cash to cover the charges.

Chapter 50

Sam's was unusually quiet for a Thursday morning. Business almost always picked up just before the weekend. This morning Sam had received an unusual heads-up from Charlie, asking for extra bacon and biscuits.

Bill, usually known for his ability to accept any circumstance with stoic Choctaw Indian neutrality, raised his bushy black eyebrows and folded his arms in noncompliance. He did not dislike Charlie quite so much as he disliked taking directions from anyone, sometimes even reasonable requests from Sam.

Sam wasn't in the mood for such an early morning argument with her partner, chief cook, and bottlewasher. She left Bill's six-foot-six frame pouting in the kitchen and proceeded to the front to open the blinds and make the first pot of coffee.

While Sam was always willing to bring coffee refills to the table, many of the regular patrons appreciated an early morning self-serve area for sweet tea and coffee, set apart beside the cashier's counter. Sam liked the constant smell of fresh-brewed coffee in the air, especially in the early mornings, mingled with the various pastries and breads baking in the ovens.

Bill, who had his own culinary quirks, preferred to fry the thick slabs of bacon in the oven, which he insisted caused less mess, risk of burning, and spatter. He also insisted on local bacon in thick slabs, hickory cured. He placed these into the oven along with his personal recipe for buttermilk biscuits, declaring that each absorbed the aroma of the other as they cooked together.

The special finishing touch, although no one was supposed to know, was the final half-teaspoon of hot bacon grease ladled into the center of each biscuit just moments before the pan was placed on the countertop to cool slightly before serving.

No one argued with Bill about most subjects, but certainly never about his culinary skills or cooking techniques. Sam glanced furtively at the door to the kitchen, just as there began a violent clattering of pots and pans. She smiled. She knew Bill was cooking extra food, although he was going to make sure that Sam could hear his protestations.

Sam had no idea what Charlie wanted or what he had planned, but if she had been included in any covert plan, she was more than enthusiastic.

Bill's curiosity, while not as well-known as Sam's, was equally strong. Being included in one of Charlie's escapades was a first for both of them, and neither one wanted to jeopardize the possibility of losing a front row seat for the show.

Once the coffee had begun to brew and clean carafes were put in place, Sam filled the crystal sugar bowls, refilled the small china pitchers with sweet cream from the refrigerator, and nestled them into the beds of ice in the cut glass bowl near the percolators. The idea of prepackaged creamer was as unwelcome as instant coffee would have been, or those tacky paper packets of granulated sugar. Sam prided herself on doing things her grandfather's way. The old-fashioned way. The Southern way.

A sudden whiff of delicious cooking aromas came from the kitchen, and the subtle sound of sizzling and added smells told her that Bill had inserted ham and sausage into the menu for the morning.

Well, good for Bill, she thought. *He's getting with the program.*

Like Sam, Bill never did things by halves. That was, perhaps, why they made such good partners.

Chapter 51

Katy stared at her cell phone for several minutes, considering the conversation she had just finished, before she went to the door of her room and opened it for the first time in three days, then headed determinedly down the stairs to find her sister. She had already had a long, difficult, introspective talk with herself when she woke in the early hours of the morning, staring at the rising sun. She had decided that the time had come to stop hiding in her sister's guest bedroom and come out to face the world.

The early morning phone call from Cora had only confirmed her feelings and steeled her resolve.

She had missed too much of her life already. She missed going to church and seeing her friends. She missed Steve, and she had cried for him until the tears were only salt. But more than anything else, she had cried for the fact that Elizabeth would never really get to know her daddy. She knew above all that Steve loved Elizabeth and had hoped, perhaps beyond any rational thought, that Steve's last-minute desire to cancel the divorce might have meant a new life for all of them.

She had tried to get Steve to see a counselor once during the last year in a futile attempt to save her marriage. She felt almost guilty that she had not tried harder. But that opportunity was over now. She knew it would not be easy, but Steve was gone, and the time had come to try to move on.

Katy paused on the steps, still a bit unsteady from so many days of rest and medication. She looked down at the familiar foyer below and thought of her sister.

Poor Amy. Poor, unhappy Amy.

Hannah was dusting the antique formal dining room when Katy reached the arched doorway. The faithful housekeeper turned and beamed her greetings.

"Good morning, Katy!" She delivered a warm hug. "Can I get you something for breakfast?"

"Thank you, Hannah." Katy inhaled and prepared to clear the first hurdle. "I was hoping to go to Sam's for breakfast."

Hannah tried not to show her surprise.

"Sam's?" she countered. "I remember your mom and dad used to go to Sam's for breakfast every Saturday morning. Of course, those were the days when Sam was her grandfather's name, and everyone called that little girl Samantha. Why would you want to go to Sam's? Is there something wrong with my cooking?"

Katy shook her head, a slight, sad smile playing around her face.

"Sam isn't a little girl anymore," she scolded gently. "She

hasn't been a little girl in decades. Time changes things, Hannah."

Hannah shook her head disapprovingly. "You aren't going alone, are you?" Her voice was full of reproach and worry. "You should ask Amy and Dan to go with you."

"Go where?" Dan asked. "What are we talking about?"

Katy turned to face her sister and brother-in-law, both framed in the doorway. Dan looked as though he had slept in his clothes, and Amy didn't look much more rested.

"I'd like to go to Sam's," Katy said, almost cheerfully. "For breakfast."

"There's plenty of food here," Amy began, hesitating. "I'm sure that Hannah could—"

"Amy," her younger sister interrupted firmly, "I want to go to Sam's for breakfast."

"I was saying she shouldn't go alone," Hannah clucked with motherly concern. "Tell her she shouldn't go alone, Amy. Not after this week."

Amy looked up questioningly at Dan.

"Of course she shouldn't go alone," Dan muttered, trying to sound agreeable. "You go with her."

"Of course." Amy looked at her husband's face. She hoped she didn't look as nauseated as she felt. The thought of food made her queasy, but she knew there was nothing she could say to get out of leaving.

"But Sam's?" she countered hopefully. "What about donuts or pastries? We could pick those up and have Hannah make coffee here."

"No, dear." Katy moved to pass between her sister and

Dan. Over the second hurdle. "I'll just run up and get my keys and purse. I want to drive. We can pretend we're children again, and it's Saturday with Mom and Dad."

"Katy—"

Katy quickly kissed her sister's cheek and faced Dan, patting the front of his shirt with feigned sisterly affection. Cora's message was clear. Charlie knew who had murdered her husband, and if she wanted to know she should meet him at Sam's with Amy and Dan. The Senator would be there with his aide Perkins and the lawyer Grayson.

"And of course you're coming too, Dan."

Her brother-in-law gave her a silent, bloodshot stare.

"I'll be right back down after I promise to bring something special back for Elizabeth and Aunt Charlotte."

Third hurdle. Time to finish the race.

Chapter 52

A similar scene was being played out in the dining room where Perkins had been organizing papers, shuffling and reshuffling, since his secretive early morning return. He had showered and changed into clean slacks and a polo shirt, but the musky smell of the lawyer's perfume seemed to haunt him and hang about his face as though he had walked into a spider's web and could not remove the sticky threads. The odor irritated and goaded him.

When the elderly housekeeper appeared, she threw up her hands in frustration at what seemed to her a paper storm of confusion, insisting that the house must be made ready for the afternoon return of the home's owners. Perkins, already short-tempered from lack of sleep combined with what might have been guilt, snapped at her for her desire to dust and dally about the rooms and insisted instead that she should temporarily suspend her cleaning schedule for the duration of the Senator's stay.

The commotion of arguing voices brought the Senator and the cook to the doorway of the room.

While the cook firmly pulled the housekeeper aside into the adjoining den in an attempt to placate the stymied domestic, the Senator entered the dining room and closed the heavy oak sliding door behind him.

"Perkins," he began with his usual paternal firmness. "I think you should take a break from all this paperwork."

"Senator?"

The younger man was quite startled at the suggestion that he should stop his work, as well as the obvious correction to what he felt was his justifiable behavior. Suddenly he felt like a small child being scolded by an authoritative father figure.

"I think," Senator Wilton continued calmly, "that we should perhaps give the staff a break as well."

"I don't know what you mean."

"Yes, you do," the Senator countered calmly. "You most certainly do."

"Well," Perkins said, folding his arms across his chest and clutching the papers he had been reading, "what are you suggesting, sir?"

"I want breakfast," the older man announced. "Buttermilk biscuits and thick hickory smoked bacon and lots of hot fresh coffee."

"I'll speak to the cook." Perkins reached for the sliding door.

"Nonsense," the Senator corrected him. "You are deliberately misunderstanding me."

"Excuse me, Senator?"

"Call the chauffeur, please. Or, better yet, we can go in your car," he instructed. "You *are* ready to go, aren't you?"

"Where?"

"We're going to Sam's."

"Sam's?" Perkins thought the name sounded familiar.

"You're turning into a parrot, Perkins. You haven't been to Sam's? Well, we must remedy that right now. Best cooking in the county. Possibly the tri-county area. Get your coat and your keys."

"But sir—"

One look at the Senator's stony face told Perkins that any objections would be futile. Perkins took the keys from his pocket, but they proved to be useless because his front left tire was completely flat.

"Interesting," the Senator said blandly. "Perhaps you picked up a nail or a screw when you dropped Miss Grayson at her apartment last night. Bad luck there, Perkins."

The aide swallowed his increasing anger and embarrassment, covering his discomfort by pulling out his cell phone to summon the chauffeur, whose cheerful assurance that he would be there within ten minutes served to further irritate Perkins.

The Senator, however, seemed remarkably pleased with the whole situation, whistling to himself as they waited for the driver to arrive. His own early morning call from Andrew Evans was still fresh in his ears. He had never been much for country preachers and organized religion, but this one seemed more practical than most. Besides, the man had promised answers.

His oddly lightened mood annoyed Perkins.

Apparently, we're going out to breakfast. At Sam's, wherever that is. No matter what else needs to be done, thought Perkins grimly, thinking of all the paperwork he needed to complete and telephone calls he needed to make.

Then, with a shock of guilty conscience, he remembered.

Sam's was where Amanda Grayson had told him to meet her on Wednesday. Perkins slapped his forehead. He chanced a furtive side glance at his employer. A thousand maybes flooded his aching head. *Maybe the Senator came to my room last night and discovered that I wasn't there. Maybe Grayson had called him this morning and told her own version of what happened last night.*

Then, the most troubling maybe of all.

Maybe someone knows something I don't know, and they're willing to use it against me.

The Senator certainly looked satisfied with himself.

The situation had gone from loathsome to lethal.

Chapter 53

Thomas and the judge arrived almost simultaneously and had settled in their standard back corner booths with fresh coffee when Katy arrived, flanked by Amy and Dan. Neither husband nor wife looked particularly pleased with the situation, although both managed to smile at Sam's effervescent greeting for Katy.

"You poor dear," Sam exclaimed, hugging the young widow to her with sincere consolation. "I'm so glad to see you. Sit here."

Without letting go of Katy's arm, she led the party of three to the back table against the wall, nearest where the judge and Thomas were sitting.

"More private," she explained. "The judge will look after you if someone comes in and tries to pry or annoy you with questions."

It never once occurred to Sam that she herself might fit that description.

Both Thomas and the judge stood to acknowledge Katy's arrival, then seated themselves once she had taken the chair against the wall. Amy looked around uncomfortably, torn between concern for her sister and her own shyness in public situations.

"Sit down, please." Katy reached out and patted her sister's hand. "Next to me."

Dan nodded awkwardly at his wife, who motioned for him to take the chair opposite hers, to Katy's right. He stood while Amy glanced around the room again, and then they sat down together. Amy twisted her hands in her lap while Dan picked up his silverware and rolled it out of the linen napkin onto the table with a clatter that made Amy jump.

Funny, Thomas noted, *I've never noticed how jumpy and nervous Amy is as a person*. He suddenly felt sorry for her. Overshadowed by her younger sister and controlled by her alcoholic husband, Thomas wondered if anyone had ever actually noticed Amy McInnis outside her own family. And if they had, he wondered not unkindly, why they would.

His thoughts were interrupted by the arrival of Andrew Evans, who was chatting almost congenially with the Senator. The two men entered together and paused, waiting to see if Sam would assign their seating. She did, placing them opposite each other at a table along the left wall with a clear view of the corner where the judge was sitting.

Thomas noticed, a bit surprised, that they seemed to be rather enjoying their conversation. Almost as old friends. A moment later Perkins entered, resembling a recently whipped puppy. He did not wait to be seated, waving Sam away with a brusque gesture and sliding into a front booth by the window, away from all the others. With a cursory glance at the other patrons, he turned his face away to the window and proceeded to stare out at the near-empty street as though bored not only with his present company, but also with life itself.

It was almost as if he wanted to be closest to the door to get out, just in case.

Now that, Thomas thought, *is even more interesting. The admirable Perkins seems to have fallen out of favor.*

Sam had delivered coffee to each of her customers with practiced ease and was just beginning to take biscuit orders when Charlie arrived with a remarkably recovered but still clingy Amanda Grayson on his arm.

The striking blonde woman had skillfully repaired the night's damage and was stunning in her gray suit and deep purple silk blouse. Her freshly washed hair was caught up carelessly in a sequined French clasp at the back of her head. Perkins took a noncommittal glance and then turned his head to the window again. The wave of perfume that had followed her into the restaurant had announced her appearance like a trumpet solo, the odor reaching out and assaulting his senses. He felt the beginnings of a migraine headache.

Amanda gave the disinterested Perkins a quick scan and was appalled to see that he was not looking at her, his nostrils twitching and his mouth sternly set in a thin line. She gripped Charlie's arm a little tighter.

Charlie, in his favorite worn jeans and sports jacket, was shorter by several inches than his female companion and considerably less fashionable, although he was certain at that moment that no one was looking at him, so it did not matter how he looked, or even if anyone noticed him. At least, not yet.

Sam greeted the beautiful lawyer with genuine Southern warmth, deliberately ignoring Charlie and instead adroitly guiding the woman away from the detective to a table in the center of the room. The gorgeous blonde sat alone, like a colorful floral centerpiece placed on white linen in the middle of fine china and crystal place settings. Sam had always fancied that she had a flare for design, and she relished the opportunity to show her expertise at staging, even if right now that meant that she was staging the cast members of this unfolding drama.

As she followed Sam, Amanda's expensive heels clicked a staccato march as she crossed to her table and gracefully lowered herself into the chair. When a cup of steaming coffee had been placed in front of her, she chanced another peek at the Senator's aide, but she was bitterly disappointed. Perkins had not stopped staring out the front window. She tapped her long pink fingernails on the table impatiently and finally looked around the room.

It was at that point that she realized Charlie wasn't with her anymore. She had only come because Charlie had called her and promised that she could go back to Atlanta today if she would meet him here at Sam's and have breakfast together. She was counting on going home today, especially after the fiasco with Perkins last night. And the whole pseudo-date with the detective seemed innocent enough. Breakfast sounded good to her, especially when Charlie mentioned that he would pay for her food.

Lost in self-absorption, Amanda looked up to find Sam

standing over her with a plate piled high with hot biscuits and another of assorted sausages, ham slices, and strips of thick, crispy bacon. Sam had already made the rounds of the other patrons, who for the most part were all already eating.

"Bacon, ham, or sausage?" Sam asked.

Amanda wrinkled her nose in distaste. She leaned toward vegetarianism, and smelling the fried meats turned her stomach.

"Just biscuits," she said, taking one of the biscuits gingerly with her fingers and putting it on the napkin in front of her. "And jam? Anything but peach."

"Of course," Sam said agreeably, sensing the cause of Amanda's reluctance and hoping no one would mention that the biscuits had been liberally doused with bacon grease. "Homemade blackberry jam in the back. Won't be a minute."

Once Sam had disappeared into the kitchen again, the front doors opened again. Another two rather well-dressed men entered the restaurant and seated themselves across from each other at a booth closest to the doorway.

Hmmm, Amanda thought absently as she pried the flaky biscuit apart and began to apply a thin layer of butter to both the top and the bottom. *Handsome. Must be businessmen.*

Sam returned and placed the small bowl of fragrant jam in front of Amanda. When she surveyed the room, she saw the two additional customers, the taller of whom gave her a quick nod of recognition. With a deliberate stride, she continued through the tables to the front doors, where she pulled the knobs toward her quickly, ceremonially flipped the front sign on the door to read *CLOSED*, and twisted the deadbolt, securely locking the principal exit from the building.

The Senator, who had been eying the two suited men with suspicion, stood almost immediately in protest, but Evans soothed him with a low, quiet whisper of reassurance. Wilton reluctantly resumed his seat.

"Can I assume that you have something to do with this?" the Senator asked gruffly. He directed his question at Charlie, who was standing inconspicuously near the cashier's counter, helping himself to a cup of coffee and licking the remnants of a sausage biscuit from his fingers. "You always were a troublemaker."

Charlie nodded in affirmation, reaching for a napkin.

"Calm down, Stewart," the judge admonished from his seat in the corner, taking a bite and finishing the last of his own biscuit and bacon. "Just listen for a minute."

Thomas wiped his own hands on his napkin and rose to his feet, leaning against the doorframe that led into the kitchen, holding the doors open while Sam made a hasty and determined exit.

"You don't have any right," began Perkins petulantly, sliding to the end of the wooden bench as if to stand. "No right at all to—"

"Oh, do shut up," said Amanda, spooning another teaspoon of jam onto her biscuit with icy coldness. "As though *you* would have any idea about what is right."

"Children, children," Charlie interrupted them with a paternal tone. "It's the grown-ups' turn to talk now."

"Charlie, get on with it," Candler warned.

"Yes, Judge." Charlie looked slowly around the room, studying each person briefly and making eye contact before moving on to the next in the sea of faces.

"Everyone has secrets," the detective began casually. "We all know that. We have a God-given right to our secrets, unless they hurt other people. We are here this morning because a secret killed Steve Wilton on Monday afternoon."

He paused and looked directly at the Senator.

"How well do you know Perkins here?" he asked quietly.

"Why you demented little vermin —" Perkins was on his feet and had assumed an awkward but obvious fighting stance. "Are you accusing me of murder?"

"Well, you have killed your own career, if that counts." Charlie ignored the angered Perkins and continued to search the Senator's face. "I'll ask you again, Senator. How well do you know your aide here? Because we've done a little digging."

The Senator let out a sigh of resignation.

"Enough of the charade, then, Perkins," he said sadly. "I've suspected that someone was undermining my reelection campaign. I got a call last night that confirmed that you've been offered a much more lucrative position with one of my opponents."

"That's a —"

"Don't say that it's a lie. I know it's true. You were the one who insisted that we hire Miss Grayson to represent my son. You knew Steven's weakness for women. Did you hope he would further disgrace me? Was that the plan?"

Amanda Grayson's face had flushed bright red, and she too stood up.

"I *never* had that sort of relationship with your son, Senator," she objected loudly. "Never."

She paused for a moment before turning to address Katy.

"He loved *you*," the lawyer offered as honestly as she knew how, all pretense gone. "We had a drink in his office before court on Monday morning, and he made it clear that he wanted to work things out with you. You and your daughter."

Amanda paused again. This was harder than she thought it would be. This town and the people in it were having a crazy effect on her. She turned back bravely to face the Senator.

"I haven't been honest with you, Senator," she said, her voice gaining strength as she spoke. "Perkins made it clear that the divorce was in your best interests, sir. I took his word that you had some reason for wanting your son separated from his wife, and I did what I could legally to make that happen. I can see now that I was wrong."

Her pain seemed genuine to Charlie.

"I'm sorry," Amanda's voice quivered slightly, sinking back into her chair and pushing the plate away.

"Senator —" Perkins began, trying to regain his bluster. "I didn't know that —"

"That I actually loved my son?" the Senator interrupted, dropping to a barely perceptible whisper. "Apparently, you aren't the only one, Perkins."

The aide slumped back onto the bench dejectedly, staring at the back of Amanda's head as she covered her face with her hands.

Charlie turned to Evans, who returned his look with calm confidence.

"So, Preacher," Charlie began. "Time to tell us all why you went to see Steve Wilton in his home office on Monday."

The Senator stared at the minister.

Evans spoke firmly. "He called me. You know that, Detective."

"Just one last time, please," Charlie said. He picked up a toothpick and slid it between his canine teeth, playing absently with the sliver of wood. "What did he want you to do?"

"He wanted me to act as a go-between," Evans admitted plainly. "I told him I wouldn't help him."

"Go-between for Steve and who else?" Charlie persisted.

"I'm not at liberty to say."

Charlie folded his arms across his chest and straightened away from the wall, his jawline growing taunt.

"A woman, yes?"

The Senator bristled.

"We've established my son's reputation," Wilton snapped. "There's no need to belabor the point, Charlie."

"But you said you wouldn't help him, didn't you, Preacher?" Charlie continued, again ignoring the interruption. "You refused to help Steve Wilton."

"Yes, I did."

"How do you feel about that now?"

Evans hesitated for a moment. The probing words hurt. He looked around the room, his gaze coming to rest on Katy.

"I think if I had done what he asked, then Steve Wilton would not be dead now."

The admission brought a collective gasp of surprise and protest.

Charlie landed his final blow to the preacher. "So, I guess your answer is that you feel guilty."

"Son," the judge said, his voice low and controlled. "I'm losing patience here. Move along now."

Charlie shifted his weight and looked at Thomas, who nodded his head grimly and stood, folding his own arms across his chest.

"Thank you, Preacher," Charlie took the toothpick out of his mouth and studied it for a moment before looking directly at Katy.

"Katy," he began. "It's true what Amanda Grayson said. Steve did love you. You do know that, don't you?"

The lovely young widow met his intense eyes, tears glistening in her own.

"Yes, Charlie. I know."

"That's the important part in all this, Katy," he continued, softening his tone. "He wanted to prove it to you. To you and to his daughter. Did you know he wrote a new will?"

She nodded her head silently. Amy reached out to grasp her sister's hand for emotional support, but Katy pushed her away.

"I didn't know for certain . . . I only suspected."

Charlie turned to Thomas.

"You're up, Thomas," he said, as though tossing a softball to a first baseman.

Thomas cleared his throat.

"Charlie asked me to go over the legal papers the police found in Steve's safe in his study," the lawyer explained carefully. "Looked like a page was missing, so I followed up by calling the lawyer who had drawn them up over in Griffith. Turns out, Steve went over to Griffith last week and had the lawyer there add an addendum to his original will last week."

There were collective gasps of surprise, confusion, and disbelief around the room, cups suddenly clattering to saucers and forks dropping.

"Oh," Thomas continued in his most soothing voice, "the bulk of the estate still belongs to you, Katy. No matter what. Divorce, no divorce. Even if you left him, Steve was going to give you everything he owned."

Thomas paused and looked back at Charlie, who nodded grimly.

"Well," Thomas said quietly. "Almost everything."

"But —" Amanda opened her mouth to speak and then stopped, a realization dawning. "Are you saying that he knew last week that he wasn't getting a divorce? That he was consulting with another lawyer?"

"Just another secret," Charlie said. "Steve had a plan, but he needed time. Steve had never really been much for plans, or for waiting, but he wanted this time to be different. He wanted to be different."

"Different?" Katy said, genuinely puzzled. "I don't know what you mean."

"I really do hate telling other people's secrets," Charlie said sadly. "I wish I knew another way to do this, Katy, but I don't."

He flipped open his notebook and found the page he wanted.

"The question really is not who killed Steve, the question is who didn't kill Steve," he began, looking down at his scribbles as he spoke.

"We know Katy didn't kill her husband. She was with Elizabeth and a number of reliable witnesses. We know that

Andrew Evans didn't kill Steve. The housekeeper saw him leave just before she was fired, and Steve was still alive."

The door to the kitchen creaked as it moved a fraction of an inch outward, and the coffee maker gurgled in the corner, but otherwise the room had fallen into silence.

"So we know," Charlie continued, at last glancing up from his notes, "that Steve was killed around two thirty in the afternoon. The preacher left around noon. The housekeeper was fired and left the house shortly afterward, and Steve's body was found in his study around three thirty when the housekeeper returned to get some of her things and to see if Steve had reconsidered."

"So you don't suspect the housekeeper?" Perkins sneered.

"No," Charlie frowned. "She doesn't have a motive. Steve's temper was epic. He was well-known for firing and rehiring the help. Besides, she's been with the family since his mother died when Steve was five, and she loved him like a son."

He paused to look at Thomas again.

"In addition," Charlie continued, "there is that revision to the will that explains what was really going on with Steve."

"So what if he changed his will?" Perkins was lost in confusion, suddenly caught up with the rest of the room, mesmerized by the drama playing out before them. "What does that even mean?"

"Steve wanted to make a special provision," Thomas explained patiently.

Amanda nodded slightly, sorting the information out in her head.

"So there was someone else besides Katy and the little girl," she said. "He wanted a guarantee that someone else would also be provided for in the event of his death."

"Exactly," Thomas agreed. "The question is who that person could be."

Charlie turned to Amy, who had lowered her head onto her hands and had begun to sob quietly.

"I have so many questions for you, Amy," the detective said gently. "Please don't make me ask."

Amy, who had been leaning toward her sister, drew away from the table and began to cry openly.

"I am so sorry," she managed, rummaging through her purse for a tissue and finding several. She began wiping her eyes as tears were replaced rapidly by more tears, and then more. "I never meant for anything like this to happen. I didn't. Please, please believe me, Katy. I would never, ever hurt you."

Unexpectedly Evans cleared his throat and stood up.

"Preacher?" Charlie rubbed his chin thoughtfully. "I wondered when you would have something to say."

"Amy came to see me on Monday after the hearing," he began, his hand on the Senator's shoulder but his eyes fixed on Katy. "We met at a coffee shop in Griffith. Your sister wanted my advice about what to do."

Katy frowned at Evans, then Charlie, and then her sister.

"She didn't know how to tell you the truth about what had happened."

"The truth?" Katy whispered, her eyes fixed on the preacher.

"Maybe Dan would rather explain," Charlie interrupted somberly. "Maybe Dan can explain the cell phone we found in

Steve's study. The only call on it was Dan's number. Not the home number, the one on his business card."

Charlie paused to let his implications sink in. The Senator had started to rise, but Evans motioned him back into the chair and sat down himself, placing his Bible between them on the table. Amy continued to sob into her hands as Katy, realization dawning, was both drawn to comfort her and full of resentment.

Her thoughts shot out one after another, rapidly swirling and tangling into one another.

So Steve had been willing to change. To come home. But why? And how is Amy involved? She's been acting strangely, and now she's crying.

Katy began putting two and two together, and her mind kept racing.

Were Steve and Amy together? Did Amy kill Steve? Is that why she's sorry? Is that why she went to the preacher? To confess?

"What did Steve say when he called you on Monday, Dan?" Charlie asked quietly. "After the preacher refused to help him. What did Steve say?"

"I don't know what you're talking about." Dan's face was flushed with anger, and he pushed his chair back furiously from the table, rattling the cups and plates. "You're just playing games now."

"No," Charlie said. "Not my games, Dan. You're the one pretending." He paused before continuing in a conversational tone. "Why don't you just tell us what happened?"

Katy stared blankly at her brother-in-law. *Dan's involved too? What do they know that I don't?* The possibilities were almost too painful to bear.

The detective paused again to move closer to the table

where the three sat, Amy still crying softly and Katy sitting like a stone statue, unable to move, frozen between them. Dan, seething in antagonism against the wall like a caged rabid animal, stood, knocking over the chair, his hands clenched at his side.

Recognizing their cue, the two pseudo-businessmen rose with military precision and took up guard at the outer doorway exit, unbuttoning their suit jackets to reveal their shoulder holsters and the shiny detective badges clipped to their belts.

"Take your time and tell us what happened, Dan," Charlie encouraged. "Burton and Dalton aren't in a hurry, are you, guys?"

Burton looked at his watch and gave the rogue detective a withering glare of distain.

"Within reason, of course," Charlie added with an easy smile. "Come on, Dan. You know you want a chance to speak your piece to everyone. You *want* to explain."

Dan slammed his thick fist onto the table, clattering the cups and spilling coffee onto the white linens, biscuit crumbs flying through the air onto the floor.

"Rich, arrogant, snotty brat—" he began.

"Steve, you mean," Charlie interrupted. "He made you angry, didn't he?"

Dan turned on Amy, whose sobs had dissolved into raw whimpers.

"You didn't tell me," he snarled. "Did you think I was stupid? That I wouldn't suspect something? All these years, Amy—and it was *him*? *Him*?"

Amy sobs began anew. Katy looked helplessly from her sister's face, buried in the tissues, to Charlie's compassionate face, her own aching heart beginning to see the truth but not wanting to believe. *Amy was with Steve. They were together. But when? For how long?*

She didn't want to believe it. But Dan seemed so sure.

Please, she prayed silently to herself. *Not Amy*.

"Talk to *me*, Dan," Charlie said calmly, giving Katy a reassuring half-smile and drawing Dan's attention back to him. "Tell *me* what happened."

Dan glared at the detective, raking his hands through his hair and chopping the words into sharp shards of rage as he spoke.

"You were all alike in high school—you, Thomas, Steve. I was older, but I saw. I wasn't smart or rich. I *had* to work." Dan stopped to take a gasping breath and stared at his wife. "All I ever had was Amy. She was mine."

"Steve didn't respect that, did he, Dan?" Charlie spoke as though Dan were a small child. "Steve didn't respect you."

Amy gave a strangled sob and covered her mouth, her husband turning on her.

"When were you going to tell me?" Dan glared at her. "Do you know how it felt coming from him? To find out from him?"

"I just found out," she said. Her eyes turned to Katy's in a desperate plea for understanding and found only confusion and pain. "It was last Friday." Amy was weeping as she spoke, completely broken now, her body slumped, hugging herself with her arms and rocking her fragile frame in the chair. Evans moved to stand behind her, his face a mask of self-control and protection, his firm hands on her trembling shoulders like a guardian angel of mercy.

Dan took a threatening step toward his wife, a move that was instinctively matched by Charlie and the detectives at the door.

"So, Dan, what *did* Steve say when he called?" Charlie firmly drew the attention away from Amy again. "He wanted to meet you, yes? Did he tell you about the baby?"

Katy gasped in disbelief, and the blood drained from her face as she went white.

"Yeah," Dan snarled. "He thought we could be bought. He thought he needed to take care of us. Like I couldn't take care of my own family." His anger turned on Amy. "He said it wasn't your fault. He took all the blame."

"I would be angry too," Charlie agreed. "Who did he think he was anyway?"

Dan nodded violently in agreement.

"I expected him to brag when I got there, you know," Dan continued, shaking his head as he remembered. "To rub it in, but he didn't. It was pitiful. He just kept saying he was sorry. That he never *meant* to hurt anybody. That was always Steve's song—the apology song. Everyone knows all the verses. He never *meant* to make such a mess of his life and everyone around him. He never *meant* to screw up everyone else's future to suit his own selfish—"

Dan paused and looked straight at his weeping wife and his shocked sister-in-law.

"I was drunk," he said simply. "I was furious that you didn't tell me, didn't trust me. And I got drunk before I went to see him. I took the gun too. The one I got for you to carry in the glove compartment. I just wanted to tell him to leave us alone.

Damn, Amy, I *was* okay until he pulled out that paper from the safe."

"The revision to the will?" Charlie offered.

"Steve said he had it done in Griffith so no one would ever know. So no one would suspect. But that paper meant *everyone* would know."

"Dan, please." Amy had found her voice amid the tears and reached out for his hand, but Dan pulled away and took a ragged breath.

"I thought about you, Amy." He stared down at his wife. "I tried for just a minute to tell myself that we could go back to the way we were. Then a picture came into my head—Steve's face at every family dinner. At every reunion. Every Sunday morning in church. Steve looking at the baby—*our* baby, Amy— and knowing all along that—"

Amy stood to embrace her husband. Before she could get close, Dan's arm raised to push her away and Charlie made himself a human wall between them. The preacher, his hands still gripping Amy's shoulders, held her upright as she swayed backward.

"Steve said he wanted you to *know*, Amy. He called the preacher to tell you about the new will, but he wouldn't," Dan spat the words. "Steve said he wanted someone to tell you that he was sorry and that he would keep the secret."

Dan tilted back his head, and an ugly, twisted, hysterical laugh escaped his lips.

"Steve Wilton! Keeping secrets," he said. "What a joke!"

"What happened next?" Charlie was standing toe-to-toe with Dan, Amy sandwiched between the detective's back and the preacher's broad chest.

Dan looked down at his hands as if he had never seen them before. His eyes had gone blank, although his mouth was still distorted with a misshapen grin.

"Steve came back from the safe with the paper. He put it on the desk and said that he was going to sign it so I could see. So I would know for certain that he was telling me the truth."

Dan paused.

"But I already knew all the truth I wanted to know. I put my gun to the back of his head and I shot him—and I watched Steve and his broken promises die."

The visual was too much for Amanda, who leaned back into her chair and felt her stomach wretch at the image. Perkins turned quickly away to stare out the window in disgust. Evans looked over Amy's crumpled form in an attempt to offer some consolation to the Senator, who had leaned back into his chair in stunned silence.

Then he turned his attention to Katy, her eyes hard as glittering stones, and he knew she needed to hear the truth too. All the horrifying truth. What Amy had really come to tell him that day. What Steve had confessed that day, and what he had promised not to reveal.

Before the preacher could speak, Dan continued.

"No more secrets, Amy." Dan had stopped laughing, and his voice was quite serene and distant. Calm. As though he had accepted whatever was going to happen to him now. As though he didn't care. "Wilton ruined his own life, and your sister's, and yours. I just couldn't let him ruin our baby's life too. You can see that, can't you?"

"Oh, Dan . . ."

Charlie's motion to the other detectives was unnecessary. They had already moved swiftly to Dan's side.

"You're under arrest for the murder of Steve Wilton," Charlie said bluntly. Dalton handcuffed Dan while Burton produced a Miranda card from his jacket pocket and began to read mechanically into Dan's ear.

"I'm sorry, Amy," Dan said quietly over the dronish voice at the side of his face, trying to look back over his shoulder as they led him away. "I *am* sorry, Amy, but not for Steve. Never for Steve."

From the slightly opened rear kitchen door of the restaurant, Sam appeared, trying not to look as sheepish as she felt, since she and Bill had been eavesdropping the entire time. She moved quickly around the detectives to unlock the front doors so they could escort Dan to Smith and the waiting squad car outside. Then she looked inquisitively at Charlie, who nodded grimly. She flipped the sign to read *OPEN*.

Charlie sighed and put away his pen and notepad.

"But what about the book?" Thomas asked curiously. "Wasn't there a missing book?"

"Preacher, here's your cue." Charlie looked over at Evans, who had helped Amy sit down again. "You probably know more about this than anyone else."

"I have the book," he admitted. "You kept asking if I took it, and I didn't lie. I didn't steal it. Steve insisted. We argued. There's a second copy of the new provision in an envelope between the pages. I decided that it was the least that I could do. He hoped I might change my mind about talking to Amy, and that she would understand when she saw the title of the book."

Thomas looked completely perplexed.

"Steve told me that he had been drinking when Amy came to talk to him about going back to Katy. He was alone and angry. Angry with you, Senator, for demanding he grow up and take responsibility. Angry with Katy and feeling guilty for how he had treated her. He saw Amy and something inside him snapped."

Evans took a deep breath and looked straight into Katy's cold eyes.

"I don't know what you're thinking, but I can imagine," he said bluntly. "You deserve the truth. The whole truth."

He glanced at Amy, who had hidden her face in her hands again.

"I also know that I promised you I would keep your secret, Amy, but you know that I can't. Not now. Steve called me not long after we talked on Monday in Griffith, and he asked me to go and see him. He admitted what he did to you. I should have gone straight to the police, but you had begged me not to tell anyone. I wanted to respect your wishes, but this is something you cannot hide."

"What Steve did?" Katy whispered.

Evans wiped his mouth with the back of his hand as if to wipe away the disgusting taste of his words.

"Your husband forced himself on your sister."

Amy began to sob again.

The Senator drew in a ragged breath and looked away.

"Why didn't you tell me?" Katy gasped, the fury on her face gone, replaced by confusion, disbelief, and finally astonishment. "You should have told me."

"What was I going to say? I thought the divorce would happen and somehow it would all just go away. I was ashamed and embarrassed by the whole thing. I was the one who went to see him. I just wanted to help you, Katy. Can you believe that?"

Amy twisted the tissues in her trembling hands.

"He called me afterwards and begged me not to tell you. Pleaded with me that he was sorry and he would make things right." Amy stopped for a moment and wiped her eyes. "I realized last week that something was—I went to the clinic in Griffith. Steve followed me to apologize and to ask me to convince you to let him come back. I shouldn't have told him that I was pregnant, but I did. I guess I hoped that Dan would believe the baby was ours. I never thought Steve would say anything to Dan."

"But why did that make a difference?" the Senator suddenly interjected. "Why did Steve care?"

There was an awkward silence before the preacher sighed and turned to the Senator, trying to remember that the man was experiencing unbearable pain and loss.

"I only know what Steve said to me," he responded quietly. "He told me that he had never known there was such a thing as going too far. At least, not until he went too far."

"You said there was a book," Amy said. "That Steve gave you a book. What book?"

"*The Portrait of Dorian Gray*," he answered gently. "I put it in my locked desk drawer in the church office with the new will inside. I can bring it with me to the services tomorrow. That is, if you want it. You don't have to decide now."

"Thank you," Katy firmly interrupted her sister's would-be

response. "Thank you."

"But, Katy," Amy said timidly, not yet meeting Katy's eyes. "Can you ever forgive me?"

Katy's eyes welled over with her own tears.

"I don't know how we're going to get through any of this," she responded softly. "All those years, I forgave Steve. I don't know how, I just did." She took a deep, painful breath. "I thought you had killed him, Amy. I'm so sorry for that. I suspected something had happened between the two of you, and I thought you were the one. I don't know how you can forgive me for misjudging you."

Thomas and the judge studied the two women for a moment, thinking essentially the same thoughts. The younger had become the elder for the first time in their lives. So much pain and deception and lies and loss. A baby that might have driven them apart might just serve to strengthen the bond of love between these two sisters and the terrible burden that was now theirs.

Charlie's curiosity, on the other hand, had gotten the better of him. "There's one thing I would still like to know, Preacher, if you can explain."

Evans drew Charlie back into the rear corner of the now almost-empty restaurant.

"How can I help you, Detective?"

"I might need to brush up on my literature, but that book . . ."

"*The Portrait of Dorian Gray*," Evans inserted smoothly. "What about it?"

"That's the point. It was part of a set of classics about . . ."

Charlie hesitated.

"About adultery." Evans was trying not to relish in the detective's discomfiture. "And what did you want to know?"

"Just what the book is about. I mean, why would it mean anything to Amy and Katy?"

"I see your question now." The preacher rubbed his chin thoughtfully. "Well, the book is about a wicked man who makes a deal with the devil to preserve outward appearances."

"Yes, that was Steve. Outward appearances. Go on."

"Well, the wicked man marries an innocent, quite beautiful young girl."

"I'm following you so far. What happens to this guy?"

"He dies, Detective. He is sorry in the end for all the pain he has caused, and he dies."

Charlie gave a long, low whistle and put his hands into his jeans pockets.

"So Steve thought he was going to die?"

Evans shook his head.

"You've missed the point, I think." He looked over at the sisters and sighed. "I think the point of the story is that a man can go too far. Dorian Gray couldn't come back. I think Steve hoped that he could."

He patted Charlie paternally on the sleeve.

"Maybe I'll see you in church on Sunday," he said hopefully. "If you will excuse me, I think I might need to talk to the Senator."

Without waiting for a reply, he left Charlie standing in the corner, waiting with less patience than appeared on the surface.

Dalton and Burton placed a defiant Dan in the patrol car

while an uncomfortable Amanda Grayson slid out just after them to make a hasty retreat to her already-packed and fully fueled rental car. The Senator skillfully intercepted Perkins, who had tried to follow Grayson out.

The two men had a quick, low-voiced, and rather one-sided conversation in which it became evident to everyone else in the restaurant that Perkins had been dismissed and was being asked to leave Balfour as soon as possible. When Perkins finally stormed out, a sympathetic Evans crossed the restaurant to the Senator's side.

"I appreciate what you did for my son," Wilton said. "For my family."

Evans nodded, ill-at-ease and self-conscious.

"They're going to need you now, Senator," the minister responded. "Their lives have been completely shattered, and you can help."

"Kind words," Wilton said gruffly. "Don't know how true they are. I didn't do my own son much good, now did I?"

Evans was considering what to say when he realized that Katy had crossed the restaurant and was standing at his elbow, extending her slender, trembling hand to her father-in law.

"Senator," she began firmly through her tears. "I'm sorry about Steve."

"Katy," he began, choking back tears.

"I know," she continued with a determination no one could have expected, taking his gnarled hand in hers. "I know."

The Senator's weathered, austere expression quickly softened.

"We'll see you at the services," she said, looking over her

shoulder and seeing the broken, bruised spirit of her sister. "Maybe we can talk more then."

Sweet Katy, Thomas thought. *Poor, sweet Katy. How can she do it? How can she possibly keep forgiving like that?*

Then Thomas realized why Cora did what she did. She believed that people could change. Everyone has secrets, and everyone has hurts and pain. Katy's secret was what Steve had known and loved about his wife. Why in the end, Steve had wanted to come home and why he had decided not to leave a woman who loved him more than he loved himself.

Somewhere in his heart, Steve knew that he could be forgiven. He believed that he could change, because Katy believed. He knew he had crossed a terrible line from which he could not return, not without help.

Cora believed.

Thomas shook his head and went back to talk to the judge.

Sam and Bill began busing the tables, bustling about and breaking what tension still hovered over the remaining members of the group. A few other early morning patrons entered and found seats and cups of coffee, enticed by the smell of country breakfast and Bill's biscuits.

Anticipating the onslaught of well-intentioned but unwanted questions from the newcomers, Evans and the Senator escorted the grieving sisters to their car. Amy leaned on the preacher while he offered whispered words of consolation and absolution, and Katy, her thin hand through his arm at his elbow, walked without speaking.

After their car drove off, Evans offered the Senator a ride back to the house where he was staying to pack his things, delaying as much as possible the time before he himself headed back to the church to dodge a full-scale inquisition from Donna and Alice. Not to mention the discussion he was going to have with Virginia over the meatloaf and mashed potatoes she was bringing for lunch.

Charlie made sure that no one was watching and that Thomas and the judge were focused on the last of their breakfast conversation in the corner booth. He slipped Sam four twenty-dollar bills, for which he intended to be fully reimbursed on his expense report by the chief, and asked for an extra two dozen assorted bacon and sausage biscuits to go. He tipped the Senator's driver another twenty to deliver the biscuits to the police station.

Charlie went out to his own battered car parked on a side street. He knew exactly what he wanted, although he wasn't quite certain how long his personal business might take. Charlie only knew that he desperately needed something positive to counteract the last few hours. As he left Balfour and headed south toward Atlanta, he formulated his own plan for recovery.

The country music station, his personal favorite, was blaring a ballad of betrayal and alcohol from the radio, an unwanted reminder of recent reality. Dan's defiant face. Amy's tear-stained pleas of remorse. Katy's firm declarations of love and forgiveness. Steve, trying at last to do what he thought was the right thing.

With an irritated jab at the dials, he turned the song off and was left in silence to continue his mission, more pleasant thoughts of the future filling his head as the brisk autumn wind flowed through the open car window onto his face.

Chapter 54

Cora sat in the den, sipping her morning vanilla coffee and eating a bacon biscuit from Sam's while she listened to the account of the morning with absentminded lack of interest. Thomas, who was well aware of all the clues she had provided along the way, was confused by Cora's unwillingness to be excited to hear just how Charlie was able to use the clues to solve the mysteries.

Right now, Thomas suspected that she was simply relieved that the dreams would be over. At least until the next time.

Thomas noted that his wife looked tired, although he knew she would not appreciate his observation.

"Missing a few nights' sleep is insignificant," Cora always insisted, "if justice is served."

"Cora," Thomas said finally, coming to the end of the morning's narrative by describing Charlie's hasty departure and omitting the number of biscuits with bacon that he himself had consumed. "Something is bothering me."

"Yes?"

"I don't know quite how to ask you this."

She tilted her head and met her husband's eyes.

"You can ask me anything, Thomas," she began, matching his almost severe tone. "I'll always tell you the truth."

"Oh," he quickly corrected himself, seeing that she had misunderstood what he was saying. "It isn't like that, Cora."

She was bewildered by the intensity of his denial.

"Then what?"

"Hasn't Amy been a patient of yours? I mean, don't you see her from time to time?" He looked away, obviously uncomfortable.

"Thomas, what is it you want to know?"

"Well," he said, hesitating, "Charlie never mentioned the ring you saw, or the apple cinnamon tea. That's how he knew it was Amy, right? I was just wondering, if Amy is a patient of yours . . ."

"You're wondering if that is a breach of privacy, aren't you?" She tapped the table top softly with the pads of her fingers. "A violation of patient privilege?"

"Cora . . ."

"Always the lawyer, aren't you?" Her voice was playful, then serious. "I did not violate my ethics, Thomas. Not at all."

"But how—"

"You also are not very observant either, love of my life. The ring isn't Amy's. The ring belongs to Katy. I remember Marjorie talking about how Steve did something different for Katy's wedding band."

Thomas tried to search his memories, but there was nothing. He was having trouble remembering that he had ever been to a wedding other than his own, and even his own was a bit fuzzy at the moment.

"Marjorie talked on and off for days about that wedding, all the details. I distinctly remember that she said how unusual it was that there were no diamonds in the ring, but how it suited Katy so well."

Thomas could remember hearing no such conversation.

"I don't understand," he said. "So the apple cinnamon tea was Katy's too?"

"The tea too. She never touched alcohol, but she also gave up coffee when she was expecting Elizabeth. I understand from Marjorie that Katy never went back to coffee after the pregnancy."

"Then how in the world—"

"Seeing the ring in color told me that Steve loved his wife. She was special to him. More than special. I knew from the herbal tea that there was a pregnancy involved. I had no idea who was expecting a baby. Charlie did that all on his own."

"Interesting leap."

"Acrobatic Charlie," she shrugged. "Anything else a puzzle to you, Sherlock?"

"No, Dr. Watson," he said, feeling awkward. The relationship she had with Charlie confused his pragmatic mind on so many levels.

Just then, Marjorie came in from the garden with Jane. Inside a wicker basket that they carried between them were several plump red cherry tomatoes and a single sweet green bell pepper, the end-of-summer harvest. As they entered, Cora and Thomas could hear Marjorie extolling the virtues of fresh fruits and vegetables to the fascinated child.

Thomas and Cora went to stand, arms around each other, in the kitchen doorway, listening to the one-way conversation. They watched Jane climb onto a step stool beside the housekeeper, her face glowing with contentment as the food was carefully washed and then put aside to dry.

Thomas looked down at his wife.

"What are you thinking?"

"About Jane," she said simply. "It's difficult not to feel selfish."

Once again, Thomas did not understand, but this time he didn't ask.

Sensing Cora's gaze, Jane turned, and with a tiny gasp of delight she bounded from the stool and into Cora's open arms.

Marjorie dried her hands and moved the stool where Jane had been sitting under the counter to give herself freer access to the wide, country-style sink. With a gentle push, she nudged Solomon away from her feet and resumed her dinner preparations.

Tonight after supper, Marjorie would make her way home to her comfortable apartment at the Piney Woods and perhaps make herself a solitary cup of hot chocolate, say her prayers, and retire to bed. She normally returned home on Friday nights, but she and Cora had agreed that she should take a long weekend. Thomas had already called Susan to tell her what had happened at Sam's and to give her the day off on Friday to spend with Harry.

Life was already changing.

Tomorrow, she knew, Marcie Jones would be at her door at a more or less respectable hour for a Friday morning, expecting a detailed inventory of the week's events. Nosy, neighborly Marcie, who was never able to extract nearly as much juicy information as she thought she did.

The two women would commiserate for an hour or so, and then they would part ways for their weekend housekeeping chores.

On Sunday morning they would dress for church and Steve's funeral service afterwards, where they would meet again, sit together on a pew near the back, and have another conversation as though they had not seen each other in a week.

Marjorie turned to take the soup bowls from the glass-front cabinets and saw Thomas watching her in his serious, studious way. She suspected that he was concerned for her because she was going home to an empty house. There was no pity, however, in his look. Neither did Marjorie feel sorry for herself because of her lone weekend existence, because those weekends were simply bookends for her weekly time with Cora, the foster children, and the young, troubled clients who came into Cora's life.

Marjorie's life was full. Every child she held was her child. Every redeemed little life was added to Marjorie's ever-growing prayer list. All neatly tucked away in her grateful heart's memories.

Cora, oblivious to everything around her except Jane, was listening intently to Jane's version of the garden adventure.

"Morrie says we are going to eat them." Jane was almost

breathless at the conclusion of her tale of butterflies, frogs, and edible plants. "Morrie says we will wash them and eat them. Tonight."

"Morrie?" Thomas took the bowls from Marjorie's hands. "Not Marjorie?"

"She says Marjorie is too hard to say," the housekeeper observed, turning to stir the homemade vegetable soup. "Besides, Morrie has a special lilt to it, don't you think?"

Thomas's eyes twinkled. He was more convinced now than ever that their entire lives were about to take a magnificent detour.

"Morrie it is, then," he agreed. "Here, let me help you scoop the soup."

"Scoop the soup?" She handed him the soup ladle with a flourish. "Renaming everything now, are we?"

Cora and Jane smiled from the high stool they were sharing, Jane straddling Cora's knee. Solomon, hungry as always, added a petulant cat yowl from under the counter at their dangling feet.

When the four of them had finished their meal, complete with slices of ripe tomato, bell peppers that Jane proclaimed to be delicious, and a small bowl of cat treats for Solomon, Marjorie cleared the table while Cora announced that she was taking Jane upstairs for a warm bath and story before bed.

At first, Jane was reluctant to say goodbye to the newly proclaimed Morrie, but both Cora and Thomas reassured her that she would indeed see her friend again on Monday. After a few minutes, Jane was almost persuaded to smile.

Thomas followed his wife upstairs, helped her run the bubbling bath water, and put the toothpaste on the waiting brush. Then he headed back downstairs.

He returned to meet Marjorie in the hallway with his own goodbyes and to give the housekeeper and confidante her weekly salary envelope.

In the beginning, Marjorie had tried to argue that she was overpaid, but those discussions were long since over. Thomas had made it crystal clear how valuable she was to him and to Cora. He had made up his mind now that Jane was an added blessing and responsibility, however long that might be, that from now on there should be an increase in what she received. Marjorie was vitally important to Jane too.

Marjorie suspected that there was more money when Thomas sheepishly handed her the heavier envelope of cash, avoiding her eyes.

"Thomas—"

"Did you talk to Charlie today?" he asked, neatly forestalling the protest he knew she was about to make.

"He came by this afternoon, late," she admitted. "Why?"

Normally self-controlled, Thomas couldn't help himself. "To see Cora?"

"No." Marjorie patted his hand. "He wouldn't even come in. Left a stuffed black kitten from some shop in Atlanta to put on Jane's pillow upstairs. The kitten looks just like the cat he gave her when she came on Monday, except the ribbon around her neck is pink instead of red."

"A pink ribbon around her neck? What in the world does that mean?"

Marjorie raised her eyebrows and smiled.

"To show that they are female kittens. Charlie says they are sisters," she added. "He said that Cat needed a sister. He mumbled something about family."

Thomas rubbed his chin and shook his head and tried not to feel resentful. *Charlie again. How could Charlie always know the right gift? Marjorie for Cora. Cat for Jane.*

He sighed.

I can be thankful for his gifts and still be glad he is gone, he thought wryly.

"Does that mean something to you? Why would Charlie think the cat needs a sister?" Marjorie said, tilting her head and looking at him curiously. "Do you know something that I don't know?"

"Not for very long, I'm sure," Thomas said with a laugh. "You seem to know things when I know things."

Marjorie's maternal patting moved from his upper arm to his tanned cheek. "You're a good man, and Cora loves you."

"Thank you, Marjorie."

"Morrie," she corrected.

From the floor at her feet, Solomon gave a plaintive meow of protest, curling affectionately about her ankles as if he could prevent her from leaving.

"Morrie," Thomas agreed. He picked up the protesting cat as he opened the door. "Have a good weekend, Morrie. We will see you Monday morning."

"Of course," she said.

Humming softly to herself, Marjorie went down the front steps and into the gathering dusk to her economical compact car.

Thomas waited until he heard the car start and saw her pull

away before he closed and securely locked the front door and went upstairs, hoping he was not too late for story time with Cora and Jane.

Epilogue

The Fifth Day: Friday

Unexpectedly, Cora found herself standing at Gramma Crawford's kitchen sink looking out the open window. The morning sun was barely visible between the branches of the chinaberry tree, full of wrinkled berries and glistening leaves. The sky was streaked with smoky gray. Glancing at her clothing, she saw that she was wearing a nightgown of some soft, cotton fabric with a light robe of the same material, and her feet were cool and bare against the worn rag mat on the floor. Across her right shoulder, there was a worn kitchen drying towel draped against her neck.

For a reason she could not define, she felt at perfect peace.

She looked down and realized that her hands were submerged in hot, soapy water and holding onto an object just beneath the surface. Lifting it from the foam, she saw that it was a child's sterling silver cup. A quick rinse confirmed what she already knew to be true. She knew this cup. Engraved with one name only. Lonora. Her Gramma Crawford's middle name. The name that would have been given to Cora's firstborn. The cup that would have been the baby's cup, if she had lived.

Before Cora could consider what was happening, she heard the sound of what seemed to be a lullaby and the familiar, recognizable sound of the wooden floors as they creaked in rhythm to the singing—a tender, compassionate melody in a language Cora did not recognize.

She turned around, still holding the dripping, freshly washed cup.

To the left of the handmade table and ladder-backed, cane-bottom chairs was the place Cora best remembered seeing her grandmother—a sturdy, handmade oak rocking chair. Seated in the center of the worn cushions was a petite Asian woman who appeared to be a little younger than Cora herself. The woman was wearing a silk kimono, her bare toes barely touching the floor as she rocked back and forth. Her hair was long and smooth, pulled to one side and over her shoulder, and she did not seem aware that anyone else was in the room.

In her arms, the delicate woman held an equally fragile-looking baby, wrapped in a quilted, homemade blanket that Cora recognized from her own pregnancy.

Stepping closer, then hesitating, she strained to see the newborn's face. Her steps caused the floorboards to creak beneath her, and the other woman looked up curiously at the noise without pausing in her song.

Cora was only mildly taken aback to see Jane's face.

Well, she thought, *Jane's face, only older. Jane's mother.*

Cora took the kitchen towel from her shoulder, dried the

cup and then her hands, and reluctantly placed the shining treasure on the table beside her before she slid closer.

Mother's eyes searched mother's eyes in unspoken love and understanding. Without hesitation, the blanket-wrapped bundle was lifted and offered to Cora's waiting arms.

"Thank you," she whispered so as not to disturb the sleeping infant. "Oh, thank you."

The woman's voice was lilting and melodious. And confusing.

Within the folds, the newborn stirred, arms and legs and tiny torso relaxing against her as Cora cuddled the precious baby closer. Cora nestled her face against the sweet-smelling softness of the beautiful, innocent face.

Lonora.

Jane's mother clucked her approval and there were more Chinese words, several still-incomprehensible sentences this time. Cora simply nodded in return.

Cora felt a strange sense of emotional unrest. Overwhelming gratitude swept through and over her, but crashing against that joy was the knowledge that she was face-to-face with another mother who had also lost a precious daughter, albeit in a different way.

Loss is always painful, thought Cora. *There is emptiness where there should be fulfillment and joy.*

Then Cora realized a truth her heart already knew.

To truly love and care for Jane, she must let Lonora go. Let go in every way so that her arms would be empty and ready to be filled. She would not stop loving Lonora, of course, but the baby must move from her arms into her heart for safekeeping to make room for another child. A child who needed her now in a totally special way.

Deep within Cora, a burden lifted and floated away.

Pressing her lips against the baby's forehead, Cora gave the baby a final long embrace and lowered a still-sleeping Lonora into another mother's waiting arms.

With a smile that Cora knew was Jane's smile too, the woman resumed her lilting song and the rhythmic rocking. The baby stirred, but she soothed her with a gentle patting and then looked up.

The words she spoke, like the others she had spoken, were unintelligible.

"I know," Cora murmured to the woman. A quiet look of understanding passed between them. An unspoken language they both knew and understood perfectly.

With a sigh, Cora dropped her arms to her side.

"Thank you," she whispered again.

And she was awake.

Beside her, Thomas was snoring softly into her ear, his face almost invading her pillow, his body turned toward her. With a prayer of thankfulness and contentment, she rolled peacefully into her husband's embrace, her head upon his strong shoulder and her arms curled against his chest.

There was no need to check to see what time it was.

There were no notes to take. The message was clear.

Cora nestled under the covers against the heart of the man she loved and returned to dreamless sleep.

to Wilton Estate

Sheland Lake to Piney Woods

Cemetery

Miss Bessie's House

United Methodist Church

Hanson's Pharmacy

Cemetery

Emmanuel Baptist Church

Florist's Shop

Parson's Funeral Home

Park & Playground

Balfour Elementary School

Nursing Home

Stone Law Firm

Post Office

Balfour, Ga est 1818

to Anson's

Dreamcatcher: Strangers

Book 2 in the Balfour Mystery Series

The dreams aren't over for Cora when she discovers that there are more than just secrets in the sleepy town of Balfour —

It may be the Christmas season, but there are strangers threatening her peaceful life and those she loves . . .

* * *

The elderly preacher cupped her chin in his wrinkled hands, his dark, piercing eyes searching hers. She felt as though he were looking into her innermost thoughts.

"I know you're afraid, Cora. You were brave before, be brave again."

"But . . ." she began aloud and then stopped. There was no sense in arguing.

I don't feel brave, she thought to herself. *I feel exhausted and frightened.*

His words interrupted her runaway train of thoughts.

"One more thing—and this is important. You must make sure Charlie has a copy of Jane's drawing. In color. You know which one."

The picture from the first dream, she thought. *The one hanging in my study. The first one Jane drew when she came to us that morning.*

As she opened her mouth for one last protest, Cora was awake.

At the foot of the bed, Solomon lifted his drowsy black head, twitched his furry ears, and stared at her with impatient, annoyed green eyes as if to protest the disturbance to his beauty sleep.

She was chilled to the bone even though she was still bundled in her thick chenille robe. An army of tiny goose bumps rose along her thin arms like a rash that cascaded up from her wrists to her shoulders.

James was right. She really had no choice.

Now the dreams were about Jane . . .

ABOUT THE AUTHOR

KC Pearcey published her first poem in the *Tylertown Times* at the age of ten, and she has been writing ever since.

At the age of sixteen, she wrote and produced her first play for her high school. While attending Mississippi College, she won the Bellamann Award for creative excellence for her five-volume poetry collection, the Southern Literary Award twice for her adult plays, and numerous other awards for her six original children's plays written for production by drama workshop classes.

Through the years, she has written and produced numerous plays, skits, essays, poems, children's programs, and murder mystery dinner theatres for churches, schools, friends, and family.

She recently retired from forty years of teaching young people how to write, perform, communicate, and think. She still loves everything about teaching—except the red pens used for grading papers.

Although she has lived in eight states and packed up all her worldly possessions a total of thirty-two times, she now lives happily in Stone Mountain, Georgia, with her husband. Between writing and spending time with her grandchildren, she also loves to travel and have exciting adventures.

Dreamcatcher: Secrets is the first in a series of novels that she always promised herself and her students that she would write when she had the time.

She hopes you enjoy Balfour, Georgia, and the people who live there as much as she does.

Email: dreamcatcherkcp@gmail.com

Made in the USA
Columbia, SC
02 July 2024